Enchanted Knight
Knights of Kilbourne, 3

KEITH W. WILLIS

CHAMPAGNE BOOK GROUP

Enchanted Knight

This is a work of fiction. The characters, incidents and dialogues in this book are products of the author's imagination and are not to be construed as real. Any resemblance to actual events or persons, living or dead, is completely coincidental.

Published by Champagne Book Group
2373 NE Evergreen Avenue, Albany OR 97321 U.S.A.

~~~

First Edition 2020

pISBN: 979-8-682263-31-8

Cover Art by Melody Pond

www.champagnebooks.com

Version_1
~~~

Praise for Traitor Knight

SFF World (online magazine)
"...a witty and action-packed page-turner that takes the classic fantasy land and adds depth, character, romance and political intrigue to brilliant effect."—http://www.sffworld.com/2016/05/traitor-knight-by-keith-w-willis/

Myths, Legends, Books & Coffee Pots (blog)
"Medieval England meets fairy-tale. I soon felt at home there. All of the characters in this book had flesh on them—their individuality shone through. There was plenty of action, romance, suspense, a murder or two, a chase across the roof tops and a dragon—did I mention a dragon?"—http://maryanneyarde.blogspot.com/2016/03/traitor-knight-by-keithwwillis.html

Praise for Desperate Knight

SFF World (online magazine)
If you haven't read Traitor Knight *and you enjoy swashbuckling, heroic fantasy with a light-hearted touch and a modern feel, go and read that – and then read* Desperate Knight. *Thoroughly enjoyable, and now with even more dragon!*—https://www.sffworld.com/2017/08/desperate-knight-by-keith-w-willis/

Dear Reader,

Well met! I'm delighted you've decided to join me on another adventure to Kilbourne. Thank you so much for sharing your time with me. I know in my own busy life just how precious that commodity is, and I don't take your purchase and reading of this book lightly.

If you're reading this tale, odds are you've already read at least one of my previous excursions into this medieval, magical world. If not, while it's certainly not obligatory, I highly encourage it. Otherwise you may be just a bit at sea (and beset by roguish pirates) as to who these characters are and what's going on. Fair warning.

Enchanted Knight *is just a bit different from my previous two novels and has given me a chance to stretch my (dragon's) wings just a bit. I've allowed myself to delve more deeply into some of the magical and mythical aspects of the world I've created. In other words, lots more magic. The King of the Dwarves. And an entire wrangle of dragons. Oh, boy, are there dragons... But hopefully still with all the humor, adventure, and romance you've come to expect from my stories. I think this book really delivers on all fronts, and I hope you'll agree.*

Please know that I absolutely love to hear from readers via email or through social media (I'm primarily a Twitter user). I also am thrilled to meet you in person at the events I attend over the course of the year—both author fairs, and especially at the Renaissance Faires my wife and I attend (see my website www.keithwillisauthor.com for upcoming dates).

One last thing before you get to the important stuff—the adventures of Morgan and Marissa (and yes, Wyvrndell) and all their friends and enemies. If you enjoy this book, or even if you don't, I urge you to leave a review. Reviews and ratings are extremely important for authors, but also important for your fellow readers who may be undecided about whether to try a new author. It could be your review that helps them make that choice to join us in Kilbourne. So thank you in advance.

And now, let's get to the story. Dragons ho!

Keith W. Willis

Chapter One

The dragon sizzled and steamed in the morning mists.

It paused at the edge of the clearing, scanning the area. For threats? Or more likely, for prey?

Morgan decided it really didn't matter. Other than a couple of squirrels chattering their indignation at this invasion of their domain, he was the only creature in the dragon's vicinity. He stepped out of the shadows of a concealing oak, pacing forward into the clearing. He set his lips in a grim line as he watched its every movement. *This is madness*, he told himself for what seemed like the hundredth time. Still, it had to be done.

The dragon's tail lashed back and forth. Its sulfurous odor marred the earthy scent of trees and decaying leaves. Morgan halted and stood his ground.

He likely would have felt much better with a squad of soldiers at his back. But this was something he had to do alone. Abandoning caution for boldness, he stalked to the center of the clearing, ready to face the beast out of legend. Hissing ominously, the dragon undulated serpent-like to meet him.

Morgan halted, his hand hovering by the hilt of his sword in its worn leather scabbard. He could draw it in the blink of an eye. But… a dragon's eye? That remained to be seen.

The beast regarded him from emerald-faceted eyes reflecting eternity. Its mouth curved into a draconic grin, displaying an impressive array of extremely pointy teeth. Delicate plumes of steam swirled on an errant air current and circled Morgan's head, a reminder of the deadly inferno presently banked within. A fire, Morgan knew, that could be called up in an instant to char him into oblivion before he could move.

Inclining his huge head toward the sword, the dragon blinked. *"Would you seek to skewer me, Morgan McRobbie?"*

His words, inaudible to human ears, rang in Morgan's head as Wyvrndell projected his thoughts. His tone held more amusement than menace.

Quirking a sheepish grin, Morgan removed his hand from the sword and stepped closer. "Sorry, Wyvrndell," he muttered. "Old habits die hard."

"For me as well. In other days I might have made a mid-morning snack of you. But I will refrain if you will."

Morgan huffed out a laugh. "Very well. You have my word on it."

"So if not to do battle, why have you asked to meet me here?"

"Because I need to understand what's going on. With Lady Marissa, I mean."

"Nothing is 'going on'. I am her teacher, as agreed."

"Yes, but—" Morgan heaved a sigh, running a hand through his close-cropped dark hair. "Look. I know you've committed to train Marissa how to use her magic. And I appreciate it. I don't want her to hurt herself—or anyone else—because she doesn't know what she's doing."

"Also, power such as hers must not go unchecked. This is why I agreed to teach her."

"What do your kin think of this arrangement? I mean, do they agree with what you're doing?"

The dragon tossed his huge head, sending another plume of smoke skyward. Then, giving a draconic shrug, he said, *"Actually, the matter has not yet been discussed."*

"Oh." Morgan pondered this for a moment. "Um, how do you think they're going to take it?"

Wyvrndell appeared to consider this for a moment. Finally he said, *"I do not foresee any difficulties."*

To Morgan's surprise, the dragon didn't seem as certain in this pronouncement as was his norm. "If you say so. I was rather under the impression dragons don't relish the notion of dealing with humans."

"Do not worry. They will see the necessity of my tutelage of Lady Marissa. It is for the benefit of all."

Morgan's brows rose at this statement. *The benefit of all? How would Wyvrndell's tutoring of Marissa benefit dragonkind?* But another thought crowded this one out. It was why he had arranged this clandestine meeting out in the forest, away from Marissa. He could easily have held this conversation from the comfort of his own study rather than traipsing out here into the forest. Instead, he'd felt an undeniable urgency to speak with Wyvrndell face to face. Which was, he realized, ridiculous. It wasn't like talking with another man, where you could gauge his reactions by watching his eyes. This was a dragon, ancient and unfathomable.

Which didn't change the strange imperative he'd felt. "So how are you able to teach her?" Morgan asked. "I just don't understand it. I mean, if dragons are unable to perform magic, then how can you…" He trailed off as the dragon regarded him reproachfully.

"Just because we can't do it doesn't mean we don't know all the arcane theories. I, and others of my kin, have studied magic for centuries, attempting to learn how to harness its power. I can teach her, Morgan McRobbie. And teach her well, rest assured."

"As you say. I suppose, all things considered, I don't have much choice."

"You may have choices to make, sooner than you think. As will your lady. Choose well. Now I will bid you farewell."

"What? Choices? What are you talking about?"

But Wyvrndell had already unfurled his wings and did not reply. With a graceful leap he mounted the sky, leaving Morgan staring, slack jawed, after him.

Shaking his head, he gathered his wits and started back to Bryntop House, the McRobbie family estate. As Duke of Westdale and lord of the manor and the surrounding lands, he had responsibilities now. Much more than he really had anticipated, which was why he was temporarily in residence.

Well, also because of the aftermath of the recent near-debacle with Xavier. Morgan still had nightmares of Marissa held hostage by the Rhuddlani. She'd only been rescued by a combination of extraordinary luck and the intervention of Wyvrndell. Once the smoke had settled, Morgan had suggested they remove themselves to the country for a bit, where she could recuperate in relative seclusion and undergo the dragon's tutelage.

She seemed to be doing much better since they'd come here. Of course, his mother fussed over her like a protective hen, although this was likely as much due to their impending nuptials as to her concern for her future daughter's mental state. But Lady Sybil was no fool, a lesson Morgan had long since learned. She had gone above and beyond in her efforts to put Morgan's betrothed at ease. When Marissa wasn't engaged in her lessons with Wyvrndell, Lady Sybil made sure to keep her occupied with discussions of gowns, flowers and banquets. Which was, all things considered, much better than allowing Marissa to dwell on such things as near death at the hands of vicious assassins. Morgan was grateful, and especially pleased the two women he loved most seemed to be getting along so well.

Once Wyvrndell had departed, the forest seemed to return to normal. Birds sang and small animals darted through the underbrush around him. Morgan hardly heard them. His thoughts buzzed like bees in a hive as he tried to make sense of the dragon's enigmatic intimations. The blasted creature was as bad as his friend Randolph when it came to beating about the bush. Why the devil couldn't people—yes, and dragons—just stick to the point?

Abandoning this line of inquiry as fruitless, he turned to considerations of a more immediate nature. Like what the near future might hold. For him and Marissa and their life together once they were wed.

For Morgan had indeed made a choice. He had chosen to marry a witch.

Well, a woman with magical talent. No, he amended, might as well call a witch a witch. This was how Marissa referred to herself now. An extremely powerful witch, according to the wizard Sebastien, who had first discovered the magic latent within Marissa. She had inherited the magical potential of both her mother and father, each of whom possessed powerful magic in their own right. Neither of them made use of it, but it was there. The combination of talent inherited from two such puissant parents had resulted in, as Marissa had put it, "A witch with a capital W."

Wyvrndell had confirmed Sebastien's assertion. The two of them, dragon and wizard, had come to a consensus: Marissa needed immediate training before anything untoward happened.

Sebastien had disclaimed any ability to properly teach Marissa how to harness and control her burgeoning powers. When Morgan had asked him if he thought she should attend St. Giles Academy for Magic, where her parents had gone, long years past, the wizard had hesitated several moments before answering.

"She could," he allowed, but Morgan noticed the emphasis on the word *could*.

"But?" he'd prompted.

"But I think she might be best served by allowing Wyvrndell to instruct her. He's eager to do so, and I'm certain he has both the knowledge and the capacity. And the patience." He gave Morgan a wry smile.

"You're telling me you'd trust a dragon before you'd trust your fellow wizards to teach her?"

"Well, when you put it that way…" Sebastien's eyes had glinted with a strange light. "Yes, I believe in this case I would."

Morgan had been unable to extract any more from the wizard. And with this recommendation, Marissa had agreed to accept the dragon as her tutor.

While Morgan was prepared to do everything in his power to protect the woman he loved, her heritage was the one thing from which he couldn't shield her. It was maddening. Here he was, a duke of the realm and Knight-Commander of the King's Legion. He possessed wealth, power, and skill at arms. But none of these mattered a jot. He growled at the thought.

Preoccupied as he was, Morgan was nearly at the manor gates before he realized he was being followed.

Chapter Two

Marissa glared balefully at the mostly empty parchment before her. Heaving a long-suffering sigh, she tossed her quill down in frustration. Splatters of black ink rained over the parchment, and she drew back hastily, lest her dress be caught in the deluge.

"I don't remember!" She groaned. "I just can't remember! I'll never get it right."

If anyone saw her, Marissa knew, they'd think her mad to be addressing such complaints to apparently empty air. Well, perhaps she had taken leave of her senses, she thought. After all, who but a madwoman would allow herself to be tutored by a dragon?

"Please, Lady Marissa, do not distress yourself unduly," replied the voice of Wyvrndell. The dragon's voice was, she reflected not for the first time, surprisingly gentle for such a large and ferocious creature.

"May I distress myself duly?" she asked.

"I do not under— Oh, yes. I see. You sought to make a jest?"

"Um, yes? Well, in a manner of speaking."

"I see. Please do not do it again. It is painful."

"Oh, I'm sorry, Wyvrndell, I had no idea."

"You see? Now I sought to make a jest in return. It is indeed painful, is it not?"

She burst out laughing. "Very well, it's agreed. No more jokes from either of us. Let's get back to it, shall we?"

"Yes. But consider this. We have only been at your lessons for a few days. You cannot be expected to recall everything we have discussed. Give it time, and the lessons I've imparted will come to you as they are needed."

"I suppose," Marissa said a bit crossly. "But I imagine it's easier to have patience when one has a lifespan of centuries."

"Indeed," agreed Wyvrndell, *"I suppose it is. I have never really given it much thought. After all, you are one of the first humans with whom dragons have had extended contact in a very long time. We generally do not take much notice of humans or their myriad shortcomings. You live such short and frenetic lives, and thus are impatient for things to happen. Having a span of centuries, as I do, tends to give one a bit of perspective. And patience. Now, shall we try again?"*

Marissa chuckled at the aspersions cast on her species. "Wyvrndell, explain to me again why I need to learn all this history. Perhaps I'm just particularly woolly-minded, but wouldn't it be easier and a lot more productive to just concentrate on actually doing magic?"

She could almost feel the draconic shrug. *"Lady Marissa, the knowing is as important as the doing. It is vital you know from where your powers come. You must also gain an understanding not only of what can be done, but what should or should not be done. For there are many things which can be done, but which should remain undone. If I am to tutor you in the arts of magic, you must allow me to do so in my own fashion. For example, my lesson today on the herb called witchbane and its effects may seem pointless, but one never knows. There is no such thing as too much knowledge."*

"Very well, I'll take your word for it. But right now, I'm in need of a brief respite. My head feels as if it's going to explode. I need to get a cup of tea and refresh myself. Then perhaps I can try again."

"Very well. As you will. Call to me when you are ready to resume."

She rose, stretching limbs stiff from too much sitting in one place. Rolling her neck to ease an imminent crick, she tossed the ink-splattered parchment in the grate and went in search of tea.

"Stupid, ungrateful chit."

Marissa recoiled as if she'd been slapped. She looked around wildly, eyes darting up and down the hallway, seeking the source of this vehement disapproval. There was no one in sight, but then she heard the voice again, although not quite so loud this time. It was coming from a half-open doorway. She crept closer.

The words cut through her like a heated knife, searing into her mind and flaying off little strips of her heart. Well, that's what she got for eavesdropping, wasn't it? Although to be honest, it hadn't been intentional. She'd merely been walking down the corridor in search of the kitchen and a cup of tea.

The speaker was Lady Sybil, Dowager Viscountess McRobbie. Morgan's mother. While she didn't know to whom Lady Sybil was addressing her words, she had a sinking feeling she could identify the subject of this censure. "Stupid, ungrateful chit?" What other female could Lady Sybil be discussing in such disparaging terms but herself, Morgan's betrothed?

"If I were you," replied another unseen voice, raspy with age, "I'd toss her out right quick and be done with her."

"I know." Lady Sybil heaved an aggrieved sigh. "But when I said as much to Morgan, he forbade it. He's rather fond of her."

Marissa staggered slightly, clutching at the wall for balance. Why on earth was Lady Sybil suddenly so dead set against her? When Morgan had brought her here to Bryntop, his ancestral home, Lady Sybil had seemed delighted. She'd gone out of her way to make Marissa feel welcome, and they'd chatted excitedly about plans for the wedding; spent countless hours discussing her gown, her thoughts on flowers, and the menu for the wedding banquet. Well, when Marissa hadn't been busy being tormented by Wyvrndell into learning every detail of the magical history of the entire world, or so it felt.

But Lady Sybil had seemed so… sweet. She'd seemed happy to welcome Morgan's choice of bride into the family. So what had gone wrong? Had Marissa done something to offend her? "Stupid, ungrateful chit" certainly sounded like it. She cast her thoughts back over the last week, trying to remember…

"My lady?"

Marissa whirled round, her hand flying to her mouth to stifle a gasp. Nearly caught listening at keyholes.

Jarvis, Lady Sybil's butler, loomed in the hallway. He was a rather small man to be able to loom effectively but managed it none the less. Marissa hesitated, unsure of herself, while the butler waited for her to reply. He practically oozed with solicitous attention.

Normally, Marissa possessed self-confidence in abundance. Yet ever since her recent encounter with Xavier, the Rhuddlani assassin who had nearly killed her, she seemed to lack her normal sense of assurance. She found herself easily distracted and lacking focus as well. As evidenced in her lessons with Wyvrndell.

Could Lady Sybil's change of heart be due to the fact Marissa would soon supplant her as chatelaine of Westdale? How did Morgan's mother really feel about this? She might be eager to rid herself of the burden. Or she might be harboring ill feelings toward the woman who would soon take up the title of Duchess of Westdale. Marissa wished she could be certain which. She swiped at her eyes and told herself not to be a fool.

And a fool she must look to this venerable figure before her. Dignity dripped from him like dew from the morning roses as he inquired sedately, "Might I be of some assistance?"

Marissa drew upon her own reserves to keep from trembling. "Thank you, Jarvis, yes. I was searching for a cup of tea and a biscuit. Wyvrndell is a hard task-master, and my head needs some clearing." *More than you can imagine.*

The butler's lips gave a slight twitch, which was as close to a smile as he probably allowed himself. "Of course, milady, right away.

But you needed only ring the bell and I would have attended you."

"I know. I really just needed to get up and walk about for a bit. If you could have tea brought into the study it would be wonderful."

"Very good, milady," Jarvis intoned. For all his dignity, his eyes seemed to light with a twinkle as he gazed upon the woman who was soon to be the mistress of Bryntop House and the new Duchess of Westdale. "If you'd care to return to the study, I shall bring your tea in momentarily."

"Thank you, Jarvis, you're saving my life." A wan smile crossed Marissa's lips. "I dare say everyone on staff is wondering what is going on, eh?"

Jarvis seemed to hesitate for a moment, to consider before he spoke. "Milady, His Grace has related to me how both the dragon and the wizard—Master Sebastien, I believe?—sensed strong magical powers within you, and how the dragon has offered to serve as a tutor so you might use them wisely and safely."

"Well, yes. I'm afraid he neglected to say I'm not a particularly adept pupil. Thank heaven the dragon has seemingly limitless patience. I'm having a terrible time recalling all the things he tries to teach me, and he says each is important. I'm afraid when I get to the point of actually using magic, I'll do something awful."

The butler's lips twitched again. "I'm certain you will master it, milady. A woman of your obvious wit will always prevail. Now, if you will pardon me, I will see to your tea." He bowed low, and Marissa smiled gratefully.

"Thank you, Jarvis. For everything." She returned to the study with a much-improved outlook. Looking about the room, she took in the desk with its mountains of ledgers and scrolls, the accounts which drove both Morgan and his mother to distraction. Morgan had vowed to hire someone to manage the accounts, but so far he'd been too busy fussing over her to worry about it. So the pile grew.

Actually, Morgan had been almost overly solicitous of late. She had little doubt this was due to her recent abduction by Xavier. Morgan, she knew, was used to such dangers to himself. As Knight-Commander of Kilbourne's Legion, he could hardly avoid them. But he'd been frantic when Xavier used her as a hostage in an attempt to bargain his way to freedom after his scheme had collapsed. If not for Morgan's quick thinking and the assistance of Wyvrndell, she might well have been killed. Now Morgan seemed determined to keep her insulated from any danger. Well, except the danger of running out of tea. It was sweet, really, but so totally unnecessary...

She just needed to let him know he didn't need to keep her

wrapped in cotton-wool and kept on a shelf, to be taken out only upon special occasions. She was not a delicate flower, but a sturdy vine upon which he could depend. And if that vine happened to twine about his neck on occasion, so much the better, eh?

A soft mental cough interrupted her. Wyvrndell, requesting permission to continue their lessons. Marissa heaved a sigh and returned to the writing desk.

Chapter Three

Morgan whirled as a tall, lean, and angular man strode toward him. "Your Grace?" the man called.

Morgan waited, observing the stranger. A wide-brimmed hat threw part of his features into shadow in the late-morning brightness. Yet from beneath its shadow Morgan noted the gleam of his eyes, which shone with an odd amber glow. Dressed in worn leathers, the stranger sported a light, dusty cloak. He appeared unarmed but carried a stout walking staff. In the right hands, a weapon of no little effectiveness.

"Duke Morgan." His voice, oddly soft and resonant, was in stark contrast to his rough appearance. "If I might take a moment of your time?"

"You seem to have already done so. Who are you, and what is your business?"

The stranger chuckled, a low rumbling laugh that seemed almost mocking. Morgan stared at him warily, his hand closing almost of its own accord upon the hilt of his sword. There was something off about this fellow, even if he couldn't put his finger on it.

The other's eyes took in this movement. "Nay, Your Grace, stay your hand," he said quickly. "I mean you no ill. I am here, in truth, hoping to do you a service."

"Oh? And what might that be?" Morgan asked. Even as he spoke, he felt a slight, invisible pressure on his hand, forcing it away from the sword. *A wizard. Great, just great.* Morgan scowled. He edged his hand away, and the pressure eased.

"I am Master Rhenn. Augustus Rhenn, Headmaster of St. Giles Academy of Magic. I have come to assess the potential of Lady Marissa duBerry for admission to the Academy."

"Have you now? A bit forward of you, don't you think? To the best of my knowledge, Lady Marissa has expressed no interest in being admitted to your academy."

"But things have changed now, have they not?" Rhenn raised a brow, while Morgan maintained a studied silence. Finally, the headmaster continued. "She was previously unaware of her talents, wasn't she? Since she—"

Morgan cut in, "Just how do you know of her talents, Master Rhenn?"

"It is my business to know," Rhenn replied, drawing himself up to his full height. He stared at Morgan, his eyes burning with a curious light. "I am the headmaster, after all. Lady Marissa has been determined to possess strong magical talents. Talents of a most interesting nature, I understand. She must enter the Academy immediately to begin her training."

Morgan stared. Finally, finding his voice again, he said, "Not only are you presumptuous, Master Rhenn, but you are also misinformed. You might as well go back to your Academy."

"What? She doesn't have the power? Are you sure? My informant was quite certain."

"No, that's not what I meant. Power she has. Both Master Sebastien of your order, as well as the dragon, Wyvrndell, seem to think so. I will certainly bow to their greater wisdom and experience in such matters. No, I meant you were misinformed as to the necessity of Lady Marissa's entering St. Giles."

"She must." Rhenn's words were gentle but firm, sounding like a rebuke for a wayward child. "It is required, both by tradition and by the College of Wizards. The charter of the College states 'None may practice magic who have not been thoroughly instructed in the arts through guidance and tuition.' So you see…"

Morgan held up his hand. "Master Rhenn, I understand your position. You wish for Lady Marissa to come to St. Giles for training. You feel she is obliged by tradition and necessity to do so. Well enough and fine. However, I fear you have failed to take into consideration the wishes of the lady herself. She has other plans at the moment. And I'm fairly certain those plans do not include haring off to the Academy of Magic. But tell me something. Why on earth have you approached me in this fashion, instead of going directly to Lady Marissa herself?"

Rhenn hesitated, obviously discomfited. "Well," he said finally, "I have heard the girl is stubborn and willful. I hoped you might be able to persuade her to see a reasonable point of view."

"Did you?" chuckled Morgan. "I'm afraid I haven't had much luck so far. I do, however, live in hope. Perhaps someday I'll acquire some amount of influence with the lady. Yet, since you've come all this way, I suppose I can at least present you to Lady Marissa. You may make your case to her, much good may it do you."

"Thank you, Your Grace." Rhenn sounded suddenly complacent, which Morgan found suspicious. "That will be all I need." His eyes gleamed from beneath the wide brim of his hat.

Morgan wondered if perhaps he had made an error. Had this man somehow influenced his thoughts, forcing such an outcome? He didn't think so, but… Well, no matter. However it had happened, he was committed. Blast it, this was why he didn't like dealing with wizards. "Come along then."

"Perhaps," suggested Rhenn, "you might tell me about the dragon whilst we walk. I've heard many tales and rumors, each one wilder than the last. To hear of it from the man who actually found and then defeated the creature would be… interesting."

His voice was soft, but Morgan could hear the eagerness underlying his words. He wondered again if he had made an error in speaking with the headmaster and decided this time, he would trust his instincts. And those instincts told him not to place too much trust in Augustus Rhenn's words. "I think it might be best if you got the tale from the true source: the dragon himself. I understand he has spoken at length with Master Sebastien. Perhaps he'll also deign to speak with you."

Rhenn made no protest but walked in silence next to Morgan. More than once, however, Morgan looked over and caught the headmaster's eye upon him appraisingly. He set a brisk pace, but Rhenn kept up with ease. Morgan was surprised. No soft academic this, but a man used to being out and on the move. In another few minutes they would be at Bryntop. Morgan decided to try a different tack, just to see what Rhenn's reaction would be.

"Tell me, Master Rhenn, I thought all wizards were required to sport robes and a flowing beard. And a pointy hat. At least by tradition, if not by actual writ." Morgan grinned to himself as he emphasized the word "tradition." "So where is yours? You seem much too clean-shaven to be a wizard, and your garb looks more mercenary than academic."

"Bah!" said the wizard. "Pure nonsense! I suppose you're basing your idiotic statement on that old fool Sebastien, with his blasted robes and whiskers."

Morgan stiffened. Whatever skills this fellow possessed, tact certainly didn't seem to be one of them. Which wasn't going to serve him well in any interview with Marissa. To Rhenn he said, "I have only the highest regard for Master Sebastien, Rhenn. He has proved himself, at least to me, to be both an able wizard and a man of no little honor and courage."

Augustus Rhenn's only reply was a contemptuous snort. Morgan's brows rose, and he wondered why Rhenn bridled so at the mention of Sebastien. All things together, he deemed it wiser not to ask. Instead he lengthened his stride and made for the manor.

Chapter Four

As Jarvis arrived with the tea cart, Marissa heard voices through the open window. Morgan, in conversation with another man whose voice she didn't recognize. Which wasn't surprising, all in all, since she really didn't know anyone in Westdale, except for Lady Sybil, Morgan, and Jarvis.

Morgan or no Morgan, she was not to be thwarted. Tea was required, and tea she would have, and anything else would just have to wait.

Well, perhaps not. She was being petty, probably in light of—or in spite of—Lady Sybil's overheard commentary. Setting down the steaming cup, she rose gracefully from the chair, smoothed out her skirts, and made for the front hallway.

Morgan was just ushering in his companion. She was about to greet them when she noticed him shoot a wary glance at the newcomer, who was handing off his hat and cloak to Jarvis.

Hmm. Interesting. Approaching, she held out her hands to her betrothed. Morgan executed a graceful bow over them. "Good day, m'lord," she said. If he'd been alone, he might have gotten a kiss. When he offered up strange men in cloaks, he got cool, if correct, formality.

"M'lady," he replied. "I beg your forgiveness, but I come with outriders, as you can see. One, anyway."

"Yes, so I see." She turned to the stranger. "Good day, sir."

Before the newcomer could speak, Morgan cut in swiftly, his tone uncharacteristically ponderous. "Lady Marissa, allow me to present Master Augustus Rhenn, the esteemed Headmaster of St. Giles Academy of Magic."

Marissa nodded her understanding. Sebastien had mentioned Rhenn, although not with any particular fondness. Turning to the wizard she said, "You've come a long way, Master Rhenn. What brings you to the wilds of Westfyld?"

"Your own delightful self," said Morgan, before Rhenn could answer. "He's here to persuade you to drop everything and take yourself off at once to St. Giles. There you would be tutored by the wizards in the arts of magic. He approached me first, thinking you would allow yourself to be guided by my own wiser counsel." Morgan chuckled. "Little does he know."

She waved a deprecating hand. "Don't be an idiot, Morgan. Of course I listen to you. Then I convince you my own ideas are just as good, if not better." She beamed up at him.

Morgan grinned, as befitted the victim of unassailable feminine logic. Rhenn stepped forward. "Lady Marissa. As you said, I've come a long way, and I don't have time to waste."

Marissa felt her mouth tighten, but she forced herself to paste on a smile. "My apologies, Master Rhenn," she said, her voice silky. "But you did come unannounced and uninvited…" She left the gentle rebuke hanging in the air.

Rhenn either didn't notice or didn't care. "I want you—" he began, but Marissa threw her hands up in dismay.

"But where are my manners?" she cried. "Please, come into the morning room. Jarvis, could you bring in the tea things?" She shooed the wizard and Morgan along the hall, flapping her hands at them like recalcitrant chickens. As she ushered the two men through the open door, she heard footsteps behind her. Glancing over her shoulder, she saw Lady Sybil approaching at speed.

"Good heavens. Did I just see Augustus Rhenn?"

"Yes, he's evidently come to carry me off. To St. Giles, I mean." Marissa rolled her eyes.

"Hmph. We'll see about that." Lady Sybil marched into the morning room with fire in her eyes. Marissa followed her in slowly, deciding both distance and discretion were indicated.

"Hello, Rhenn," Lady Sybil said.

Marissa missed Rhenn's reply, for suddenly the voice of Wyvrndell was in her head. *"Be wary, Lady Marissa. I fear this wizard means you no good."*

"Morgan says he's come to take me off to St. Giles for training," she replied silently.

"Do not trust him. He has something in mind, something hidden. He has power, and he may well attempt to use it. Be on your guard."

"Thank you, Wyvrndell. I shall."

Stranger and stranger. She returned her attention to the tableau in the morning room just as Lady Sybil said, "How nice to see you again, Headmaster. I think the last time was at the coronation of King Rhys. Such a grand affair, was it not? I do hope you've been keeping well. And here you are, come to pay us a visit without even a word of warning, or we would have had a splendid banquet laid on." She extended her hand.

Rhenn took it, wincing visibly, and bowed with forced politeness. "Your Ladyship," he murmured. "How charming to see you again."

Marissa watched from the door. She was certain from Rhenn's expression he was anything but charmed. Lady Sybil beamed.

"Tea will be served momentarily," Marissa chirped. "Now, Master Rhenn, what's all this about hauling me off to St. Giles?"

Rhenn turned his attention back to her. "Your Ladyship, the training of those with magical talents is the sole responsibility of St. Giles Academy. As headmaster, it is my duty to ensure all with such talent come to us for appropriate instruction. I will expect you within the week, of course."

The wizard's gaze focused on her eyes with a fierce intensity belying his casual tone. Marissa felt the sudden force of his will pressing against her own. The dratted wizard was trying to somehow compel her to accede to his demands.

"This can't be good," she thought wildly, as she struggled to resist. In the back of her mind, she heard Wyvrndell say softly, *"Remember our lessons, Lady Marissa."*

What? What was he talking about? Oh, right. One of her recent lessons had been on how to block out all external stimuli. Which might, she realized, include unwanted persuasion of a magical nature. She steeled herself, focused, and felt the pressure of Rhenn's will ease. She hardened her own will, bringing it up as a soldier raises his shield. The pressure faded until it was almost unnoticeable.

Marissa met Rhenn's startled gaze, giving him a curt nod. With a heroic effort, she forced a gracious smile. "I'm so sorry," she said, "but I'm afraid that just won't be possible. I have other commitments. Such as my impending wedding to the duke, you know. I'm sure you'll understand these will prevent me from accepting your gracious offer of tuition. Honestly, I find my current tutor quite well suited to the bothersome task of training one so uneducated. I wouldn't wish it on you, Headmaster. Of course, since you already know about my 'talents,' as you put it, you also know that the dragon Wyvrndell has agreed to give me the benefit of his knowledge regarding the magical arts. So kind, don't you agree?"

Rhenn narrowed his eyes and intensified his gaze. He was making another attempt to exert his will on her. Well, he'd find she wasn't so easy a target as he expected.

Morgan glanced from Rhenn to Marissa with a puzzled frown. Then he stiffened, sending a dark glare toward Rhenn. Perhaps Wyvrndell had told him what the wizard was up to? Whatever the reason, she saw Morgan swiftly catch up the teapot and a delicate china cup. Stepping directly between the headmaster and Marissa, he offered up the cup.

"Some tea, Headmaster?" he inquired pleasantly. "You surely must be in need of refreshment after your long journey."

Rhenn glowered at him, trying to focus on his target. The distraction was enough. The pressure of his will eased slightly as Morgan continued to play the genial host. Marissa staggered, and Lady Sybil came to her side, placing a hand on her shoulder. Marissa nodded, while Morgan plied Rhenn with tea and cakes. The wizard's expression was grim as he tried in vain to peer around Morgan to where Marissa stood. Wondering, no doubt, why he hadn't been able to exercise his control upon her.

"Lady Marissa, am I to understand you refuse to come to St. Giles for the required training?" demanded the wizard, his tone as frosty as a January morning.

Marissa gathered her wits and stood ramrod straight. "My good sir, it is not a matter of refusing. I simply have neither the time nor the inclination to do so. So many things to do preparatory to a wedding, you know. And of course, with the king and queen in attendance, one must make certain everything is just so. Plus, as I said, my current tutor is most satisfactory. Call it a refusal if you wish, but I'm afraid I cannot accept your most kind offer of tutelage at St. Giles. I'm sorry you had such a long journey for naught, but then a letter would have sufficed, don't you think? I hope your trip back will be swift."

"Hmph!" Rhenn seemed to be taking his dismissal with ill grace. "I must say I am not surprised, considering."

"Considering what?" asked Marissa. She kept her voice calm but allowed it to evidence icy undertones that heralded impending doom. She saw Morgan cringe. Good—he'd evidently already learned the warning signs.

"Well, I have heard all about your father's dismissal in disgrace, and..." Marissa stiffened, and Rhenn trailed off as her lips tightened into a thin line.

Taking a deep breath, she managed to maintain her composure. It wasn't easy. "Headmaster Rhenn," she said through clenched teeth as she moved to stand before the wizard. "I think you'd best leave now, before I lose my temper. My father's 'dismissal in disgrace' from St. Giles was, as I am certain you are aware, a shameful miscarriage of justice on the part of the former headmaster." She stepped closer to Rhenn and gave him her most ferocious scowl. "However, it was a long time ago. As my father bears no ill will, neither will I."

Rhenn opened his mouth to speak, but Marissa gave him no quarter. Closing the distance between them she poked his bony chest with her forefinger. "But I will not have you bringing up painful memories in order to shame me into doing what you want. I don't know why you are so eager to have me at St. Giles, considering your opinions about my family, but your methods of persuasion leave much to be desired. You may go."

Turning on her heel, she made for the door. She paused to glance back just as Lady Sybil sprang into action again. She was instantly at Rhenn's side. "So nice of you to drop in," she said, her voice hearty with forced cheerfulness. "Safe journey home now. Jarvis will show you the door."

"This way, sir," said Jarvis, presenting Rhenn with his cloak and ushering him out. Rhenn sniffed, muttered something unintelligible under his breath, and followed him out, shrugging on the cloak. As soon as he was out of the room, Lady Sybil sank onto a chair.

"Make sure he's gone," she ordered Morgan breathlessly. "Marissa, go up to your room and collapse. This was terribly hard on you. I do hope you're all right."

They obeyed. Marissa stumbled toward the stairs. Clutching the banister for support, she started up. Morgan stalked toward the front door and peered out after the departing wizard. Looking back, through the open door she saw Rhenn descending to the drive. She turned back to the daunting task of mounting the stairs.

Chapter Five

After watching as the wizard jammed his hat back onto his head and stalked off down the drive, Morgan slammed the door and headed upstairs. When he reached Marissa's bedchamber, he gave one perfunctory knock. Flinging the door open without waiting for an invitation, he stepped into the room.

She reclined on a settee, her eyes closed. Her maid was applying a damp cloth to her forehead.

"Are you all right?" he asked. "What in the name of heaven just happened down there?"

"I'm fine." She sat up and gave him what he reckoned was intended to be a reassuring smile. It didn't work. It had way too many teeth and very little in the way of actual smileage.

It obviously wasn't working for Briana either. "She is not fine," objected the maid in stout defense of her mistress. "She is exhausted and needs rest and quiet."

"Briana, I really am fine." Marissa pushed the maid away, sounding a bit more convincing this time. Nearly indestructible, Morgan thought. At least so far.

Although she must have a charmed life. Some of the things she'd been through in the last few weeks flashed through his mind. Captured by a dragon. Kidnapped by Xavier, twice. Tangling with spies and murderers. Morgan shook his head. Indestructible indeed.

Marissa went on, "I just need to sit for a few minutes and collect myself. And perhaps have a bit of wine to steady my nerves. As for what happened just now… It's a bit difficult to explain."

"Give it a try," Morgan urged.

"Mmm. Well, that blasted wizard tried to exert control over me somehow, to force me to do what he wanted."

"What? Are you serious? In my house?" Morgan felt outrage rising like an ocean tide.

"I was able to resist him, barely," she continued. "And only because Wyvrndell was assisting me, giving me guidance and support. Rhenn is fantastically strong, Morgan. He would have just overwhelmed me and bent me to his will if Wyvrndell hadn't shown me how to stop him. But why? I don't understand why he's so determined to have me come to St. Giles. I mean, he comes all the way down here and goes to all this trouble. Especially considering his views on Papa."

"I've no idea." Morgan's mouth was tight. "But I certainly intend to find out."

"How?"

"I think perhaps we should consult with Sebastien. Rhenn seems to hold similar views of him as he does of your father. Although I think Sebastien feels pretty much the same way about Rhenn."

"Headmaster Rhenn," she said as she fended off Briana's attentions, "is not a particularly likeable individual. And yes, talking with Sebastien is an excellent idea. I'd have landed on it myself if I weren't so played out. I'll speak with Wyvrndell and ask him to contact Sebastien. Should he come here, do you think?"

He considered. "There's no way for him to get here easily or quickly. None of your magical transfer portals or anything." He grimaced at the thought of how Marissa and Sebastien had been trapped in such a portal not so long ago.

Marissa must have seen the look on his face. She quirked a smile. "It all worked out," she reminded. "I was fine. Just a bit shaken. Like now."

"I know, I know. I just… worry. About you. Anyway, Sebastien would have to come by horse, and I know he's not keen on it. Perhaps it would best if I went up to Caerfaen for a bit. I should probably check in with Rhys anyway, and see how Aartis and the Legion are getting on."

"Mmm. Perhaps you're right. I'll come with you. I'm due for a fitting soon." She brightened. "Also, I need to see what mischief Clarisse has gotten up to now."

He groaned inwardly. Lady Clarisse, Marissa's close friend and chief conspirator in the making of wedding plans, had no trouble getting up to mischief. She would be certain to have horrible things scheduled for him. Like making him plan the wedding breakfast. And forcing him to try on innumerable articles of fancy clothing. It was a bit much for a simple soldier to bear. Still, the prize was worth the cost.

"If you'll excuse me, then, I'll leave you to rest. I'll go make preparations for the trip back to Caerfaen." He bent and pressed a kiss to her forehead. She wrinkled her nose at him.

Morgan headed back down to the first floor. Jarvis waited at the foot of the stairs, bearing a salver with a decanter of brandy and a snifter.

"I took the liberty of anticipating you might wish a libation, milord," the butler said, following him into the study. He deftly poured a liberal amount of the amber liquor into the snifter. Morgan took it gratefully. He swirled it about for a moment, then took a healthy sip.

"Thank you, Jarvis. Two things. First, would you have a bottle of wine brought up to Lady Marissa? I think the '87. She'll enjoy that."

"Certainly, milord. I'll attend to it at once."

"After that, please, locate Henry Dawkes and tell him I want to see him."

"Very good, milord. Shall I leave the decanter?" Morgan nodded, and the butler left, closing the door behind him.

He'd just finished the brandy when a tap on the door heralded the arrival of Dawkes, the coachman. Morgan gave him instructions and he departed to prepare for the next day's journey. Dawkes was replaced almost immediately by Lady Sybil.

"All right, my boy," she said. "I didn't like to disturb Marissa, so tell me all. What the devil happened? I've never liked that man. He always looks as if he feels superior to everyone around him. I said as much to Lord Barston at the king's coronation. And now, for him to come into my home and attempt to bully that sweet, innocent girl! Ooh, I could just spit!"

"Have a brandy instead," recommended Morgan.

"I've already had two," replied his mother. "Another and I won't be fit to travel tomorrow."

"Ah, you've anticipated that, eh? You're coming up to Caerfaen with us?"

"I am. Someone's got to keep the two of you out of trouble." She flashed him a grin.

"Naturally. Well, hopefully Master Sebastien will be able to shed some more light on the situation. Marissa is asking Wyvrndell to alert him to what's just happened and to say we'll see him as soon as we get into town."

The dinner gong sounded. Lady Sybil looked up in dismay. "Drat! I was going to ask Jarvis to have Cook put back dinner for a bit. I haven't even changed and I'm sure Marissa is still resting. Oh well, it'll have to be endured, eh? Will you go up and see if Marissa would like to come down for dinner or prefers to take a tray in her room?"

"Certainly." Morgan made to rise, but Lady Sybil waved a hand at him, signaling him to stay.

"Morgan, I want to say something." When she sounded this serious, Morgan knew it was time to pay attention. "I know you'll think I'm interfering in your business. And yes, I am."

He smiled inwardly. His mother had few equals when it came to the fine art of interference. But it was always with the best of intentions. Besides, her instincts were normally sound, so he was inclined to give credence to what she had to say. "Go ahead."

She eyed him suspiciously for a moment, then nodded once. "I know how concerned you are about Marissa. Especially after everything she's been through lately. I don't blame you one bit."

"Life has been... interesting," Morgan temporized.

"That's putting it mildly. Anyhow, this intrusion by that dratted wizard doesn't make matters any easier. But take a hint from your mamma. Don't try to keep Marissa under lock and key just to keep her safe. She is an exceedingly intelligent, very determined young lady, and she's not about to let anything stand in the way of what she wants. I'm sure you know it, but it may not have fully penetrated that thick head of yours."

Morgan looked at his mother in surprise. "But I'm not—" He stopped. "Well, all right, perhaps I am," he admitted. "But it's only for her own protection. I came so near to losing her when Xavier captured her this last time, and..."

Lady Sybil nodded vigorously. "So you must aid and protect her, should she find herself in trouble. But you also have to let her be her own person and make her own decisions. I didn't raise any fool, my boy. You know what I'm saying. I don't want to see you hurt, either of you. I care too much about you both."

Morgan nodded slowly. "Thank you, Mamma," he said. "Your concern is noted and appreciated. I'll check with Marissa. After dinner, we need to pack."

Chapter Six

"Wyvrndell?" called Marissa.

"I am here. Did you take any injury from your encounter with this wizard?" inquired the dragon. Marissa found herself strangely touched by his concern.

"No, I'm fine, thank you. Although if you hadn't been here to guide me, he would have had me under his control almost instantly."

"You had the power to resist, but lacked the knowledge or the discipline," said Wyvrndell. *"I merely provided you the appropriate knowledge."* He paused for a moment, as if for reflection, and then added, *"You did well."*

"You sound surprised. I have an excellent tutor. But have you any idea why Rhenn would do such a thing? He came an awfully long way just to attempt to force me to attend St. Giles Academy."

"I am sorry, but I have no notion of the wizard's reasoning. His mind is shielded from me."

"Drat. I'd hoped you…"

"I would venture a supposition, however. If your talent for magic is as powerful as I believe it to be, this wizard would undoubtedly want you under his control, rather than running about loose. Wizards are a wily bunch and brook no interference in their plans. You have a well-developed sense of fairness and honor. For a human, I mean. Ultimately, you might seek to oppose and possibly thwart some scheme of his. This move might be his attempt at forestalling such an eventuality. If you were ensconced in his school, you would be under his eye. As well as under his control."

"Mmm. You may well be right. He does seem a scheming sort of chap. Anyhow, that's neither here nor there at the moment, as between us—and Lady Sybil—we've managed to send him packing."

"For now," the dragon replied, and Marissa could sense a feeling of distaste in his tone. It was the feeling one got when a foot lands unexpectedly in something soft, squishy, and smelly. She wrinkled her own nose as Wyvrndell continued.

"I do not think you have seen the last of this wizard. Be on your guard. I will not always be close by to aid you as I was today. Another reason for us to continue your lessons apace."

A grin bubbled its way to her face. "An extremely polite way of saying to get busy and apply myself, eh? Are all dragons so tactful, I wonder? But first I have a request. Could you contact Master Sebastien? He needs to be informed of what has occurred. Tell him Morgan and I would like to meet with him to discuss the matter. We're leaving for Caerfaen tomorrow morning."

"I will be happy to. I enjoy speaking with Sebastien. He is intelligent, for a wizard."

"Excellent. Let him know to expect us late on the day after tomorrow. Oh, I suppose we really can't see him until the day after that. Blast, more time gone. Oh well. Again, my most sincere thanks, Wyvrndell."

Francesca, the cat to whom Marissa belonged, emerged from beneath the bed, gave a full-body wriggle, and twitched her tail before leaping up to the top of the bed. She peered curiously into the trunk into which various articles of clothing were being stowed and gave a thoughtful "Mrowr."

"Yes, we're leaving for Caerfaen tomorrow," Marissa told the feline. "Does that meet with your approval?"

Francesca cocked her head as if in cogitation, then sat up straight. Her bright green eyes glowed with an almost fey light. "Mrowrrr," she replied.

Briana laughed, but to Marissa it sounded a bit nervous. "My heavens, you'd almost think the cat understood you," the maid said.

Marissa smiled. "Having conversed with a dragon, it wouldn't surprise me one bit. Now, let's finish this trunk, shall we?" Together they returned to the task of packing Marissa's wardrobe. Francesca, her mission accomplished, jumped back down to the floor to begin a serious investigation of a corner of the room, to forestall any possibility of mice that might trouble her mistress.

Chapter Seven

A coach and four clattered along the North Road, its wheels churning up the late afternoon dust. The driver seemed determined, as far as Kiara Northram could tell, to test both the coach's springs and its occupants by hitting every rut and hole between Rhuddlan and Caerfaen.

She had spoken to him about it earlier in the journey. Quite sharply, in fact. The driver had just shrugged laconically. "Beggin' yer pardon, yer ladyship," he'd responded, "but t' only way I could miss them holes would be t' not bother takin' the road at all, if ya gets my meanin'."

She had to admit, if grudgingly, he'd probably been correct. Still, she didn't see how Liza managed it. She directed a glare toward her maid, who lay sprawled on the opposite bench, up against the side wall with her eyes closed and gentle snores sounding in counterpoint to the rhythm of the coach wheels.

"Thank God, we should be there soon," Kiara muttered.

The maid yawned and opened her eyes. "Gracious, Your Ladyship, I'm sorry. The coach got to rockin' and before I could say 'scat' I was off to sleep."

"I didn't realize I'd spoken aloud. It's fine, Liza. Go back to sleep if you want. It's hours yet before we're due to arrive."

"Oh, no, I'm right as rain now. A bit peckish, though." She rummaged through a basket and pulled out an apple. She looked a question, and Kiara nodded. Liza crunched a large bite. Kiara returned to her contemplation of the countryside passing by.

"Are we nearly to Caerfaen?" asked Liza around a mouthful of apple.

"A couple of hours, I think. Perhaps a bit more. We should arrive before nightfall, though."

"Good. Me backside's never goin' to be the same after this." She rubbed the offended appendage and shot Kiara a reproachful look. "Weren't nothing wrong with Penllwyn. I don't know why we had to come traipsing all the way to Caerfaen. I ain't never held with foreign parts."

"Perhaps I should have just come alone," Kiara said. It was a well-worn topic by now, eight days into the journey. "You did insist on accompanying me, you know."

"Well, of course I did," Liza said, as if explaining to a particularly dimwitted child. "I wasn't about to let you go running around in this wild place all alone, now was I?"

"Your concern is duly noted. Have another apple."

Liza obliged, crunching heartily. Finally, tossing the core out the window, she asked, "I guess I'm dim, Your Ladyship, but I just don't understand why we're here. Why you wanted to come all this way. Home was nice and comfortable, 'tweren't it?"

"For the last time, Liza, there's something here I have to do. It doesn't concern you. It's a private matter I must see to. And I can only do what I need to do here in Caerfaen."

"Will we ever go home again?"

The question took her off guard. She shot a surprised look at the maid. "I hope so, Liza. I certainly hope so," was the only answer she could give.

Sometime later, as they rolled through the North Gate and into Caerfaen, Kiara looked out the window at the buildings they passed. They were all unfamiliar now, after her long-enforced absence. Not that she'd ever spent that much time in the capital. When she was sixteen, her parents had left the Kilbourne province of Westdale and moved the family to the northern kingdom of Rhuddlan. Her father, through the unexpected bequest of a long-forgotten uncle, had come into a title. A baronetcy, in fact, and a minor country estate called Penllwyn. And so off they'd gone, emigrating to the north and away from everything Kiara had known.

She had missed Kilbourne with a fierce, longing ache. Still, as time passed, it had all become like something in a dream, or from another life: vaguely remembered, but not really substantial. Eventually she had acclimated and even come to love her adopted land. And once she'd managed to catch the eye of Lord Jermaine Northram at a ball, things improved immensely.

Jermaine had been a young noble of impeccable lineage and fortune. Her parents had enthusiastically approved the match and would have moved heaven and earth to see it accomplished. Even her older brother, Harvil, had seemed pleased, and practically nothing pleased him.

After they'd wed, she'd been happy with Jermaine. They had even dreamed of starting a family. Then the fateful news arrived, shattering her world into splinters of despair: Jermaine had been killed in the war with Kilbourne, at the siege of Noordstrom.

She'd been more than devastated, taking to her bed and even

refusing to see her mother, who'd tried to comfort her. She had cried until there were no more tears left, and then cried some more. Dry, heaving, wracking sobs that rattled the windows and disconcerted the servants. Finally, drained and shaking, she'd left her bed, tottered to the window, and stared up at the stars. And by those stars, she had sworn to wreak vengeance on the man who had robbed her of her chance at happiness.

Vows of vengeance, she reflected with a bitter smile, were becoming a habit. She'd done so once before, when the same man, then a boy, had spurned her affections. Then she hadn't really meant it. Now she did. And by luck and calculated cunning she now had the means to achieve her aim.

The coach pulled to a stop. Kiara stepped down to the street. She tottered in small circles for a few moments while the driver and his helper unloaded the trunks. Once she'd regained the full use of her legs, she walked up the stairs of the Royal Arms Inn. A clerk sat behind a large desk, engrossed in a book. Kiara gave a soft cough and the clerk looked up.

"Yes, may I be of assistance?" he inquired, eyeing her travel-stained clothing and no doubt disheveled hair.

"I am Kiara, Lady Northram," she said with more confidence than she actually felt. "I believe you have a suite of rooms for me."

The clerk sprang to attention. "Indeed we do, Your Ladyship," he cried. "Our finest. Welcome, welcome. If you'll just sign here…"

With much bowing, scraping and summoning of servants to assist with the luggage, Kiara was installed in a suite of bright, comfortable rooms on the third floor of the inn. Windows looked out upon the town, and the towers of St. Basil's were visible several blocks away. So too were the spires and turrets of the palace. Kiara looked around the room and said, "This will do nicely."

"Very good, Your Ladyship," said the clerk. "If you should need anything, anything at all, please just ring the bell. A servant will attend you at once."

"I should like dinner sent up right away," said Kiara. "My maid and I have been long on the road, and we're famished."

"At once, Your Ladyship," said the clerk, bowing his way out of the room. Liza was busy unpacking trunks and hanging gowns in the wardrobe. A chambermaid was turning down the bed, while another lit a fire in the hearth in the adjoining sitting room. Kiara removed her travelling cloak and handed it to Liza, and then went to the window. Looking out upon Caerfaen Town, she wondered if she had been mad to come here. Her plan now seemed to lack some of its original luster. Then memories of Jermaine flooded back, and her resolve hardened. She would not be denied vengeance against the man who had caused her world to crumble: Morgan McRobbie.

Servants soon arrived, bearing platters and pitchers. Kiara sat down at a small table to eat her dinner and plan her next move for the morrow.

Chapter Eight

Tobias Albert Fanshawe sat at his desk, chewing thoughtfully on a scarred knuckle. With a sigh he completed his tally of a long column of figures.

Those figures represented the booty taken from the latest Rhuddlani vessel he and his crew had plundered. A percentage of the spoils—a small percentage, to be sure—would be divvied up amongst the crew. The remainder of this substantial sum would be Toby's share. As captain, it was his right.

Of course, not all of it would be his. Not that much of it, in the long run. There were bills to pay, always more bills, and of course there was… Toby shook his head as he made the final entry. He wasn't a pirate; he was a bloody bookkeeper. Well, looting and pillaging was all good fun, but someone always had to do the paperwork.

He whistled softly as he wrote the total and signed it with a flourish. A nice haul indeed; the crew would be pleased. He glanced out the window to the dock where the *Mad Maudie* rested at anchor. Most of his men were on shore leave. A token crew remained behind as punishment for some infraction or another. They were swabbing decks and polishing brass. Making the vessel shipshape.

At least, he amended, she was ship-shaped. That was about the best that could be said for her. She wasn't sleek, she wasn't fast, and she wasn't pretty. In point of fact, she was ugly and wallowed through the ocean troughs like a pig. But she was serviceable and reliable. Which meant she hadn't sunk out from under him. Yet. Unlike some vessels he could mention but wouldn't. He grimaced at the memory. That incident had brought him right to where he was today, a scurrilous pirate.

A movement from the doorway gained his attention. Toby sighed and put down his quill. "Yes, Sharkey?"

The mate had come by his name honestly. No man had ever looked more shark-like. A wide sloping forehead, beady eyes, a broad mouth filled with teeth filed to points, and a body that was pure muscle. If he'd ever had a real name, it was lost somewhere in the swamp-like depths of Mr. Sharkey's own memories. No one Toby had ever met knew it.

"Cap'n," grunted the mate. "Wonderin' when we'll be setting

out, sir. Men 're getting a bit antsy, beggin' the cap'n's pardon."

"Soon, Mr. Sharkey, soon," Toby said. "But this should keep them happy." He turned around the tally sheet, pointing to the total.

Sharkey's eyes glinted with a dark light as his mouth split into a toothy grin. "Aye, sir, that it should," he agreed. "Nice bit o' plunder. I still thinks ye made a mistake 'bout the girl, though. She'd have brought a nice bit o'ransom. The lads right fancied 'er besides."

Toby fixed him with a gimlet stare. "I'm quite certain I have made my position known, Mr. Sharkey. More than once. Pirates we may be. We loot and plunder, certainly. That is our business. We do not, however, ravish maidens. Ever. There will be none of that on my ship. No. Ravishing. Got it?"

"Yessir," mumbled Sharkey, the picture of piratical contrition.

"Spread the word, Mr. Sharkey, starting with yourself. Any man who treats a lady captive with anything less than the utmost respect will be subjected to stringent punishment. Keelhauling and plank-walking will be involved, but that will be on the mild side. Things will get, um, interesting from there." Tobias found himself breathing a bit hard after this exchange, and he took a moment to calm himself.

He couldn't remember the last time he'd been involved in any such activities. Well, actually never, he acknowledged with a sour grimace. Oh, there'd been a good bit of cajoling, along with a surfeit of raised brows and not-so-subtle innuendo. And on occasion quite a good deal of pleading—on his part. But he did have a reputation to maintain, and a conscience to keep. Plus, he'd promised his Aunt Maudie, the old harridan and a scurvy pirate herself. And his word was his bond.

That went for his crew as well. Any man caught in, to put it politely, activities disrespectful of a lady on company time was subject to severe disciplinary action. Of course, he couldn't be responsible for what they did on their own time. But on board, the captain's word was law, and woe to the man who broke it.

"I know you fellows find me a bit odd, Sharkey," he said at last. "I have my little habits and rules. That's just the way I am."

"Ah, but you're a good pirate, Cap'n," Sharkey said.

Toby waved a hand. "We've done all right, I suppose. But tell me something. Why do you and the rest of the crew stay on? I mean, this new scheme, now. It's absolutely insane. But I don't see anyone jumping ship. I expect you fellows think I'm a bit crazy, don't you? Why do you all keep on?"

"Oh, we know you're mad all right, sir. Madder 'n a pack of weasels at the bottom of the rum barrel."

Toby winced at this descriptor, but Sharkey paid no heed. "But you're lucky, that's the thing. I've seen you dice with the devil hisself and come home in the mornin' with his trousers. That's why we stick with you. Sure your plans are crazy, but they always seem to pay off right handsomely."

Toby smiled. "Why thank you, Mr. Sharkey. Coming from you, that means a lot to me."

With an avaricious grin, Sharkey waved the tally sheet. "All right if I post this, Cap'n?"

"Post away, Mr. Sharkey. Then start getting us ready to sail. We leave for Caerfaen tomorrow at dawn to begin this new venture. Anyone not aboard will be left behind."

~ * ~

"She must be kept under our control."

Nardis Cardion sucked in a breath with a little gasp. He'd been sitting at a quiet table in his favorite tavern, sipping a glass of wine and thinking about little except maybe another glass of wine.

But the familiar voice of Augustus Rhenn, Headmaster of St. Giles Academy of Magic, carried just enough to reach his ears and make him sit up and take notice.

It was a voice Nardis had learned to dread during his time at St. Giles. It had constantly berated him, chided him, mocked him. The headmaster had displayed an intense and overt distaste for those of "his kind," which Nardis had taken to mean anyone who looked even remotely different than the typical fair-skinned, blue-eyed, light-haired men so predominant at the academy.

Which Nardis, with his dark complexion, dark hair, and glittering dark eyes, most certainly was not. Actually, he'd been amazed and a bit shaken when his application to the academy had even been considered. He'd spent the voyage from Orsk wondering if he'd manage to fit in, and had quickly discovered that no, he didn't at all. But he'd been dogged and done his best to maintain a low profile while doing the best work he could in his classes. He'd managed somehow to achieve his journeyman's certificate, thanks to the intervention and support of one of the Masters.

He thrust this line of thought away, turning his attention back to Rhenn and his companion. The man to whom Rhenn had been speaking had his back to Nardis. His voice had been too quiet to overhear. But Rhenn, gesturing emphatically, said, "If she is allowed to operate unchecked, there's no telling what course she may pursue or the damage she might cause."

"Rhenn, does she really have such power as to be a concern to us?"

The second man spoke in a more normal voice this time, and Nardis was able to both hear his words and recognize his voice. Arjin Skarlatos. Nardis rolled his eyes. He should have known. Skarlatos, a stout and well-bearded wizard, had seemed to delight in tormenting Nardis during his time at the Academy. He'd shown himself time and again to be one of Rhenn's inner cadre. What was this pair up to? And who was the woman they were talking about?

"She has no training, does she? No real ability to use whatever power she may possess?" Skarlatos cut the air with a dismissive wave of his hand. "So why should such a trifle as this even concern us?"

"I could feel the stirring of great power within her," reported Rhenn. "Truly, it was unlike anything I've ever encountered. Untrained, yes, of a certainty, and unharnessed. Yet it would be foolish to forget about the dragon. He seeks to instruct her. To what purpose, I wonder? And with this tutelage, she will soon acquire both the training and the ability to wreak all manner of havoc on our—"

Skarlatos quickly held up a hand, no doubt to keep Rhenn from divulging secrets in such a public place. Nardis edged deeper into the shelter of the wide wooden beam which had thus far concealed his presence. If they knew he was here, had overheard their conversation… the consequences of that just didn't bear thinking about. Being turned into a croaking toad was the best he could hope for.

The headmaster, Nardis had heard, had been quietly maneuvering toward the removal of Foxwent, the Chief Wizard, from his position. Men like Rhenn often played such dangerous games in pursuit of power. Those who stood in their way, or were perceived as antagonists, were often casualties.

"Yes, of course. Well, no matter. We must either gain control of this woman and her powers, or…." Rhenn left the sentence dangling ominously.

"Or? You have met with her, have you not? Weren't you able to induce her to come to St. Giles?" inquired Skarlatos archly. Rhenn's flush of anger was visible even from where Nardis sat. He winced, waiting for a dire reaction. Rhenn somehow managed to keep control of his legendary temper, for when he answered his voice remained calm and measured.

"Aye, I've met with her. And despite my efforts at persuasion, she was able to fend off my attempts to influence her."

"But you said she has no training." Skarlatos sounded incredulous. "How?"

Rhenn's voice lost its calm, and his words came out as a growl. "I'm positive that blasted creature was aiding her somehow."

"But it's proven fact dragons are incapable of performing magic."

"Hmph. You know it, and I know it," he replied in tones that could curdle milk. "But has anyone bothered to tell the dragon? I only know what I saw. This Lady Marissa was able to resist my best efforts at coercion."

Both men appeared to ponder over this statement. Nardis hardly dared to breathe for fear they would notice his presence.

Finally Skarlatos leaned back, took a deep drink of his wine, and gave a little shudder. "Do you really think the dragons have somehow learned to perform magic? Could it be why they are returning after all this time?"

Rhenn slowly shook his head. "I've no idea," he admitted. "But one thing at a time. My concern at the moment is this confounded woman. I'm not sure just what the dragon's interest in her is, but it seems intent on keeping her under close control. Which is not something we wizards should take lightly."

"What are you proposing to do?"

"I've given it quite a bit of thought," said Rhenn. "I have arrived at the only logical conclusion. If she will not submit to my authority, she must be eliminated."

Nardis heard the sharp intake of breath that was Skarlatos's only response. Rhenn went on, "Drastic times call for drastic measures, eh?"

"You're talking about eliminating the betrothed of Kilbourne's Knight-Commander," Skarlatos protested. "That's pretty damned drastic."

Drastic indeed. Nardis's mind churned with fear. They were talking ever so casually about murder. The murder of Lady Marissa duBerry, Commander Morgan McRobbie's betrothed. Nardis had always felt a sense of pride in his fellow Orskan. If McRobbie could rise to such lofty heights, Nardis had thought on more than one occasion, then perhaps he could as well.

Now more than ever he pressed himself back into his hiding spot, hoping against hope he'd remain unnoticed. Any slip on his part, and his own life wouldn't be worth a penny.

Skarlatos muttered something Nardis couldn't hear, and Rhenn barked out a sharp laugh. "If the time comes, I will deal with her," he assured his companion. "And no one will ever know it was me."

Nardis bared his teeth. *Not if I can help it.*

Chapter Nine

Sebastien duPre Tarvryn pushed aside the scroll he had been perusing and rubbed his smarting eyes. The candle lighting his work had guttered and hissed down to a nub and appeared in imminent danger of expiring. He could faintly hear the bells of St. Basil's Cathedral chiming away another hour. He stopped to count. Seven bells.

Good heavens! He'd been down here nearly the entire bloody night. He looked at the scrawled notes he'd made from documents he'd found in the Archives. It was, he decided, enough to be getting on with. Slotting the last scroll back in its niche on the shelves, he gathered up his notes and neatened them into a ragged semblance of order. After a welcome stretch to relieve a crick in his shoulders, he placed the notes carefully into an inner pocket of his robes. Whoever had decided robes should have pockets, he thought for not the first time, was an absolute genius and deserved a special place in heaven.

He took up the remains of the candle and used it to light his way out. This necessitated a climb up three flights of stairs, since the Archives had been relegated to a sub-basement chamber. At least it was relatively dry and rodent free, Sebastien mused. He had seen worse, much worse.

As Sebastien emerged into the morning light, he winced at the blinding glare. Pulling his hat low to shield his eyes, he trudged toward the docks, where he'd let a room in a cheap boarding house. His mind reeled at the import of his discoveries. A few hours' time to organize his thoughts and write up his notes would allow him to process what he'd learned. In addition, it would provide more clarity when he explained his discoveries to Commander McRobbie and Lady Marissa when he met with them. They were due to arrive later today, and he was to meet them tomorrow at a café at one o'clock.

That would be enough time. Wyvrndell had relayed their encounter with Augustus Rhenn, and Sebastien was concerned—no, make that deathly afraid—of what the Headmaster was up to. And why.

He passed a stall selling fresh-baked bread, and the enticing aroma caught his attention. Just the thing to break his fast, Sebastien decided. He had a few coins in his purse and he bought a small loaf. The warmth of it felt wonderful to his old hands. If he hurried, it might still be warm by the time he reached his room.

He arrived at his lodgings, and the bread was indeed still warm. Now to brew up some tea. As he entered the room, he pulled a bit from the loaf and popped it into his mouth.

A movement in the corner caught his eye. Sebastien nearly dropped the bread, gasping as a figure rose up out of the shadows. He began to utter a defensive spell, but the other man said quietly, "Wait, Sebastien."

Panting slightly from the sudden rush of adrenaline, he halted the spell. "Nardis! What in the name of all the saints are you doing here?"

"Waiting to see my old friend and mentor," Nardis replied. "I need to speak with you."

"How did you know where to find me?"

"You're not that hard to locate," said the younger wizard. "You haven't made any real efforts to conceal your presence here in Caerfaen."

"No, why should I?" Sebastien shrugged as he pulled off another hunk of the loaf and bit into it. He chewed, swallowed, then said, "I've no need to slink about. But what brings you here, my young friend?"

Nardis looked around as if to check for eavesdroppers. Lowering his voice, he said, "I overheard something yesterday. Something I thought you needed to know."

Sebastien cocked his head and took another mouthful of bread. He held the loaf out to his guest, but Nardis waved it away. Finally, the young man continued. "I was sitting in a café when I saw Rhenn and Skarlatos at a nearby table. They didn't realize I was there, and I inadvertently overheard what they were discussing." Nardis related the conversation between the two senior wizards. Sebastien sank into a chair, so intent on Nardis's tale that he nearly dropped the loaf of bread again.

"… and Rhenn said if this Lady Marissa couldn't be controlled, he would take it upon himself to eliminate her. Skarlatos didn't seem enthused with the idea, but Rhenn was adamant."

"Anything else?" Sebastien inquired.

"Isn't that enough? Good Lord, Sebastien, they're talking about murder."

"Yes, they certainly are. Careless of them, too, allowing themselves to be overheard."

Nardis sucked in a breath. "You—you don't think it was intentional?"

Sebastien shook his head. "No, no, not at all. I merely think the headmaster is too confident of his own abilities. No, if he'd noticed you eavesdropping, you wouldn't have been allowed to just calmly stroll away."

"I wasn't calm, I can assure you." Nardis grimaced. "I was

shaking like a leaf. I must have sat there a good twenty minutes after they left before I even dared to move. Then I came straight away to find you. And had to wait forever, I might add."

"Yes, I'm sorry about that. Actually, the errand that kept me up all night now appears to have even more importance."

"Meaning what?"

"Meaning nothing. At least nothing you need to know. You know entirely too much already, I'm afraid." Sebastien sighed. "If I were you, I'd think about taking a nice long holiday somewhere as far from Caerfaen as I could get."

Nardis narrowed his eyes. "You're not going to tell me? After I've taken the risk of coming here, of telling you all this? I trusted you, Sebastien."

"I know, Nardis, and believe me, your trust is not misplaced. As much as I would like to tell you what Rhenn's up to, it's best if you remain secure in your ignorance. The less you know, the less chance you'll get caught up in something unpleasant." He looked up sharply. "No one knows you've come to me, do they?"

Nardis shook his head. "Not likely. You, who are anathema to those in positions of power on the Council? No, Sebastien, I made damned sure no one knows I'm here. I'm only a very junior member of the Council, and it's more than my life is worth if they discovered I'd come to you. Yet you have always been a source of inspiration to me, and I value your wisdom and counsel. Very well, I will trust you know what you're doing."

"I'm not sure of that in the least."

"Shouldn't you go to the Chief Wizard and tell him what you suspect?"

Heaving a sigh, Sebastien shook his head. "No, that wouldn't help. I'm afraid Foxwent in his own way is just as bad an option. I don't trust any of them in this matter. I'm not even sure I trust myself. There's too much at stake. But if my hunch is correct, the Headmaster plays at a most dangerous game, and hazards much on one turn of the cards. He feels that he holds the aces; yet it may be a single pair shall best him in the end."

"As usual, you speak in riddles," laughed Nardis. "Yet I will trust you know best."

"I only hope that I do," said Sebastien. "For all our sakes…"

~ * ~

Catching a convenient updraft, Wyvrndell soared happily on the warm air currents wafting up from the city below. The sun beat on his wide-spread wings, he'd recently fed upon a succulent ox, and he was on his way to visit R'gm'l. Wyvrndell the dragon found himself content.

It was an odd feeling, he acknowledged. Dragons were, by both nature and tradition, solitary creatures, prone to brooding alone in their mountain aeries over hoards of treasure. They gathered only infrequently, and when they did—well, not for nothing was a group of dragons termed a wrangle.

But Wyvrndell, youngest of his kind, had discovered that he actually enjoyed companionship. He liked speaking with Morgan McRobbie about deeds of valor and the concepts of honor. He liked tutoring Marissa duBerry in the arts of magic. He was eager to learn about humans, to understand them as few dragons had done. So he conversed with other humans as well—soldiers, farmers, merchants, and any others bold enough to wish to make his acquaintance.

He also spoke on occasion with Rhys Gwynfallis, King of Kilbourne. It was, he reasoned, only proper, since Rhys had so thoughtfully provided the oxen upon which he snacked when the mood struck him. This arrangement obviated the need for Wyvrndell to swoop down and snaffle some poor farmer's livestock, a fact tactfully left unmentioned by all parties.

Finally, there was R'gm'l, son of King K'var'k of the Dwarves. Who was currently waving furiously to him from one of the high windows in the tower of the palace. Wyvrndell dipped his wings in acknowledgement and began a slow, spiraling descent toward the tower and his—yes, he would say the word—his friend.

He landed near the window, talons scrabbling to clutch at a wide ledge seemingly constructed for dragon roosting. R'gm'l leaned precariously out to greet him. "Good morning, my friend," called the young Dwarf, his face wreathed in a broad grin. "How much gold have you stolen today?"

"*Vast storerooms full,*" replied Wyvrndell. "*Yet how much have you stolen back, good Dwarf?*"

"Oh, almost all of it. But then I had to go in for breakfast."

It was a game they played, hearkening back to the day they first met. Each had felt the ingrained fear and loathing of the other, based purely on their own legends and prejudices. Thanks to Morgan McRobbie, both dragon and prince had come to realize just how silly the whole thing was and had determined to put aside past grievances and form an alliance.

They'd each vowed to work to bring peace between their races. R'gm'l, as heir to the Dwarf throne, hoped to convince his father that continued conflict with the dragons was pointless. Wyvrndell, for his part, intended to persuade the Council of Dragons to end centuries of enmity with the Dwarves. It was a daunting task, but each felt the outcome worth the effort.

But today was simply a day to enjoy one another's company. And to fly.

"May I?" asked R'gm'l politely.

"You may," Wyvrndell replied, arching his long neck toward the window. R'gm'l scrambled out, albeit cautiously, as befit the fact they were several dragon-lengths high. He slid onto Wyvrndell's neck, clambering down to a seat just above the dragon's wings.

"It's a beautiful day," R'gm'l said.

"To fly!" finished Wyvrndell, slipping off the ledge.

Dragon and Dwarf dropped like a stone, plummeting downwards toward the hard earth far below. R'gm'l yipped out a wild cry in Dwarvish as they fell.

Then, before they could wind up in a splattered heap, Wyvrndell unfurled his great wings and they soared upwards to the blue sky. And around his neck, on its slim silver chain, the dragon felt a warm glow from the ring called Dragon's Fire, the token given to him by R'gm'l as a symbol of friendship and alliance.

They flew for a long time, soaring high over the city, swooping down over rivers and meadows, startling sheep and shepherds alike, and playing tag with the clouds.

As they leveled off and soared after a particularly thrilling nose-to-tail loop which, if R'gm'l's minders had seen would have caused them no little distress, the Dwarf observed, "I received a letter from my father yesterday."

"Indeed? And how fares the King of Dwarves?"

"Well enough. He says the rebels, those who wish to have no dealings with men, have been quashed for now, so he is able to govern in peace. At least for the moment."

"And had he anything to say on the subject of... dragons?"

R'gm'l chuckled. "He said I am impetuous, headstrong, and will no doubt come to a bad end."

"Oh."

"He also said I have acted against centuries of Dwarf tradition."

"I see." Wyvrndell's spirits sagged at this news. He had to make a conscious effort not to allow his flight to turn into a nosedive. Blast and scorch it. The Dwarf king wouldn't—

"He also," R'gm'l went on, "said I acted exactly as he could have hoped, and that he is proud of me."

"Truly?"

"Truly. My father says he finds both my conclusions and my

actions acceptable. He considers a formal peace with dragons something to be hoped for."

Wyvrndell's heart soared again at this news, and he likewise spiraled upwards, chasing after a particularly fluffy cloud.

R'gm'l went on, "He says it will not be easy to achieve. There are still many Dwarves who will balk and wish to hold their hatred of dragons just because their forefathers did so. But my father believes the time is right to pursue a course to an accord."

"Now," Wyvrndell observed, *"if only the dragons can show half as much sense."*

On they flew, until finally, with a reluctant sigh, R'gm'l said, "I think perhaps we'd best head back. My arms are starting to tire."

"And the clouds are darkening quickly," Wyvrndell added as he banked westward toward Caerfaen. *"It will be no weather for flying soon."*

"I like flying in the rain."

"I don't. Besides, this looks to be more than just rain. 'Lightning and thunder, wings split asunder,'" he quoted. *"And my wings are getting tired as well."*

"Liar," R'gm'l said, but his voice held not scorn but affection. He gave the dragon a fond slap on the neck. "You're afraid I'll fall off. You worry worse than any old Dwarf auntie."

"Mmmph. Be that as it may," the dragon replied equably, *"we will return to the palace."* His words were punctuated by a distant rumble of thunder and he increased speed.

They landed in the palace courtyard just as the first fat raindrops spattered down, puffing up little clouds of dust. "Thank you, mighty dragon," R'gm'l said, sketching a bow.

"It was my pleasure, mighty prince," Wyvrndell replied. *"Please extend my compliments to King Rhys."*

With a wave, R'gm'l dashed off through the rain. Wyvrndell shook out his wings and took flight for the warmth and shelter of his rocky lair.

Chapter Ten

"Look!" cried Marissa, tugging on Morgan's arm with such vigor he was nearly thrown off balance.

Their journey back to Caerfaen had taken a day and a half. After dropping Lady Sybil off at the home of a friend, Morgan had suggested he and Marissa stop to get something to eat. Now, all thoughts of lunch forgotten, he scanned the street for threats. His hand reached instinctively for a sword he wasn't wearing at the moment. It was generally looked upon as bad form to wear armament while escorting a lovely lady to lunch.

The only thing out of place seemed to be a wagon, gaily painted and sporting colorful banners, rumbling up the street. It didn't appear particularly menacing.

"Look at what?" he asked finally.

"The Tzigani," she said, cocking her head to look at him as if he were a complete dullard. Then her eyes took on a glow of excitement. "Can we go see them?"

A couple more wagons, pulled by sturdy if rather tired looking horses, rolled by. From their vantage point on the adjacent cobbled walkway, Morgan noted people gesturing and exclaiming over the wagons. Some looked as excited as Marissa, while others grimaced in evident disapproval.

Several mounted men followed the wagons, in a tight formation that would have made any cavalry sergeant proud. Except instead of military uniforms, this lot sported a collection of bright orange, blue, and purple tunics with flowing sleeves, loosely cut linen trousers, and an abundance of sashes. One, whom Morgan presumed to be the leader, wore a grand hat with a red feather dancing proudly from its band. His companions wore brightly hued scarves to cover their heads. And to a man, old and young, each bore a sweeping moustache which wouldn't have looked out of place on one of the old-time mountain brigands of legend.

A final wagon, this one with a cage housing a huge, shaggy brown bear, was followed by another squad of mustachioed Tzigani, each with a short, curved sword in his sash. Morgan turned back to look at Marissa, who appeared ready to give immediate pursuit.

"Tzigani?" he repeated.

"Oh, Morgan, yes. They used to pass through Vynfold when I was a girl. Father would take Mother and me out to their camp to talk to them, and sometimes they'd tell my fortune. I remember how one year, she told me I would fall in love with a dark handsome man."

"Well, she got it half right, anyway," Morgan demurred.

"Pooh. She got it all right." Marissa squeezed his hand. "Will you take me to see them? After they set up their camp, of course. And"—she gave him a pitying look—"after we've had some lunch. Poor Morgan, starving away to nothing."

He stared thoughtfully after the line of wagons. "Mmm? Oh, yes, I suppose so, if that's what you want."

"You don't sound quite so thrilled with the idea." Marissa regarded him, her eyes dark with concern. "Is there a problem?"

Morgan shrugged one shoulder. "No, not at all. It's just where I come from, Tzigani have always been looked on with suspicion. Most folks were eager for them to just move along."

"Nonsense," Marissa protested. "Oh, of course, say 'Tzigani' and everyone immediately locks up their chickens and guards their purses extra carefully. But all the ones I've ever met have been enchanting. They're wanderers, that's all. People just have a hard time understanding their lifestyle."

"So if they're wanderers, just how do they earn those chickens?"

"You're terrible." She poked him in the arm. Hard. Well, at least it wasn't a slap, which he took as a good sign. "They earn their keep entertaining people wherever they stop. They'll set up camp and dance. They'll do conjuring tricks and tell wild stories of their adventures. And hope that the crowd will show their appreciation by tossing coins in the hat."

"And they tell fortunes?"

"Yes, they also tell fortunes," she agreed. "Many of the Tzigani folk do actually have the sight, as they call it. Did you know Briana is from Tzigani stock?"

"Your maid Briana?" He thought of the maid's appearance and temperament. "Yes, I could see that."

"She's told me some wild tales of her grandmother's mother, who she says was a highly regarded seer. I'll get her to tell you about it some time. She says she even occasionally gets flashes of 'the sight.'"

"I'm all agog," he assured her.

So it passed that in the evening, after they had dined, Morgan found himself escorting his lady to the bustling encampment. The day was drawing toward dusk, the fading sun painting the sky with rosy hues.

The Tzigani had drawn their little caravan of wagons into a half circle so they provided a backdrop to the open area which had, Morgan assumed, been cleared off for dancing and other entertainments.

A large fire crackled cheerfully off to one side, its flames leaping and dancing as if in anticipation of the evening's pleasures. A small boy stood there, engaged in industriously turning a brace of rabbits on a spit over glowing coals raked to one side. The smell of the roasting meat was enticing as it wafted over the camp.

Everywhere they looked presented a riot of color. The wagons, the banners, and especially the colorful garments of the Tzigani all jumbled into a festival atmosphere that soon had him smiling appreciatively. "It's like the midsummer faire," he said.

"Except without the jammy tarts," Marissa lamented.

Silently Morgan directed her attention to a crude but well constructed brick oven just beyond the last of the wagons. A young woman in a riotously colored skirt and a white linen blouse which bared her tanned shoulders was just extracting the oven's contents.

"They must have heard you were coming." He chuckled as the heavenly aroma of freshly baked pastries permeated the air. In short order the woman had a small wheeled cart laden with steaming tarts. Before she could trundle it off toward the crowd of townspeople, Marissa rushed toward her, dragging him in her wake.

The woman looked up with a welcoming smile. She appeared to be around Marissa's age, Morgan thought, perhaps even a bit younger, though it was hard to tell exactly. "Hello," she said. "Would you like to buy a jam tart?"

She exuded an impression of alluring mystery, even in the simple act of displaying her wares, and there was a sensation of smooth honey in both her voice and complexion. His brows rose as he realized that, given the right clothes, Marissa might easily pass for one of the Tzigani.

"We'll take two—no, make it four," she said, her words tumbling out as she gazed at the array of bubbling, flaky tarts with a covetous eye. "Please," she added.

The Tzigani laughed, her eyes bright with mirth. "Ah, I think you've tasted our tarts before."

"Many times, as a girl in the south," Marissa told her. "How much?"

"Normally four tarts would be eight pence. But, for a connoisseur…"

"Give her half a crown," Marissa instructed. Morgan obeyed; when she spoke in that tone, there was no arguing. He cheerfully handed over the coin. The girl accepted it, tossed it into the air, and caught it like a conjurer in a suddenly open pouch on her sash. With a saucy wink at Morgan and a half-curtsey to Marissa she closed the pouch and gestured to her cart.

"Cherry, raspberry, peach, and blackberry," she said, pointing to each row in turn.

"One of each, please," Marissa requested. To Morgan she said, "If you behave yourself, you may have one."

He rolled his eyes as the baker, chortling, wrapped up their tarts. Soon they were strolling around the camp, watching with interest as the Tzigani prepared for the evening's entertainment. Marissa took a bite of tart, her sigh of pleasure encouraging him to do likewise. The pastry was golden, flaky, and sweet, and the tartness of cherries flooded his tongue. The filling was cooled just to the point where it was still perfectly hot, but not so much as to scald his mouth.

"Mmm," she breathed. "W'n'erful." She smacked her lips. "Say, did you snitch the one with the cherry jam?"

"I didn't snitch it," Morgan replied with righteous dignity, or as much as he could muster through a mouthful of jammy tart. "You gave it to me."

"But I didn't know it was the cherry."

"M'lady, I surrender my tart in your favor," he replied with a bow. He handed over the remaining half.

"Oh, you do love me." She accepted his offering with regal graciousness. Then, with a happy shiver she bit the tart, the cherry jam squishing out to coat her lips and fingers. And in the rapidly fading light, Morgan McRobbie took tribute for his sacrifice, kissing traces of jam from her already sweet lips. She shivered again, but he didn't think it was due to the tarts this time.

They emerged from the shadows to the strains of music, passing the tart-baker, who flashed a knowing grin. In the center of the space before the wagons, three men played a fiddle, a lute, and a small harp. Four Tzigani girls danced, their brightly colored skirts swirling to reveal a flash of tawny legs as they twirled and kicked. Each of them had small metal disks on her fingers which chimed in time with the musicians.

A crowd of townspeople had gathered, drawn by the music and the aromas and colors. Morgan and Marissa joined them to watch.

After a bit the women were replaced by several of the Tzigani men in their bright silk tunics, flowing trousers, gaily colored sashes, and boots polished to the standards of any Legion sergeant. As the music began, they moved slowly, then faster as the tempo increased. As they danced, two women began to strike tambourines in time to the music. As if this were a cue, each of the men drew his curved sword with a shout. They leapt and whirled, waving their blades, striking them together in a clash of steel in time to the music. Two of the dancers held their swords in outstretched arms, while a third, tossing his own blade to one of the others, leapt through the swords in a diving roll, rising to catch his sword as it was tossed back to him.

As the men completed their dance to thunderous applause and cheers, two burly Tzigani opened the cage and led out the bear. The musicians changed their tune. The bear reared upright, stepping in time. Then, to Morgan's astonishment and excited murmurs from the crowd, the Tzigani baker moved to join the beast, taking one of its paws in her hand and dancing with it.

A collective gasp escaped the crowd as she led the bear in a tender waltz. The beast towered over her, but maintained a stolid, stately grace. The music slowed, and the woman stepped away from her incongruous partner, her head turning as if she were scanning the crowd. Her stare fixed on Marissa and she walked sinuously toward her.

The woman held out her hands in invitation. Eyes wide, Marissa began to move forward.

"Marissa, no!" Morgan said. But a burly Tzigani with flashing white teeth and a luxuriant moustache blocked him from reaching her.

"Do not worry, soldier," he said as the woman led Marissa into the clearing where the bear waited, still upright. "She is chosen, no? No harm will befall your lady. Indeed, she is honored."

Morgan longed to thrust the man aside and dart forward to stop her from doing something stupid. As if sensing his thoughts, the Tzigani stood aside. "Do as you feel you must," he said quietly. "Just remember, my friend, that one day we must all dance with the bear."

Morgan halted, feeling as if he'd crashed into a wall as the Tzigani's words sank in. Had he not, on so many occasions in his own life, danced with the bear? Dared fate, risked his life? Slowly, reluctantly, but with understanding, he nodded. "Very well," he said, taking a calming breath. "I won't interfere. After all, she has braved a dragon and survived. What terrors could a mere bear hold for her?"

The Tzigani stared at him hard. "Braved a dragon?" he sputtered. "Then she is none other than the famous Lady Marissa duBerry, the Witch of Caerfaen? And you? You are the redoubtable Commander McRobbie?"

"Yes, and yes," Morgan replied with a sigh.

The Tzigani extended a hand. "I am Radivan," he said. "Later, Commander, I would very much like to speak with you, if you will. But for now, watch the dance."

With that he whirled and was gone. Marissa, led by the Tzigani woman, was dancing slowly with the bear. The music increased in tempo again, and another woman joined them. Then another, and another, their skirts flying as they swirled around Marissa and her ursine partner.

Then the harp sang out, a resounding note that echoed off the wagons. The male dancers stepped into the clearing once more, weaving in and out among the women with great cries and leaps. And in the center of it all, skirts swirling and looking ecstatically happy, Marissa danced.

Morgan watched, a smile spreading across his face. The music came to an end, the crowd clapping and whistling and stomping their feet. And loudest of all was Morgan McRobbie. Laughing, gasping for breath, Marissa fell into his arms. He cradled her for a moment, then tilted her head up with a finger under that resolute chin and gave her a kiss.

Chapter Eleven

Marissa could hear, vaguely in the background, appreciative sighs from some of the ladies present as Morgan kissed her. One of those sighs, she realized, might have been her own.

Finally he released her from his embrace. She took a step back, swayed, and might have fallen if Morgan's strong arms hadn't come to the rescue once more. "Was that due to your dance, or to my kiss?" he inquired.

"Yes," she said, recovered enough to flash an insouciant grin. She took his arm and they strolled around the camp, pausing to watch a man juggle three, then four, and finally five daggers in a twisting whirl of razor-sharp steel. They gasped with the rest of the onlookers as the blades flew faster and faster through the air, until finally the Tzigani laughed and plucked them from the air one by one to drive them into a stump at his feet.

Next was a conjurer who made scarves disappear, ropes seem to dance upright, and coins to appear and vanish out of thin air. As they watched, Morgan asked, "Am I losing my place as your dance partner to your shaggy friend back there?"

Marissa eyed him with an appraising glance. "Well, he did dance quite elegantly," she replied, doing her best to keep her face straight. "But I think, all things considered, I'll stick with you. At least if you tread on my foot, I might come out with only a sore toe. If he did…" She gave an expressive shrug.

He laughed and circled his arm around her. "I'm relieved. I was quite sure you were going to throw me over."

"Hah! You can't get out of marrying me that easily, I'll have you know."

He pulled her close. "I would never wish to," he said, and the conviction in his tone sent a thrill coursing through her.

Before she could reply, a young Tzigani woman—one of the ones from the dance, Marissa thought—approached them. "My lady," she said, dropping a curtsey. "My mother, Elbethesba, who is leader of our band, asks if you would join her. She wishes to read your fortune."

"I would be most grateful for the honor." Marissa gave an answering curtsey. "Will you take us to her?"

"This is for you alone, my lady," the girl said. "As for you, Commander, Radivan wishes a word with you. He awaits you by the fire."

"Good fortune, m'lady," Morgan murmured, squeezing her hand. He turned toward the fire. Marissa followed the Tzigani girl, who led her briskly toward one of the wagons.

"Excuse me," Marissa said. "If it's not terribly rude of me to ask, what is your name?"

The girl gave her a shy smile. "I am called Antonettia." She giggled. "But it's such a mouthful, everyone just calls me Toni."

"I think Antonettia is a lovely name," Marissa said. "But Toni is much easier for a boy to whisper in your ear, eh?" She'd noticed the way the eyes of several of the younger men followed Toni's lithe form appreciatively.

Toni flushed, but didn't answer. Instead, she pulled aside a curtain at the end of a wagon to reveal an entrance. "My mother awaits you inside," she said. "When you are done, I will guide you back to your betrothed."

Before Marissa could ask how Toni knew she and Morgan were betrothed, the girl darted away, calling out something to another woman. Marissa supposed their public displays might well have given her a clue. Smiling fondly, she mounted the three steps up to the door of the wagon, gave a quick rap, and called, "Hello?"

"Come in, my dear," came a low, sonorous voice. Marissa obeyed, plunging into the interior of the wagon.

It felt much more spacious inside than she would have ever envisioned. A pair of bunked beds, with storage cupboards above and below, took up one side wall. A small washstand and more cupboards, along with several trunks, lined the opposite wall. In the center stood a round table, with two chairs facing each other, one on each side. The far chair was occupied, presumably by Toni's mother Elbethesba, leader of the Tzigani.

Elbethesba was, Marissa saw, younger than she'd expected. This was no wizened crone, but a vibrant woman of her own mother's age. Where most of the Tzigani were swarthy and dark-haired, Elbethesba had a crown of red-gold hair piled atop her head. Her face was fair, with a sprinkling of unexpected freckles and a mouth curved into a welcoming smile. Her eyes, bright green like a cat's, watched her visitor with intense interest.

Dropping a curtsey, Marissa said, "Thank you, Madame Elbethesba, for your kind invitation."

"Sit down, please. Time is fleeting, Lady Marissa, Witch of

Caerfaen. We must use it wisely."

Marissa stiffened. "You know about me?"

"Oh yes. I know much about you. The question is, do you wish to know about yourself?"

Silently, Marissa nodded, pulling out the chair to sit across from her. Elbethesba cocked her head, as if listening to a voice only she could hear. Seeming to arrive at a decision she gave a curt nod and said, "To do this properly, we must follow tradition. Please, if you have a coin, place it on the table. Large or small, it matters not. What matters is the exchange."

Fumbling in her reticule, Marissa produced a coin. She placed it on the table. Elbethesba glanced at it, nodded once, and picked it up. Turning it over in long slim fingers she said, "I told you before time is fleeting. More fleeting, even, than this gold." She flipped the coin into the air, where it seemed to vanish.

"Give me your right hand." Marissa extended her arm, and Elbethesba took her hand, turning it so the palm faced up. Gently she traced the lines there, murmuring to herself, almost a croon as a mother does to her child.

She stopped so suddenly Marissa almost jerked her hand away. When Elbethesba raised her head, her eyes were wide, and her breathing seemed labored.

"What?" demanded Marissa. "What did you see?"

Still holding her hand, Elbethesba spoke in a low, hollow voice, as if from a great distance. "You have braved great dangers," she began. "You have snatched joy from the jaws of sorrow. Yet I see even greater dangers besetting you, dangers you do not understand. You are near the cusp, and all will hinge on the choices you must soon make. Hard choices, in hard times. To save what you love, you will need to choose what you are to become."

"You speak in riddles, Elbethesba," Marissa protested. "Could you be a bit less murky? What danger will I face? What choice must I make? Can you not tell me more?"

"I wish I could, my child." Elbethesba's voice was tinged with regret. She released Marissa's hand. "I'm sorry. My sight will not show me all things that are to come. Only shadows of what may be."

"But—"

Elbethesba held up her hands, and Marissa quieted. When she spoke, it was in a voice of authority. "Yet this I say to you, Marissa, Witch of Caerfaen. There is more than one power at work in you. It may yet be that this power, when all seems darkest and lost, will be the one which informs your choice. Your destiny."

"I-I see."

"No, you don't. One day soon you will. Go now. You have a good heart. Use it. Follow it. Toni is waiting outside. She will lead you back to your enchanted knight."

Marissa rose and bowed her head. "Thank you, Elbethesba. Your words are puzzling, unsettling even, and I do not understand what they mean. Yet I will remember them, so that when the time comes, I may choose wisely."

The Tzigani's face was wreathed in a smile. "Go in peace, my child. I believe you just may do so."

~ * ~

Morgan paced back and forth by the fire, waiting for Marissa to return from her audience with the Tzigani fortune teller. He earned nervous glances from the boy who, freed from his spit-turning duties, was now engaged in dodging Morgan while stirring the contents of a large iron kettle.

Radivan had been a congenial, if somewhat mysterious, host. He had led Morgan to a wagon, provided him with a glass of something that tasted like liquid fire, and proceeded to enumerate the caravan's recent travels.

They had, Radivan related, been most recently up in the northern provinces of Cormaine and Dunstanshire, meandering here and there, stopping as they needed to take on supplies and earn a bit of coin.

Morgan, considering this, said, "If you don't mind me asking, what do you earn on a night like this?"

Radivan laughed, his moustaches twitching in high good humor. "Not at all. We don't do so bad for ourselves. I saw many of your townsfolk tossing coins in the hat as it passed by. I won't know the total until later when we count it all up. But I'd be willing to wager we took in a good five crowns or better tonight. And we'll be here for a several days. Caerfaen is a large city, and first night is always a bit slower. Word of our arrival hasn't spread yet. Tomorrow we'll have twice the crowd."

Morgan's brows rose precipitously. "Five crowns? For one evening? Seriously?"

Radivan shook with laughter. "Yes, I am quite serious. Plus, all the chickens we can carry."

Morgan opened his mouth to object, realized Radivan was merely having fun at his expense, and sat back with a grin. "All right, all right, well done. I've no doubt you come by your poultry supply honestly."

"We do, we do. All in all, Commander, our life is not such a bad one. We have food, we have family, we travel and see the world. Perhaps you'd like to join us. You'd likely be a star attraction in the sword dance. Can you grow a moustache, do you think?"

"Thanks for the offer, but right now I'm satisfied. Perhaps someday, if I tire of my position as Knight-Commander, or more likely the king tires of me. But come, you didn't ask me here to ply me with potent spirits—what the devil is this stuff, by the way?—and convince me to take up the Tzigani life. What's on your mind?"

"The drink, it is a Tzigani brew called jalzani. Clears the sinuses, eh?"

"If clearing the sinuses is achieved by blowing the top of one's head off, then yes, it does a marvelous job." Morgan held out his hands, palms up, making a "give me" motion with his fingers.

Radivan's expression grew serious. "You have a reputation, Commander, as a man of honor. I respect that. While my people give no allegiance to any monarch but our own queen, still it is sometimes prudent to have a friend in the right place."

Morgan waited silently for him to continue. Radivan sighed and said, "In exchange for your good will, and the favor of your lady, I offer a—how should I put this? I suppose you could say I offer you a large network of informants."

Morgan's mouth worked, but no words came out. Shaking his head in an attempt to clear the fog he said, "I don't understand. You're offering to spy? For me?"

"Not spy. Not as such. Merely provide information we think might prove useful. To you, as an agent of your liege." He tugged on his moustache. "Look, we travel all over. Not just in Kilbourne, but across the Devil's Teeth, up into Rhuddlan as well. Wherever we go we are tolerated at best, ignored, or reviled and chased away at worst. Those chickens, you know…"

Morgan waved away chickens. Radivan nodded and continued, "But in our travels, we see much. We take the back roads, the ways known only to ourselves. And, for example, if across the Devil's Teeth we see many men marching south, with horses and weapons and supplies for a long journey, we might pass word of this to a man of honor who would know what to do with such information."

Morgan nodded slowly. "Yes, I see what you mean. Advance knowledge of something like that could be crucial to mounting a counteroffensive before they're prepared. But, as you say, you owe no obligations to Kilbourne. What do you gain from this?"

Radivan held up a finger. "First, as I said, we gain your goodwill. You are a man not only of honor, but of power and influence in this land. Your word has sway, and to be under your protection, even if not overtly, is nothing to be sneezed at."

He raised a second finger. "In addition, a prolonged conflict between Kilbourne and your neighbor in the north is not in our interest any more than it is in yours. It makes it much more difficult for us to travel around, much harder to earn our bread. And," his teeth flashed white under his moustache, "it gets much more difficult to steal all those chickens."

Morgan rolled his eyes. Radivan raised a third finger. "Finally, there is also the favor of your Lady Marissa to consider. My wife is a most intelligent woman, Commander. Ha! She must be, for she married me. But, all jesting aside, she senses the power residing in your betrothed. She feels that the future Duchess of Westdale will be a most puissant power in the land. And it never hurts to have a friend with such powers."

"The Witch of Caerfaen?" Morgan grimaced.

"As you say. You doubt her power, then?"

"Oh, no, I don't doubt it at all. Both the dragon and a fairly trustworthy wizard are agreed that she has magical powers in great abundance. I suppose I just sometimes wish she didn't."

"As does she, I've no doubt. Yet some rise to power, like yourself. Others find power thrust upon them unbidden. But both must do their best, should they not, to use what they have for good?"

"You are wiser than I, Radivan."

"No, just more experienced. For my wife possesses no little power herself. So I understand. Love your lady, my friend, and give her support and encouragement as she has need. This is my advice to you."

"Thank you. I accept both your advice and your most generous offer. In return, I pledge on my honor that you have my goodwill, for whatever that may be worth to you. And I shall encourage Marissa to look upon you and your kin with favor as well."

Radivan beamed and clapped his hands together. "Excellent. I can ask for no more. Come, to celebrate our agreement, we shall toast with another round of jalzani."

Morgan's sinuses had never felt clearer, even if his brain didn't.

Chapter Twelve

As Toni led her back to meet Morgan, Marissa asked, "Isn't this a difficult life for you?"

The girl looked at her with puzzled eyes. "Difficult? How do you mean?"

"You have no home, no roots. You're always on the move. Isn't it hard for you?"

Toni shook her head vigorously, sending her red hair cascading about her face. "Oh, no." She swept her arm out to encompass the camp. "This is my home. It moves about, yes, but it is home. For this is where my family is. I travel about, I meet new people, see new places, and my family is always here to protect me and care for me. My roots, as you say, are firmly planted in these wagons and in that love. I may not live in a fancy house, with servants to see to my every wish, yet still, I count myself most fortunate."

All Marissa could say to this was, "Yes, I see. You are right, Toni. You are truly fortunate. Accept my apology."

She waved this away. "You are of that other world. You could not know what it is like for us. But I tell you, even now we are making our way to Renais. There, bands of Tzigani from many different clans will gather for a conclave. There will be much celebrating, feasting, and drinking. And much dancing and singing." The girl's face lit at this prospect. "I will see my aunts and uncles and cousins. And many boys will come to ask if they may pay court to me, for my family is well regarded. To make such a match would bring honor to both houses." She gave Marissa a shy smile. "Perhaps, if I am lucky, I will find one as handsome, brave, and honorable as your betrothed."

"I hope you do." Then they were back at the fire, and across the dancing flames she saw Morgan and her heart leapt within her. "Goodbye, Toni," she said. "Thank you for helping me to understand." Giving the girl a quick embrace, she darted around the fire and into the safety and shelter of Morgan's arms.

"Are you all right?" His voice sounded concerned, and his eyes were wary in the flickering light of the campfire.

"I'm fine," she told him. "At least I will be if we go somewhere and eat these." She held up the parcel containing the two remaining jam tarts.

Morgan produced a similar parcel. "I anticipated you might have such a plan. I managed to acquire two more."

"Ah, how nice. You've learned so well in so short a time. Are they…?"

"Cherry," he confirmed. "Both of them."

"My hero."

"Come, m'lady, let us away with our prize. Or is that pies? The carriage should be just over here."

She gave him her arm and allowed him to assist her over the rough terrain. After all, she reasoned, there was no point in taking chances with the safety of the tarts. Once they were settled and underway, with their precious cargo stored safely away, she asked, "So what did your Tzigani want with you?"

"Radivan? He was…interesting." He described his interview with the Tzigani leader. Marissa listened agog.

"But that's wonderful," she exclaimed when he'd finished. "How exciting. And how wise the Tzigani are, to recognize you for what you are: a man of honor and influence."

"I think," he said with a wry look, "it's less my favor they wish to cultivate, and much more yours."

"Mine? Good heavens, what do I have to do with—" Realization struck like a hammer blow. "Oh."

"Witch of Caerfaen?" Morgan suggested.

"I'd really, really like to find out just who started that name and make them eat it. It's getting old very quickly."

"Don't look at me," he said, holding up both hands in mock terror. "By the way, tell me about your fortune. What did the fortuneteller see for you?"

Marissa waved a dismissive hand. "Oh, the usual."

"Wealth, health, happiness, and romance?"

"No such luck, I'm afraid. She was all full of mysteriously dire warnings of unseen dangers besetting me from every side, and difficult choices to save what I love. Or some such blather."

"You don't believe it?"

Marissa considered this question seriously. "She did sound awfully convincing at the time. But, here with you, and these tarts, I seem to have come across with a dose of healthy skepticism. Besides, I've had my full share of dangers and disasters already. I don't want any more, thank you."

"We rarely do," Morgan pointed out. "It's not really a question of what we want, is it?"

“Well, no, I suppose not.” She grimaced. “Oh, Morgan, I—” She broke off with a harsh laugh. “I guess I’m being foolish, aren’t I? If there are more dangers ahead we have to face, well…”

He pulled her into the security of his arm around her shoulders. “We’ll face them. Together.”

She forced out a wan smile. “Together,” she echoed. “That has a nice ring to it. And after all, what can stand against the two of us?”

“What, indeed?”

Chapter Thirteen

Marissa paused in her reminiscences of the previous evening's encounter with the Tzigani, a piece of toast halfway to her mouth. Morgan strolled into her breakfast room. She placed the toast back on her plate, saying, "Good morning. I didn't expect to see you here. At least not so early. Would you like some breakfast?"

He grinned. "You shall make an excellent soldier's wife, my love. Always keep him well fed, that's the right idea." He ducked as she feigned flinging her toast at him. "Thank you, I had a bit of breakfast. Although," he eyed her plate with an appraising stare, "those sausages do look quite tasty." He leaned in to give her a kiss. "As to my coming by so early, well, I just couldn't stay away."

She rolled her eyes. "Hmph. I'm not really sure if you love me or just my sausages."

He considered this question until she threatened him with more toast. "You," he said. "Definitely you. But the sausages do come a close second."

She waved him to a chair and rang the bell. He detoured to pour a cup of coffee. "More for you?" he asked.

"Yes, please." She held out her cup and he filled it.

Rose, the housemaid, entered. "You rang, m'lady? Oh, good morn, Your Grace."

"Please ask Cook if there are any more sausages left," Marissa instructed. "The duke is looking malnourished."

"Right away, m'lady." Rose departed at speed. By the time the coffee had cooled enough to sip, she was back bearing a tray laden with a surfeit of sausages and a tower of toast.

"Cook says she can have more ready in a jiffy," she reported.

"This will be more than enough, thank you," Morgan said. Rose colored prettily and left them alone again.

"Suborning my servants," Marissa observed. "And eating my sausages."

He pushed the plate toward her. "There's more than enough here, have another."

She shook her head with a smile. "But on the subject of servants, I suppose we need to discuss how we're going to handle things."

"Oh? How so?" Morgan asked through a mouthful of toast. He chewed, swallowed, and said, "I beg your pardon. I'm afraid I'm more used to eating on my own, or with the fellows in the Legion. I'm going to have to relearn my table manners."

She waved a hand in dismissal. "You didn't seem to have a problem when we were at Bryntop."

"Good heavens, no. If I'd talked with my mouth full there, Mother would have thrown me out and told me to have my dinner in the kennel." He grinned. "I shall take this under advisement for my future conduct."

"Well, since you're a duke now…"

"Might serve to act like one?"

"Just a thought. Back to the subject of servants. I assume Kevin wishes to stay on with you? After we're married, I mean."

"I—" Morgan stopped. "Well, I suppose so. I haven't actually asked him. I'll do so at the earliest opportunity."

"I've gotten used to Rose and Cook," Marissa went on. "I'd really like to keep them on when we're in town. I doubt if they'll want to come all the way out to Westdale, though, and the estate is simply rife with staff."

"All under Jarvis's watchful eye."

"He's a dear," Marissa said. "But tell me something. Have you given any consideration as to where we're to live? When we're in Caerfaen, I mean. Of course, when we're in Westdale we shall reside at Bryntop."

Morgan cocked his head and halted his sausage consumption.

"We can't live here," she said by way of explanation. "This house actually belongs to my parents. They've been kind enough to let me use it, but it's theirs. We certainly can't stay in your lodgings. It's much too small. So…"

He leaned back in his chair. "Good Lord, you're right. Obviously I've neglected to consider a most important point." He slathered jam on a piece of toast. "Where am I to bring my bride?"

"Where indeed? While I may make a good soldier's wife, I have no intention of sleeping in the open with naught but a bedroll to keep me warm. I've become accustomed to my creature comforts."

He nodded. "I shall make inquiries at once. I wonder if Rhys would consider moving out of the palace?"

She choked out a laugh. "I don't think we need go quite that far. I said creature comforts, not opulent luxury. We don't need anything huge, just something a bit larger than your current lodgings."

"Right. I know you have a lot of things to organize already.

Leave this to me."

"Oh, I shall," she said. "I shall also remind you of your appointment with Master Bergeron, the tailor."

"When did I make that?"

"You didn't, I did. Eleven o'clock today. He's doing final measurements. I have a lesson with Wyvrndell this morning, and then I'll meet you for lunch at the café where Sebastien is to join us."

"One o'clock?"

"Yes, but plan to get there early. It's quite busy at lunchtime, so it might be hard to get a table."

"I shall use my influence as a grand duke of the realm." Morgan struck a gallant pose.

"Bosh. You shall wait like everyone else. Now finish that sausage, give me a kiss, and be off. I have things to do. I can't spend my whole morning chatting with stray dukes."

He did as instructed.

~ * ~

"More history?" Marissa rolled her eyes. "Wyvrndell, when do I get to do something fun?"

There was a marked silence. Finally, Wyvrndell said, *"Just what is it you would consider 'fun,' Lady Marissa?"*

"I don't know." She waved a hand, which seemed singularly pointless considering the dragon was nowhere nearby and completely unable to see what she was doing. "Perhaps actually perform some magic. Do a spell. Make a potion. Something besides this deadly dull history and theory."

"Ahh." Wyvrndell sounded almost amused. *"I suppose it would not be amiss to put your focus to the test. It might even aid with our lessons."*

"Focus? What do you mean?"

"Magic is not simply accomplished by the words you speak. The words of a spell are there to guide you toward what you intend. They are merely a construct. It is your focus, your intention, which provides the spark to any magic."

"I see." She didn't, really, but it seemed something was required here. Wyvrndell must have sensed her confusion, for he gave a draconic chuckle.

"Open your hand," he directed. *"Hold it out in front of you."*

Well, she'd asked for this, so best to get on with it. "All right. What now?"

"Now, imagine a ball of light in your hand. Um, a small ball of light," he cautioned. *"Something the size of your closed fist, perhaps."*

She concentrated. Nothing happened. She reported as much.

"No, of course not. We are merely preparing. Now, the common spell to do this is 'Lluminas acciadio.' You may say it if you wish. As I said, the words are merely a mnemonic to help you remember what needs to be done."

There was a pause, and she asked, "And just what is to be done?"

"Create the ball of light in your hand. You must concentrate on it, desire it to be so, and make it so. The light is within you, as is the power to bring it to fruition. It requires focus and intention. You have the tools to do this thing. You simply need to find them within you."

Marissa looked at her palm, which remained free of any trace of light. In truth, her arm was trembling a bit from the effort of holding it out in front of her. "So, I merely focus my mind on a ball of light, and intend it to appear?"

"Correct. If you wish to say the spell, you may. In your own time…"

She swallowed, regarded her hand, and concentrated on the idea of a ball of light residing there. *"Lluminas acciadio,"* she muttered.

Her hand remained empty of any balls of light, or anything else. "Nothing," she reported.

"Of course not," Wyvrndell replied. *"I said it requires focus. This is not something achieved in an instant. It comes from practice. From the secure knowledge you have the light within you to be called upon. From the surety of the needed intention. These are all things which must be developed."*

She let her arm relax down by her side again. "So, this is something I should practice later?"

"Yes, I think it might be an excellent exercise for you. Perhaps you might try it in a darkened room, when you actually require the light."

Marissa nodded. "Yes, I can see how that might make a difference." She hesitated, and then said, "May I ask you something, Wyvrndell?"

"You may ask. I cannot guarantee an answer."

Hmmm. Interesting. "When Sebastien and I traveled by the portal, he was able to enter my mind, show me what to do. Why can't you do so as well?"

The dragon didn't answer right away. She waited, not saying anything. She wanted to hear what he would say.

Finally, Wyvrndell spoke. *"Lady Marissa. When the wizard Sebastien was allowed access to your thoughts, did it disconcert you at all?"*

"Well, yes, a bit. I mean, it's not something I'm used to, having someone else in my head.”

“Mmm. Yes. Now, when I speak to you as we have been doing, does it bother you?”

“It did a bit a first,” she admitted. “Not now I’ve gotten used to talking with you.”

Wyvrndell was silent for a moment, and then said, *“Sebastien is human. A wizard, but human, nonetheless. You were able to allow him to enter your mind because of this. But I am a dragon.”*

“Indeed you are. No doubt about it.” She shivered just a bit, remembering their first encounter.

“But for me to enter your mind as Sebastien did… it would be completely different. We may converse together, but our minds are not really alike. If you allowed me to enter your mind, it would be catastrophic.”

“Oh.” There wasn’t much more she could say.

“In addition,” Wyvrndell went on, *“I actually could not do so. Sebastien could, by means of his magic, but…”*

“But you’re a dragon, and dragons can’t do magic.”

He sighed. *“You are correct.”*

She thought for a moment. “But I do have magic. I could enter your mind.”

“Yes, in theory. In practice, not such a wise idea.”

“Nooo, I suppose not.”

The dragon’s voice, when he spoke, was harsh. *“There is no ‘suppose not’. Trust me on this, if you trust me for anything. Joining our minds would be a terrible thing. Please do not even contemplate it. Ever.”*

Marissa shivered at both Wyvrndell’s words and tone. “As you say, of course.”

He seemed almost relieved. *“Thank you.”*

Chapter Fourteen

The bells of St. Basil's chimed two. Marissa looked around for what Morgan estimated was about the tenth time and set down her tea cup.

"He said he'd meet us here at one o' clock. He's—"

"Late. Yes, you've said so several times already. Obviously he was delayed."

"Well, yes, it's… Oh, look, there he is." She pointed toward the window of the café.

He turned to look. Through the glass he could see Sebastien striding along the street toward them. His hat, as usual, was pulled low over his forehead, and its jaunty red feather danced in time to the wizard's steps. Morgan wondered, not for the first time, just how old Sebastien was. His gait was surprisingly quick for—

A man stepped directly into Sebastien's path. The wizard changed course to avoid a collision. As he did, the other man brought his arm up, and Morgan caught the telltale glint of steel. A knife.

He leapt from his seat, the chair crashing into a man sitting at the next table. He raced toward the door, ignoring the man's shouts of protest and sidestepping a pair of serving girls balancing trays filled with tankards. The girls shrieked, spinning in circles and sending a foaming fountain of ale skyward. Morgan dashed on toward the door. Their accompanying cries of indignation centered on Morgan's morals, ancestry, and upbringing. He ignored them, at last managing to dart out into the street with a lanky waiter in hot pursuit, demanding he return and pay his bill.

Sebastien lay crumpled on the ground, a circle of horrified spectators gawking helplessly. No one made any effort to help him, to staunch the flow of blood pooling on the ground around him. Or to detain the attacker.

A crash of shattering glass caused Morgan to spin around, hand reaching for the knife secreted at his back. He relaxed slightly as Marissa stepped through the broken window, a chair in her hand and fire in her eyes.

"Go after him," she ordered. "I'll take care of Sebastien."

He hesitated, not wanting to leave the wizard just lying there.

"Go!" she shouted. "He's getting away!" She waved him on.

Morgan scanned the milling crowd, searching for—there! He caught a glimpse of the assassin sidling eel-like through the throng. Forcing his way through, he saw the man glance over his shoulder. The attacker's eyes narrowed momentarily, and he redoubled his efforts to slip through the crowd.

Morgan pressed on, intent on keeping his quarry in sight. The crowd was thick here, everyone milling about in confusion, and he was losing ground. The assassin broke free of a knot of pedestrians and dashed toward the corner.

Entangled in a group of elderly ladies and their parcel-laden footmen, Morgan swore. He tried to slither between them, muttering apologies as he went. One of them cracked him across the shoulders with her parasol, a stinging blow that nearly sent him sprawling. He just managed to stay on his feet, arms windmilling as he struggled to keep upright. Finally he disentangled himself and sprinted for the corner. His quarry had a long lead, but Morgan had a clear field at last. He broke into a sprint.

Turning the corner, a scene of chaos met his eyes. This was a market street, or had been until moments earlier. Now overturned carts spilled fruits, vegetables, and crusty loaves of bread into the street. Morgan hurdled over a merchant who was kneeling, swearing vehemently as he tried to corral his rolling potatoes. A squawking contingent of chickens flapped into his path, their owner offering curses skyward as he attempted to shoo them back toward a wrecked cage.

A potato whizzed by his ear. He instinctively ducked and the missile struck the chicken's owner on the back of the head. Another potato caught Morgan on the shoulder. He yelped, as much in surprise as in pain. The blasted things were hard as rocks.

At last! He spotted a pair of watchmen approaching the melee, drawn by all the commotion. As he opened his mouth to instruct them to seize the assassin, his quarry rushed up to them, shouting, "That man in black tried to attack me. Help! Stop him!"

The watchmen turned to focus on Morgan. As they did, the assassin dashed away. Laughing, no doubt. The watchmen blocked Morgan's path, starting to reach for their weapons.

He did the only thing he could. Lowering his left shoulder and accelerating, he hit them at full speed, slamming between the two startled constables and sending them sprawling. Morgan raced on, striving desperately to gain on the fleeing man.

A whistle shrieked from astern. One of the constables, no doubt summoning reinforcements. But Morgan's only thought now was pursuit. He fled down the street ahead of a thunderous clatter of footsteps.

Risking a quick glance rearward, he spied one of the constables running after him, at the head of a pack of braying fruit vendors, potato purveyors, chicken wranglers, and bakers. Small boys and dogs cavorted in their boiling wake, uttering gleeful cries and happy howls. He ran faster.

More whistles sounded from all around. They were closing in, converging, tightening the net. And while he wasted time trying to explain things to officious constables, the assassin would make good his escape. Morgan put on a final burst of speed.

His quarry, he reckoned, must be in fine shape to lead him such a chase. As he closed the distance between them to a few steps, he realized the fellow didn't even seem to be breathing hard.

Morgan resented this bitterly. With everything going on over the past few weeks, his own training schedule had gone by the wayside, and he was paying the price now. His tortured lungs made furious complaints as he gasped for breath in this final push. But the end was near. He stretched out his arm, straining to grab the fleeing man's collar. He closed his fingers as…

With an excited yip a small black dog darted right between Morgan's churning legs. He and the dog both went tumbling tail over teakettle in a whirling mass of flailing limbs and anguished howls. They finally rolled to a stop, still entangled. The dog was evidently determined to show he had no hard feelings about the affair and, on the whole, reckoned it a great lark. He licked Morgan's face enthusiastically.

Gently removing his newfound friend, Morgan pushed himself upright with a groan. He shook his head, trying to stop the world from spinning around. A beefy hand fell on his shoulder.

"You," panted the constable, "are nicked."

He heaved a sigh dredged up from somewhere in the vicinity of the soles of his boots. "Fine," he said. "I want to see Captain Jenks."

Chapter Fifteen

As Morgan dashed off after Sebastien's assailant, Marissa dropped the chair she was still holding. Kneeling by the wounded wizard, she saw blood oozing from a long cut in his side. His breath was rapid and thready, his face drawn and pale.

Looking up, she cried, "Someone get a surgeon, quick. He'll die if he doesn't get help."

The ring of spectators closed in, lured by the grisly prospect of death by violence. A burning rage blossomed within her, sudden and unfamiliar, and she suddenly wanted nothing so much as to call up fire and scorch them all.

Taking a deep breath, she smothered her anger. She needed to channel it into something productive. Something which might help save Sebastien. She gripped his robe where it had been sliced open and ripped it wider, exposing the bloodied wound below.

As she reached in with both hands to hold the deep cut closed, she said through gritted teeth, "I'll give three crowns to the first person who can bring me a surgeon."

Avarice acted where compassion had failed. Several of the bystanders took off in different directions. She growled in her throat and tried to concentrate on keeping her friend alive.

"Oh, Sebastien," she breathed. "Hold on." The blood seeped through her fingers, his life slipping away with it.

She grabbed his tattered robe, jamming it against the wound to staunch the flow.

If only she could do something useful. There were old tales, she knew, of healers with magical powers who could repair broken bones, even heal deadly wounds such as this.

She tried to focus, to channel her magic into her hands to close the cut. But it was no use.

A man in the white robes of a surgeon knelt at her side. "What's happened here?"

"Oh, thank God," Marissa breathed. "He has a knife wound, in his side. It's deep, and he's lost a lot of blood already."

"So I see." The surgeon's voice bore no trace of irony as he knelt in the ever-spreading pool. "You're trying to keep the wound closed?"

She nodded, suddenly unbelievably weary. "Help him."

He moved in closer, pausing to glance up at the ring of onlookers. "Move back, you vultures. No, wait, you!" He pointed at a balding man. "You just hustle in there and fetch me a basin of hot water and a bunch of clean cloths. Move!"

The man stared, dumbfounded. Then, to her surprise, he headed into the café.

The surgeon edged closer. "Move the cloth for a moment—just a moment, mind you—so I can see what I'm up against here. Ready?"

She nodded.

"Now," he said, and she gently pulled the bloodied robe away. The surgeon sucked air through his teeth in a sharp hiss as he made a brief examination. "Put the cloth back and try to keep it closed," he directed.

"Aren't you going to take him somewhere?"

"No time. If we move him, he'll die for sure. If I work on him here, there's the devil's own chance I might manage to keep him alive."

The bald man returned bearing a sloshing basin. He was accompanied by outriders holding relatively clean rags.

"Set the basin down here," the surgeon ordered. Once it was positioned to his liking, he plunged his hands in, pulled them out again, and grabbed up one of the cloths to dry them.

"Push my bag over here, will you?" he asked the bald man, whom he'd evidently conscripted as assistant.

The man complied, opening up the bag when directed.

As the surgeon brought out a pair of shears and began to cut away a substantial portion of Sebastien's robe, Marissa's mind was inexplicably flooded with memories of the night Morgan had been attacked and badly wounded by an assassin. They'd been leaving the Black Swan Inn, on a night seemingly ages ago. She'd only known him a few days.

His wound had been ugly, but not nearly as deep as this one. Marissa had washed it and bound it up, despite the fact Morgan had effectively kidnapped her and carried her off to that lovely, romantic, secluded inn...

She was recalled to the exigencies of the present by the surgeon—Dr. Carnavon, he informed her—who instructed her to position her hands a bit to the side so he could work.

The bald man, seeing the wound up close, turned a charming shade of puce and began to edge away. "Oh, no you don't," Carnavon said brusquely. "I need you."

"But—" the man held up his hands in protest.

Marissa favored him with a sunny smile. "But I haven't paid you your reward yet. And I'll add another two crowns if you'll assist Dr. Carnavon."

"Oh, what the hell," the man muttered. He moved closer, trying not to look at the ghastly cut.

"Dip one of those cloths in the water and hand it to me," Carnavon directed as he dug through his bag.

Things proceeded quickly from there. Carnavon worked with quiet efficiency, bathing the wound and tossing in some sweet-smelling herbs which, he explained as he worked, were an old wives tale, but no less effective for it. Finally, as Marissa held the edges of the cut together, he sewed it shut.

"Hmm. Need something to bind him up and help keep the wound clean," Carnavon muttered.

Marissa had anticipated this. She washed her hands in the basin, an effort which at least made her feel a bit better even if it didn't accomplish much toward cleanliness. Then she resignedly hiked up her skirts a bit and ripped off a swath of petticoats. Wordlessly she handed it over to Carnavon, who nodded gravely and set to work on his patient.

Sebastien moaned softly. Marissa placed her hands on his forehead to soothe him. His eyes fluttered open, but his gaze seemed unfocused. He blinked several times, then rasped hoarsely, "I do believe I'm still alive."

"Oh, Sebastien," she cried. "Yes, you're still with us."

"Mmmph. I must be. I don't think one would hurt quite so much if one were dead."

Carnavon spoke. "Don't try to move about, old chap. You're not far from death's tender embrace yet, and I loathe having my handiwork undone." He turned to his erstwhile assistant. "You, go fetch some chair men to transport this fellow." Seeming relived to be anywhere else, the man dashed off.

"Hoy," declared a strident voice. "Ain't no one going anywhere 'til we discuss my broken window, eh?"

"Oh, bother your window," Marissa muttered. "I'll see to it, don't you worry. But—"

Carnavon cut her off, barking at the newcomer, "But first you just hump it and fetch me a large pitcher of water. And two, no make that three, stiff brandies."

The café owner opened his mouth to protest but Carnavon flapped a hand at him in a shooing motion. "Now," he bellowed.

In the face of such forceful authority, the man fled, calling orders through the broken window. "Three brandies?" Marissa asked, her curiosity at last getting the better of her. "Doesn't three seem a bit excessive? He'll be drunk as a hedgehog in the moonlight."

Carnavon grinned. "Only one is for the patient. One is for me. And one," he said, handing her a glass, "is for you, m'lady. I don't like your color at the moment."

"And the water?" she asked, taking a sip of the spirits.

"To wash down what I've no doubt will be absolutely foul brandy." He sampled, pursed his lips, and nodded. "Yes, no question, this will need all the help it can get."

She knocked hers back, to Carnarvon's evident surprise, and declined the water. "I've had much worse," she assured him. She rose, shook out her skirts, and set off to collect her reticule from where she'd left it at their table in the café. She set about distributing largesse to all concerned.

Finally she approached the surgeon, who was giving little sips of the brandy to Sebastien. "What is your fee, Doctor?"

"Half a crown will suffice. You did a good bit of my work before I even got here. If not for you, I wouldn't have had a patient at all, odds are. Is he a friend of yours?"

"Yes, he is. A good friend."

The wizard's eyes flickered open again at this. "Lady Marissa," he croaked. "I came…to warn you. Beware…" he trailed off into a gasping wheeze. Then he sat up, opened his eyes wide, and said, "Beware the wizard's prophecy."

He slumped back down and was still.

Carnavon raised a brow. "Well now. Quite melodramatic, isn't he? And did him no good. Do you know where he lives, Lady, um, Marissa, is it?"

"Yes it is, and no, I'm afraid I don't."

"Lady Marissa, Marissa," the doctor mused. He snapped his fingers. "Oh. You're the—"

"Witch," sighed Marissa. "Guilty as charged."

Carnavon shrugged. "As you will. I was going to say you're the woman Commander McRobbie is to wed. I served as a surgeon in the Legion, you see."

"Oh." Her cheeks warmed. "Sorry. I'm just getting used to being notorious. It's a bit of a shock to the system when I'm suddenly not. Speaking of Morgan, I wonder where he's got to. He dashed off to try to catch the man who did this." She waved toward Sebastien. "I'm sure he's managed to find some manner of trouble. He usually does. Oh, good, here are the chair men. Let's take him… Oh, bother. I guess they can take him to my townhouse."

While Dr. Carnavon supervised the loading of Sebastien, she mused on his final enigmatic words. "Beware the wizard's prophecy." *What on earth does that mean?* She sighed and climbed in beside Sebastien.

Chapter Sixteen

Harlan Jenks, Captain in the Caerfaen City Watch, leaned back in his chair. Narrowing his eyes, he regarded the prisoner and heaved a long-suffering sigh. "All right, all right. I know full well anything you and your lady involve yourselves in is going to be—" he searched for the appropriate word and finally settled on, "—messy."

He'd just finished listening to Commander McRobbie's account of the attack on the wizard Sebastien and his subsequent pursuit of the assailant. Jenks had received numerous reports from a veritable host of constables detailing carnage, mayhem, assault with deadly potatoes, and—he'd had to read this one twice—a madwoman who'd flung a chair through a café's window. Which, he was fairly certain, must have been Lady Marissa's handiwork. She was, as he knew from their previous encounters, a woman of forceful personality. Window smashing would be all in a day's work for her.

McRobbie shrugged and gave him a sheepish smile. "Sorry, Jenks," he said. "I'm just a fellow things seem to—well, to happen to."

This was, Jenks had to concede, nothing less than the gospel truth. Still… "They just seem to happen a lot oftener, and a lot stranger, when Lady Marissa is involved, don't they?"

McRobbie managed a deadpan expression, although his eyes twinkled with suppressed mirth. "You know," the duke mused, "the thought had never occurred to me. Do you really think so?"

Jenks had always harbored a sneaking sense of admiration for the Knight-Commander. McRobbie was a genuine hero, after all, not only for his efforts during the war with Rhuddlan, but also for helping foil a dastardly plot to start a war between Kilbourne and the Dwarves.

But, he now realized, he also actually liked the man. McRobbie wasn't the type to put on airs or flaunt his title and pull rank. No, instead he sat here meekly, drinking awful coffee without complaint and apologizing for wrecking half the city.

"You're a brave man, Commander," Jenks observed. "I hope you know what you're letting yourself in for."

McRobbie arched a brow. "Why, Captain," he drawled, "whatever can you mean?"

They both burst out laughing at the same time. Jenks finally subsided into choked snorts, managing to compose his face when a knock sounded at the door.

"Come," Jenks called, and Sergeant MacGwyn entered with a sheaf of papers.

"Afternoon, Your Grace," he said with a pleasant nod toward McRobbie. To Jenks he said, "Got a report in, sir." He handed over the papers. "The wizard's all stitched up, and the surgeon thinks he might make it."

"Thank you, Sergeant. Anything else urgent?"

"No sir, nothing that won't keep for a bit."

"Very good. That'll be all for now."

MacGwyn tossed off a casual salute and departed. Jenks handed the report to McRobbie, saying, "He's lucky. They found Dr. Carnavon to work on him. He's a damned fine surgeon."

McRobbie nodded, still scanning the report. When he looked up, he said, "Yes, I know Carnavon quite well. He served in a couple of my units in the Legion. A very capable man. Ah, and I see they've taken Sebastien to Marissa's. Good."

Jenks considered, "It might not be a bad idea to have a couple of my constables hanging about there. This fellow, whoever he is, might decide to come back and try to finish the job."

"I would be grateful, Captain."

"Anything you can add to your description?"

McRobbie grimaced. "I'm afraid not. I never really registered his face at all. When I was chasing him, I only saw him from behind. I do know he's fast, though, and in damned good shape. Runs like the bloody wind and wasn't even puffing at the end." He paused for a moment, concentrating. He looked up and said, "There was one thing: his ears."

Jenks raised a brow and waited for elucidation. McRobbie's forehead creased in thought. "His ears were odd. The one on the left side was all right. But the top of his right ear was bent over a bit, rather like a dog's will. Like this." As Jenks watched, McRobbie grabbed his own ear and bent the top of it by way of demonstration.

"I can't really do it justice," he said, releasing his ear. "But it's very distinctive. I'd know the fellow if I came across him again. At least if I saw him from the back."

"That's something, at least," Jenks allowed. "Hopefully the wizard can give us a better description once he's able to talk. Helps to know who we're looking for. I'll go 'round and see him."

"For what it's worth," McRobbie offered, "I'd just stop anyone trying to get into Marissa's house. Make certain they actually have business there.”

“Like yourself?”

McRobbie grinned. “Well, yes, I suppose so. Can’t be too careful, you know. After all, you’ve had your suspicions of me before.”

Jenks opened his mouth to protest, then barked out a laugh instead. “With good cause,” he pointed out.

“With good cause,” McRobbie agreed. “No hard feelings?”

Jenks took his offered hand. “None, Commander.”

“Good. Anyhow, since I don’t reckon I can be of any further use, I think I’ll push off.”

“Be careful yourself, Commander. This fellow knows who you are, even if you don’t know him.”

This appeared to take McRobbie by surprise. His brows lifted and his face took on a thoughtful expression. “Thank you, Jenks. I’ll take your warning under advisement.”

~ * ~

Toby surveyed the docks of Caerfaen from his position at the stern of the *Mad Maudie*. The ship was anchored in the harbor, well away from most of the other merchant and navy vessels. Even though the *Maudie* currently flew the Kilbourne ensign, he wasn’t taking any chances. He was probably crazy to have come back here. But the lure of this scheme, mad though it might be, was too strong a siren’s call to ignore.

He clambered down the rope ladder and into the dinghy. A couple of men were waiting to row him ashore. The rest of the crew was already off on leave, but Toby had allowed himself to be detained by various unimportant chores. *Get on,* he finally chided himself. *If you’re afraid to set foot on Caerfaen soil again you might as well go back to your island and forget the plan.*

The men rowed vigorously, eager to divest themselves of their captain and begin their own leave among the myriad entertainments of Kilbourne’s capital city. Once they’d landed Toby dismissed them, and the pair bolted off with whoops of delight. He set off across the docks at a more sedate pace, making his way through grimy alleys. He emerged at last into a street at least marginally more palatable. He stepped gingerly over the worst of the debris in the gutters. He no longer had a boot boy, and if his boots got soiled, well, it was up to Toby to clean them himself. Perhaps after this latest haul he’d hire himself a valet.

Contemplating this notion, he made an unerring line past several taverns of dubious pedigree, stopping at last under a weather-beaten sign depicting a fluffy, if angry, sheep. The Mean Ewe. He opened the door, allowing the raucous noise echoing off the tavern’s walls to spill out into the street. Along with it came a well lubricated sailor, staggering toward the gutter. Toby dodged aside to avoid being bowled over and stepped through the door.

Scanning the common room, he spotted several of his crew already there. A few were at a table drinking. A couple were in a corner throwing dice. One was endeavoring to toss a dart at a target. Toby jerked his head to one side as an errant missile thudded into the wall not more than a foot away.

A barmaid sailed by, pert and pretty. "Are you going to let all the flies out?" she inquired.

With a laugh, Toby pulled the door closed. He'd no sooner seated himself at a table than the barmaid had a tankard of ale in front of him. Nodding his thanks, he took a sip and sighed happily. It was excellent ale. Surprising to find in such a place, but he certainly couldn't complain. The Mean Ewe had no charm. It had no class. What it did have was excellent ale, fairly private tables, and a rather attractive barmaid.

"I think this place will do nicely," he said to himself. "Yes, this will do." He leaned back in his chair, sipped his ale with a contented sigh, and began to formulate his plans.

Chapter Seventeen

After his interview with Jenks, Morgan headed back to his lodgings long enough to get cleaned up and change his muddied clothes. Then he made his way back to Queen Street. There were no conspicuously lurking Watchmen about, although he didn't think Jenks would have had time to detail them yet. He was admitted by Rose, who informed him Her Ladyship was in the back parlor where the dying man was laid out.

He met Marissa coming down the hallway. "How's Sebastien?" he asked. "Rose says he's dying?"

"Pooh. Don't mind Rose. He was badly wounded, but the doctor says he should pull through."

"Dr. Carnavon, I heard. Good man."

"Yes, he is. He said he knows you from the Legion."

"He served in a couple of my units over the years. His skills have saved more men than I can count."

"So what happened?" Marissa asked. "Did you catch the assassin?"

"No, blast him. I chased him across most of Caerfaen, with half the Watch in hot pursuit of us both. He managed to give me the slip, the constables hauled me away, and I ended up having a nice cuppa with your friend Captain Jenks."

She beamed. "Such a nice man, when he's not arresting the wrong people." She gave Morgan a sly glance, and he burst out laughing.

"He's going to place a couple of constables around here to keep an eye on things. Just in case the fellow who attacked Sebastien decides he wants another go."

Her eyes widened. "Oh. Do you think he might? Do I need to be prepared to repel boarders? I could heat up the boiling oil…"

He chuckled. "Bloodthirsty wench." Then he grew serious. "I really don't know. My instincts say no, but who knows what this fellow might try? Hopefully Jenks' constables will give him pause. Did Sebastien say anything? Give you any idea of what this was all about?"

"No, he didn't. He roused long enough to mutter some nonsense about 'beware the wizard's prophecy,' and then promptly lapsed back into unconsciousness again. The doctor sewed him up and we brought him here. He hasn't said a thing since. But how did you know he was here?"

"Jenks," Morgan replied. "His sergeant, MacGwyn, kept popping in with updates." Morgan took her hand and gave it a gentle squeeze. "How are you doing? Are you all right?"

"Fine, I'm fine." She gave him a wan smile. "Although I have to confess it did shake me up a bit. Reminded me of the night you were attacked coming out of the Black Swan…" She shivered. "Blood everywhere, and me trying to bandage you up."

"Ah, those were the days, eh?"

She pulled her hand away and poked him in the chest with her forefinger. "I'm serious. Even though you'd kidnapped me, I still didn't want you to die of your injuries."

"Yes, I remember." He grinned. "You were determined to save me so you could do me in yourself."

She started to scowl but it turned into an answering grin. "Well, yes. With just cause, I might add."

"With just cause," he agreed. "Thank you for your forbearance." Catching her hand again he pulled her into an embrace. "I do appreciate when you don't murder me."

"Don't get used to—mmph!" Morgan cut off her words by the expedient of kissing her. Marissa struggled for a moment, then relaxed into the kiss.

At last she pulled away and straightened her hair. "I suppose, under the circumstances, I can put up with your continued existence. You do kiss rather nicely."

"You say the sweetest things." He tried to enfold her into his arms again, but she slipped away.

"No more. A girl can only take so much at one time, you know. Besides, since you're joining me for dinner, I'll need to go let Mrs. Handley know to set another place."

"Am I joining you for dinner?"

"Did you have something more important to do?"

He didn't even hesitate. "Never."

Marissa favored him with a smile. "I thought not. Why don't you go into the parlor and pour us each a glass of wine? I know I could use one, and I imagine you could as well."

"Beauty and brains. How did I get so lucky?" He ducked back as she aimed a swat at him. "I'm going, I'm going."

Much later, after they'd finished off Mrs. Handley's offering of roast fowl, potatoes, and peas, topped off with a delectable cherry crumble, Morgan asked, "Do you have any idea what this prophecy

Sebastien warned you of is all about?"

"Not a clue. And other than Sebastien, I'm not really on speaking terms with any wizards of whom I might inquire."

"Augustus Rhenn?" he offered.

Marissa shook her head vigorously. "No, definitely not him. And yes, I know you were only joking, but honestly, he gives me the jitters. I'd be just as happy if I never saw him again. But I do have an idea."

"Of course you do. You always have an idea," he said. "It's one of the endearing things about you."

"Idiot. I want to go back to the Tzigani camp."

"Ah, I'm crushed." He feigned swooning. "You do prefer the bear as a dance partner. I knew it."

"Oh, be quiet and listen! I'm serious, Morgan."

"I'm sorry, I'll quit playing the fool. You have my complete attention. Why do you want to visit the Tzigani again?"

"Because, unlike some people I could name, Elbethesba is no fool. I think it's possible she might know something about this wizard's prophecy."

"Aaaah, I see." Morgan nodded approvingly.

"Also," she pointed out, "there will be more tarts."

He drained his coffee cup and set it down with a clatter. "We leave at once."

As they approached the camp, the sky was turning an azure shade of blue, reminiscent of Wyvrndell's scales. The sounds of stringed instruments and voices raised in song melded with the aromas of baking tarts and roasting meat to create a festive welcome.

Morgan spotted Radivan near a cheery fire, watching the crowd. He led Marissa around the ring of dancers until they could approach the Tzigani chief. Radivan waved them over.

"Good evening Lady Marissa, Commander," he said. "I am delighted to see you back. You've come for more tarts, perhaps?"

"Yes indeed. But also to ask Elbethesba a question, if I might trouble her for a few moments of her time," Marissa replied.

Radivan glanced over his shoulder toward the wagons. "Wait here while I check. She may be doing a reading." He darted off through the milling crowd and was back in moments.

"You are in luck," he reported. "She is free and will see you."

"Why don't you wait here?" she told Morgan. "I think it might be best if I speak with Elbethesba alone."

"As you wish," he said.

"Come, Commander," Radivan said with a huge grin. "You and I, we will visit the bakers and get some tarts for you and your lady." He grinned broadly. "And for me."

~ * ~

"The wizard's prophecy, eh?" Elbethesba looked thoughtful. "Interesting. Tell me, how did you learn of this?"

Marissa recounted the events of recent days, beginning with the appearance of Headmaster Rhenn, and concluding with the attack on Sebastien and his enigmatic warning. When she was done, Elbethesba poured them each a cup of tea and uncovered a plate of tarts.

"Oh, how lovely," Marissa said. "I smelled them, but I didn't want to ask."

Elbethesba sipped tea. "The wizard's prophecy. I have heard of it, certainly. Unfortunately, I don't know what it actually says. I'm not sure anyone does."

Marissa cocked her head in surprise. "What do you mean?"

"It's a legend, a fairy tale told by the wizards. Of course, I'm not privy to their secrets, but from what I've heard, no one really knows what the prophecy says. They just know there was one. It seems to have been lost over the ages."

"So I should just forget about it?"

"I cannot say. This wizard Sebastien, whom you say you trust, warned you about it. This makes me wonder if perhaps he discovered something. Perhaps he managed to learn just what the prophecy says."

"But why would he warn me about it? I mean, why would the wizards care about me? And a prophecy? It seems a bit ridiculous, doesn't it?" She picked up a tart and bit into the flaky crust, capturing the berry filling on her tongue. She swallowed. "Doesn't it?"

Elbethesba waggled a hand. "There are many strange things in this world. But consider this: you are a woman who possesses extraordinarily strong magic. You are young and untrained, of a certainty. But you will not remain either for long. As you grow in wisdom and power, you may choose to become involved in things the wizards would rather you didn't."

Marissa waited for her to go on. Elbethesba sipped more tea. "The wizards, they wish to maintain control over things. You are an unknown quantity. So they may wish to control you, as this Rhenn has already attempted to do. They might intend to use this prophecy to justify some action against you. I wish I could tell you more, or give you some reassurance, but I just don't know."

Marissa nodded. "I understand. I suppose I just have to be patient, and hope Sebastien recovers so he can tell me what he was talking about."

"In the meantime, be vigilant. Continue your lessons and learn to manage the power you have been given. I have already told you of choices you may have to make. I do not know what those are, or what the circumstances will be. But it may well have something to do with all this. The sooner you can learn to harness your magic, the better."

"Thank you. I shall apply myself to my lessons. And thank you for talking with me."

"I wish I could be more helpful. Some things are only revealed in the fullness of time. I fear this is one of them."

"Hopefully when it comes, I will be ready."

Elbethesba smiled. "I believe you will. Now come, let us talk of more pleasant things and do something about these tarts."

Chapter Eighteen

For a wonder, Morgan found himself left to his own devices the next day. Marissa was planning to immerse herself in wedding preparations, which evidently did not require the encumbrance of the mere bridegroom. This was a fact for which he felt grateful, for he needed to call in at the Knight-Commander's office. He still had important duties which needed attention, and he'd been seriously neglecting them of late.

Then the note arrived, and everything changed.

He crumpled the heavy, cream-colored parchment and flung it viciously into the grate. It was immediately consumed by the flames. This served two purposes. First, his action erased any evidence of the note's existence. Second, it made him feel at least a little better.

He glared as the last bits curled, caught, and flared, settling quickly into a fine ash. The message had been short, but its point was that of a sword at his throat. Just a few innocuous words he'd known would one day show up, unannounced and unwelcomed. The knowing didn't make them more palatable.

"Please call on me at your earliest convenience. Taggart."

When he sought Ian Taggart's help during the d'Eastmond affair, Morgan had known full well he was making a deal with the devil. But he'd been out of options, on the run from the Watch, and hadn't been able to figure any other way out. Striking a bargain with Taggart, the most notorious criminal in Caerfaen, was the only way Morgan could see to identify the man he was after. Taggart had been as good as his word, using his network of informers and petty crooks to help unmask a traitor. Now he was summoning Morgan to repay the debt.

What will the price be? A chill, like walking into a sudden fog, ran through him as he contemplated the myriad answers to this question. None of them were particularly appetizing. Still, his sense of honor required he satisfy his obligation to Taggart. Rising from his chair, he prepared to get the distasteful business over with as soon as possible.

He decided against donning his sword. He wasn't going to a fight, merely a parlay. Besides, he'd just have to hand it over to one of Taggart's guards before gaining admittance to the rogue's inner sanctorum. He didn't relish the idea of trusting his weapon into a stranger's keeping. So, no sword.

Still, there was no point in being a complete idiot. Walking into Taggart's lair without a single weapon would be akin facing down a dragon unarmed. So Morgan possessed himself of several sharp, lethal objects, secreted in various places about his person. Suitably prepared, he stuck his head into the kitchen to alert Kevin he was going out. The valet, absorbed in the task of mending one of Morgan's tunics, merely nodded abstractedly.

Stepping out into the morning sunshine, he breathed in the scents of the city. Wood smoke, the faint fragrance of late-summer flowers, and the unmistakable, aromatic scent of something baking all floated on a cool, soft breeze. He smiled for a moment before his mood faded as he recalled his destination.

He glanced around, searching the surroundings for any sign of surreptitious watchers. He had no reason to assume anyone was keeping him under observation, but it would be foolish to take any chances. He needed to be certain no one knew where he was heading or whom he was meeting, so he meandered for a bit, doubling back across his tracks several times, until he was positive no one dogged his trail. Then, by an even more twisted route, he made his way to Taggart's lair.

Morgan eyed The Hound and Hare from a place of discreet concealment across the street. The last time he'd been here, he had been on the run from the Watch. He'd been framed for a murder but managed to escape from his dungeon cell in order to find the real killer. He'd snuck into the Hound and Hare through the kitchen in the back, forcing his way in to see Taggart at the point of his weapon.

Today he walked into the common room, made his way to the bar, and told the squint-eyed bartender, "Taggart's expecting me."

The man gave Morgan an appraising glance at odds with his own appearance but didn't utter a word. He just jerked his head toward a set of stairs at the back of the room. Morgan tossed a coin onto the bar. You never knew when a bit of bread cast upon the waters might come home to roost. "Thanks," he said, and made for the stairs.

His upward progress was checked at the first landing. A beefy individual whose breakfast must have contained an appalling quantity of onions blocked the stairs. Morgan was pleasantly surprised at the sentry's demeanor and diction.

Instead of grunting and gesturing, the man asked with the aplomb of a seasoned butler, "Might I inquire your name, sir?"

"McRobbie," he replied.

Apparently, this was the correct response, for the beefy man gave a toothy grin and stepped aside. "Thank you, Commander. You may proceed," he said with a flourish of his arm.

Morgan moved up the staircase. Another sentry waited on the next landing, but he simply waved Morgan on. The final landing was a different story. The guard posted there eyed him suspiciously, as if wondering how such riff-raff had been allowed to penetrate The Hound and Hare's defenses so far.

Morgan nodded amiably. "He's expecting me."

The sentry held out a massive hand. "Weapons," he rumbled in a voice which sounded as if sired from an avalanche out of an earthquake.

Before the man could even blink Morgan had the stiletto from his wrist sheath out and to the guard's throat. He reversed the blade just as quickly, placing the hilt in the still outstretched hand.

"Any more tricks?" The guard remained stoically unimpressed. Morgan shrugged and pulled a second knife from his boot, a third from a sheath on his opposite calf and handed them over into safekeeping. The guard raised a brow, but this seemed to be the extent of his reaction

"That's the lot," Morgan said. The sentry gave him one final, appraising stare, as if wondering whether to grab Morgan by the heels and shake him to see what fell out. Finally, evidently deciding against this course, he stood aside, opened the door, and muttered, "Get 'em here when you leave."

"Thank you, my good man." He grinned, bestowing another coin. "A pleasure, I'm sure."

Taggart was waiting for him. The last time he'd been here, Morgan had forced his way through the Hound and Hare's defenses at sword's point, bursting in to find Taggart relaxing in a dressing gown and slippers. Today, prepared for a guest, he was dressed all in silk: dark trousers, soft tunic, and an elegantly embroidered jacket. He stood as Morgan entered. Tall and lean, Taggart had a calculating look in his eye.

"Welcome, Commander," Taggart said. His voice carried the slight lilt which betrayed his highland ancestry. He extended a hand. Morgan only hesitated a moment before he took it.

"Taggart," he said, treading with care. "It's been a while."

"Ian, please," his host suggested.

Morgan gave a nominal shake of his head. "No," he replied. "I'll stick with Taggart, if it's all the same to you."

His host chuckled, appearing to take no insult. "As you wish, as you wish. The last time you were here you were only one step ahead of the Watch. Ah, what a time, eh?"

So he was going to bring up the debt Morgan owed him. No great surprise there. It would just be a matter of whether he could bear the price while managing to maintain at least a few tattered shreds of his honor.

"Come in, come in, sit down. I shan't bite you."

Morgan wasn't so sure of this, but he allowed himself to be led to a comfortable chair and handed the claret bottle. He splashed a bit into a goblet, took a fortifying sip, and asked, "To what do I owe the pleasure of your invitation?"

Taggart smiled lazily. "Well, Commander, not so long ago I did you a favor."

Morgan's lips compressed tight. Taggart went on, "You did make good on the thousand crown fee I set. Right promptly too." His eyes lit with amusement at Morgan's obvious discomfiture. "I do appreciate prompt payment. It's so rare in my line of country."

Morgan said nothing. His host said, "But now, I'm afraid, it's my turn to ask a favor of you, Commander."

Morgan still said nothing. He merely raised a brow. If Taggart could maintain such a bland demeanor, he'd match him as best he could.

Taggart sat back and grinned. His eyes, glittering like a cat's, watched Morgan with keen amusement. He was like a cat, Morgan reflected, playing with a nice juicy mouse. He just didn't relish being the mouse in this particular game.

He took another sip of the wine, savoring the robust tang. *But not too much of this, good as it is,* he admonished himself. He needed a clear head to have any hope of coming out of an encounter with Ian Taggart and keeping his shirt. Or his integrity.

"You're learning." Taggart beamed. "Always wait the other fellow out. Very well, I'll make you wait no more. Caerfaen is in danger, Commander. I need your help to protect it."

Unable to help himself, Morgan found his mouth dropping open. He took a deep breath to calm himself. To say this was unexpected would be the understatement of the year. "Protect it?" he managed to croak. "Protect it from what?"

Taggart flashed a smile, all teeth and little in the way of humor. Now that he had Morgan's rapt attention, he was at ease again. He poured himself some more of the claret, sipped, and regarded his visitor with those glittering grey eyes. Then he uttered one word: "Pirates."

"What?" Morgan rocked back in his seat.

"You heard me. Pirates."

"Here? Right in Caerfaen?" Morgan gaped at Taggart in bemusement. Of all the things he might have expected to hear, pirates weren't anywhere on the charts. But with an unexpected suddenness, he found himself seeing his own distant past.

He'd been all of ten, serving as cabin boy on his father's fast cutter, *HMS Raven.* Coming alongside a becalmed vessel whose crew lay apparently dead on the decks, *Raven* had been taken by the definitely not-dead pirates. Morgan had led his fellow cabin boys in escaping detection. He'd then staged a daring raid to free Commander McRobbie and his crew, who had in turn rounded up the pirates.

As this memory flashed through his mind in the space of an instant, Morgan shook his head. He'd never imagined he'd have to deal with pirates again. He returned his focus to Ian Taggart. "Pirates?" he repeated dully.

Taggart leaned back in his chair, took another sip of claret, and allowed a grim smile to play across his lips. "I know, McRobbie, you think I've gone a bit daft. Trust me, I haven't. There's a pirate crew in port. I don't know where they hail from, and I don't know why they're here. But I do know they're here, and I've no doubt they're up to no good."

"And you know all this because…?"

"Oh, I hear things. In this case, because of my, um, shipping interests, as you might call 'em."

"Shipping interests." Morgan was quite aware this actually meant Taggart's smuggling operations. But smuggling was beside the point. "And you're telling me this why? I'd think you'd want to inform the Watch. Not me."

Taggart quirked a crooked grin and drank a bit more claret. "The Watch and I remain on, shall we say, equitable terms. And normally yes, if something of a criminal nature was going on, I'd drop a word in the proper ear."

Morgan nodded. Taggart's expression changed to worried.

"This is a bit beyond the Watch, I think. I've sent a couple of lads to snoop 'round a bit, see which way the wind's blowing. They never came back."

"I see. That doesn't bode well, does it?" Morgan squeezed his eyes shut for a moment. When he opened them again, he found he was still in Taggart's sitting room, with a nearly-full glass of claret in his hand. He took a healthy swig. "You're not suggesting I go snooping around, are you?"

Taggart managed to look almost affronted at this suggestion. "No, no, not at all." He held out his hands in a calming manner. "No, Commander, you're much to, ah, distinctive."

He couldn't argue the logic of this statement. And to be fair, Taggart had never seemed to consider Morgan's heritage and skin color a factor in their previous dealings. To him, unlike a lot of the so-called gentlemen of Rhys's court, a man was judged solely on his actions rather than on the size of his estate or the color of his skin. In this, at least,

Morgan counted Taggart as an honorable man.

"Then what?"

"The last time we met," Taggart began, seeming to skirt round the question, "you came to me in need of a favor."

Morgan felt his heart sinking rapidly toward his boots. This was it. Still, he nodded in agreement.

Taggart's mouth quirked up at one corner. "Well, now it's me who's asking a favor in return. Actually, the loan of an asset."

Unable to speak, Morgan just goggled at him. Finally he pulled himself together a bit. "A loan? You want a loan, from me?"

"Not money, Commander. An asset, I said, and an asset's what I meant. Actually, I want the loan of a man. A particular man, who can do the job as needs doing."

His mind raced as he calculated possibilities and figured Taggart's angle. "Aartis Poldane?" he guessed, his voice dull.

"Ah, well done. Got it in one." Taggart smiled like a teacher pleased to have such an astute pupil.

Morgan crossed his arms. "Before we get to the why, tell me the why behind the why. What is there between you and Aartis? You mentioned it before, during the d'Eastmond affair. With one thing and another, I've never gotten around to finding out from him. If you've compromised him somehow…"

"Now, Commander, furl your sails. 'Tis nothing like that. Aartis and I are friends, nothing more, and that's the truth of it. It's his story to tell. I'll just say I was by way of doing him a good turn a few years ago. He bought me a drink by way of thanks, and we got to talking. We found we have rather similar views of life and of our fellow man. We've been friends ever since. And before you go leaping to any conclusions, I do not trade on our friendship. Not one bit." Caerfaen's most notorious criminal looked Morgan dead in the eye as he said this, his gaze unwavering.

"All right," Morgan said. "Taking it at face value for the moment, what do you want with Aartis? I may not be the sharpest sword in the armory, but I presume it has something to do with these pirates. But Aartis is a soldier, not a naval officer. I'd think…"

His host huffed out an aggrieved sigh. "McRobbie, the city's in danger somehow, real danger. There's more of these damnable pirates slipping in every day. I don't know what they're planning, but we need someone to find out."

"You said you've already lost two men over this. What makes you think Aartis will be able to do what your lads couldn't?"

Taggart grinned. "Because Aartis is part pirate himself."

Morgan's brows rose with the velocity of an ascending catapult missile. "Just what the devil do you mean?"

Taggart cocked his head. "Merely a figure o' speech, Commander. I was referring to his way of looking at things. Women, for example."

He couldn't fault the logic in this statement. Aartis definitely had something of the pirate in his nature as he set sights on some new beauty. One could almost picture him hoisting the black flag and grinning a buccaneer's smile of anticipated conquest. "All right, point taken. So, obviously you've thought this through. What's your plan?"

Taggart grinned again, and Morgan suddenly realized the man was more than half pirate himself, if a land-bound one. That's what he meant when he said he and Aartis had similar outlooks.

"He's a bright lad, is our Aartis. We'll let him figure it out. We just need to get him pointed in the right direction."

"And you know the direction, I take it?" Morgan scrubbed a hand across his face, suddenly weary.

His better judgment cried out this was a horrible idea. Yet his instincts—the feeling deep in his gut, the one he trusted above all else—told him it might be the only way. Besides, Taggart was playing more than fair. Oh, he had his own interests in mind, of course. But he was serious about wishing to protect the city. He was a son of Caerfaen. He wasn't born and bred here, any more than Morgan was. But they both looked on Caerfaen as their adopted home and would do whatever it took to defend it. At heart Taggart was a loyal, if dishonest, citizen.

"Very well," Morgan said, abandoning judgment for instinct. "I'll send him along to you. Brief him with whatever you know and set him in motion."

"Thank you." Taggart looked genuinely grateful. He rose and extended a slim hand. "We'll consider all debts honorably discharged, eh? Another drink?"

~ * ~

As Morgan left The Hound and Hare, the sunshine that graced the morning had given way to dark storm-laden clouds. A light mist swirled about his ankles like an affectionate cat. He thought about hailing a chair, for he'd ended up having a bit more of Taggart's claret than was strictly sensible. However, he decided the air and the walk would do him better, helping to clear the cobwebs from his brain.

Pirates. What were they up to here in Caerfaen? The very question Ian Taggart wanted the answer to, wasn't it? Why he'd summoned Morgan and inveigled the loan of Captain Aartis Poldane.

Morgan still wasn't sure how he felt about the notion but, all things considered, sending Aartis down to the docks for a bit of reconnaissance work was far preferable to a lot of things Taggart could have reasonably demanded in repayment for past favors. If this was what it took to wipe the slate clean, the cost seemed acceptable.

He strode on, oblivious to the people in the street around him. He just wanted to get back to Kingston Street, strip out of his clothes and take a long hot bath. Dealing with Taggart, as necessary as it might be, still left him feeling just a little dirty.

But as he focused on this homey objective, his attention was drawn to a man walking ahead of him. Morgan noticed the man's silhouette. In particular, his ears. One stood out at an unusual angle, just as he'd told Jenks. Morgan sucked in a breath as he lengthened his stride, intent on discreetly closing the distance between them without alerting his quarry. Could this really be the fellow who had attacked Sebastien? Just strolling along the street as if he hadn't a care in the world?

As Morgan edged closer, his objective dodged around a group of men just emerging from a tavern, all laughing and slapping each other on the backs. They weaved into Morgan's path, milling about like a land-bound flock of starlings. Over their heads he could see the man he'd been following drawing farther way, his steps quickening.

Morgan thrust his way through the group of men, eliciting cries of, "Oy, watch who yer pushing about there, laddie," and "Quitcher shovin', mate." He broke though, just catching a glimpse of the odd-earred man nipping around a corner.

But when he got to the corner himself, there was no trace of his quarry. He scanned the short alleyway. Its only occupant was a lanky alley cat that arched its back and hissed before slinking into the shelter of a doorway. The fellow must have sprinted to get out of sight so quickly. Which, Morgan realized, meant he'd not been as discreet in his pursuit as he'd imagined. The man had known he was being followed and was taking steps.

No point in being cautious now. Morgan trotted swiftly down the alley, emerging into another more major, albeit almost deserted, street. Up ahead, he caught a quick glimpse of the man just rounding the next corner. Morgan broke into a run.

Even as he turned the corner, skidding slightly on the debris littering the street, Morgan realized he'd made a serious mistake. His quarry had tucked in tight against the building, right at the junction of the alley. As Morgan came barreling along, he gave him a hard shove. Morgan went sprawling, and as the world whirled by he saw the fellow taking off in the opposite direction.

But a lifetime of training in combat techniques came into play.

Morgan managed to turn his forward momentum from a precipitous sprawl into a roll. It certainly wasn't graceful, but effective enough to keep him from plowing up the street with his chin. He kept the roll going, pushing off with the strength in his arms garnered from wielding a heavy sword in battle. Staggering to his feet, he turned back toward the mouth of the alley. He made sure to keep his turn wide enough this time.

But there was no one waiting to send him sprawling. His quarry had a good lead and was rounding the next corner. This disappearing around corners business, Morgan decided, was getting damned old. He ran.

The sound of his boots pounding on the street had the same effect as trumpets to a racehorse. With a startled glance over his shoulder, the man's eyes widened, and he took to his heels. But Morgan, already in motion, had the advantage this time, and was closing the distance between them. In another few moments he'd be close enough to grab the fellow's arm.

But as Morgan had told Jenks, the man could run like the wind. He put on a sudden burst of speed, leaving Morgan hurtling along in his wake but losing ground fast. Not to be outdone, he dug deep into his reserves, quickening his pace.

A man stepped out of a doorway, whistling a cheery tune. Morgan altered course, tacking like a sailboat rounding a buoy to avoid a collision. There too much man and too little time. Morgan caromed off him, spinning uncontrollably into the wall with a thud. The man, solidly built and unmoving, swayed slightly and shook his head with a bemused air. "Sorry," Morgan called, peeling himself off the wall.

"As you should be," his victim replied loftily and retreated back through his doorway.

Morgan trotted off down the street, but there was no sign of the assassin.

Chapter Nineteen

Rhenn strode up the Broad Way of Caerfaen, staff in hand and his hat pulled low. He should, he knew, get back to the Academy. But somehow he couldn't bring himself to leave. Not while Marissa duBerry was here, just within his grasp. He had to do something about her before Chief Wizard Foxwent co-opted the witch's powers for his own use.

But what to do? Ah, that was the question, wasn't it? She'd proved impervious to his efforts at McRobbie's home. Or, if not impervious, at least more than adequately resistant. It was all because of the blasted dragon, he had no doubt. The creature was instructing the woman in how to manipulate her powers. He had certainly shown her how to shield herself from Rhenn's attempt to exert control.

Was there a way to get to her without the dragon's knowledge? Probably not. Since he'd tipped his hand and expressed an interest in her, she'd be on her guard. And the damned dragon had already shown her what to do. Not to mention the fact she was incredibly powerful. Rhenn had his doubts he could overcome her shielding through brute magical strength. So, what do to?

Rhenn made his way amid a tangle of people along the street, giving them little notice. He didn't have time to bother with mere people, not with problems of such magnitude on his mind. He strode onward, his face set in concentration, and the crowd parted before him like a flowing stream parting around a rock.

A woman sidled by him, her cloak brushing against his sleeve for the briefest moment. Rhenn barely managed to stifle a gasp.

A sudden jangling tingle of latent power resonated through him. He felt it suffusing the air all around him. The magic was untrained and unused, but there nonetheless. And whoever this woman was, she had large quantities of power at her disposal.

Rhenn stopped short, casting his senses about to locate the source of this unexpected font of magic. A man walking behind caromed into him. Rhenn ignored his protests, whirling to stare wildly up and down the street.

There. He centered his focus, following the traces of power to their owner. A dark-haired woman, strolling on down the street, casually gazing all around.

He followed her.

It wasn't hard. She was meandering, looking about her, staring up at the palace spires and the dome of the cathedral. To all appearances, she was a stranger to Caerfaen. Perhaps, he mused, some country girl in for a visit and taking in the sights.

He quickened his pace, drawing closer in order to make certain she was the one he had sensed. Yes, it was her. No question at all.

The question was, what was she doing here? Anyone with any trace of talent was supposed to be evaluated for potential and sent to St. Giles for instruction. Of course, there were always a few who slipped through the wizards' net, but this woman shouldn't have been missed. Her font of magic was too potent to have been missed.

But that was a problem for another time. Right now, Rhenn needed to find out who she was, and what she was up to. He followed along in the woman's wake, not too closely, but staying near enough not to lose her in the bustling crowd choking the street.

The woman was obviously in no hurry. She wandered along, peering into shop windows and gazing at some of Caerfaen's impressive architecture. Finally, somewhat to his relief, she hesitated outside a tea shop.

"Go in!" he urged silently, for the day was warm, and he was feeling rather dry himself. Whether or not she heard his unspoken command, she did indeed enter the establishment. Rhenn heaved a sigh of relief. After waiting for a few moments, he followed her in.

The shop, which proclaimed itself to be Madam Muriel's Tea Shoppe, was pleasantly shabby. Worn chintz graced the windows, while once-snowy linen, now gone slightly yellow with age and hard usage, covered the few tables. A stout woman with a face like a forlorn bulldog stood to attention next to Rhenn's mystery woman, taking what was no doubt a request for tea and biscuits. Yes, it would have to be biscuits, he decided, noting the buns oozing gelatinously under a glass cover on the counter. There was enough sugar there to satisfy the needs of every ant in the kingdom, with plenty left over in case of an ant invasion from foreign parts.

Rhenn hung up his cloak on the stand, placed his hat on the shelf, and waited for the bulldog-faced individual to deign to notice him. She was engrossed in the mysterious female and so had yet to realize she had another customer. When she finally turned and saw him, she shied back.

"Oh, sir, I'm terrible sorry," she cried. "You was so quiet, I didn't know you was there. Please, sit down. Can I bring you tea?"

"And biscuits," he said. "The molasses ones, with crinkles, if you have them."

"Oh, bless you sir, I do indeed. I makes 'em meself. Very particular 'bout his molasses biscuits was my husband, him as been dead these past five years. He used to say 'Muriel, there's no dabber a hand at a molasses biscuit than you.'"

As Rhenn digested this vital intelligence she bustled off, muttering to herself. No doubt wild tales of the biscuits of yore, he decided. He hoped the ill-fated husband hadn't expired of an overdose of molasses biscuits. More likely it had been an overdose of Muriel.

He seated himself where he could unobtrusively observe the woman. They were the only patrons currently occupying the shoppe, which he deemed a fortunate circumstance.

She was younger than he first imagined, probably only five and twenty. She was quite attractive, too, with a heart-shaped face and hair the color of a raven's wing. Her eyes were the blue of an evening sky, and though her nose was just a bit longer than current fashion deemed beautiful, Rhenn found her enchanting.

Muriel the bulldog emerged from her place of concealment in the rear of the shoppe, where she likely slaved away over her biscuits. She carried a tray with a tea pot and cup, a scone and a small jam pot.

Ah, he hadn't considered scones. Well, the biscuits would no doubt win the day. Rhenn watched as Muriel delivered her cargo intact to the mystery woman, who thanked her in hushed tones and sent her away.

Interesting. The young woman spoke with a slight accent, one he couldn't quite place. She definitely wasn't from Caerfaen. This made him even more curious.

"I'll be right out with yours, sir," Muriel assured him, departing at speed like a barge before a heavy tide. Rhenn watched with unconcealed interest as the young woman poured tea and slathered jam on a bit of scone. She popped it into her mouth, and her eyes widened.

"That bad?" he asked, sotto voce.

The woman, still chewing, glanced over at him. Swallowing, she said, "No, it's marvelous. A treat, and no mistake." Her tongue flicked out to capture a bit of crumb which had attached itself to her lower lip. It was an unconscious motion, but he found it strangely alluring.

Nonsense. He was here on business. To find out about this woman's magic, not to engage in idle flirtation. Wizards didn't do such things. He thrust all other thoughts from his mind and concentrated. "I'm glad to hear it," he said. "I've taken my chance on the biscuits."

She smiled encouragingly. "If they're half as good as the scones, you'll be fine."

Muriel returned, bearing gifts of tea, cup, and biscuits. Rhenn poured tea into the chipped china cup, picked up a biscuit, and…

"Good Lord, they're still warm," he marveled. He examined the biscuit in question. It was a lovely golden brown, the edges crinkled to perfection. He took the first bite and felt his eyes widen just as his companion's had. "Amazing," he murmured, taking another bite. "Who would have guessed?"

He washed the biscuit down with what turned out to be excellent tea and took up another. Then, as if coming to a sudden decision, he looked over at the young woman. "As we seem to be the only ones here," he said, "might I join you? I'll even share what's left of these most excellent molasses biscuits."

She considered. Then shook her head. "Thank you, but no. Not even for molasses biscuits."

"They have crinkles."

Her eyes narrowed. "Not even for crinkles."

Rhenn shrugged. "I merely thought it might be interesting to talk with you, since I am a wizard, and you seem to possess an aura of magic about you."

The woman's mouth formed a perfect "O" as she stared at him in surprise. She quickly regained her composure, and her hand was steady as she took another sip of her tea. Wiping her mouth with the napkin, she scrutinized him. "And just what make you think I possess any magic at all?"

"I can feel it," he assured her. "It is my business to sense these things. I am the Headmaster of St. Giles Academy of Magic, where all with magical talent come for training and instruction. I am surprised to find you here, and not at the Academy. Your magic is quite strong. I sensed it as you passed me on the street, so I followed you in here."

"You foll—Of all the impudence!"

"No offense was intended, miss…? I'm afraid I don't know your name."

"And you won't learn it from me. Go away. I…" she shook with indignation. "He followed me," she announced to the air. "I don't believe it." She rounded on Rhenn, a fell light in her eye. "Tell me, sir, do you often pursue young women into tea shoppes?"

"I—" He cleared his throat. "Only when I discover said young woman with powerful magic and no training roaming about loose. Then, yes, I follow them into tea shoppes."

She tilted her head and managed to look down her nose at him. "Well, follow me no more. I have no interest in your magical academy. I do not live in Caerfaen, or even in Kilbourne. I'm only visiting here a short while, and then will return to my home in the north. So you needn't bother yourself about me or any magic I may or may not possess."

It was his turn to narrow his eyes. He drew himself up in wizardly indignation. "You do not realize—"

He was cut off by a haughty sniff from the young woman as she swiftly gathered her belongings. "What I realize," she said in clipped tones, "is that you are being exceedingly rude to a visitor to this city. I do not wish to see you near me again."

Opening her reticule, she tossed a few coins on the table and turned to leave. As she did, a small book fell out onto the table. Uttering a sharp cry, she made a grab for it, but Rhenn was quicker. He sent forth a quick burst of power, sending it skidding away from her hand. With a word and a flick of his finger, he brought the book sailing through the air, into his outstretched hand. He turned it over to read the title and dropped the little volume as if he'd been suddenly burned.

"Where did you get this?" he demanded, his voice a harsh croak.

"It's mine," the woman said. "Give it to me." Her own voice was commanding, carrying with it a compulsion he nearly found himself obeying. Surprised at the strength of her coercion, he still managed to shake off the impulse to comply. He stood, blocking her path to the book.

"Where did you get this?" he repeated.

The woman grabbed for the book, but he remained in her way, preventing her from obtaining the volume. "It was the book's aura I perceived," he said grimly. "Not yours. I should have realized. This little volume is quite powerful, not to mention extremely dangerous. So I'll ask once more, nicely, before I begin to get irritated. Where did you get it?"

She pressed her lips together, then made another frantic grab for the book. Rhenn sighed. She was going to be tedious. And he really didn't want to go into this in front of Muriel, who was watching the proceedings in horrified fascination from behind the shelter of her counter. But this was the second woman who'd defied him in the last few days, and it was getting old. He stretched out his right hand, preparing to loose a tiny bit of his power at this obstinate female. Not to actually hurt her. He'd merely stop her in her tracks for a few moments so he could get some answers. He began the spell—

The door opened, and three elderly ladies crowded into the shoppe, chattering and cackling like a flock of hens. He glanced up at them. In the instant of his distraction the woman darted around him, snatched the book from his hand, and bolted from the shop. He started to give pursuit, but the three women managed to cluster steadfastly in his path, even as they'd parted for the fleeing female. He was foiled again by Muriel, who loudly demanded where he thought he was going without paying for his tea and biscuits.

Scowling ferociously, Rhenn pulled coins from a pocket and tossed them into the blasted woman's outstretched palm. He dodged around the intruding gaggle of hens and rushed out to the street. He scanned right and left, but the woman and the book were gone.

At least that's what she thought. He had no doubt she figured she made a clean getaway. He smiled to himself. The book was leaving a trail of residual magic a blind man could have followed. He started on its trail.

Chapter Twenty

Kiara Northram hurried down the unfamiliar street, glancing repeatedly over her shoulder to make sure the wizard wasn't following her. She turned another corner, nearly caroming into a stout matron laden with parcels. Kiara dodged around her with a dancer's grace, her skirts swirling around her legs. The woman dropped a bag of onions which rolled off in every direction. She hastened on, ignoring the woman's protestations and curses.

Eventually she slowed her pace, finally pausing to catch her breath. She was still clutching the book in white-knuckled fingers. She tucked it back into her reticule. She'd been in such a swivet she'd just darted out of the tea shoppe without pausing to stow it safely away. She couldn't afford to lose it. How had the wizard realized she had it? He'd prattled on about the book projecting some kind of aura. Which was sheer nonsense. It was just a book. Wasn't it?

Still, she felt better with it tucked safely away in her reticule. Her own power was so negligible as to be practically non-existent. Surely the wizard couldn't find her now.

Although she wasn't sure why she'd run. Her scheme, after all, did require the assistance of a wizard, or at least someone with much stronger magic than the tiny bit she possessed. She'd never been able to do anything with it, much to the dismay and eventual disgust of her tutors. She'd tried and tried, but to no avail. Now it didn't matter. Because now, she had the book.

And the book was the key to everything. Kiara doubted it had any mysterious arcane powers of its own, despite the impertinent wizard's warning. What it did have was the instructions for several powerful magical spells. For the book, obtained by perseverance, bribery, and a great deal of gold, was a grimoire. An ancient tome wrought by sorcerers in the dark distant past.

One spell, and only one, was of interest to her. It didn't look particularly complicated or dangerous. Of course, any magic was inherently dangerous, if one was careless or cavalier. Her tutor had at least managed to drill this lesson into her admittedly thick head. He hadn't had much luck with teaching her to perform any spells despite the fact she did possess the talent. After she'd wed Jermaine Northram, he'd encouraged her to pursue her magic, but she'd been otherwise occupied. That had been before. When they'd been so happy and so wildly in love. When they'd been so completely besotted with one another. The magic of love had overshadowed magic of a more prosaic nature.

Before. They had only been wed six months when Jermaine had received the summons from King Varsil, directing him as Baron of Southingshire to muster his troops and rally for the assault on Noordstrom.

He'd looked so handsome and gallant, his long hair flowing in the breeze as he'd kissed her and mounted his steed. He'd promised to be back soon, covered in glory and honor.

He'd come back all right, but instead of honor and glory, he'd been covered in a shroud. His men, the few of them left, bore Jermaine's lifeless body back to Harringhall and related to her his valiant deeds. They'd also told her of his defeat and death at the hands of the Kilbourne commander, Morgan McRobbie.

Kiara had been dumbfounded when Morgan's name had bounded out of her own distant past into an inconceivable present. This bolt from the blue had set her senses reeling, nearly as much as the knowledge of Jermaine's death. The two, combined, had nearly killed her.

With effort, she'd managed to rally, pull herself out of the dark and deadly miasma of despair, at least for the moment. She'd taken charge, arranged for the priest and for Jermaine's interment in the Northram family crypt in the manor churchyard. She'd waited until everyone had gone, taking their platitudes and sorrows and wailing with them.

And then she'd simply…gone mad. She'd wept, and raged, and cursed. Thrown crockery at the walls and screamed into the blackness of an uncaring night.

Finally, spent, weary, and aching in body and spirit, she made a vow. One which had led her to find the book. One which had brought her step by unwilling step back to Caerfaen. One which she now sought to fulfill.

A vow to wreak vengeance on Morgan McRobbie. Both for Jermaine's death, and for the death of her own girlish, foolish dreams so many years before.

Nearly ten years, she reflected. She'd been only fifteen, Morgan seventeen. Her father's small estate had lain not far from Bryntop, the holding of Viscount Martin McRobbie, Morgan's father. Kiara had loved those rolling green meadows and pastures, the rocky cliffs jutting out into the endlessly crashing sea. And she'd loved Morgan, albeit from afar.

They'd met at a ball. He danced with her, as he had dutifully done with all the fawning daughters of all the other nobles in the county. But he smiled at Kiara, his teeth flashing white against his dark skin, so intriguingly different. His mother hailed from the island nation of Orsk, where everyone was dark skinned, or so she'd heard. Kiara's mother, who bore an unrelenting loathing for foreigners and anyone different, gnashed her teeth in silent disgust at having to defer to the lovely, charming, exotic Viscountess McRobbie, Lady Sybil.

Kiara didn't care. He bore his mother's coloring, certainly, but she thought him so handsome and dashing. She was certain he held her hand a bit longer than the dance required, smiled at her just a bit more brightly than he had the other girls. She'd fallen head over heels in love with him that night, and made up her mind, then and there, to capture his heart. The proximity of her father's land had made it easier for her to "accidentally" meet him when he was out riding. He always had greeted her cheerfully on those occasions, inviting her to ride with him.

Kiara had thought Morgan the most wonderful boy ever. She'd eagerly encouraged him when, one glorious, brilliant afternoon, he tried to kiss her. They'd both been awkward, but she still recalled how her heart had soared like an eagle, rising up on ever-spiraling currents of sweet young love.

She'd begun to make plans for their future together, all on the basis of one messy kiss. Then, he had gone off to school and she'd never heard from him again. She'd written him letters, so many letters, declaring her undying affection and pouring out her tormented soul.

No letters had come in reply. At first, she passed his silence off as the newness of St. Colin's, then to the busy schedule he must be keeping. But as the months dragged on with no replies, love had begun to sour and taste bitter on her tongue. Eventually his name, once breathed with such longing, became something of a curse.

Soon afterward, her father had received news of his uncle's demise and the inheritance of an estate in the kingdom of Rhuddlan. Kiara had been even more eager to leave than her father. Eager to leave behind the shattered girlish fantasies and aching hole in her heart Morgan's betrayal had wrought.

She had adjusted well to their new home in the north, never once regretting having left Kilbourne. Jermaine Northram, newly come into his title after his father had been thrown from a horse and died, had filled the hole Morgan had left. He'd been caring, kind, and filled with an almost boyish exuberance. Their brief time together had been joyful, loving, and so very right.

Only now, everything was wrong again. All thanks once more to Morgan McRobbie. He'd crushed her heart not once, but twice. And now she would crush his, make him watch as she destroyed what he loved most. She had the means to do it. The little book tucked into her reticule. She—

Kiara jumped, letting out a piercing shriek as a familiar voice said, "Ah, there you are."

Breathing hard, heart pounding, she turned slowly to face the wizard from the tea shoppe.

Chapter Twenty-One

Rhenn pinned her with a steely stare. She raised a defiant chin and said in the tones of one finding a mouse in her soup, "Oh. You."

"Augustus Rhenn, at your service."

"I've no need of your service." But he saw her gaze waver, as if she were not as certain as she sounded.

"My lady, anyone in possession of such a volume is likely in need of all the aid they can get. I mean you no ill, please believe me. I only want to help you. And to ensure nothing—um, drastic—happens. Possession may work more than one way, you know."

She heaved a sigh, her stance chancing from prospective flight to reluctant acquiescence. Rhenn almost sagged with relief but managed to control his emotions. "Perhaps you're right," she muttered at last.

"I am," he replied. "Come, let's go somewhere a bit more congenial, so we can talk."

"Not back to the tea shoppe."

"No," he agreed. "Definitely not back to the tea shoppe. I doubt I'd be welcome to darken their door again any time soon."

The woman gave a wan smile which ultimately turned into a choked giggle. "No, I don't imagine so. Where, then?"

Rhenn glanced around to get his bearings. Montrose Street, not far from The Royal College of Wizards. He nodded once. "There is a public house, right down this way. There are tables in the back where one may converse in privacy. I believe it will suit our purposes."

Her mouth turned down at the corners. "A tavern? I don't particularly care for ale, Master Rhenn."

"The barman keeps a nice selection of wines and spirits on hand as well," he assured her. "And I think a drink might be just what you need. I as well. You've led me a merry chase, Lady—" He left the question of her name hanging between them like a wall. If she gave it, he was almost assured she'd not run again. If not, well…

"Kiara, Lady Northram." Rhenn noticed a pained expression as she said this. "I'm sorry," she said, choking on the words. "I'm newly widowed."

He bowed solicitously, murmuring, "My condolences, Lady Kiara, on your loss. Please, come with me. A glass of wine, perhaps, or a drop of brandy. Yes, I think brandy is called for."

"Perhaps you're right. Very well, Master Rhenn, lead on to this tavern of yours."

He did so, and in short order ushered Lady Kiara into the Sword and Crown. They took a secluded table in the rear of the common room. Once refreshment had been provided—ale for himself, brandy for this odd young woman—he glanced meaningfully at her reticule. "Please, tell me about the book."

"It is a book of magical spells," she said quietly, hiding the lower half of her face behind the glass.

"No, it's a grimoire," he corrected. "I meant tell me how you came into possession of it. And more importantly, why?"

She took another sip of the amber spirit, grimaced, and set the glass down with a sharp thud. Brandy sloshed up, nearly escaping the bowl of the glass.

Taking a deep breath, Lady Kiara squared her shoulders, closed her eyes, and spoke. "You were correct when you said I possessed magic. But very little, it seems. My tutors were unable to teach me to perform even simple spells. Still, I did listen and learn, and I heard tales of this little volume from one of them. Recently, after my husband died, I realized I had need of one of the spells it supposedly contained."

Rhenn winced, trying to recall if this particular grimoire contained any spells of necromancy. Surely she couldn't be intending to...

Lady Kiara went on, oblivious to his racing thoughts. "I set out to acquire it. It took a lot of time, and a lot of gold, but I achieved my goal."

"I imagine you usually do," he muttered.

She raised one sardonic brow. "Not always. Some things in life have eluded me."

He pursed his lips, almost holding his breath. "Which spell?"

She smiled. Well, her mouth smiled. Her eyes remained cold and hard as she said, "Domelindos's binding spell."

Rhenn's eyes widened in surprise. Not necromancy after all. Far from it, in fact. "Really? Do you realize what this spell does?"

"Oh, yes." Her eyes were bright now, eager, almost manic. "The subject of the spell is bound helpless, but fully aware. And the first person to touch them after they are bound...will die."

"Correct," he said approvingly, reverting to his role as headmaster. "You have learned your lessons well. But tell me why. This is a most dangerous, ultimately a killing spell. Who has done you such an injury—"

He halted as her eyes went first wide, and then black with fury. A sharp exhalation of breath, the nearest thing to the growl of a wounded animal, escaped her. One hand clutched the edge of the table until her knuckles went white with strain. The other hand gripped the stem of her glass, squeezing so hard he thought it might shatter.

All color drained from her face. Lady Kiara closed her eyes and shrank back behind the wide oaken pillar which provided seclusion to their table. A series of shudders wracked her body.

Rhenn risked a glance over his shoulder toward the door. A pair of men strolled in, intent in conversation. He only knew one of them…

"Morgan," he heard Lady Kiara hiss.

Rhenn turned back to face Kiara. "McRobbie?" he asked, so softly as to be almost inaudible. "That's who you want to use the spell on?"

She nodded once, never taking her storm-tossed eyes off the pair of men.

"Why?"

"Later." She dismissed his question with a curt wave. "I-I need to get out of here. I don't want to be seen." Her breath came quick and shallow, her voice sounding panicked.

Rhenn glanced over his shoulder again, to where Morgan and his companion had taken over a table on the other side of the room. "We can't," he said. "There's only one way out, and we'd have to pass right by them. I've no wish to encounter Commander McRobbie either. So, if we wish to remain unobserved, I think we'd best remain right where we are."

"But—" She started to protest, then subsided.

He indicated the brandy snifter, still half filled. "Drink that," he directed. "It will steady your nerves."

She looked at him with blank uncomprehending eyes. He pushed the glass toward her hand.

~ * ~

Kiara took the snifter, almost instinctively, raised it to her lips, and drank. She thought she might gag and spit out the brandy, but with an effort of will she controlled her reflexes, swallowed, and wiped her mouth with the back of an unsteady hand.

Rhenn reached out a hand as if to comfort her, then drew it back.

She straightened her shoulders, and her gaze came back into focus. "Help me," she said. "Help me make him suffer."

"You can tell me all about it later. Right now, let's see what we can do about getting you—us—out of here." He picked up his tankard, drained the last of his ale, and set the oaken vessel down on the table.

Fishing coins from some inner recesses of his dark robe, he placed them neatly next to the tankard.

"That should more than suffice," he said. "As to whether I can do anything, the answer is yes. We are going to walk out the door, right past the good commander and his friend, and none will be the wiser."

"How—?" she began, but Rhenn put a finger to his lips.

"Patience, Lady Kiara. And a bit of trust, if you please. Both are in order at the moment. Now, I'm going to stand and edge fully behind this lovely old pillar which so conveniently shields us from view. When I do, I'll need you to stand as well, and take my hand. Ah, don't question, just do as I say."

She fought down the instinctive protestations, gave a sharp nod, and bit her lower lip as an aid to silence. He pushed back his chair, rose, and moved so he was completely blocked from view of the rest of the room by the pillar. She stood, took his outstretched hand...and gasped.

Rhenn was gone! Well, not gone, but certainly not visible. She could feel his hand, large and warm, holding hers. She looked down and realized she was invisible as well.

Rhenn's disembodied voice murmured in her ear. It was a rather eerie feeling, like being spoken to by a spirit. "We shall move together toward the door. Taking great pains not to bump into any furniture or any patrons of this fine establishment. And for God's sake, whatever you do don't let go of my hand."

"Anything else?" Her tone was just this side of acerbic.

He must have noticed, for he gave a soft chuckle. "Yes. Don't sneeze."

Kiara immediately felt her nose give a little twitch, along with an urge to do that very thing. "You just had to say that, didn't you?" she muttered darkly.

"The way toward the door is fairly clear at the moment," Rhenn advised. "Hold tight to my hand, and let's go."

They set off through the maze of mostly deserted tables. The hour was still early enough that the tavern wasn't particularly crowded, which was fortunate. A mad crush of people milling about would have made their unseen journey much more prone to discovery.

After a couple of minutes, which seemed to Kiara to span a couple of centuries, they stood beside the door. It was closed, and she realized that if it suddenly opened, seemingly of its own accord, people might take notice and investigate.

Rhenn's voice, soft as a thistledown next to her ear, said, "We'll wait 'til someone enters and leave as the door closes. Don't dawdle. And—"

"I know," she whispered back. "Don't let go."

She prepared herself to wait another eternity or two, but it was only about a year and a half before the door swung open and two men entered. She felt Rhenn move and followed in his wake as he sidled through the rapidly narrowing opening. She was nearly through when the door closed with a thump—catching the hem of her dress.

"Come on," he urged, tugging on her hand.

"I can't. I'm caught. The door closed on my dress!"

"Rip it!" he snarled.

Kiara looked wildly around. A pair of men were approaching the Sword and Crown. They would be at the door in only a moment. She and Rhenn would be discovered. Or, if not actually discovered, at least the men would raise an outcry if they ran into spectral bodies as they tried to open the door. Perhaps that would swear them off drink for a while, she thought, stifling the urge to cackle.

Rhenn pulled her to the side of the door, as far as the taut fabric of the dress would allow, just as one of the men reached for the door. He stumbled suddenly, falling heavily against the portal with an oath.

"Oy, why'd ye push me, ye ninny?" he demanded. His companion, protesting injured innocence, blamed his fallen comrade's clumsiness on his haste for refreshment. They debated this hotly as the still standing fellow helped his companion back onto his feet.

But his stumble, which Kiara assumed must have been courtesy of a shove by the wizard, had done the trick, nudging open the door just enough for her to pull her dress free. She kept a firm grip on Rhenn's hand as he led her away from the tavern and around a corner into an alleyway. There he released her, and they were both visible again.

Kiara examined her dress. There was a slight rip where she'd been caught in the door, but nothing her maid couldn't repair easily enough. At least she hadn't had to shed the dress to get away, scampering down the street in naught but her chemise. She'd have made Rhenn keep them invisible if that had been the case, until she could get back to the inn where she was staying.

Done with her examination she glanced at the wizard. He was practically smirking. "Yes, yes, well done," she said, irritated by his supreme overconfidence. It might be nice, just for a moment, to see him nonplussed. She'd have to think on how to do that. But right now, she had other things to worry about.

"Shall we go?" he said, offering his arm. "I believe we have much to discuss."

~ * ~

"All right, what's so blasted important?" Aartis asked as he and

Morgan entered the Sword and Crown. "I had a rather interesting and quite pleasant evening all lined up. The young lady," he went on, "was most disappointed when I had to cancel."

Morgan quirked a grin as he led the way to a table near the wall. Here they'd be out of earshot of most of the tavern's patrons. "No doubt. Unfortunately, your evening is about to get a lot more interesting. Although I have a feeling pleasure may be in short supply."

Aartis eyed him, his expression wary. "This," he muttered, "doesn't bode well. Not at all."

Any reply Morgan might have made was precluded by the advent of Rajan Turksa, the barman and owner of the tavern. Rather than delegating the chore to one of the serving girls as he normally would have with any other customer, Rajan stumped over himself to wait on Morgan and Aartis. After an exchange of pleasantries and backchat, Rajan ambled off to get their drinks. Morgan turned back to his companion.

"Before we get to the actual reason I've asked you here, there's something I need to know."

Aartis's eyes narrowed, and his expression grew grim. "I was right. This doesn't bode well."

Rajan delivered their drinks—foaming tankards of ale from the reserve he kept for special customers—and Morgan raised his tankard in salute. Hesitating for a moment, Aartis returned the gesture and they both drank.

"Ahh." Morgan wiped foam from his lips. "Now I remember why I keep coming here. All right, so tell me. What's between you and Ian Taggart?"

Rather than answering, Aartis took another long pull from his tankard of ale. When he set it back on the scarred oak table, he looked Morgan in the eye. "I've done nothing wrong," he said. His voice was quiet, but firm.

"I've not said you have, Aartis. But this—" He waved an expressive hand. "This mess Taggart's just dumped into my lap—well, I just need to know exactly how things stand. This is nothing official, no court of inquiry. This is just me, asking you as a friend, to tell me what your relationship with him is."

Aartis drummed his fingers on the table for a moment, his expression distant. Finally he took another fortifying sip of ale, set the tankard down with a thump, and spoke.

"We first met, Taggart and I," he began, "in a tavern not unlike this one. Well, no, actually, not at all like this one. Rajan would skin me. The place I'm talking about was a dump. But in point of fact, most of our time together seemed to have been spent in one tavern or another. But that first one… It was a seedy dockside place whose name I can't recall. I think it burned down long ago. But it should have been something along the lines of The Drowned Rat. The smell of the place, and of the patrons…" He grimaced.

"I was a newly minted knight, and a fresh recruit to the Legion. My unit had been on a training maneuver which involved landing on some island and taking control of it. I didn't enjoy the sea voyage in the least, short though it was. I've never been a particularly good sailor. I'll leave the sea to the chaps in His Majesty's Navy, and they're welcome to it. Anyway, several of us spent most of the voyage hanging over the rail and praying for a quick and merciful death."

Morgan laughed, and Aartis quirked a wry smile. "I was green, in more ways than one. Well, once I got my feet back on dry land, I dived into the first tavern I could find, disreputable as it was. While I was downing a much-needed glass of ale, a couple of pickpockets nipped my money pouch. When I realized what had happened, I started to go after them. Taggart was sitting nearby, and he stopped me. Well, actually he tripped me. Probably prevented me getting my throat cut. But it turned out he'd lifted my pouch off the thieves, neat as you please. Said he didn't like seeing 'em take advantage of a king's soldier like that. I bought him a drink, we got to talking, and well, that's pretty much it. Even when I learned about his criminal activities, I still maintained our friendship. I just took care not to get involved in anything dodgy. And Taggart never asked me to. And that's it."

Morgan nodded as Aartis finished his tale. "Pretty much what Taggart implied."

"Morgan. No, Commander McRobbie," Aartis said. "On my honor as a knight, I've never done anything untoward. Nor has Ian ever asked me to. I don't see him often. I just—well, I just enjoy his company."

"He can certainly be charming when he puts his mind to it," Morgan agreed. "And I have to say he's dealt more than fair with me. I just needed to know, for my own peace of mind."

"You believe me, then?" Aartis looked surprised.

"Of course I believe you. And it's up to you whether or not you tell Taggart we've had this little chat. As far as I'm concerned, it never happened."

Aartis heaved a sigh of relief, picked up his tankard, realized it was empty, and signaled for another. "So," he asked. "What's this all about?"

Morgan told him.

Chapter Twenty-Two

"Lluminas acciadio."

"Lluminas acciatio."

Marissa took a steadying breath, let it out slowly, and raised her hand once again, palm open. She could barely see it in the darkened room. *"Lluminas acciadio,"* she muttered.

To her complete surprise, a tiny gleam of light blinked into existence in the hollow of her hand. "Oh!" she cried. And then, "Wait! Come back," as it winked out again.

"I did it," she crowed. She held out her hand once more, uttering the spell. The gleam of light bathed her hand. She remained still this time, concentrating on holding the light steady. The glow grew stronger, brighter, finally spilling out of her hand to fully illumine the room.

"I did it," she said again, marveling at the little globe of light dancing and flickering in her hand. It looked hot enough to singe her flesh. Instead it was almost chill to the touch. She'd have to ask Wyvrndell about that.

Marissa closed her hand, and the ball of light winked out. She stood there in the dark for a moment, basking in her accomplishment. She'd done magic, all on her own. No dragon or wizard to guide her steps. She'd done it.

Now, could she do it again? She raised her hand, concentrated, and whispered the words. The ball of light, not much larger than an apple, blossomed once more. It flickered tentatively at first, then settled down into a steady glow which bathed the room in a warm, rosy patina.

Marissa jumped as the door opened, and Briana entered, saying, "M'lady, the doctor is—ack!" The maid ducked as the ball of light flew from Marissa's hand, swooping and darting about the room, nearly colliding with Briana's smooth dark hair.

Transfixed, Marissa watched as the light caromed off a picture of some long-distant duBerry ancestor, circled a vase of flowers, and finally came to rest next to Briana's horrified face. With a start she closed her hand and the light winked out once more. Enough light came through the open doorway for her to see the maid shaking her head and muttering imprecations at mistresses thoughtless enough to send balls of fire to attack innocent people.

"I'm sorry, Briana," she said. "It's harmless, just a bit disconcerting."

"The doctor is here to see you, m'lady," Briana said stiffly. "He is waiting in the front parlor." She turned and fled.

Marissa heaved a sigh. Then she opened her hand just a bit and whispered, "*Lluminas acciadio.*" A warm glow suffused her palm. With a satisfied smile she closed her hand once more and headed down the hall to where Dr. Carnavon waited.

The doctor stopped pacing as she entered the parlor. "Good morning, Dr. Carnavon," she said.

"Good morn, Lady Marissa. How is my patient?"

"You'd better judge for yourself."

"Mmm." His brows rose. "Something wrong? Is he feverish?"

"No, not that I could tell. But he just…lies there. Doesn't move, doesn't even stir. He doesn't appear to be any worse, but he also doesn't really seem to be recovering."

Carnavon grimaced. "Very well, let's take a look at him."

Marissa led him down the hall to the room she had appropriated for Sebastien's sick room. The curtains were drawn against the morning sun. Carnavon strode to the window and flung them open. "Let's get some light in here. If he does wake up, we don't want him thinking he's been stuffed into a crypt."

Marissa refrained from pointing out that chintz curtains, a patchwork quilt, and a shelf overstuffed with books hardly seemed crypt-like. Even if she had, she reckoned the doctor wouldn't have noticed. He was fully engaged in examining Sebastien. He listened to the old man's low, even breathing. He placed an ear to Sebastien's chest. To check his heart, she supposed. Carnavon pulled open the wizard's eyelids, bending close to peer into his eyes.

Nodding to himself, Carnavon said, "Could I get a basin of hot water and some clean cloths? I want to change this dressing and take a look at the wound."

"Of course. I'll tell Cook." Marissa stepped out into the hall, found Briana hovering nearby, and dispatched her on the errand instead. Back in the room she asked, "How is he?"

Carnavon shrugged. "From a cursory examination, he seems…fine. I want to check the wound, see how that's healing up. But…"

"But you're concerned about something?"

He glanced up at her. "I am. He should have regained consciousness by now. He needs to be eating, trying to walk around a bit, regaining his strength. Instead, he's just lying here, limp as an old rag. No fever, which is good. But I don't understand why he's still like this."

"He is quite old," she suggested. "Even by wizard standards, I think he's pretty old."

"Yessss." He didn't sound convinced. Any further discussion was forestalled by the entrance of Briana with the tea cart. It was loaded with the requested hot water and cloths.

"Good," the doctor said, busying himself with unwrapping bandages. Dipping a cloth into the steaming bowl he gently laved Sebastien's wounded side. Marissa winced in sympathy as the wizard stirred restlessly.

"Ah, that's actually a good sign," Carnavon observed. "At least he's responding a bit. The cut is healing up nicely too. Another couple of days and he should be practically jumping out of bed. Except he's not, is he?"

"No," Marissa sighed. "It certainly doesn't seem like it."

"Mmm." He regarded his patient, a pensive look on his face. "I just don't know. Why aren't you awake, you old duffer?" He rummaged in his bag, extracting bandages and herbs, and set about dressing the wound again.

Task completed, he pulled the quilt back over the wizard and tucked him in with surprising gentleness. "I'm going to do a bit of research," he said. "See if I can figure out why he's not awake and grouchy. A wound like that must hurt like blazes, especially as it heals."

"What can I do?" Marissa asked.

"Continue to drown him in broth and brandy. And call me at once, day or night, if his condition changes, for better or worse." He shook his head in a gesture of frustration. "Any time," he repeated. "I'll come."

Gathering up his bag and muttering under his breath, the doctor cast one last aggravated glare at his patient and stalked out.

Chapter Twenty-Three

Aartis wrinkled his nose at his reflection in the grimy window of an unsavory tavern. It wasn't merely his appearance that evoked this reaction. He not only looked like a dock rat, he smelled like one. He exuded a piquant fragrance mingling old fish, cheap ale, and sweat. In point of fact he bloody well reeked.

Turning away from his momentary scrutiny, he shuffled along past seedy alehouses and ramshackle warehouses. He glanced at a once-grand inn, fallen on hard times and reduced in circumstance to a shabby boarding house.

Rather like his own condition, Aartis mused. *How the mighty have fallen.* Only yesterday he'd been the dashing Captain Poldane, second in command of the King's Legion, and an object of desire for more of Caerfaen's beauties than he could count. Today he was Arn Pitcher, disreputable dockhand. And prospective pirate.

One corner of his mouth twitched in what might have been a grin had he allowed it. When Morgan had told him of his meeting with Ian Taggart and what they wanted him to do, he'd been incredulous. "Play at pirates?" he'd demanded. "You're not serious."

Taggart, Morgan had informed him in acid tones, had seemed exceedingly serious. The pirates were a threat to the city, and someone needed to do something about them. That someone was Aartis.

He growled, garnering a suspicious look from a passing Watchman. He'd have to remember to thank Taggart for thrusting him into this little adventure. Assuming he survived it.

His briefing by Taggart hadn't amounted to much more than a directive to present himself, in disguise, to the dockside tavern known as The Mean Ewe. Where, supposedly, the pirates could be found. Then all he had to do was figure a way to insinuate himself into their company, learn their schemes, and foil them. Simple, a mere bagatelle. Right. He growled again, more quietly this time. The Watchman was still keeping a jaundiced eye on him.

Aartis halted his shuffling progress along the street as he came to one of the less seedy taverns in a progressively appalling bunch. To say The Mean Ewe was a more desirable environ than its neighbors was giving it more credit than was due. The Mean Ewe was simply less dilapidated, having seen a coat of paint applied to its exterior sometime within the last couple of years. In addition, Aartis noted with approval as he inspected the place, the windows had been cleaned since that last coat of paint had been applied.

Pulling the door open, he started to step inside. He was immediately propelled back into the street, courtesy of a rapidly moving figure that came hurtling through the door. Aartis sprawled in the dirt as the man gave a yelp of pain, leapt over him, and tore off down the street.

Staring bemusedly after him, Aartis jerked around as a voice from just inside the tavern's door called, "And stay out, ya scallywag!" He peered up to see the owner of the voice.

A young woman stepped out, glaring after the dearly departed. In one hand she held a short, sturdy club. In the other was a scrap of cloth which, Aartis realized with a grin, must have been ripped from the fleeing man's shirt.

She grimaced in apparent frustration at not being able to wield the club. She was just turning on her heel when she noticed the prostrate form at her feet. She looked down at him, eyes widening in surprise. Dropping her weapon, she reached out a hand to help him up. "Are you all right?"

Aartis, who had managed by now to achieve a sitting position, found himself paralyzed. He stared at the woman, his mouth opening and closing soundlessly.

The girl narrowed her eyes. "Are you having some kind of fit? Do I need to summon a physician? Or do you just make a habit of sprawling about in the gutter?" She started to move her hand out of reach, but Aartis forced himself out of his trance and grasped it.

With a long-suffering sigh the girl heaved. Aartis found himself jerked off the ground like a recalcitrant stopper pulled from a bottle. Finding his voice at last, he said, "Thank you. Just a bit winded after that fellow bowled me over."

"Sorry about that," she said. "I have to run him off about once every couple of weeks or he doesn't feel he's gotten good value for his coin."

Aartis chuckled. "Don't worry 'bout it, miss." Back on his feet, he eyed his angel of mercy. She was tall, the top of her head coming nearly level with his own. She was striking, with dark curls, piercing blue eyes, and a pert nose. And perfect cupid's bow lips, which at the moment were twisted into a sardonic half-smile.

He allowed his gaze to travel a bit lower, to bared shoulders and a tightly laced bodice, to shapely hips upon which her hands rested akimbo. He found himself reddening as she asked, "Well? Will I pass?"

Aartis, who never found himself at a loss for words, did so now. He managed to stammer, "Uh...I..."

"If you're done staring, be off with you. I've no time to stand here like a blasted painter's model. Got a bar to tend to, don't I?" She turned her back on him, heading into The Mean Ewe.

"I... wait," gasped Aartis. "You're—I mean, are you Kate? I was told to ask for Kate at The Mean Ewe."

She turned to face him, her ripe mouth forming into an impossibly thin line. "Oh, really? By who?"

"Taggart. I'm, um, Arn Porter."

"Are you now?" She stooped to retrieve her fallen club. "Well, you'd best go 'round back. Better if you're not seen coming in here with me. Shoo!"

Aartis ducked his head, muttered, "Sorry, miss," and shuffled away.

"Don't you come back, either," she called at his retreating back. He glanced back as she brandished the club. He moved faster.

Entering an alleyway he figured would lead around to the back of the tavern, Aartis allowed his reeling brain to focus on Kate the barmaid. What the devil was a girl like that doing down here in a dockside tavern? It was like turning over a rock, expecting to find crawly things, and discovering a sapphire—the color of her eyes—instead.

It wasn't that she was beautiful. Aartis had dallied with a lot of beautiful women and considered himself something of a connoisseur. No, this Kate was different. Oh, she was comely enough, but what had caught his interest—had in fact made his breath catch in his throat—was something more than sheer physical attributes. He wasn't quite sure what it was, but it would certainly bear further investigation. He smiled for the first time that day.

Then he came out of the alley and any trace of a smile faded. He had a mission to complete, a pestilence of pirates to thwart, and a city to save. He had no time for dalliance, no matter how intriguing this girl might be. He needed to focus.

But when he saw her waiting at the back entrance, he felt a fizzing in his blood. He took a steadying breath and flashed her a brilliant smile.

It was not returned. "Come in, and be quick about it," she snapped.

Aartis trotted up the stairs, but Kate had already turned away. He followed in her wake as she strode purposefully through a dimly lit store room and down a narrow passageway. There were doors leading off on both sides, but Kate passed them all, aiming for the stairway at the end of the hall.

At the stop of the stair, she produced key and unlocked and opened a door. She motioned Aartis inside with a preemptory wave. Once he'd entered, she followed, pulling the door closed and locking it again. He stood aside to let her pass in the small entranceway and had to brace himself against the wall for support. The very nearness of her was more intoxicating than the finest wine.

The interior room was dark, the windows covered so no daylight entered. Aartis was momentarily blinded as Kate struck a spark and set a lamp glowing. As his eyes adjusted, he made out what appeared to be a lady's boudoir. The room was remarkably neat and tidy, except for a pair of stockings draped with casual abandon over the back of a chair. She must have seen him notice. She huffed out an aggravated breath and caught them up, stuffing them into a drawer.

Then she turned to face him, arching one brow. "Well, Captain Poldane?" she inquired.

Chapter Twenty-Four

Morgan made his way to St. Basil's Cathedral. With all the things going on, he needed to talk to Randolph. Perhaps his friend could help him to gain some perspective. The bishop was often infuriatingly insightful.

"So, what's on your mind?" Randolph inquired as he poured claret.

Morgan gave him a brief recap of events, in order of occurrence, beginning with the arrival at Bryntop of Augustus Rhenn. He carried on through the attack on Sebastien and his own meeting with Taggart. Randolph leaned back in his chair, eyes more than half closed, until Morgan wasn't sure if his friend was even awake.

"If I'm boring you," Morgan said at last, "I can go."

"Bah." Randolph sat up and took a sip of claret. "I've heard every word. Most interesting. I wonder what the wizard's prophecy is."

Morgan shrugged. "I suppose I could just corral a wizard and ask, but I'm not sure how that would be received."

"Not well, I'm sure. Getting information out of a wizard is like trying to change the mind of a priest. Which brings me to our next topic of discussion. It's my turn to tell a story. We'll call this one Randolph's Nightmare, or An Interview with Father Dmitri."

"Should I know this Father Dmitri?"

Randolph barked out a laugh. "Not if you're lucky. He's a hidebound old priest who… No, I shall refrain from further comment on the foibles of Father Dmitri. But our conversation was interesting."

~ * ~

Randolph heaved a sigh and rubbed the bridge of his nose.

He had known, when he decided to enter the priesthood, that the Lord would send him a good many trials and tribulations in the course of a lifetime. Today's just happened to be one he hadn't quite managed to anticipate.

"You can't allow her to marry in the cathedral," his visitor yammered. "You can't allow her to marry at all. She's a witch! She's tainted. A—"

Randolph held up a large hand to stem the floodtide of words gushing from Father Dmitri's pinched mouth. "Thank you for your concern, Father," he rumbled. "Well founded, I'm sure. However, if you reflect for a moment, you'll recall that over the years numerous wizards have plighted their troth under the auspices of the church. The cathedral's roof," he mused, "is still standing."

"Wizards?" sputtered Dmitri. "Sophistry, Randolph, pure sophistry. This is much different and much more dire. She is…" he forced the word out, "a woman."

Randolph closed his eyes for a moment. When he opened them, the sullen face of Father Dmitri was still there. Patience, he told himself, was a virtue. Besides, bellowing at the old codger wouldn't help the situation, and certainly wouldn't change his mind. People like Dmitri rarely changed their minds.

"Yes, she is," Randolph agreed, for something to say. He didn't say, "She's a very nice woman, who loves Kilbourne and has risked much to keep it safe." He didn't say, "She never asked for magic, never wanted it." He also didn't say, although it was a near thing, "You're a bloody old fool, Dmitri."

Instead, he said, "I'm afraid I have another appointment, Father. If you'll excuse me."

It took another five minutes of grumbling and admonishments from the old priest before Randolph was able to usher him out of the room. Closing the door and locking it, just in case, he made his way to the small cabinet that held a bottle of claret intended for just such exigencies. Pouring a sustaining quantity into a glass, he huffed down into his chair and sipped thoughtfully.

~ * ~

When he'd finished speaking, Randolph topped up his glass and held the bottle out to Morgan, who scowled and shook his head.

Randolph held up his hands, palms out. "Before you start swearing and calling down thunderbolts, yes, Father Dmitri's a hypocritical old duffer."

Morgan's mouth twitched at the corners. Randolph knew him well enough to know a grin was lurking in there. He went on, "That being said, his attitude doesn't surprise me much. After all, the word 'witch' has always had negative connotations. Makes people think of cackling crones, moldering cottages, and cauldrons loaded up with bat wings and eye of stoat."

"Marissa doesn't cackle," Morgan said through gritted teeth. "And I think eye of newt is the generally accepted ingredient."

"Mmph, as you say. And no, the girl couldn't cackle if you offered her a ruby to do so. That's not the point. The point is people, and the stupidity and prejudices of same. They see witches as bad."

"But not wizards?"

Randolph leaned back in his chair and steepled his fingers thoughtfully. "Interestingly enough, there does seem to be a difference. If a feller grows a beard to his knees, slaps on a pointy hat with a couple of stars on it and calls himself a wizard, folks say, 'Oh, right ho,' and don't give it another thought. If a woman puts on a black dress and a pointy hat and calls herself a witch, people figure she's firing up the oven to roast somebody. Look here, it ain't fair, but there it is."

"Growf," Morgan replied.

"Growf, indeed. Although saying it doesn't help things any, for all it may make you feel better. Something constructive might be more in order."

"I suppose." Morgan scowled, but then scrubbed a hand across his face and settled back in his seat. He lifted his glass and realized he'd already drained it. With a grin Randolph poured him a healthy portion and passed it over.

"It's not like Marissa wanted this," Morgan said. "But she's stuck with it."

"Stuck with it? Why? I thought you said her parents gave up their magic?"

"Nooo, they didn't actually give it up. They just gave up using it. There's a difference."

"Well, what if Marissa did that? Just made a conscious decision not to use the power she has?"

Morgan shrugged one shoulder. "According to both Wyvrndell and Sebastien, she must be trained how to use it, or she might accidently do something awful."

"Right. I can certainly see how knowing what to do, or not to do, would be beneficial to all concerned. Prevents people, present company included, from being turned into something small and furry, eh?"

"Well, there's that," Morgan agreed. "But seriously, from what I gather, this magic she has is serious stuff. Enough so to concern the headmaster of St. Giles, who claimed to be speaking on behalf of the Royal College of Wizards."

Randolph pondered this for a moment as he sipped claret. Finally, heaving a sigh that came from somewhere in the vicinity of his toes, he straightened and looked Morgan in the eye. "What we need," he said, "is a way to change people's notions. Word has obviously gotten around that Marissa is a witch, right? That frightens people, or offends them, or threatens them, depending on their perspective. So perhaps we need to change things up a bit."

Morgan screwed up his face as he attempted to follow this train of logic. "Change things how?" he asked, shaking his head in bemusement.

"No one seems to have a problem with wizards, do they? So all we need to do is cast her as a female wizard. Problem solved."

"Female wizard? Right, of course. Why didn't I think of that?"

"You don't sound convinced," Randolph said reprovingly. "It's brilliant. Which, m'boy, is precisely why you didn't think of it."

Morgan rolled his eyes, which Randolph chose to interpret as, "Please continue with your brilliant ideas."

"As I see it," Randolph went on, "we have to put it about that Lady Marissa is a… a… what? A wizardess? That sounds kind of silly, even to me."

"Sorceress," Morgan supplied.

"Sorceress? Mmm, no. Not quite what I was looking for. Still sounds a bit—well, I don't know, but that ain't it. What else have you got?"

"Me? I've got nothing. This was your idea. I'm—"

He stopped as Randolph held up one finger. "All right. Lady Marissa isn't a witch. She's an enchantress. No cackling, no cauldron, no broomstick. And she's enchanting," he went on, "so it's perfect."

"Randolph, you're crazy," Morgan protested. "No one will believe this. And even if they did, I don't think it'll make a blasted bit of difference. Witch, enchantress? It's all the same under the hat. Damn it, what am I babbling about? She doesn't even have a hat, pointy or otherwise."

"Ha. That's where you're wrong. I've got the stirrings of a plan. You just leave this all to me. Uncle Randolph will fix everything. An enchantress," he said, caressing the word on his tongue. "I like it. It'll work. Trust me."

"If you say so." Morgan wasn't convinced.

"I do." He sat back, a smile spreading over his face. It soon faded, to be replaced by a troubled look.

"What's wrong? Your plan spring a leak already?"

Randolph waved this away. "No, not that. It's… I ran across someone yesterday, and…"

Morgan raised a brow. "Are you waiting for me to ask who? All right, I'll bite. Who?"

"Kiara."

"Who?" Morgan's face was a study in puzzlement. "Kiara? I—oh."

"Yep. Kiara Farsten. Well, she was Farsten back then."

"Really? I haven't thought of her in years," Morgan confessed.

"No doubt."

Morgan's brow wrinkled. "Just what's that supposed to mean?"

Leaning forward, Randolph said quietly, "Well, you did rather leave her hanging, all those years ago."

He stared. "Leave her hanging? Randolph, there was never anything between Kiara and me. Oh, a little casual flirtation that summer before I went off to St. Colin's, but... serious? No, not at all."

Randolph heaved a sigh. "Morgan, I was still in Westfyld when you left. I heard things then. Things I've not mentioned to you since." He hesitated. Morgan made a 'get on with it' motion with his hand.

"Kiara was—distraught, I guess is the best word for it—when you left. And even more so when you never answered any of her letters. She was mad for you, Morgan. And I mean that quite literally."

Morgan gazed off into the distance. "Randolph, it was just an innocent summer flirtation. Like I said, I never made any promises to the girl. None. I never even gave her a hint of anything remotely promise-like. We danced together at balls; we went riding together. And yes, I snuck her off behind the stables once and kissed her. But that's it."

Randolph held up both large hands. "Morgan, I believe you. I'm just telling you what I observed and heard. What about her letters?"

"As God's my witness, I never got any letters from Kiara once I went off to school."

"Hmm. Interesting. According to what I heard at the time, she wrote you letters. Lots of 'em, to the point where it was almost daily near the end."

"Perhaps she wrote them, but I damned well never got any. Not even one." Morgan frowned. "I mean, even though there was nothing between us—at least as far as I was concerned—if I'd gotten a letter from her, I would have answered."

"Do you think," Randolph mused, "the good brothers of St. Colin's might have intercepted correspondence of an, um, amorous nature?"

With a shrug, Morgan said, "I suppose it's possible. I certainly got letters from home. Even a few from you."

"That's true," Randolph allowed. "You even deigned to answer them on occasion. But why wouldn't you have received any of Kiara's letters, I wonder?"

"Pardon me if I'm being dull again, but what possible difference could it make now? This is ancient history. Her family upped and moved to Rhuddlan that fall. Her father inherited a title and an estate up there. Perhaps if she'd still been in Westfyld when I returned, I might have picked up where we'd left off. As it was, I moved on with my life, and assumed she'd done the same. If I thought about it at all."

"Hm, yes, I suppose so." Randolph squeezed his eyes shut for a moment, then opened them and regarded his oldest friend. "My spies," he said, "tell me that she's been married, and was widowed not six months later. Her late husband, Lord Jermaine, Baron Northram of Penllwyn, was killed at the battle at Noordstrom."

Morgan was silent for a long time, likely remembering his own comrades who perished in the conflicts with the Rhuddlanis. Noordstrom had been particularly devastating for both sides. Randolph waited, and finally Morgan said, "That's too bad. Most unfortunate, certainly. But I still don't see what this all has to do with me."

Randolph drained his glass, wiped his lips, and said, "I don't know why she's come back to Caerfaen. But my intuition, such as it is, tells me it's not for any good purpose. Stay away from her. I said before that she was mad for you when we were all young. I didn't speak in jest. The people I've talked with, those who knew her better than I, felt she was actually deranged at the time. Yes, this was all a long time ago, and probably long forgotten. But still, better safe than sorry. Avoid her if you can. If you do meet her, tread carefully."

Morgan nodded slowly. "Good Lord, Randolph, you almost frighten me with such talk. Very well, I won't be such a fool as to ignore your counsel."

"Good." Giving Morgan a nod, he set the empty claret glass on the table, rose and stretched. "It's getting late and I've got an early mass tomorrow."

Morgan laughed. "All right, I can take a subtle hint."

Randolph laid an arm across his shoulders. "Don't worry, Morgan. All these things will sort themselves out. Just focus on your upcoming nuptials like a good bridegroom. Do whatever your lady love tells you to do, and you'll be a happy man."

"Oh? How do you figure that?"

Randolph grinned. "Because she'll be happy, and if she's happy, everything else will fall into place."

Chapter Twenty Five

Aartis's brows rose. He somehow managed to keep from sputtering as he said, "You know who I am?"

Kate shrugged. "Ian Taggart sent word to expect you. He—let's just say he trusts my discretion."

"So I gather," he murmured, even as his mind raced at just what she might have done to gain such trust. The implications were a bit staggering. "And did he tell you why I'm here?"

She gave a low growl and uttered a single word. "Pirates."

She said it with such vehemence Aartis took an involuntary step back. She must have noticed his reaction, for she gave him a quick, sheepish grin. "Sorry. I promise not to kill you. I just get so angry when I think about it. About them."

"Why?"

"Because this is our city, damn it. We don't need any stinking pirates sailing in to do God knows what. Taggart has things under control in Caerfaen. He runs a tight operation. Even the Watch knows it. But if a bunch of pirates starts causing trouble, things will get out of hand right quick. Bad for business, bad for the city, bad for everyone."

Aartis stared. Finally, shaking his head bemusedly, he asked, "Who are you? You're no barmaid, that's for certain. You know too much. And you sure don't talk like any barmaid I've ever met. And before you ask, yes, I've met my fair share." He swept a hand around, gesturing to the room. "And this isn't the room of any lowly barmaid. I know I'm supposed to trust you too, but... talk."

A slow smile spread across her face. It was a genuine smile this time, lighting her with an almost childlike glee. "Ahh, well done. You've seen through my little disguise, just as I've seen through yours."

"But you already knew," Aartis pointed out. Somewhat uncharitably, he realized, and wished he hadn't said it. But he pressed on. "I repeat: who are you?"

"Hmm. Well, my name really is Kate. Would you believe me if I told you I own The Mean Ewe?"

Aartis considered this. "I suppose I'd have no reason not to."

"In fact, I own just about every building on this block. And a few more besides."

"Be serious," he chided.

Her eyes darkened like a summer sky when a storm sweeps in out of nowhere. Nostrils flaring defiantly, she demanded, "You don't think a woman should own property? Run a business? Should they just serve as barmaids, or wives, or mistresses?"

"No, I didn't say that. Don't think that. I…"

"Liar." But her expression lightened as she said it, and Aartis relaxed. Just a little. After all, she was still carrying that cudgel, although he had no doubt she could do quite a bit of damage even without it.

"Well, perhaps," he admitted. "Let's just say it's not something I've ever really been forced to consider before. Most of the women of my acquaintance are not so very, ah, industrious. They toil not, neither do they spin, as it says in holy writ."

"I manage to keep myself occupied." She cocked a skeptical eye at him. "I wouldn't have imagined you to be so familiar with holy writ."

Aartis started to bridle, and then shrugged. "Well," he said with an expansive wave, "how else would I know all the 'thou shall nots' that might be interesting to 'shall'?"

She gave a delighted laugh. "All right, point taken."

"And so, how does one learn to become a woman of business?"

"The same way a man does, I imagine. In my case, I found someone to teach me what I needed to know. The fellow who sold this place to me was most helpful. Actually, he still comes in to tend bar a couple of nights a week. He likes to chat up his old regulars."

Aartis regarded her thoughtfully. "He didn't balk at selling the place to a woman?"

"I reckon my money's as good as anyone else's. Besides, I can be a bit—persuasive." She opened those sapphire eyes wide, with such an ingenuously innocent expression that Aartis barked out a delighted chuckle.

"Perhaps I should just ask you to find out what our pirate friends are planning," he said.

Her smile faded as quickly as it had appeared. "I'll pass, thanks. I shouldn't wish to deprive you of the honor."

"Very well, if you're sure. I was obviously sent to you for a reason. They just neglected to tell me what it was. Not," he added, "that I'm complaining in the least."

"Flatterer," she said, but her grin appeared genuine this time. "The reason you were sent here is that the pirates are using this place as a base of operations. If you're going to get in with them, this is the place to do it."

"Interesting. Any idea why?"

She shook her head. "I just know they're here. They don't pay much attention to me. I'm just the stupid little barmaid, after all."

"Right. But you've no idea what kind of dastardly scheme they're hatching?"

"Dastardly scheme, eh? You like words, don't you? To answer your question, noooo..." She trailed off, her expression pensive. "At least—"

"What?"

"You'll think me silly."

"Can't be done," he assured her. "I know you now. Tell me."

A corner of her mouth turned up. "A couple of times, when I've brought their drinks, they've been talking about the dragon."

Aartis shrugged. "Who hasn't? It's been the talk of Caerfaen for weeks."

As indeed it had. As second in command of the Legion, Aartis knew more about the dragon than most. The tale of how the dragon Wyvrndell had carried Morgan McRobbie and the Dwarf prince R'gm'l to Caerfaen just in time to foil a plot to ignite a war between Men and Dwarves had spread like wildfire.

What most citizens of Caerfaen didn't know was how the dragon had saved Marissa duBerry, Morgan's betrothed, by gobbling down the Rhuddlani assassin Xavier. Even fewer knew that the dragon was now instructing Lady Marissa in the arts of magic so she could safely wield her newly discovered powers.

He realized Kate was watching him, her head cocked to one side. "Sorry," he said, "I was just thinking."

"It looked painful."

"Ouch. All right, so they're talking about the dragon. You think that's significant?"

"It seemed to be more than just idle chatter. I don't know why, but I do think it's important somehow."

"Right. We shall file the dragon under 'Clues, Important'," he said.

"You're making fun of me." She cast him a baleful look.

Aartis shook his head. "No, my lady. For you are a lady, aren't you, for all you pretend you're just a barmaid or a woman of enterprise. I'm treating your observations and intelligence with the respect they're due. You have eyes and ears—both quite nice, by the way—and a brain. And you put them to good use. If you say the dragon is important, we'll take that as gospel."

Kate's look was searching, as if she still suspected him of mocking her. Finally she said, "You're the first man to ever complement my ears. Most don't seem to get that high."

Aartis could understand why. He manfully refrained from allowing his gaze to lower to her bodice, instead giving her ears careful scrutiny. They looked eminently nibbleable, but that didn't seem the kind of thing to mention, at least not at the moment. Instead he asked, "So how do I insinuate myself with these pirates of yours?"

She waved away any ownership of pirates. "Not mine, not ever. The only reason I didn't run 'em out is so I could keep an eye on them."

"And report to Taggart."

"To… Taggart, yes. As far as you getting in with them?" She surveyed Aartis and shook her head. "You'll need to get cleaned up a bit. Surprisingly, these are pirates with standards. At least their chief seems to be. A dock rat wouldn't cut it with this lot."

"Seriously? Ah, all my boyhood illusions shattered."

"Well, let's just say they appear to bathe more frequently than many of my regular customers. Their captain is almost by way of being a gentleman. I've a notion he might have been in the Royal Navy once upon a time. He seems to have that air about him."

"Cashiered out?" mused Aartis. "Quite possible. Very well, I get myself cleaned up to piratical standards. Then what?"

Kate's expression was triumphant. "You've met the dragon, haven't you? There's your ticket in."

Aartis blinked. "My lady," he said gravely. "I can see I shall be well served to leave all strategic planning in your capable hands."

She threw a cushion at him.

Chapter Twenty-Six

"Wyvrndell!"

Wyvrndell trembled as the morning's stillness was broken by a roar tinged with thunder. The voice sounded again. "Wyvrndell. Answer me!"

Wyvrndell began to retreat hastily into a corner of his cave. Which was pointless, as the owner of that voice was miles—likely hundreds of miles—away. Wyzandar couldn't eat him from such a distance. Only flay him with words and scorn.

"Yes, Father," he replied meekly. "How are you?"

"Never mind the pleasantries. You, my son, have much to answer for."

Wyvrndell raised his head. He'd known this day would come eventually. An early arrival didn't serve to make it any more palatable. Still, better to play innocent, at least for the moment. "Oh? And what egregious sins have I committed this time, Father?"

The older dragon snorted. "Do you really wish me to catalogue them? All right. To begin with, consorting with humans. Even serving as steed to one." Wyvrndell could sense his shudder. "What were you thinking?"

Wyvrndell said nothing.

"Well?"

His sire's tone indicated he would brook no further dissembling. If that was the case, the young dragon decided, it was time to speak frankly. "You know what occurred, Father. I've told you more than once. In the beginning, it was simply a game of catch the maiden. When that knight, Sir Morgan, showed up, that's when things went a bit… awkward."

"So you've said. Your hiccups. They betrayed you once again."

"Yes, Father, as you say."

"I do wish you'd let Ventrailiox treat you. He says he could likely remedy the problem."

"Thank you, but no. I do not care to be 'treated.' It is not normally an issue."

His father sighed. "Until it is."

"It doesn't happen often," Wyvrndell protested. "And anyway, it didn't happen when I met Sir Morgan again. He simply was clever enough to have noticed my weak spot and exploit it. He would have slain me had I not yielded. We made a bargain: he would spare me, and I would leave his kingdom and never return."

"Yet you did return," his father pointed out.

"Yes, I did. He called to me, asking for my aid. I felt I owed him a debt of honor. Would you have it said one of our line refused to satisfy such an obligation?"

"But to serve as his steed? To carry him on your back? By the Elders—"

"The Elders," Wyvrndell pointed out, "are no longer with us. We must make our way as we see fit. I had a debt to discharge, and I did so."

"The Elders," replied Wyzandar, "are always with us."

Loath to debate draconic legend and philosophy with his father, Wyvrndell refrained from challenging this pronouncement. Instead, he said, "As you have taught me, Father, I did what I deemed necessary and right in the circumstance. I am sorry if you feel shame because of my actions. But I would do it again."

"No doubt." Wyzandar replied. Wyvrndell could feel his father sigh right down to his talons. "Which," he went on, "is likely why the Council insists that you present yourself before it. Immediately."

"T-the Council?" Wyvrndell had expected this, but hearing it wasn't something to rejoice over. The Council of Dragons would not look kindly or with understanding upon his actions. Even his father's membership on the council would be no protection.

"Very well, Father. If the Council has summoned me, I must certainly attend. Will you be there?"

"Yes. But not as a sitting member. I cannot be involved; it would not be proper. You must deal with this on your own."

"As is only right. You have, after all, instructed me to always stand up for what I believe, have you not?"

"Yes, but—"

"It will be all right, Father," Wyvrndell said. It felt strange, trying to give comfort to his sire instead of the other way 'round. "I am not afraid of the Council."

"Mmm. Perhaps you should be, Wyvrndell. Do not be hasty or say things to antagonize them."

"I will only tell the truth, Father. I will try to make them understand the truth beyond that truth."

"What do you mean? Do not speak in riddles, my son."

"Never mind, Father. Wait and see, that's all I ask."

"I suppose I have no choice, do I? Make haste, Wyvrndell. Do not keep the Council waiting. Delay will only provoke them further."

"I will come, Father. Soon."

~ * ~

"Lady Marissa?"

Marissa jerked, her quill carving a jagged black slash across the parchment she'd been inspecting. "Bother," she muttered.

"Lady Marissa." The call was more preemptory this time.

"Yes, Wyvrndell?" she said with forced cheerfulness. In the time since the dragon had declared his intention to instruct her in the arts of magic, she still hadn't gotten used to that disembodied voice echoing in her mind. It was, she knew, the only way they could converse, but still… Oh, he was always pleasant, consistently courteous. He was just…there. In her head. Where no one but her should be hanging about.

She schooled her thoughts, hoping Wyvrndell hadn't heard. He had pledged he would only hear thoughts directed specifically to him. But she wondered if that included thoughts about him. Well, she couldn't help what she felt.

She glanced at the clock. It wasn't yet time for their daily lessons. "Do you mean to start now?" she asked. She hadn't even had her second cup of coffee yet. Could witching lessons be endured on only one cup?

"No," came the reply. *"I am sorry, but we will have to forego your instruction for today."*

"I see." She struggled to keep the note of jubilation from her tone. "Is something wrong?"

"No, no," replied the dragon, sounding almost distracted. *"I may be gone for a few days, however. I'm… not certain."*

A few days? Marvelous! This would give her time. Time she desperately needed to prepare for the wedding. She had so many things to do, so much to arrange… She ground this line of thought to a halt as Wyvrndell went on, *"During my absence, I would ask you to work on your focus and centering. You are still a bit shaky."*

A bit shaky was an understatement. Her mother had been right when she'd said learning magic was hard work.

"I shall do so."

"Excellent. Hopefully I'll only be gone for a day or so. Continue to practice. I expect to be impressed when we resume our lessons."

"Impressed. Yes, of course." She rolled her eyes, and thought she heard a faint mental chuckle from Wyvrndell.

"Farewell, Lady Marissa," he said, and his presence was gone.

Odd. There seemed to be a note of resigned finality in his words. She nearly called out to him again but held herself in check. Whatever was bothering him, it wasn't any of her concern. And this respite from her lessons couldn't have come at a better time.

She would be able to attend to the thousand things necessary to orchestrate a wedding, every one of which seemed to require her undivided attention. She heaved a sigh. Morgan, blast him, got off easy. All he had to do was show up at the church.

Oh, he'd offered to help her. But she was pretty certain his notion of arranging the wedding feast would be to order in capacious quantities of ale and wine, let the guests get rousingly tipsy, and steal her away for their first night together as man and wife.

Which, she admitted with another sigh that was less aggrieved and more anticipatory, didn't sound like such a bad idea, all in all.

"Mwrowr."

Marissa looked down. A pair of emerald green eyes stared into hers. Lady Francesca, the sleek black cat who resided with her—there was an ongoing, if minor, dispute about who was mistress and who was minion—sat regarding her with a patient, inscrutable gaze.

"Did I forget to feed you, you poor thing?" She leaned down to stroke the cat.

Francesca butted her head against Marissa's hand. She instinctively stroked the smooth fur, giving little scritches behind Francesca's ears. The cat wriggled in luxurious ecstasy, purring vociferously and giving forth small mews of cat-like appreciation.

"Oh, I do wish you could answer," she murmured, her hand resting on Francesca's head. She felt a sudden unfamiliar tingle and jerked her hand back. "What was that?"

Francesca blinked once, her eyes suddenly huge and luminous. She stretched her jaws in an enormous yawn, wiped a paw across her face, and said, "It's about time."

"Um." Marissa shook her head. This couldn't be happening. Could it? "Excuse me?"

"I said 'It's about time'," Francesca repeated, speaking slowly and enunciating each word, as if to a dullard. "I thought you'd never do that."

"I-I made you speak? That's not possible."

"I believe the fact belies any doubt," Francesca replied. A bit snippily, Marissa thought. "Do you disbelieve the evidence of your own ears?"

Marissa opened her mouth to say, "Yes, that's it exactly." Then she closed it again, biting off the words. Because no, she couldn't doubt her own ears. Unless she'd gone mad. Which wasn't outside the realm of possibility, but she'd have thought someone might have noticed.

"But how?" she said instead, suppressing a rising urge to laugh at the incongruity of holding a conversation with a cat.

"Hellooo. Witch, remember? Lots of magical powers. Just stands to reason."

"But…" Marissa heaved a sigh and scrubbed one hand across her face. "Well, yes, I suppose it does. But I've not really been able to do any spells. I think poor Wyvrndell despairs of me as a pupil."

"Ah, but with me to help you along, you'll be up to scratch—if you'll pardon my saying it—in no time."

"With—you—helping me?" Marissa asked helplessly. She wasn't sure whether to laugh, cry, or start screaming.

"Of course. I am your familiar. Although I must say, it's taken you quite long enough to get on with finalizing the arrangement. I finally had to take matters into my own paws."

"You…what?"

"When I rubbed up against your hand, you inadvertently released a bit of power. And then you wished I could talk. Well, what did you think would happen?"

"Honestly? Not this." Marissa waved a hand in the cat's general direction. Francesca instinctively arched her back, and Marissa suddenly found herself stroking her fur again. "But as it seems to have happened, I suppose I must accept it. Very well, familiar. What now?"

"A bit of fish wouldn't be turned away." Francesca's voice carried a hint of eager desire.

Marissa chuckled softly, shook her head, and picked up the bell with the hand which wasn't engaged in cat-stroking. She rang it, and in a few moments Briana knocked and entered.

"Briana, could you ask Mrs. Handley to send up a bit of fish? Lady Francesca seems a bit peckish. Um, and some milk as well," she added as an afterthought. Francesca purred happily. "Oh, and Briana?"

Briana eyed the cat, her mistress, the cat again. "Yes, m'lady?"

"You'd best bring up a bottle of the '78 as well."

The maid gave her a horrified stare. "You're going to give wine to the cat?"

Marissa choked back a gurgling laugh. "No, you goose, the wine is for me. It is sorely needed at the moment, so don't dawdle."

"Peckish," Briana repeated in dark tones. Then seeming to recall herself, she murmured, "Yes, of course, m'lady, at once."

"Thank you. Most kind," said Francesca once the maid had departed.

Marissa narrowed her eyes. "Is this to be one of those things where you only talk when no one but me can hear you?"

Francesca's eyes became tiny green slits. "Of course. What would be the fun otherwise?" Marissa threw her hands up in the air, huffing out an aggravated breath, but the cat continued, "No, I'm only joking. If you don't mind if others hear me speak, I don't either. But consider. First be certain you're ready for the world to know you have a talking familiar."

"Hmm, yes," she mused. "I see what you mean. Let's keep this between us, at least for now."

"As you wish," Francesca purred. A knock on the door heralded the arrival of Briana with a plate of fish, a bowl of milk, and a bottle of wine with accompanying glass, all balanced on a tray.

Marissa hastened to take the fish and milk from her, placing it on the floor. Francesca leapt sinuously from the bed, circled around the offerings, evidently found them acceptable, and began to feast. Briana placed the bottle and glass on a table, regarded both cat and mistress with a quizzical expression, and silently turned and left the room.

"Wha's her problem?" asked Francesca around a mouthful of fish.

"She likely thinks I've gone mad. Honestly, I'm not so sure I haven't, so I don't reckon I can blame her much. Also, I'm drinking wine before lunch. Which is definitely not a sign of anything good." She reached for the bottle and poured.

"All right," Marissa said some time later. She set down the empty wine glass and contemplated the cat, who was industriously grooming herself. "Would you mind telling me what a witch's familiar actually does?"

Francesca, having at last completed her toilette, sat back on her haunches, her green eyes fixed unwaveringly on Marissa. "An excellent question," she replied, battling idly at a discarded stocking. "But you're the witch. I assumed you'd know."

Marissa's mouth opened, closed, and opened again. For several moments she remained speechless. Finally she managed, "I regret to report I'm rather new at this witching business. I suppose I shall have to make inquiries."

"Yes, please do. Why don't you ask the big lizard?"

"He's not a lizard. He's a dragon."

"I ate a lizard once," Francesca went on dreamily, seeming oblivious to the differentiation. "It crunched something fierce. Although," she added, "it might take me a while to get that big one down."

Marissa tried her best to maintain an appropriately solemn expression, but it was no use. The mental picture of Francesca stalking the enormous dragon was just too much for her, and she succumbed to a fit of giggles. The cat bestowed a cold, indignant stare on her and retreated under the bed.

"I'm—I'm sorry," Marissa gasped, struggling mightily to keep from another spate of laughter. "It's just…Wyvrndell is so big," she finished lamely, spreading her hands in apology.

"Mmph," replied Francesca, materializing on the bolster. "I may not be large, but I am sufficiently fierce, I believe. After all, consider the youth in holy writ, who slayed the giant against all expectations."

This reference to sacred text was so unexpected as to cause Marissa's brows to rise to the point where she felt they might keep right on going and fly off her forehead altogether. "You study the scriptures, do you?"

"No, don't be silly. Cats can't read. But I have heard you read the story before, and I have a particularly good memory."

"And you have recalled it to good use. Perhaps you should discuss it with Bishop Randolph."

Francesca gave a luxurious wriggle. "I like him," she confided. "His hands are very large. Quite excellently suited for stroking. You may invite him here again, soon."

"As you wish." Marissa displayed her own hands. "And how are these for stroking?"

Francesca flowed around her, allowing Marissa to pet her sleek fur. "Mrowvelous," she pronounced.

A rap on the door heralded the entrance of Briana, bearing the luncheon tray. As she placed it on the little table beside Marissa's bed, she inquired, "Were you talking to yourself, m'lady?"

She exchanged a look with the cat. "Oh, just conversing with Lady Francesca," she said airily.

"Ah, you will have your little jests, m'lady."

Marissa poured coffee, added cream, then weighed the half full pitcher. "Hand me that bowl, will you please? I'm sure Francesca would enjoy the rest of this cream." A loud purr confirmed this opinion.

"Most kind of you," said the cat once Briana had departed. Her eyes glittering with anticipation as she eyed the cream. Her tongue flicked out to lick her lips. "Most kind indeed."

Marissa inclined her head regally, poured in the remainder of the cream, and set it upon the table. Francesca levitated in the manner of cats, and only little mews of pleasure punctuated the sound of her lapping tongue.

Marissa said, "Perhaps I should speak with Wyvrndell and inquire as to the role of my familiar."

Francesca scrubbed her face with a paw, blinked slowly, and said, "I have called to the big lizard, but he does not answer. I think perhaps he's frightened of me."

"I've no doubt whatsoever this is so," Marissa replied deadpan. "As I am less fierce, perhaps he will answer me."

Francesca spoke thoughtfully. "I was wondering," she said, "if perhaps we haven't got this whole business the wrong way 'round. Might it be that you are intended to be my familiar, not I yours?"

Marissa hid a smile behind her hand. She managed to inquire, "Just what would this arrangement entail, do you suppose?"

"Ah, I believe you have already made a good start on it. Cream upon request, a fish for my dinner. Scritches as required, a lap to curl up on in the sunshine. Oh, and you may read to me."

"Most kind, your majesty," murmured Marissa. Whatever Francesca had been about to reply was interrupted by Briana's return. But, having finished off the bowl of cream, the cat vanished in pursuit of more congenial occupations.

Marissa, for her part, was left to consider this new and uncertain arrangement as she ate her lunch.

Chapter Twenty-Seven

Wyvrndell emerged from his cavern in the hills not far from Caerfaen. Spreading his wings, he looked to the sky. A few clouds, fluffy and plump as the sheep on the nearby hillside, dotted the sky. Wyvrndell sternly cautioned himself against swooping down to snaffle one of those sheep. That could come later, assuming he got out of this mess with his wings and talons intact.

A light westerly breeze stirred the leaves into a whisper of late summer. Perfect flying weather. The young dragon leapt into the sky, his massive wings beating the air as he rose. Soon he was high above the ground, with the city laid out below him. Humans looked skyward as he passed overhead, pointing and shouting. Wyvrndell paid them no mind. He had no time to swoop down toward them or spray out gouts of flame as he often did. Today his mind was on the Council, and what he would say in defense of his actions.

The Council, he was certain, would be unwavering in their condemnation of his actions. Consorting with humans. Well, they didn't know the half of it. He felt the weight of the ring fastened around his neck, a gift from the Dwarf prince R'gm'l. The Council, when they learned of it, would probably call for his death for that alone.

Wyvrndell shivered as he flew. He would only have a few moments, once they caught sight of the ring, to make his case. To explain why he'd done what he had. Not for himself, but for all dragonkind.

He had a feeling no matter what he said, they wouldn't understand.

The flight to Ervantium was long but uneventful. Which was, in its own way, more aggravating than flying through a thunderstorm. With no distractions, Wyvrndell had time to fret.

It wasn't a question of whether or not he was in trouble. He was. The only question was, how much? And what would the Council do about it? He had broken the Laws.

Well, he'd certainly bent them pretty far. This wasn't something which happened often. Wyvrndell couldn't recall any instances in his relatively short lifetime, but stories were whispered of Morzain the Black, who had turned traitor and sided with humans in some centuries-old conflict. When Morzain had finally been captured and brought before the Council, he'd been sentenced to death.

He shuddered. Morzain had been killed for allying himself with humans. Wyvrndell had delved even further into the realms of the unthinkable. He had befriended a Dwarf. This was certain to earn the Council's displeasure, putting it mildly. His father's position would be no protection.

He could have—probably should have—removed the Dwarf ring before making the journey to Ervantium. The Council couldn't know for certain the extent of his treachery. Still, he might as well be hanged for a sheep as for a lamb, as the human expression went. He flew on, wings straining as he hastened through the cloud-strewn sky. His father had urged him not to keep the Council waiting. Wyvrndell deemed this sound advice. He flew, steady in his resolve.

Which promptly wavered as the lights of Ervantium twinkled in the distance. The hall of Petrandius, King of the Dragons, occupied an enormous cavern near the top of the Velthorn, tallest peak in the range the Dwarves named, appropriately enough, the Dragon's Teeth.

Unless he was extremely lucky, he'd be seeing more dragons' teeth than he cared to. They would not be smiling.

He had one chance—albeit a slim one—to convince the Council of his good intentions. And if they refused to listen? At best, he'd be imprisoned in Ervantium. At worst, they would destroy him.

With this less than comforting thought, Wyvrndell approached the entrance to the king's hall. The ledge was already thick with dragons arriving to watch the proceedings. He circled, waiting for a space to clear so he could land. Another dragon hailed him.

"Wyvrndell," called Aireantha. "Come to watch them tear some poor fool apart?"

Wyvrndell gave a rueful snort. "I'm the poor fool."

She flew closer, her head swiveling on its long graceful neck as she regarded him with suspicion. "You're joking. Aren't you?"

When he didn't reply, she blinked, her amber eyes clouding with distress. "You mean it?"

"I am afraid so. I have been consorting with humans. The Council, in its infinite wisdom, does not approve."

Aireantha spewed a jet of fire in his direction. "No, I'm sure they don't. I can't say I see any harm in it. Times have changed, for men and for dragons as well. Even if the Council has not changed with them."

"Thank you," said Wyvrndell. "But don't say that too loudly. I fear the Council will not share your tolerance. I wouldn't want you subjected to their attention. Ah, there's a spot to land. I'd best not keep my elders waiting."

They landed, close together. Aireantha unexpectedly twined her neck around his. "Good luck," she said quietly.

Wyvrndell looked into her eyes, dark golden pools reflecting concern. He felt his spirits lift suddenly, a wellspring of hope coursing through his body. If he made it out of this, perhaps…

"Thank you," he said again. "It's best if I go now. They're waiting."

"I'll go with you," she said. "As far as I'm able."

They walked together, the ranks of dragons parting before them, until they reached the entrance to the main hall. With Aireantha beside him, Wyvrndell walked erect and proud. Even if these should be his final moments, he'd count them well spent.

Two dragons waited to take him in charge. One, an old green whom Wyvrndell knew only by reputation as a despiser of humans, sneered disdainfully as only a dragon can sneer. The other, a younger brown called Fendarel, looked sympathetic. Wyvrndell halted, turning to Aireantha.

"You'd best go, before you become tainted by association," he muttered. "But if I should somehow make it out of this with my wings and scales intact, expect to see me upon your ledge."

"I shall count upon it." A trace of warmth tinged her words. She turned and hastened away. Wyvrndell turned back to his escorts.

"I am ready," he said. They led him out into the hall of Petrandius, to be examined and judged.

Chapter Twenty-Eight

The throaty rumbling of the dragons increased as Wyvrndell approached the great dais. The two guard dragons flanked him, cutting off any retreat. Which was rather silly, he thought. Where would he run? There was no escape from this place. If he tried, a hundred dragons would be on him before he got to the tunnels. He walked on, to stand before the king.

Wyvrndell bowed his head in obeisance to the Lord of the Dragons. Petrandius, an enormous black dragon whose scales glittered like a thousand cracked mirrors, regarded him with interest. Around Petrandius, but lower, were ranged the members of his Council. One spot was noticeably vacant. It was the seat his father, Wyzandar, normally occupied. His sire, Wyvrndell observed, was instead among the crowd, near the front line of spectators. His dam was there as well, and… Wyvrndell felt a slight frisson as he saw Aireantha slip into a space next to them. Well, this was interesting. Now, he just had to get out of this mess alive, so he could find out what it all meant.

A stentorian bugle from old Storvold, the king's seneschal, brought the rumbling throng to silence.

"Let the prisoner approach," he directed.

Might as well begin by upsetting the powers that be. "A point," Wyvrndell said. "I am no one's prisoner. I came here of my own free will, at the behest of my revered sire, Wyzandar. If I am under arrest, none have informed me of such."

"Silence!" bellowed Storvold. But from the king's dais came a rumbling chuckle. Wyvrndell approached, bowing his head respectfully.

"Your Majesty," he said.

"Well said, young one," the king said, motioning the seneschal to subside. "No, you are not charged. Yet. But there are many here who think you should be. What say you to that?"

Wyvrndell's mind raced. The king valued forthrightness. Therefore, forthrightness he would get. "Your Majesty," he said, inclining his head once more. "If my actions have brought shame to you, or to my family, I humbly beg forgiveness."

"He consorts with humans," cried Jakarian, one of the Council.

"He even acts as steed for them," growled Bobokus.

Wyvrndell turned to face them. He longed to lash out, to roast them with fire. But he held his temper in check. They said nothing that was not true. So he nodded politely and said, "Yes, I have done these things you say. I have done as I saw fit. Some may see them as ill advised, while others call them crimes against dragonkind."

Petrandius's eyes gleamed with interest. "And how do you answer, young Wyvrndell, scion of Wyzandar?"

"I say that my actions in 'consorting' with humans were acts of expediency rather than any disrespect to our race and our Laws." He held his head high.

This might have been a mistake, for it brought the Dragon's Fire into clear view. A cry of outrage filled the hall as the other dragons saw it and realized what Wyvrndell bore.

"Silence!" bellowed Petrandius. Eyes narrowed, steam hissing ominously, he beckoned Wyvrndell closer. "What is this?" hissed the king. "And just where did you get it?"

"It is the ring called the Dragon's Fire," Wyvrndell said. His voice trembled slightly, but he went on. "It was gifted to me in token of respect—and friendship as well—by Prince R'gm'l, son of the Dwarf King K'var'k."

A collective gasp sucked the air out of the cavern. Petrandius shook his ancient head. "Wyvrndell," he said at last. "Consorting with humans might have been overlooked or forgiven. But this?" He gestured to the ring, which winked in emerald splendor in the light of a hundred torches. "This is beyond reason."

"Your Majesty," Wyvrndell said. "I meant no disrespect. Far from it. I sought, in fact, to bring an end to the conflict between our race and the Dwarves. R'gm'l has pledged to me to petition his father to bring an end to such discord in the future. He wishes our peoples to live in peace."

"Peace?" came an outraged cry.

"With the Dwarves?"

"Never!"

Petrandius ignored these shocked outbursts. Keeping a sharp eye on Wyvrndell, he said, "Would you then have me turn against centuries of tradition? Have me abandon the policies of my ancestors?"

Wyvrndell squared his shoulders, raised his head, and looked his monarch in the eye. "Yes, Majesty," he said.

The silence that filled the cavern was excruciating. It was as if the entire assemblage of dragons waited for the king to strike down this insolent hatchling.

Instead, Petrandius simply said, "Indeed?"

"Yes, Majesty. For tradition is all it is, isn't it? There is no real point of conflict between dragons and Dwarves."

A chorus of "Gold!" and "Thieves!" rang out from the crowd. Wyvrndell looked around, and then back at Petrandius. "That's all it is, isn't it? Dispute over stolen property? Are we so petty as all that?"

"Is it not enough?" The king's eyes gleamed and glittered as he waited. Waited for Wyvrndell to commit himself, to utter the ultimate heresy.

"No. This ring I bear is the chance for peace, freely given in friendship. Why should we wish to pursue a senseless war?"

"They stole our gold!" came a cry from one of the watching dragons. Others quickly took up the call, and soon the hall reverberated to earthquake proportions as dragons yelled and jeered.

Finally the tumult died away. Only then did Wyvrndell dare to say, "Are we not the thieves? Did we not steal the Dwarves' hoard first?"

The dragons' earlier reaction was a mere pebble bouncing down a hill compared to the avalanche of outrage which greeted this statement. Calls for banishment, beating, and even death rang out. Wyvrndell paid the crowd no heed. Instead, he focused on Petrandius.

As the cries finally died away, Wyvrndell remained silent. When Petrandius made no move to speak, he said, "There is one thing more, Your Majesty."

The king looked at him with eyes that seemed focused on some distant prospect. "Even more heresy, young one?"

"Perhaps. But I think not. For not only do I bring a good-faith offer of peace. I also bring the hope of magic."

The king's head, which had bowed under the weight of troubles, suddenly jerked up. "What? Magic?" he hissed. "What nonsense do you speak now?"

Wyvrndell knew he had only one chance to make his case, to make Petrandius understand what was at stake. He regulated his breathing, forcing down an impulse to hiccup. That would be all he needed right now to turn his slim chance to make the king see into a catastrophe.

He said, "Lady Marissa, the human female with whom I've been 'consorting,' is gifted with extremely powerful magic. She was unaware of her power until recently and is thus untutored. I have been training her in the arts of magic…"

"You will get us both killed, you young fool," muttered Petrandius quietly. Aloud he said, "This action is unconscionable."

Undaunted, Wyvrndell said, "I have looked into her mind, seen her potential. And I believe she is the one of whom our prophecy speaks.

The one who holds the key to unlocking magic for dragonkind. Magic which has eluded us for the long centuries of our existence. And because I am her friend," he finished, "I believe she will be willing to help us."

Jakarian rose, inclining his head to the king. Petrandius nodded his permission, and the counselor, with a baleful glare at Wyvrndell, began.

"Your Majesty, I speak on behalf of the Council. This young fool goes too far. Heresy. Blasphemy! Peace with Dwarves? Magic? If he is not merely deluded, he may well be mad. We can listen to no more of his lies and dreaming."

Wyvrndell was about to erupt, but at a slight gesture from the king he subsided. "Perhaps you are right, Jakarian. I think for now, young Wyvrndell, you shall remain here in Ervantium, under our hospitality, as it were."

Wyvrndell glanced over to where his sire and dam and Aireantha sat watching. Waiting for his doom to fall. "I will, of course, abide by Your Majesty's decision." He caught a flash of triumph in Jakarian's expression.

Petrandius instructed the guards who had escorted Wyvrndell into the chamber, "Take him away."

But as he turned to go with them, Wyvrndell heard the old dragon murmur, almost as if to himself, "Yet who would not wish for peace? Or… magic?"

And as he left the halls of power, the young dragon felt an unexpected surge of hope.

Chapter Twenty-Nine

Toby plopped down in his normal seat in The Mean Ewe. Within twenty seconds he was taking his first sip of ale. Kate, the barmaid, flashed him a brilliant smile and sailed away again toward the bar. He watched her slither like a lithe serpent through the tumultuous throng. It was an effort worth his attention.

None of his crew had come in yet, so Toby sat alone, nursing his tankard and listening with half an ear to the conversations going on all around him. A pair of sailors from a merchant vessel argued over the respective faults of their first mate and cook. While the mate was a nasty brute, quick tempered and heavy fisted, they decided the cook was the worse threat, for while his demeanor might be pleasant, his cooking was the worst on the sea.

Toby grinned to himself. The *Mad Maudie*'s own cook, Mr. Ramsey, was a raucously foul-mouthed giant with the temper of a devil. But he cooked like an angel. It was, the crew had decided, a fair trade. Toby had to agree.

Then his attention was caught by another conversation at a nearby table. This one piqued his interest with one word: "Dragon."

He edged over a bit in his chair and cocked an ear. He'd done a bit of surreptitious questioning of the local populace, with little hard information to show for it. The dragon, wherever he might be, was keeping a pretty low profile. Hadn't tried to eat anyone in ages. By the same token, the dragon hadn't invited anyone 'round for tea, either. Which meant, all in all, that no one really knew where it was holed up.

That was the information Toby wanted. Needed, if his plan was to come to fruition. If he didn't find out where the dragon's lair was, his latest scheme would die aborning. If that happened, he'd have a lot of angry pirates to deal with.

His grin, when it arrived on his face, was more rueful than cheerful. They weren't just pirates. They were his men. His crew. He owed them a plan that would work, that would make them all rich. This one might be crazier than most, but it also had the benefit of being extraordinarily rewarding. If he could pull it off.

And so he eavesdropped. Shamelessly.

Well, he was a pirate, wasn't he? He could plunder information as easily as he could treasure. Much more easily, in fact. The man at the next table was telling his less-than-rapt audience, "...and thash how I beat the dragon." He held up his tankard, tilting it helpfully to show its state of near emptiness.

"Gwarn wit'cha," laughed one of his companions, spitting on the floor. "You ain't never fought no dragon, Arn. Prob'ly ain't never e'en seen the beast. 'E only fights knights, don't he?" Still, he waved over the barmaid to refill the conquering hero's tankard.

"Lot you know," said the hero, wiping foam from his lip with a satisfied smirk. "Those knights, wi' all their armor and their horses, they need foot sojers too, don't they? Thash me. Foot sojer. Or at least, I used t' be."

"Foot sojer," jeered another. He examined the hero's large boots with a judicious eye. "Well, ye got the feet for it right enough," he declared, laughing raucously at his own wit. "But c'mon, did ye really see that monster?"

The hero nodded gravely. "Aye, I'us there. Righ' there when C'mander McRobbie fought the beast and bested it."

Toby leaned closer as the hero spun his tale. He told it well, having no doubt done so many times before, lubricated by prodigious quantities of ale provided by his audience. Interestingly enough, Toby mused, he didn't try to embellish his own role in the tale but gave all the honor and glory to Knight-Commander Morgan McRobbie. This fellow actually relegated himself to the role of chronicler of mighty deeds, despite his earlier braggadocio.

Toby nodded to himself as he listened. He needed to talk to this man. It seemed likely this—Arn, was it? —possessed the information Toby needed to put his plan into action. He'd just have to be judicious in his questioning, so as not to arouse any suspicions about what he was really after. At least not yet.

A couple of his crew meandered into the tavern and started toward him. Toby discreetly waved them off. He wanted to talk to this potential ally without a crowd around. The men took the hint, snagging seats at a nearby table which had just been vacated.

As the hero's companions began to drift away, Toby caught the fellow's eye. He raised his tankard suggestively and said, "I'd like to hear more of your tale of the dragon. Sit here, let me buy you another pint."

"I wouldn't say no to that," the man replied with a wide grin. He moved to the seat across from Toby, his empty tankard thumping down on the oak table top.

He signaled the barmaid who was passing by, and in short order two more tankards graced the table. Toby's companion took up his and took a hearty drink, wiping the foam from his mouth with the back of his hand.

"So, ye want to hear 'bout the dragon, eh?" he asked.

"I do indeed. I overheard a bit of your tale before, but I'd definitely like to know more. But first, what's your name?"

Taking another pull on his ale, the man replied, "Arn. Arn Porter. You?"

"Toby Fanshawe, at your service."

Porter looked thoughtful. "Seems like I've heard that name somewhere," he mused.

Toby shrugged. "I, um, get around. So, about the dragon…" He raised his own tankard in a gesture of encouragement. Porter nodded, took another pull on his drink and settled back in his chair then began to speak.

Chapter Thirty

"How's Sebastien?" Morgan asked. He'd stopped by Marissa's house after spending several hours at the Knight-Commander's office, catching up on reports, paperwork, and Legion gossip. Because, as he wryly acknowledged, soldiers were worse than the ladies for spreading tales of the foibles of their mates.

"The same," she replied, but Morgan could tell she was anxious. "The doctor thinks he should be recovering, but he's not."

"But he's not getting any worse, is he?"

"No, no worse. He just…lies there. We've managed to get water and a bit of brandy into him. But the doctor thinks by now he should be at least sitting up and eating something." Her brow wrinkled in concern.

Morgan folded her into an embrace. "Carnavon's a good man," he assured her. "If anyone can pull Sebastien through, it's him."

She hugged him back, burying her face in his shoulder. "I know," she said, her voice muffled. "I just hate this. Why would anyone attack a nice old fellow like Sebastien?"

"A good question. I thought perhaps you'd like to come with me to see if we can get some answers."

Marissa moved out of his arms. "Where are we going?"

He told her.

On the way, he related his interview with Ian Taggart. "Pirates?" she mused. "What on earth do pirates want in Caerfaen?"

"Hopefully Aartis can find out." Morgan shrugged. "And put a stop to whatever it is. Taggart seems to think so, but I'm not so sure. Aartis isn't used to this type of assignment."

"Neither were you," she pointed out. "When Rhys and Lord Holman sent you off on that crazy assignment, pretending to be a traitor."

"True." Morgan grimaced at the memory. "But it's done, and we both made it through, so…"

Marissa gave him a wry smile. "You're not the only one who's had an interesting time of things."

"Oh? How so?"

"You're going to think me mad," she warned.

"I know better. There's no one saner."

"What if I told you my cat now talks to me?"

"Um. Perhaps I'd better revise my last statement?"

She poked him. "I told you. But I'm serious." They strolled along, and Morgan listened, astonished, as she related what had occurred with Lady Francesca.

"If I'd heard this from anyone else," he said when she finished, "I would have agreed they might be a bit mad. But under the circumstances, I guess it makes sense. In an odd sort of way." He led her into a side door of Kilbourne Palace, down several stairways, and toward the subterranean lair of Lord Holman and his Office of Spies.

"Good afternoon, Mr. Barlbent," Marissa said to the spymaster's clerk when they entered the outer sanctum.

Barlbent leapt up from his seat behind a desk laden with files. "Lady Marissa. Commander McRobbie," he said. "Please, come in. But I'm sorry, if you're looking for Lord Holman, he's away at the moment. All very hush-hush."

"Something big on?" Morgan asked.

"Actually," confided Barlbent, his eyes gleaming behind his spectacles, "he's off to Cormaine to visit his mother. Who invariably seems to threaten to expire about this time each year. Things around here are actually fairly quiet at the moment, thanks to you and Captain Darby. And you of course, Lady Marissa."

"Why, thank you, Mr. Barlbent," Marissa replied, favoring him with a beaming smile.

"Thinking of offering her a commission in the service?" Morgan chuckled. "Where you find spies and assassins and doers of evil deeds, you'll likely find her in the thick of things, wreaking mayhem."

"Pooh," replied Marissa. "You make it sound like I go about looking for trouble."

"No, trouble finds you," Morgan said.

Barlbent chuckled. "Well, Commander, you have to admit, she did manage to unmask d'Eastmond. And foiled Xavier, not just once but twice. And put paid to a plot to foment a major conflict between us and the Dwarves."

"I helped," he protested.

Barlbent waved away this inconsequential triviality. "Is there a message I can give to His Lordship?"

Morgan pulled up a chair for Marissa, then sat and stretched out his legs. "Actually, Barlbent, it was you we wanted to see."

The secretary's brows shot up to a point just below his sandy cowlick. "Me? Commander, I'm merely a clerk."

Morgan snorted. "You're just a clerk like Aartis Poldane is just a chap who enjoys feminine companionship. You're Barzak's clerk and know pretty much everything he knows. And," he went on, holding up a hand to stem any protestations, "I've seen you in the field. Captain Darby has boasted of your work in helping to capture Thrawnly. So don't try this 'just a clerk' business with me, laddie."

"All right," Barlbent acknowledged. "I do see most of what Lord Holman sees. But I can't divulge any of that information without his approval."

"Good heavens, no, we're not asking you to reveal any secrets. I probably wouldn't know what to do with them if I got them. Actually, we're hoping you might be willing to assist with a little investigation. Especially since Barzak's off in the wilds of Cormaine."

Barlbent's eyes took on a calculating glint. "Tell me more."

So Morgan told him, with Marissa adding in pertinent details. About Rhenn. About the attack on Sebastien. About the warning to "Beware the wizard's prophecy."

"My word," the secretary said once he finished. "It is a bit intriguing, I must admit. Hmm. Essentially, we need to learn if the attack on Master Sebastien is related to Rhenn's interest in Lady Marissa. And what this prophecy is, and how it ties in."

"That pretty much sums it up. Of course, Captain Jenks is investigating the attack on Sebastien."

"But unless he can find the assailant and force him to talk, he's really not going to get anywhere."

"Exactly." Morgan stood, pacing the floor a bit. "I thought perhaps your agents—Lord Holman's, but you know what I mean— might sniff around a bit, see if they can find any connection."

"That doesn't seem unreasonable," Barlbent allowed. "Especially considering Lady Marissa is viewed as vital to the security of the kingdom."

Marissa stared at the clerk. "Me? Whatever do you mean, Mr. Barlbent?"

Morgan leaned over the desk, looming over Barlbent. "Vital to… What are you talking about, man?"

"Just quoting His Lordship." Barlbent said, edging back just a bit more behind the tenuous safety of his desk.

"Oh, stop it, Barlbent, I'm not going to pounce on you," Morgan assured him. "Although I can't speak for Lady Marissa. But if she turns you into something, I'll ask her nicely to change you back. All right, tell us the worst."

"Lord Holman seems to think Lady Marissa's unquestionable loyalty, reputedly unparalleled magical powers, and penchant for trouble…" he trailed off under the force of twin gazes.

"You mean her penchant for poking her lovely little nose into things, don't you?" Morgan translated with a grin.

"You said it, Commander, not I. Anyway, with all those qualities together, His Lordship has inferred that Lady Marissa may have a vital part to play in the security of Kilbourne."

"The Witch of Caerfaen." She rolled her eyes.

"As you say, m'lady. Of course, this is merely His Lordship's interpretation of available data."

"But he's normally spot-on, isn't he?" Morgan pointed out.

"Well, yes, now you mention it. I've rarely found him to be anything but exceedingly astute about matters of this nature."

Morgan heaved a sigh. "I suppose I knew the job was dangerous when I took it."

"Beg pardon? You mean the job of Knight-Commander?"

"No, that bit's easy. I mean falling in love with Marissa duBerry."

"Dangerous? I like that," she observed to the air. Barlbent's bland countenance became, if anything, blander than ever. Morgan was certain he was chortling inside. He decided to press his advantage. "So, does this 'vital to the security of the kingdom' bit mean you'll help us?"

"I'm in," Barlbent assured him.

"Thank you. So, what else do you need to know?"

Barlbent's eyes grew distant. At last he said, "Nothing at the moment, Commander. Obviously if Sebastien recovers, he can shed a lot more light on the whole affair. Especially the prophecy bit. But in the meantime, I'll see what I can do."

"That's all we can ask. Thank you, Barlbent." Morgan extended a hand. The clerk took it, gave a firm handshake, and turned to make notes. Morgan offered his hand to Marissa. She turned her nose up at him at first, but then broke out into a broad grin.

"Beast," she muttered, but she took his hand and let him escort her back out into the passageway.

"Blast, I forgot," Morgan said. "Hang on a moment." He led her back into the Office of Spies.

Barlbent jerked in surprise, splattering ink across his papers. "Commander?" he ventured.

"I say, Barlbent, have you heard any rumors of increased piratical activity recently around Caerfaen?"

It took the other man a few moments to mentally shift gears. "Um. Are there pirates after Lady Marissa, too? Not that it would surprise me, but..."

"Mr. Barlbent, really," she protested, but she smiled as she said it.

"No, just something a fellow mentioned in passing, and I'd wondered."

Barlbent searched his memory. "Actually, there's been very little pirate activity of late. The Navy seems to have pretty much managed to squelch most of 'em operating in our waters. The only one who still seems to be active is this fellow Fanshawe. But as he only targets Rhuddlani vessels, no one really bothers about him too much. Of course the Rhuddlanis would probably love to get hold of him and tickle his insides with a boat hook or something equally dreadful. But our chaps don't really concern themselves about him."

"Fanshawe," Morgan repeated. "Seems like I should know that name."

"Former naval officer. Cashiered when his ship, the *Sea Hawke*, was sunk out from under him. He'd been a rising star in the fleet. On his second command, I believe. It was all a bit sketchy, but Fanshawe never made any defense, and so out he went."

"And turned pirate," Morgan mused. "Hmm. All right, thanks again, Barlbent. We'll leave you to your machinations now."

Chapter Thirty-One

Aartis regarded Fanshawe over the top of his ale tankard. It was nice to have a name to attach to the pirate. He'd definitely heard the man's name before. He'd have to find out where and why. Perhaps Kate had been right about Fanshawe being a cashiered naval officer. If that was the case, he might well have heard of him along the way. News from the different branches of service did tend to spread. Especially when it was juicy gossip.

For now, he needed to find out just what this fellow was after. He hadn't expected it to be so easy to connect with the pirate, but he wasn't about to look a gift dragon in the mouth. "What did ye want to be knowin'?" he asked.

"Everything. Tell me all about it. You said you were there when McRobbie fought the beast. What does it look like? How does it fight? Does it actually fly? How does it communicate? And…where is its lair?"

Aartis—no, Arn, he needed to remember he was Arn—allowed himself a brief internal moment of congratulations. Fanshawe had leaned forward just a little too eagerly as he'd asked the last question. He pondered the significance of it as he spun out his story of the dragon and its fight and final surrender to Commander McRobbie. Despite what he'd told his earlier companions, he hadn't actually been present. But he'd heard enough over the course of the last few weeks to be able to convince this pirate he had.

So he related everything he knew about the dragon, even mentioning its name. Which should count for something. The number of people who actually knew the creature's name was Wyvrndell was fairly small. As Aartis talked, he watched Fanshawe to gauge his reactions. The pirate listened intently, nodding to himself as Aartis spoke, as if he were making mental notes.

Aartis leaned back as he finished. He peered into his nearly empty tankard with abject suspicion, as if wondering who had made off with the contents. Fanshawe took the hint and waved the barmaid over again for a refill. Kate whirled by, an overloaded tray balanced on one hand, and plunked another drink in front of each man.

"Fascinating," Fanshawe murmured after taking a sip of ale. "Who'd have thought dragons would return, after all these many long years?"

"Aye, who indeed," Aartis agreed. "But they're back all ri'. At least this one is. I don' know 'bout any others. Nobody's seen any others, for which I reckon we ought be thankful."

"But you never told me where the dragon's—Wyvrndell, is it?—where his lair is."

Aartis hid his smile behind the conveniently placed tankard. So he really was after the location of the dragon. Interesting. Not to mention puzzling. Wiping his mouth on his already well soaked sleeve, he said slyly, "Ach, why would ye be wantin' to know that, now? Are ye plannin' to pay a social call on the monster? A bottle o' wine in one hand an' a bunch o' poseys in the other?"

Fanshawe threw back his head and laughed with delight. Finally, seeming to recover himself, he said, "No, nothing like that. I just think it would be interesting to see the creature, that's all."

Aartis tapped the side of his head meaningfully. "Aye, if ye've a hankerin' to end up as the beastie's supper, I reckon. Just 'cause C'mander McRobbie defeated the creature don't mean it ain't still mad dangerous. It's lying low, is what I thinks. But if folks go out into t' forest lookin' fer it, well, I wouldn't be surprised but what ol' Wyvrndell would just gobble 'em right on down."

"Aye, I suppose you're right," Fanshawe said with a theatrical sigh. "Although I would love to see the dragon. And would pay well for someone to lead me to its lair."

Aartis made a show of perking up at the notion of payment for services rendered. "Would ya indeed? Now, I reckon s'long as we didn't get too close, I might think on it. I don' relish bein' gobbled up by the beast, do I? But for the ri' price, I might consider takin' you out so's you could see ol' Wyvrndell."

"Is it far?"

"Nay, not so far. But it ain't no stroll in t' park, neither. Pretty deep forest, ya know."

Fanshawe looked surprised. "The dragon lives in the forest? That seems…odd."

Chortling, Aartis asked, "Where'd ya think he'd live? A cottage on the edge o' town, wi' a little white fence an' a couple cats layin' on t' hearth?"

Fanshawe tried unsuccessfully to stifle his own laugh. "No, I guess the forest's as good a place as any. I suppose I just figured he'd be in a rocky cavern somewhere."

"Got it in one," Aartis told the pirate. "He lives in a cave all ri', just out in the middle of the forest. Right up in the side of a big hill. If ya really wants to go, I reckon I could take ya there." He was trying to think two or three jumps ahead, so they'd have time to make plans, figure out what Fanshawe was up to. He needed to delay the pirate. "Can't go now, it'll be dark soon. Tomorrow's no good, got some business to attend to. Could go next day, I reckon. Wednesday."

"Good, good. Wednesday would be fine." Fanshawe cocked his head, as if something had just occurred to him. "Tell me something, Arn. I heard you say you were a foot soldier in the Legion. You're not anymore?"

Aartis grimaced. "Banged up me leg pretty good in the fracas wi' the dragon," he explained. "Couldn't take all the marchin' no more. Nor carryin lot's o' gear up hill 'n down. So they discharged me. Gimme a bit o' coin to ease me way a bit, though I reckon tha's 'bout drunk up."

Fanshawe nodded. "I see. Well then, allow me to buy you another pint."

"Nah, not t'night. One more 'n I'd ne'er find me way home again. Prob'ly shouldn't ha' had tha' last one."

"Another time then," Fanshawe said. "So where shall we meet on Wednesday?"

"We could meet here," Aartis suggested with a grin. "Then ya could buy me tha' pint."

"All right. Meet me here at noon?"

"Aye, that'll do. Thanks for the drinks. I'd best be gettin' on home." Aartis rose, a bit unsteadily, and tipped Fanshawe a wink.

It took him a moment to get his bearings. His unsteadiness wasn't all an act. He hadn't consumed so much ale in one go since he'd been—well, actually never. He swayed like a young tree in a stiff breeze, then managed to collect himself, focus on the door, and maneuver through the crowd toward it.

Kate, passing by with another tray of drinks, gave him an inquiring look. Aartis nodded briefly and managed to make it out the door without falling down. He breathed in the night air, redolent with the scents of Caerfaen. Those scents were an array of the more pungent variety, like spilled drink, unwashed bodies, and manure, but at the moment it didn't matter.

It only took a minute or so for his head to clear. Aartis straightened and made his way down the street. Reaching the corner, he checked to see if anyone was taking notice of him. A couple of old men lounged across the street, feet stretched out into the gutter as they smoked their pipes, but no one showed any interest in him.

He darted around the corner, trotted down the alleyway, and in another moment was at the back entrance to The Mean Ewe. He entered, gave a cheery wave to Stuart, the cook, and passed through the kitchen and up the stairway that led to Kate's room.

~ * ~

"So, what did he say? Did you find out what he's up to?"

It was well after midnight. While The Mean Ewe wasn't by any means closed for business, Kate had managed to slip away for a bit, handing off her duties to a couple of the other barmaids while things were marginally quieter.

"You were right. He's extremely interested in the dragon."

"I told you, didn't I? Did you doubt me?"

"No, not at all. I have complete faith in you." Aartis favored her with his most engaging grin, which she waved away.

This girl is a tough nut to crack. Aloud he said, "I don't know yet exactly what Fanshawe—that's his name, Toby Fanshawe, in case you're interested—is up to. But I should soon. He's really eager to know where the dragon's lair is, and I'm supposed to lead him there."

Kate arched a brow. "Interesting. Why on earth would he want to see the dragon?"

"That's what I intend to find out. I think he would have had me go tonight. I managed to put him off for a day so we could make plans."

"What kind of plans?" Kate looked amused, and Aartis bristled a bit.

"How should I know? I'm just a simple soldier. Someone points me in a direction and says 'go,' and I go. You're the one with the brains, remember? At least that's what you keep telling me. I've managed to worm my way into Fanshawe's confidences. Well, maybe not his confidences, but at least he's talking to me, and has hired me to lead him on this little expedition to the dragon's cave. Anyway, I've done my bit. Now it's up to you to come up with a brilliant plan."

"It's a rare occurrence," Kate said as if speaking to the air instead of to Aartis, "when a man actually acknowledges that a woman might have a brain. I like that in a man. It's…refreshing."

She wrinkled her nose at him and Aartis felt his heart skip a beat. It was such an adorable nose, perched over a pair of such luscious lips. And yet, when he thought about it, what really attracted him to Kate was her intelligence and determination. He'd never noticed that in a woman before.

To be honest, he'd never really taken the time to look. He'd generally been concerned with more earthly aspects. But Kate—well, Kate was different. She was vivacious and smart and sure of herself and needed no one. Not even Aartis. More than anything else, this was what intrigued him. What made him want her to like him. To need him. He shook his head, banishing such thoughts. They had pirates to foil.

"So, oh woman of brains," he said. "What is our next move?"

"You really are allowing me—expecting me—to come up with a plan?" The surprise in her voice was palpable.

"Absolutely," he said. "I'm all agog to hear it."

"Hmmph. I wish I had one. Right now, the only idea I have concerns going to bed." Aartis brightened, until she said repressively, "Alone."

He deflated and she let out a throaty laugh. "You're cute, Captain Poldane. If circumstances were different, perhaps..." She reached over and ruffled his hair. "Go home. Come back tomorrow evening. Hopefully by then I shall have a brilliant plan hatched."

Aartis gazed into her eyes for a moment. Eyes which seemed to hold something he couldn't quite fathom, depths he couldn't plumb. Best not to press his luck, he decided. He took her hand, bowed over it, and bestowed on it the briefest whisper of a kiss. "Sleep well, m'lady," he said gravely. "I shall count the hours until we meet again." With that he turned and fled, before he could do or say something he might come to regret.

~ * ~

Kate watched Aartis depart at speed, a smile tracing its way across her lips.

He was rather adorable. Oh, she knew all about his reputation. So very handsome, so very dashing, and so very, very available. He was the passionate object of desire of almost every lady at court. Even if only half the stories were to be believed, he'd managed to bestow some passion on quite a fair number of those fair ladies.

Which didn't bother Kate in the least. After all, who was she to cast stones? Anyway, such reputations were tricky things. So much of what was sworn to be gospel truth was often either wishful thinking or malicious twaddle. The passion of all the ladies at court? She rolled her eyes. So far he seemed more lamb than lothario. He couldn't even form coherent thoughts half the time, just watched her with those bright blue eyes, as if seeing something precious for the first time....

No! No, no, no. She couldn't allow that. He could not be permitted to think he was falling in love with her. She didn't need the distraction, especially not now. There was too much at stake. Besides, what would her father say?

Hmm. What would her father say indeed? That was an excellent question, and one which would bear some thinking about. Perhaps at some other time. It was getting awfully late, she still had to close The Mean Ewe, and hopefully get a few hours sleep. And come up with a brilliant plan. Mustn't forget the brilliant plan…

Kate jerked as she realized her eyes were drifting shut. She got up, walked around the room in an attempt to wake herself up. When this failed to have the desired effect, she stuck her head out the window in hopes the cool night air would set her senses into motion again.

When she looked down, she noticed a glimmer of gold in the moonlight. Golden hair. Aartis, standing across the street, staring up at the window. With a quick intake of breath, she ducked back inside.

What on earth? He… She shook her head in only partially mock despair. This couldn't be happening. Could it?

Swearing softly, she headed back downstairs to the tavern. She had things to do, plans to make, and Aartis to…

"No!" she remonstrated again. "Do not go there." Reaching the bottom of the stairs she braced herself, opened the door, and stepped into the cacophony of noise, smoke, and odors that made up the atmosphere of The Mean Ewe. It acted as a bracer, waking her fully, and Kate put thoughts of pirates and Aartis aside as she was swept up into the world she occupied.

Chapter Thirty-Two

Wyvrndell ignored the noise from the corridor. He'd seen few other dragons since the guards had brought him to this dank chamber. The few who had deigned to visit had only come to jeer.

With justification, certainly. Perhaps he was mad, as Jakarian insisted. If so, Wyvrndell was certain he'd prefer madness to Jakarian's own insular, narrow-minded folly. At least Wyvrndell's brand of madness held the tantalizing hope of fulfillment of a long-cherished dream of dragonkind: a chance to obtain magic for themselves.

It almost seemed as if Petrandius might be, if not convinced, at least open to the idea. The king was, or so his sire had said on more than one occasion, nothing if not a pragmatist. If something might benefit dragons, Petrandius would consider it. Wyvrndell held out hope the king might be intrigued about what he had suggested. At least enough to prevent him from spending the rest of his days in this cell. Or worse.

"Wyvrndell?"

He looked up in surprise. It was Aireantha. Stepping to the entrance, he eyed the lithe female dragon. "Hello, Airie," he said. It was the name he had used since they were hatchlings together, oh so many years gone by.

"Hello," she replied. Then she looked down at the ground. Around the corridor. Anywhere but at Wyvrndell.

"I hope you haven't come to mock me, too," he said.

She looked up sharply. "Of course not. I would never do that."

Wyvrndell heaved a gusty sigh of relief. "Thank you. I really didn't think so, but…"

"But you doubted me."

He gave a steam-laden snort. "Doubt you? No, Airie, I did not doubt you. I merely worried you might have been troubled by my so-called madness."

"What troubles me is those old fools who don't see what you are trying to do for us."

Wyvrndell's eyes widened. "Really?"

"Yes, really. Oh, Wyvrndell, if you could get magic for dragons…" She let the words trail away, as if even the prospect was too much to contemplate.

"I do think it's possible. This human, Lady Marissa, is unbelievably powerful. And she, like her mate, Morgan McRobbie, is both honorable and just."

"And you truly think she would be willing? To help us gain magic?"

"Yes. I think she would help, if I asked. Asked her to help not just me, but all dragons."

"You would be known as the giver of magic," Aireantha murmured. "You would be legend."

"Yes, well… I have to make it through this first, don't I?" He tossed his head to indicate the cell he occupied. "At the moment, my legend will be as a dead dragon, vilified as insane, unless I can convince the king to listen."

"I think he'll listen," she said.

"Yes, perhaps he will," came a voice from the darkness.

The deep, resonant voice of King Petrandius startled both the young dragons. Aireantha squeaked, skittering awkwardly away from the cell's opening. Wyvrndell stepped back into the illusory safety of the darkened cell. "Y-your Majesty," he managed.

"Yes, I think I will listen," Petrandius repeated. "So tell me, young Wyvrndell, scion of Wyzandar. Just what do you envision?"

Wyvrndell stepped forward again. He took a deep breath and mustered his courage. "It's as I said to the Council, Your Majesty. This human woman, Lady Marissa, whom I am tutoring in the arts of magic, is an exceedingly powerful sorceress. I believe she might hold the key which would unlock magic for dragons."

"This is something which has eluded our finest minds for centuries, young one. What makes you think you can best them?"

Wyvrndell took a deep breath before speaking. This was it. His fate, and perhaps the fate of all dragons, would depend on the next moments.

"Two things, Your Majesty. First, as you are aware, the study of magic has long been my avocation. I have been guided by Erkarna, a dragon of great wisdom in this discipline. He has taught me much. I have used my knowledge to assess the power and capabilities of Lady Marissa while I have been instructing her."

"Go on."

"I believe the power this human female possesses is unprecedented. If we could but harness it, we could indeed find a way to channel magic for dragons."

"Mmmm. Does Erkarna concur with your assessment?"

Wyvrndell shook his head. "I have not yet consulted with him. I wanted to continue to work with her, gain her trust, and learn just what she might be capable of. I…I didn't wish to get his hopes up prematurely."

"You didn't wish him to rush in and ruin what you've begun, you mean." Petrandius's voice was tinged with a certain amount of amusement. "Yes, I know what Erkarna is like, young one. You don't need to hedge with me."

"Yes, Your Majesty. You are correct. I knew if I told Erkarna, he'd be ready to fly off and do something drastic. And foolish."

Petrandius sighed. "Yet you broached this matter before the council. Was that a wise course, do you think?"

"He had no choice," Aireantha declared hotly. "You saw what they were…" She stopped suddenly, realizing she was speaking to the king of all dragons. "I…perhaps it's best if I just go now."

Petrandius chuckled, the sound rolling off the walls in rich echoes. "No, stay. You are only defending this young troublemaker, and he certainly needs a champion, doesn't he? Consorting with humans, befriending Dwarves. Scales and talons, you don't do things by halves, do you, Wyvrndell?"

"My sire has taught me well, Your Majesty."

Petrandius was silent for so long Wyvrndell feared he'd at last gone too far. Then he realized the ancient black dragon was shaking with laughter. He glanced over at Aireantha, who was watching the king in fascinated horror.

Finally Petrandius shook himself from head to tail. "Wyzandar has indeed taught you well. Although perhaps just a bit more deference to your elders—and your monarch—might serve you well. Ah, no matter. I see a bit of myself at that age in you. Can I then fault you? But you said two things. What, pray tell, is the second?"

Wyvrndell felt a hiccup rising in his treacherous gut. He took a deep breath, managing to force it down again. "This is not the time," he silently ordered his stomach. Not in front of the king. And not in front of Aireantha either.

Wyvrndell marshaled himself and spoke. "My second point is this, Your Majesty. Until now, there has never been a human with any reason to help us achieve this goal. The relationship I have established with Lady Marissa, and with her mate Sir Morgan, changes this."

Petrandius looked thoughtfully at nothing in particular for a long while. Wyvrndell and Aireantha maintained their silence, waiting for a sign. At last the king spoke softly.

"Young dragon, if what you believe is true, you will indeed go down as legend. As magic-bringer, certainly. But perhaps also as peacemaker. Tell me about this prince of Dwarves who gifted you the ring.”

"He is called R’gm’l, son of K’var’k, the Dwarf king.” Wyvrndell related his encounter with the prince. Petrandius and Aireantha both listened intently to his tale.

Chapter Thirty-Three

Marissa peered into the darkened room where Sebastien lay, still and unmoving. His eyes had fluttered open a few times when they'd brought him here after the attack, but he'd never regained his wits enough to speak again. Now he lay, still and pale, his breath thready and with a little wheeze at the end of each shallow cycle.

Dr. Carnavon had promised to check in on his patient later in the day. She could only hope the wizard's constitution was up to holding out until he returned. How old was Sebastien, anyway? She knew wizards were blessed, or perhaps cursed, with a much longer life than mere mortals.

Hmmm. That rather begged the question: was her own lifespan impacted by the advent of her magic? How would Morgan react if she discovered she had a much longer than normal life? Come to that, how would she react?

Perhaps she could ask Wyvrndell. Would he even know? While he seemed well versed in magical history and theory, was this something dragons would even consider? They seemed to generally regard humans with disdain, her own tutor proving the exception.

"Well, I suppose it couldn't hurt to ask."

"Ask what?" came a voice.

Marissa gave a little shriek and whirled, nearly toppling a small table. She found… no one? Looking wildly around the room, she finally spied Francesca. The cat—her familiar, she corrected—sat nearby, looking up at her while placidly washing her own face.

"Don't startle me like that," Marissa chided.

"Oh, I beg your pardon. How should I startle you?"

"I—oh, just meow or something to let me know you're here before you start talking. It's very disconcerting."

"Hmmph." Francesca delicately cleared her throat, uttered a preemptory "Mrowl," and arched her back sinuously. "Was that to your satisfaction?"

"You're making fun of me," she grumbled.

Francesca assumed an inscrutably innocent look. "Me? How could you think such a thing? Anyway, what would it not hurt to ask?"

Oh, why not? Aloud, she said, "I was wondering if witches have a longer lifespan due to their magic? I've heard wizards do."

"Oh yes," Francesca replied, flicking her tail. "Anything wizards can do, witches can do. And generally do it much better."

"And you know this because…?"

"Because I was once a witch."

"I see." Marissa considered for a bit, and then added, "I think."

Francesca levitated to the top of the table and bumped her head against Marissa's hand. "This is why you need a familiar. Oh, I suppose the dragon is fine as a tutor, but he doesn't really know anything beyond theory. There are things you need to know. Such as how to actually navigate the world of magic without—"

"Ending up as a cat?"

"Yes. Got it in one. Which is why I'm here."

"Yes, I'm glad you brought up the subject. How did you end up with me? I mean, were you sent? Or is this just happenstance? You've been with me much longer than I've been a witch."

"No, I haven't. I've been with you much longer than you've known you were a witch. I've known all along. I just didn't have the ability to tell you. And may I say it's been quite frustrating, all this waiting about whilst you played around with lizards and chased spies and assassins and such. And what were you thinking, falling in love?"

Marissa choked on this last question. "What was I thinking? I'm not sure thinking had anything to do with it. Like the spies, the assassins, and the dragon. It just happened. Like discovering I'm a witch. I certainly didn't intend it. Any of it. Truth be told, falling in love was the furthest thing from my mind. But—"

Francesca snorted. This, Marissa realized, was a rather disconcerting habit in a feline. "I suppose you may be forgiven, given the circumstances. He is rather dreamy. And he gives good ear scritches."

"I-I'm glad you approve," Marissa managed weakly.

"Looks like he's a pretty good kisser, too."

"What? You've been watching?" Heat crept over her face.

"Well, you haven't exactly been discreet about it, have you?"

"I certainly thought we were. I just didn't realize we had an audience. Um, Francesca, can we please stop discussing this, and get back to more important things."

"More important than kissing? You have a distorted sense of what's important, but very well." Francesca uncurled herself and leapt lightly to the ground. "Back to your original question. Yes, you have a much longer lifespan than the normal human. Probably about double, unless you do something stupid and get yourself killed."

"Or turned into a cat," Marissa muttered.

"Ah, but now I have nine lives," pointed out Francesca smugly.

"Seriously? That's not just—"

"Don't get all excited, I was only jesting. I think. I haven't really wanted to try it out, in case I don't. But yes, your own situation is something you'll need to discuss with your betrothed, since he is strictly mortal. He is strictly mortal, isn't he?"

"Oh yes. At least as far as I know. Of course, I thought I was too until a few weeks ago. And I thought you were just a cat."

"Just a cat? Mrowr. There is no such thing as 'just a cat.'"

"Pardon me. I'm still learning. And it would appear I have much more to learn than just the history and theory of magic."

"You certainly do."

She digested this information in silence. Francesca continued her grooming, seemingly oblivious to her mistress's surprise. After a long moment, Marissa ventured, "You were a witch? And now you're a cat? Um, pardon me if it seems like I'm prying, but exactly how does that work? And should I be concerned? I mean, might I unexpectedly be turned into a cat?"

Francesca arched her back and flowed toward Marissa. "Ear scritches would not be unwelcome," she said. "And no, you needn't be concerned for yourself. At least not at this point. I was turned into a cat because I broke the rules and was punished."

"Rules? What rules?"

"Oh my whiskers! Hasn't that overgrown lizard taught you anything yet?" The look of disdain on the cat's face was so palpable that Marissa was hard-pressed not to laugh. "You'd better sit down." Marissa obligingly sat. Francesca leapt up into her lap, curled into a furry circle with her tail covering her front paws, and cocked her head.

"Oh, yes, ear scritches," Marissa murmured, suiting word to action. For a few moments the only sound was a loud rhythmic purring. Finally she said, "About rules, and the breaking thereof?"

"Many years ago," Francesca began, "before I was a cat, I was a witch. Like yourself, I was young, and beautiful, and in love."

"Yes?" Marissa murmured encouragingly.

"Like you, the man I loved was also quite a good kisser," she went on.

A bit dreamily, Marissa thought.

"Unfortunately, it turned out I wasn't the only one he was kissing." The cat's ears flattened back against her head, and her eyes narrowed into a dangerous glare. "It came as quite a shock, to be honest, when I learned of his betrayal."

"I'm sure it did. What did you do?"

"Something terrible. Although to me, at the time, it seemed quite justified. I determined to be revenged. Not just on him, but also upon the girl. You see, I judged she had stolen him from me."

"And you used your magic?"

"Oh yes. I came up with a spell. A binding spell."

"Ah. To bind this man to you? But I don't see—"

"No." The cat's voice was a sharp hiss. "You don't see. But you will. The spell was not intended to bind him to me. Oh, no…"

Marissa listened in silence as Francesca explained what she, in her misery and rage, had done. When the cat finally fell silent, Marissa shivered in horror at the destruction this creature had wrought. Francesca's eyes searched her own with a penetrating gaze, as if seeking…what? Forgiveness? Scorn? Revulsion? Marissa felt each of these in turn yet could not put voice to any of them.

She stood up, dislodging Francesca from her lap. She paced the room for a minute. Finally, she said, "I'm surprised you got off with only being turned into a cat."

Francesca sniffed. "Say that after you've eaten a mouse. Still, you're correct. By rights I should have been put to death for my crime. I'm still not sure, even to this day, why they decided to be lenient. Not that I'm complaining, mind."

"No, I shouldn't think so," Marissa agreed. "So how did you end up with me?"

"Oh, just lucky for you, I guess."

"Francesca?" Marissa assumed a tone of command. "Why are you here?"

"I was…sent."

The cat, thought Marissa, seemed suddenly and strangely reticent. "Right. Sent. By whom?"

"By the Council." The words sounded forced, as if dragged unwillingly out into the open.

"What Council? The Council of Wizards?"

"No, not the wizards. By…by the Council of Venerable Enchantresses."

"Enchantressess?" She looked down at the cat, hands on her hips. "Would those be witches when they're at home?"

"Certainly."

Narrowing her eyes, Marissa asked, "And these wit—these enchantresses, sent you to me? Why?"

"I'm not allowed to tell you."

"What do you mean you're not allowed to tell me? What are you and these witches up to? Why does it involve me? And just let me remind you there won't be any more fish or cream served until I get some answers."

The cat heaved a long-suffering sigh. Which was in itself a rather odd experience. Francesca sat back on her haunches, curled her tail around her feet, and managed to look as if her feelings had been mortally wounded. "You don't have to get all snippy," she said. "If you really must know…"

"I really must know."

"All right, all right. If I tell you, you'll still come through with the fishes?"

"Extra, if you tell me everything."

Francesca purred happily. "Very well. The leaders of the Council seem to feel that you are the one about whom the prophecy speaks. But as you hadn't actually demonstrated any powers, there was a good deal of disagreement among them. The Council likes to remain behind the scenes, so they didn't want to approach you directly. A decision was reached, to send me to keep a discreet eye on you."

There were so many things in this précis requiring further explanation, Marissa wasn't even sure where to begin.

"Fish?" suggested Francesca hopefully.

"Oh, no. You still have a lot of explaining to do. I'm going to regret this, I'm sure, but…tell me about the prophecy."

"The prophecy has been handed down for generations. If I recall correctly, it was given by Mistress Ephebra Attlesby, a witch of no little repute in her day. She was evidently a first-class diviner. This was ages ago, I believe, around the year ten-eighty or thereabouts. The prophecy has been entrusted in turn to each of the succeeding heads of what has now become the Council."

Marissa flapped an impatient hand. "I really don't need the history lesson," she said. "I get enough of those from Wyvrndell."

"Well, you did ask." Francesca managed to shrug, something Marissa hadn't thought cat shoulders could do. "But here's the thing. The Council believes the fate of Kilbourne is at stake. Here is what the prophecy says." The cat's eyes became slits for a moment. Then she opened them wide to regard Marissa as she spoke.

"'*Dark daughter of magic, long hidden, long awaited. Arise now, Witch of Caerfaen. Take your rightful place. Shepherd your sisters when all languish in hopelessness. With power and mercy, scour the land of evil, and uproot the tree of the usurpers of true power who seek to grind the witch beneath their boots. Thus shall a new era of peace and jubilation reign.*'"

Marissa stared. "Good heavens. Isn't that a bit…um… vague? Not to mention overly dramatic? And this council of witches honestly believes all this refers to me?"

"Prophecies, unfortunately, tend to be quite dramatic. And yes, vague as well. The nature of the beast, as it were."

She tilted her head. "But just what makes you—or rather, this Council—believe it has anything at all to do with me?"

"Well…" Francesca seem to consider her next words. "The fact you seem to have earned the title Witch of Caerfaen is a pretty good start."

With a fierce scowl Marissa said, "Bah. That's just people being people. Besides, I'm still a very novice witch, as it were. I don't really know how to do anything even the tiniest bit, um, witchy."

"Haven't taken up cackling lessons yet?"

"I'm fairly sure that's not on Wyvrndell's curriculum. But seriously, I'm completely inept. I can't imagine this prophecy refers to me."

Francesca leapt up to the top of a small table, so her eyes were on a level with Marissa's. Her gaze was steady as she said, "One may have great power and not be trained in how to use it. The lack of training does not diminish the power that lies within."

Chapter Thirty-Four

"Absolutely not!" Fanshawe uttered a curse and thrust away the blindfold Aartis held out to him.

"Reckon we'd best just forget the whole thing, then," Aartis drawled laconically. "If I just take you out there, you'll know the way and won't have no need o' me again. And I like to be, um, useful."

Fanshawe appeared to be on the point of either drawing his sword or walking away. He must have thought better of either course. With an aggrieved grunt he gave a curt nod. "Very well, we'll do it your way. But no tricks."

Aartis sniffed. "I never play tricks. Mount up an' put on the blindfold."

Fanshawe regarded the mule with distaste. The animal returned his gaze with mutual repugnance. It seemed even more dubious of the whole affair than Fanshawe, if such a thing were possible.

Aartis had to work hard to suppress a grin. "Wha's wrong?" he inquired solicitously. "This one too tame for you? Yer welcome to t'other one."

The second mule grumbled, stamped and lashed out with all four feet at anything that moved in its vicinity.

"Nooo," Fanshawe said with a glower. "This one's fine."

"Right, then. Let's be on our way. Up ye go."

The pirate mounted competently enough, which Aartis filed as interesting for a seafaring buccaneer. Fanshawe adjusted the blindfold over his eyes and felt for the reins.

"No peepin', now," Aartis advised.

"Can't see a damned thing," growled his companion.

"Just as should be." Aartis waved a hand right in front of Fanshawe's face. No reaction. He turned away, then whirled back, waving his hand again. Fanshawe sat still as a stone. As still as a man can on the back of a mule who really isn't into the whole spirit of the thing. But Aartis was satisfied, at least for now.

He produced a large carrot from the recesses of a pocket, proffering it to his own mule. It evidently decided Aartis might be someone interesting to know, at least in the carrot department. Aartis mounted, took the reins from his companion and led him off toward the forest.

It was a slow journey over rough terrain. It was made slower by the fact he was essentially leading a blind man. Slower still as Aartis crossed and recrossed his own trail several times.

Still, it had all the hallmarks of a jolly outing. Aartis was just thinking they should have brought a picnic lunch when Fanshawe said through gritted teeth, "If one more branch whacks me in the face, I'm going to start drastically reducing your fee. You're doing it on purpose."

Not bothering to suppress his grin this time, since Fanshawe couldn't see him anyway, he called back, "Sorry, Mr. Fanshawe, accidents all. But no fear, we're nearly there."

A terse, muttered, "Thank God" was the only reply.

After another five minutes, Aartis brought both mules to a halt. "You can take th' blindfold off now," he said. "But hang on to it. You'll be needin' it again in a bit."

Fanshawe, who had already ripped off the blindfold, rolled his eyes and muttered something unintelligible—and likely unrepeatable in polite company, Aartis suspected. Although, he supposed, pirates didn't often get invited into polite company, did they? Well, no matter.

"We'll leave the mules here. Far enough away they shouldn't scent the ol' dragon and bolt."

Fanshawe took in their surroundings. Probably in an attempt to figure out where they were, Aartis reckoned. He wished the pirate luck with that. The immediate prospect was trees, more trees, and a few stubby ferns scattered about. Certainly nothing in the way of helpful landmarks. Aartis motioned for Fanshawe to follow.

"Quietly," he cautioned. "We don't want the beast t' hear us crashin' 'round amongst the underbrush and decide we'd make a tasty, toasty snack now do we?"

His companion stopped, stepping on a twig which immediately snapped with a muffled *crack*. Aartis winced. "You think that's possible?" Fanshawe asked.

With a muffled snort, Aartis replied, "'Tis a bloody great dragon, ain't it? Full of fire and fight. He's used to taking on armored knights, man. And winning, normally. The pair of us have naught but your little cheese slicer." He pointed to the short sword sheathed on Fanshawe's belt. "Yeah, I reckon if we're not just a wee bit this side o' cautious, it's right possible."

The other man muttered, "I must be mad." Then he seemed to steel himself. "Proceed," he said. "With all due caution."

They followed a nearly invisible track through the towering trees, traversing a bit less than a mile to where the forest began to thin appreciatively.

"Up there," Aartis whispered, pointing ahead. "Across the clearing, in the side of the hill. If ye look close, ye can just see ol' dragon's lair. Nice and slow, now, and not a sound."

He led the way to the edge of the clearing, silently pointing out the entrance to the cave opposite. Fanshawe stared intently, then stepped out from the shelter of the trees. Aartis grabbed his arm, pulling him back. "Are you mad?" he demanded in a barely audible hiss.

Fanshawe cocked his head toward the cave's opening. "Doesn't look like anyone's home," he whispered back. "I want to see…"

He broke off as a shadow swathed the clearing in midday darkness. The dark shape grew, and Fanshawe's eyes widened as he scanned the sky.

Above them, a great eagle soared toward the trees. Fanshawe heaved a sigh of relief. Aartis jerked his head in the direction of the mules. "Might well ha' been the dragon," he murmured. "I don't reckon either of us wants to meet him close on. Come on, we're leaving." Fanshawe nodded once, and they set off back the way they'd come.

Once they'd reached the mules Aartis inquired politely, "Well? Did ya get value for yer money?"

"Yes, I think so."

Aartis handed him the reins. "Then let's go."

Fanshawe glanced back toward the dragon's lair, and then looked resignedly at his mount, who sneered in that way only mules can. He mounted, adjusted the blindfold over his eyes, and said, "Lead on."

Aartis led on.

Chapter Thirty-Five

"Very well." Rhenn handed a glass of wine to Kiara. "Just how do you propose to get McRobbie someplace where I can administer the spell?" His bushy brows lowered as he stared at her across the table.

Kiara's answering smile was not a sight designed to warm the heart, Rhenn noted. No, this was the smile of a predator. A slight shudder ran through him, like the beginnings of an earth tremor. He managed to keep his expression neutral and forced himself to show no revulsion. He couldn't afford to display weakness in his dealings with her; he had to maintain control at all times.

"Simple," she said. "We just lure him there."

"Of course." He found himself fighting off the urge to roll his eyes. Didn't this woman understand anything about conspiracy? "What, if you don't mind me asking, are you planning to use for bait?"

"The bait no hero can resist. A damsel in distress."

"Mmmm. Perhaps." He stroked his chin pensively. Then he sat up straight. "Don't you think it might be much simpler to just snatch McRobbie from his lodgings? Knock him out, toss him in a closed carriage, and take him to where I can administer the spell?"

"I suppose." Kiara made a half-hearted effort to keep a tone of petulance out of her voice. It still came through loud and clear. "If you want to go all prosaic on me."

His mouth tightened. When he spoke, it was through partially clenched teeth. "I am merely trying to get the job done with a minimum of fuss. I've already agreed, albeit reluctantly, to your choice of locale to stage your most theatrical revenge."

Blast. He hadn't meant to say that. He really didn't want to antagonize her. But she was just so bloody focused on getting everything done her way. Acquiescing to a woman's demands wasn't something which came naturally to a wizard.

"The tower is perfect," she protested. "It's deserted, and far enough away from Caerfaen that no one will notice us there. But not so far as to keep the girl from coming."

"It's a moldering old pile, likely inhabited by bats, and located on the seacoast. Sea air bothers my rheumatism something terrible. Perhaps I should just give the whole thing a miss."

"Bah. You want this as much as I do. Maybe more. We both know you want to get rid of Marissa duBerry. Here I've given you the means to do so. But only if you do it my way."

Rhenn nodded. "All right, we'll do it your way. But you do realize we'll have to kill McRobbie as well, do you not?"

"Kill Morg—why? I don't want him to die! I want him alive, and suffering as I have, knowing he's lost what's most precious to him."

Rhenn steepled his fingers as if he were about to begin a lecture. "Of course he has to die. While he will be bound by the spell and unable to move, he'll be aware through the entire thing. He'll see what you're doing. Which, I realize, is what you want. Otherwise, at least from your point of view, the entire exercise is pointless. But if he's aware, he will see both of us. He will, in fact, watch the murder of his betrothed before his eyes. Not by our hands, precisely, but caused by us."

"Oh. Well, yes, I guess when you put it that way."

"Were you planning to just let him go after that? Don't you think he might be a bit…obstreperous at that point? Seek some sort of retribution? And I don't imagine he would just report what we did to the City Watch."

Kiara took a few moments to contemplate. "Yesss," she sighed. "I suppose you're right. Very well, we'll kill Morgan too. I don't suppose the spell can be modified so he'll die after she has sprung the trap?"

"Modify that spell? By the stars, no! It's dangerous enough as it is without any mucking about."

"All right, I was just asking."

Rhenn pressed his advantage. "I urge you to allow yourself to be guided by me in this matter. If you insist, we'll use the tower. But please, no false damsels in distress. Let us be simple and straightforward and do this neatly, with as little fuss as possible."

"Oh, all right. Though I think my way would be much more…," she licked her lips, and finished, "interesting."

"No doubt. Let efficiency be our watchword. Just leave the details to me. Go back to your inn for tonight. I will attend to everything."

He finally managed to get rid of her, after a bit more carping and complaining. Rhenn sat back, poured himself a glass of port, and began to consider his options.

Taking McRobbie should be simple. They'd do it late at night. Use magically induced deep sleep for both his manservant and McRobbie. Dump him into a carriage and haul him out to that confounded tower on the seacoast. His joints twinged at the thought, and Rhenn scowled.

Once at the tower, he would cast the Domelindos binding spell, which would turn McRobbie into a living trap, deadly to the next person to touch him.

Which in this case would be Marissa duBerry. He'd have a message delivered, instructing her to come alone to the tower. Once she rushed to her hero's side, she would trigger the killing portion of the spell. He'd be rid of Lady Marissa and Kiara would have her petty revenge on McRobbie.

After that it would be a simple matter to cut the commander's throat. All the loose ends tied up.

Almost, anyway. Rhenn drained his wine glass. The last detail would be the third body discovered in the tower. The body of Kiara Northram. The whole thing would be a baffling mystery.

When it was all over, he'd be in a position to take control of the Council. Without the duBerry woman's powers, there would be no one strong enough to challenge him. As an added bonus, he'd have the book. With all those lovely, forbidden spells. And no one would ever know.

Chapter Thirty-Six

Toby stalked through the crowded streets of Caerfaen as a smoky dusk fell on the city. All around him vendors shouted, animals barked and brayed, and people chattered. But lost in his own schemes, he took little note of it. All he heard was the gentle tinkle of gold and jewels.

His vision of what the dragon's hoard would yield had grown exponentially over the last several days. He was now almost certain there would be more loot than his crew would even be able to carry off. Gold was heavy, after all, and it stood to reason all that gold would be difficult to manage. Unfortunately, he wouldn't be in a position to ensure things were done properly, with only the choicest pieces taken.

He would instead reluctantly have to rely on Mr. Sharkey. While Sharkey might be an excellent first mate, Toby had his doubts about whether the man possessed a discerning eye. He'd just have to hope for the best. He turned the corner, neatly avoiding a pair of strolling watchmen, and spied his objective ahead. The Mean Ewe. He allowed himself a brief smile.

He'd come to grow fond of the place. It possessed none of the finer qualities, yet it felt almost—well, homelike. The raucous darts tossers, the harried serving girls. And most of all Kate, the barmaid, who had even favored him with one of her exceedingly rare smiles the previous evening.

Toby's steps grew a bit quicker as he neared his destination. If he pulled off this job, he'd have enough booty to settle his debts, pay off the crew, and give up this crazy life he'd taken on. Maybe even become respectable. Again.

It was easy to forget he had once been respectable. An officer and a gentleman. It seemed a long time ago, even though it was in reality only a couple of years since…

Toby's mouth twitched into a fierce grimace. Two ladies approaching him emitted little shrieks and fled back the way they had come. Good heavens, was he really as bad as all that? He caught a glimpse of his reflection in The Mean Ewe's window. Yes, he really was. With good reason.

Ever since the trumped-up incident on the *Sea Hawke*, which had resulted in his being cashiered, he'd felt his soul turn to bitter ice and his heart harden like a stone. There was no justice in the world, or at least not in the Royal Navy. With no prospects and no reference, he'd begun a downward slide toward a life of penury and dishonor.

Until he'd been approached, very quietly, by an obsequious little man with a most outlandish offer. One which Toby couldn't and didn't want to refuse. It allowed him to get back in the game, and while his honor might still suffer, his bank account wouldn't. He could live with that. He—

His ruminations were interrupted. Toby shied like a skittish colt as Mr. Sharkey stepped out of a shadowed doorway, muttering, "Ev'nin' Cap'n."

Taking a deep breath to steady his nerves and slow his racing heart, Toby said crisply, "Mr. Sharkey. A fine evening indeed. Shall we proceed?" Sharkey showed his teeth in what he must have thought passed for a cheerful grin. It didn't. He followed Toby into the tavern.

If the street was a noisy din, The Mean Ewe was a veritable maelstrom of sound. It washed out through the open door, overflowing into the street and back again like an incoming tide. Even Sharkey winced, something Toby had never seen him do in the entirety of their association. To Toby, the sounds wrapped around him like a comforting blanket with which to keep the troubles of the world at bay.

He led Sharkey toward the rear of the room, dodging roistering patrons and weaving serving girls. At the very back table, in a dim alcove with but a single guttering candle on the table, Arn Porter waited, a mug of ale at his lips. He set the tankard on the table when he saw Toby, licked foam from his lip, and gave a casual nod.

Toby slid into a chair, motioning his companion to do likewise. Porter's brow rose slightly as he regarded the mate. "Evenin', Fanshawe. Who's this, then?"

Not belligerently, Toby noted, but just because he wanted to know. "This is my, um, associate, Mr. Sharkey. Sharkey, this is Arn Porter."

Both men nodded. Porter affably, Sharkey with the curt brevity with which he accomplished any task before him. Toby plunged ahead. "Thanks for coming this evening, Porter. I—"

He paused as a serving girl swung by to take their orders. "Another ale for my friend here," Toby told her.

"Thankee," Porter said. He looked back and forth as if trying to determine the reason for their meeting merely from facial expressions. Toby managed to keep his own face closed; Sharkey's, he knew from experience, would give away exactly nothing.

The noise of the tavern swept all around them, like leaves before an autumn wind, but back here at least it was quiet enough to carry on a conversation without screaming. "Porter," Toby began. "I have a proposition for you."

"'Nother trip out to visit yon dragon, perhaps?"

"Actually, yes. I'd like you to escort Mr. Sharkey and some of my friends to view the creature's lair."

Porter looked doubtful. "'Twas one thing, just taking you out there. But a whole group? 'Tain't exactly a jolly picnic, is it? I don't know..."

Sharkey growled low in his chest. Porter glanced at him, cocked a brow, and waited for Toby's reply.

"See here, Porter. This isn't a game," Toby remonstrated. "I—"

"No, it ain't. Not a game at all. I ain't takin' a whole passel o' folk out into th' forest just to gape at the dragon."

"I don't want you to take these men out to gape at the dragon, Porter," Toby said, staring into the man's eyes. "I want you to lead them out there so we can make off with the dragon's hoard."

That shut him up. Porter's eyes bulged out alarmingly. His mouth, which had been open to utter another protest, closed with an audible snap. He made a little whimpering sound, like a dog who's just been kicked. Toby waited.

Finally Porter said in an awestruck tone, "G'on, pull the other one." Toby sat like a cat guarding the cream. Porter finally sputtered, "Yer mad. Yer gonna rob the bloody dragon?"

"Not so loud, we don't want everyone doing it, do we?" Toby grinned. "That's exactly what we're going to do. And you're going to help us. And for that help, you'll get a share of the spoils."

Toby could see avarice warring with common sense. Avarice, it appeared, was in the lead by a nose. "Don't ya think the dragon's gonna take issue with you lot just waltzing in and taking all his—wha'd ya call it?"

"The hoard."

"Right. I can't see as he'd just sit idly by. And when a dragon don't sit idly by, he tends to get right forceful 'bout things, as you might say."

"He won't be there," Toby explained.

Porter looked incredulous. "Why ever not? You gonna invite him out for tea?"

"Something like that. I have a plan to ensure that the dragon will be nowhere near his cave at the appropriate time."

"A plan, eh? What kind of plan?" Porter's eyes lit with curiosity.

Toby shrugged. "That, I'm afraid, is information you don't really need to know. Either you trust me to do my job as I trust you to do yours, or you don't. And if you don't, then ..." He glanced meaningfully toward Sharkey, who chose this moment to show off his pointed teeth in a menacing glower.

Porter ignored the tacit threat. He really, Toby thought, was either much braver or much more foolish than he gave the man credit for. Porter took another long sip of ale, assumed a thoughtful expression, and said, "How much?"

Toby chuckled. "That's like asking 'how long is a piece of string?' There's no way to know until we actually do the job. But based on historical records of dragon hoards over the ages, let's just say the total will be a substantial amount. And you'll receive one share of the total."

"Hmph. 'Storical records is all well and good, I reckon. But it's 'free ale tomorrow', sounds like to me. So I think I'd prefer cash on t' barrelhead, as 'twere. You just pay me to lead your little band o' robbers out to dragon's cave, and I'm yer man. But for a share o' somethin' that may turn out to be nothin'?" He shook his head. "Don't rightly think I'd be game."

Toby considered. "I think you're making a mistake, Porter. This could make you a very rich man."

"And might not. I'll take me chances, an' take cash. One hun'red crowns, up front, an' ye got yerself a guide."

"A hundred crowns? You can't be serious," Toby sputtered. Beside him, Sharkey emitted a low guttural sound. "Twenty-five or take a share like the rest of us."

Porter shrugged. "Well, p'rhaps you can find somebody else fool enough to go dragon huntin' for tw'nty five crowns. Though there ain't so many, outside the Legion, who knows where the lair is."

"You have a point," Toby admitted. "All right, I'll go as high as fifty."

"And I'll go as low as seventy-five."

Toby considered, then nodded. "All right, seventy-five. Up front." Porter nodded, spit on his palm, and held it out. Toby winced, but did likewise, and they sealed the bargain.

Porter set his tankard down with an empty thump. "When?" Now that money was involved for real, he was all business.

Toby, likewise, assumed a businesslike demeanor. "Almost all the pieces are in place. I had to make sure I had you on board before we could proceed. Now that you are, I just need another day or so to finalize my part."

"Tha's the part where the dragon's two other places?"

"That's right."

"I'd surely love to know how you plan to do that. Might come in right handy, case we end up wit' a dragon infestation."

Toby shook his head. "Sorry, Porter, but you don't need to know. Not for your part of the job. Leave it to me. If I fail, the job's off, that's all."

"A'right, fine, I's just curious. Don't matter none. Ye gonna send word when ye want me to lead yer lot out to the cave?"

"Well, not exactly." Toby spread his hands. "Since you know what we've got planned, I really think I'd prefer to keep you around. Not from any lack of trust, Porter, I just can't risk a word of this getting out."

"Oh, I'd never tell," Porter protested. "If'n I did, I'd ne'er see them crowns, now, would I?"

"No, you wouldn't. And while I'm sure you wouldn't talk, at least not intentionally, I can't take any chances. So my associate here, Mr. Sharkey, is going to keep his eye on you."

Porter sagged in his seat. Mr. Sharkey, Toby knew, could have that effect on people.

Chapter Thirty-Seven

Rhenn glanced at the clock. It was time. He stood, marched over to remove his cloak from its peg and swirled it around so it settled on his shoulders. "Let's go."

Kiara flashed a smile that was all teeth and made him think of some predatory animal. "My cloak?"

He held it for her. "Ah, such a gentleman," she breathed. "You'd think we were on our way to the theatre instead of to a—"

She hesitated, and he filled in, "A kidnapping and murder?"

"Well, yes, when you put it that way." She tossed her head. "And I can hardly wait."

Her eyes, he thought, shone just a little too bright and eager, her voice just a little too brittle. She was near the edge of madness. As long as she held together for another day or so, it would all be over. He smiled to himself as he ushered her out into the night. Yes, it would all be over.

The carriage he'd hired was waiting. Of course, he'd have to do something about the driver later. He didn't really care for the way the plan was laid out, but he had to go along with Kiara in order to have access to the book. She still hadn't relinquished her control of it. Initially she had only given him a brief glance at it, to prove it was actually what she claimed. She kept the book, allowing him to see the page that outlined the binding spell. But there were so many more interesting things in the book, if only he could read it.

It didn't matter. He'd have it all to himself soon enough. Then things would be quite different. He just needed to get through the next couple of days.

They were both silent as the carriage clattered through the darkened streets. Only as they neared McRobbie's lodgings did Kiara venture to say, "What about the driver? He won't talk?"

Rhenn shook his head. "He won't remember a thing."

"Altering memories? That's against the wizard's code, isn't it?"

"Considering what we're about to do, altering this fellow's memories is the least of my concerns."

"Yet you have no compunctions about doing any of it?"

He shook his head. "Do you?"

"None at all. This is why I came. I intend to see it through. But for me it's personal. For you, it's only about the game. About power and control. You don't really have a stake."

Hmmm. Perhaps she wasn't quite as mad as he had thought. She understood him. Few people did. It was unusual. Not that it would change the outcome any. "We each have a goal," he told her. "You get what you want. I get what I want. Then we each go our separate ways."

"And never look back, eh?"

He raised a brow. Was this a prelude to blackmail? If so, she was barking up the wrong tree. Aloud he said, "Why would you want to?"

She nodded as if this answer satisfied her. The carriage slowed. Rhenn had directed the driver to a location around the corner from McRobbie's lodgings. Even though the driver wouldn't remember his passengers, there was no point in parking the conveyance right outside McRobbie's door. Others might see and remember.

Once they'd come to a halt Rhenn assisted her from the carriage. Together they melted into the shadows, making their way silently toward McRobbie's lodgings. Kiara led the way, having scouted out the area earlier in the day. Rhenn had been reluctant to show his face there, in case McRobbie returned and recognized him.

The streets were quiet, with only a few hardy souls out and about. Most were already inside and in bed at this late hour. In fact, he could just make out the sound of the big bells of the cathedral tolling the hour of one.

"Not midnight?" she asked, amusement tinging her eyes.

"Bosh. Much too passé. There'll be less of a chance of anyone seeing us, and much more likely we'll catch McRobbie sleeping."

And just as he predicted, all the windows in the house were dark. Rhenn allowed himself a satisfied smile, and—

"Hssst!"

He turned and saw why she was hissing like an overworked teakettle. A pair of City Watch constables was approaching at a leisurely pace. He started to draw back into the shadows, but Kiara tugged on his arm.

"No, you'll just make them suspicious for sure. This way." And giving a girlish laugh, she darted away from him.

Rhenn goggled for a moment, then realization struck. He was supposed to follow like some moonstruck lover. "Great stars," he muttered. Then with a too-hearty chuckle he hurried after her, calling, "Wait, darling, come back."

He caught up with her just as the heavy boots drew near. With another laugh she fell artfully into his arms. "Kiss me!" she hissed.

"What?" He almost dropped her.

"Kiss me, damn it. Do you want them wondering about us?" She wrapped her arms around his neck and pulled his face down toward hers.

And for the first time in more years than he could count, Augustus Rhenn kissed a woman. Wizards, he tried to tell himself above the sound of the blood rushing in his head, were above this kind of thing. They didn't go around kissing attractive young women…

But her lips were on his and she was kissing him with apparent abandon. All such thoughts fled.

He straightened as the constables turned the corner. She was staring at him, her eyes glittering. Her tongue flicked out, and she looked serpentine and dangerous. Rhenn took a step back, "Umm. Yes, well done. Your little deception was certainly…convincing."

Her laugh was throaty. "What makes you think it was a deception? Didn't you enjoy kissing me?"

He had, he realized with no little astonishment. Quite a bit, if he were to admit the truth. Although in retrospect, kissing Kiara Northram was rather like kissing a snake. You could never be quite sure you were going to get out of it alive.

"No. Now, let's get on with what we're here to do."

A pout marred her expression. Rhenn ignored it. "Come on. We need to get closer to McRobbie's lodgings if my spell is going to have the desired effect." He strode off, leaving her to follow in his wake.

They encountered no other wanderers. Soon they were standing in the shadows outside McRobbie's lodgings. The house was a surprisingly neat little place, with a bit of garden in the front behind a small fence. From the shelter of a hedge Rhenn stood watching for several minutes.

There were no lights visible at any of the windows. This hopefully meant the occupants were all fast asleep. He figured only McRobbie and a manservant would be in residence, which would make his task easier. The spell he planned to use would certainly work on more people, but with only two it would have greater impact, keeping McRobbie in a deep state of slumber.

Kiara watched eagerly, impatient for him to act. He nodded, as much to himself as to her, and prepared to cast the spell. Gathering power, he formed it to his wishes and sent it speeding toward the house. A faint glow illuminated its path. Once the kernel of power reached the interior of the house it blossomed like a flower, encompassing the interior and its inhabitants.

Rhenn felt the spell activate. "We'll give it a moment." He held up a hand to stay his companion, who appeared ready to bolt for the house.

She settled. He chuckled silently to himself. *Excellent. She thinks she's in control of the situation. Soon she'll find out differently.* He bared his teeth in a vulpine smile.

"All right," he said, once he was certain anyone in the house would be completely incapacitated. "Let's go."

They moved together from the shadows toward the door of McRobbie's house.

There they encountered another obstacle. The door was firmly locked. Rhenn grunted in dismay. This was something he hadn't foreseen. Who locked their doors at night?

Actually, he did, but only because he didn't want anyone with ill intent gaining easy entrance. But mere mortals? Bah. It was…maddening.

"Can you open it?" she whispered.

He hesitated. "Only by brute force," he admitted. "I've not trained as a burglar. I'd have to blast the thing off its hinges."

"Maybe around back?" she suggested.

With an aggrieved sigh, he nodded. He hated when things didn't go exactly to plan. Little of late had. It was starting to get to him. "Yes, let's try the back."

Too late. They heard the sound of boots on the cobbles. Looking up, Rhenn saw a dark figure approaching. "Hey!" the man called. "What are you doing? Get away from there!"

"It's Morgan!" she snarled. "Do something."

Before he could act, another figure darted from a darkened doorway on a course to intercept McRobbie. Light glinted off a knife in the second man's hand.

"Do something!" she cried in panic. "Stop him. He'll ruin everything."

Rhenn did something. He flung a spell at both men. It happened to be the same one he'd used a few moments earlier, since it was fresh in his mind. The spell did its work. As it activated, McRobbie and the man with the knife both went limp, slumping bonelessly to the ground next to one another.

Together Rhenn and Kiara moved to stand over them. "Why?" she asked. "What was he doing?"

"Who knows?" Rhenn replied. "I'm sure McRobbie has made some enemies along the way. Other enemies, I mean. Perhaps…" The tread of more booted feet broke the stillness. He sucked in a breath.

"Damn!" This was devolving into farce. Who the devil was this fellow with the knife? Well, it didn't matter now. They had to move quickly before the Watchmen came tramping back around the corner.

He bent down, grabbing McRobbie's attacker by the shoulders. With a grunt of effort, he managed to drag him behind a conveniently placed hedge. He'd have a nice little nap th—

Rhenn caught a glimpse of the man's face in the moonlight and sucked in a sharp breath through his teeth. *Bloody hell! It's the chap who was supposed to take care of that nuisance Sebastien.*

No time for that now. He hurried back to where Kiara was standing over Morgan, her eyes wide with…what? Fright? Anger? Madness? He couldn't decide which, and it didn't matter. "Help me get him up," he instructed. "Get your shoulder under his left arm once he's standing. Quick, the Watchmen are coming back."

She gasped, bending to help lift the prostrate McRobbie to a standing position. By the time the constables strolled around the corner, they had McRobbie between them, supporting him relatively upright.

"Here now, everything all right here?" asked one of the constables.

"Fine, just fine," Rhenn said hoarsely, trying to keep his voice unrecognizable. "Our friend here's had a bit too much to drink. We're just helping him home to bed."

"Ah, all right then. Carry on, carry on." Laughing at his own wit, the constable led his companion down the street, leaving Rhenn and Kiara holding an extremely limp McRobbie.

"Now what?" she asked once the Watchmen sauntered out of earshot.

"Now, we do what we were going to do in the first place. Get him out of here, off to that tower of yours. I'll hold McRobbie. You go fetch the coach."

She wriggled out from under McRobbie's arm and dashed off, leaving him to support the man's full weight. McRobbie wasn't an overly large man, but he was solidly built. Rhenn hoped she hurried back with the coach before he ended up dropping his burden.

It was only a couple of minutes, but he was beginning to sweat with effort, something which didn't happen often. She threw open the door. Between them they managed to get McRobbie inside and stretched out onto the floor. Rhenn clambered in, stuck his head out the window, and laid a quick enchantment on the driver.

"He'll take us to the tower, drop us off, and come back," he said. "And won't remember a thing about any of it."

"You're sure?"

"Quite sure," he replied a bit huffily. This constant questioning of his competence was becoming quite annoying. The driver shook up the reins and the team started off.

Chapter Thirty-Eight

Lady Sybil didn't arrive with the dawn, but it hadn't seemed all that much later to Marissa.

She'd really intended to sleep until at least noon. When Briana awoke her to say the viscountess was waiting for her in the morning room, Marissa had groaned and tried to burrow back under the quilt. Briana had chivvied her out of bed, gotten her dressed in a fine flurry of flounces, and hurried her downstairs to greet the guest. Rose wheeled in the tray with coffee and rolls immediately after, giving Marissa a brief moment to rub the sleep from her eyes and try to paste on a bright smile.

Lady Sybil regarded her over a steaming cup of coffee and ventured, "I do apologize. I really shouldn't have descended on you at this unholy hour."

"Oh no, I've been up for simply ages," Marissa lied, desperately trying to conceal a jaw-cracking yawn.

The older woman gave her an appraising look. "Bah. I roused you from your bed and we both know it. Sit down and drink your coffee. I'll try not to keep you long, but there's something I wanted to talk to you about."

Marissa's stomach clenched.

"I couldn't say this back at Bryntop," continued Lady Sybil. "Morgan was always underfoot, and I never seemed to get you alone for a good chin-wag."

Marissa swallowed. Hard. A lump the size of a boulder seemed lodged in her throat. Her mouth was dry as a desert, but her palms felt curiously clammy. Managing not to croak like a demented frog, she said, "Lady Sybil, I know you must think Morgan's making a terrible mistake by marrying me. But I—"

Lady Sybil set down her cup and narrowed her eyes. "My dear girl, whatever gives you such a ridiculous idea?"

"I mean, he is a duke, and my father is only a very minor baron. I'm well aware he could have made a much more advantageous match."

Lady Sybil regarded her thoughtfully. "Yes, I suppose he could have," she said after a lengthy pause.

"And—what about the other day, back at the estate? When Headmaster Rhenn showed up? I overheard you talking to another lady that morning…”

“Oh, you heard that, did you?” Lady Sybil raised one elegant brow.

Marissa stumbled on, hastening to explain. “I didn’t mean to listen, really I didn’t. But it certainly sounded as if you were talking about me. The other woman said to ‘chuck her out,’ and you said you couldn’t because Morgan was fond of her.”

Her companion’s eyes glittered. With malice? Or something else? Marissa wasn’t sure she wanted to know the answer. But Lady Sybil scowled ferociously. Finally she said, “Umph. I’m sorry you overheard that. You’ve been worrying about it all this time, haven’t you? Well, you don’t have to believe me, but I wasn’t speaking of you that day.”

It was Marissa’s turn to raise a brow. Lady Sybil, looking a bit sheepish, said, “One of the housemaids found herself in the family way. Old Lady Trantorn, who’s as big a tartar as ever lived, was sticking her nose into my household affairs. As usual. She was determined to convince me to turn the poor girl out onto the streets. So I told her I couldn’t and blamed it on Morgan. Not the baby!” she added hastily.

Marissa smiled. “No, of course not.”

“Thank you for asking me, instead of just continuing to stew about it.” Lady Sybil gave a rueful shrug. “So often this type of misunderstanding just festers like a boil, because no one bothers to actually find out what was really going on. Rather like those silly girls in the books by—oh, what’s her name? The one who writes all about those oh-so-tragic heroines without a brain in their heads?”

“Oh, I know who you mean!” Marissa wracked her memory. “Lady Bertilde, isn’t it?”

“Yes, that’s the one. I shouldn’t even admit to reading the things, utter trash that they are. But they are rather fun, in a kind of horrid way.”

Marissa nodded. “You’ve found me out too. I knew at once who you meant.” They both laughed.

“I must say that’s a relief,” she said at last. “I’ve been a bit frantic ever since I heard that conversation. And I guess I really couldn’t have blamed you. After all, you’re getting stuck with a witch in the family.”

“Ah, I wondered when we’d get ’round to that.”

“Does it… concern you?”

Lady Sybil shrugged. “Well, yes, it does, a bit. But not for the reasons you might think.”

Marissa looked a question, and the older women leaned back in her seat as if to collect her thoughts. She picked up her cup and took a cautious sip. Making a face, she set it down again. Finally, when she spoke her voice seemed almost distant.

"Marissa, you can't help what you are. This power is in you, courtesy of your parents. You can't change it, any more than Morgan can change the color of his skin." She gestured to her own coffee-and-cream complexion. "He got that from me, and there's not a damned thing he can do about it. He's fought many a battle about it over the years. Especially as a boy. I think he's finally gotten to the point where he's accepting of it."

"He is," Marissa said. "We've talked about it."

Lady Sybil nodded. "Good. I'm glad to know that. It means he trusts you. Always a good trait in a husband. But my point is, neither of you can change what you are. It would be like that bloody great dragon trying to become a fish. The difference comes from what you do with those gifts, or those challenges you're given in life. Those choices are what will determine who you turn out to be."

"You are wise," Marissa said softly.

"No, just practical. So, here's the thing. Neither you nor my son are what might be called, for lack of a better word, normal. He says he loves you, in spite of the fact you might turn him into a stoat if he doesn't behave himself." She grinned. "A most useful talent. Helps to keep your man in line, eh?"

Marissa choked out a laugh, and Sybil continued, "So now I'll ask you. Do you love him?"

Marissa didn't even have to think about the answer. "Yes, I do. Very much. Madly, in fact, although if you tell him I said so I'll deny it."

Lady Sybil grinned conspiratorially. "He'll never hear it from me. But that's all to the good. I'm delighted. Oh, people will say awful things, how Morgan should be expanding a dynasty, or forming some type of meaningful alliance. I say love each other and have fun. It's what Martin and I did, and it worked out all right for the two of us while I had him."

Marissa looked down, not wanted to delve into the subject of Martin McRobbie's untimely demise. But Sybil said, "Yes, I lost my husband and best friend. Morgan lost his father. We both took it hard. But there wasn't a damned thing we could do about it. We both just had to accept it and move on. Worrying about 'could have beens' or 'should have beens' is never very productive. Much better to just look to what is. And look to the future."

Marissa nodded, not trusting herself to speak. She knew if she did, she would likely burst into tears. She was blinking them back now.

"Speaking of Morgan," Lady Sybil said, "where is the boy? I've not seen hide nor hair of him since we arrived in Caerfaen."

"I don't know where he is. He hasn't been 'round for a couple of days. Probably tied up with Legion business. Although I'd have thought he'd want to check on Sebastien's condition."

"He is a stickler for duty. It's something you'll get used to. His father was the same way." Then the older woman blinked. "Wait. Sebastien? What are you talking about?"

"Sorry, I guess I figured you'd heard all about it from Morgan." She gave a précis of the attack on Sebastien, Morgan's pursuit of the assailant, and her own efforts to keep the wizard alive. "I had him brought here," she said. "Dr. Carnavon has been coming by to check on him."

"And you say this wizard was on his way to meet with you and Morgan to discuss what happened with Augustus bloody Rhenn? Then someone tried to stop him. Interesting…"

"You think it's related?"

"Mmmph. Wouldn't surprise me. One doesn't just randomly attack a wizard, does one? That kind of thing can lead to…consequences."

"Perhaps the attacker didn't know he was a wizard," Marissa offered. But even as she said it her words rang hollow.

"Some madman who just wanted to knife a random stranger?" Lady Sybil's mouth quirked in gentle derision. "Do you really think so?"

"No, I think he intentionally went after Sebastien." Marissa was remembering everything she'd seen that day. "It wasn't at random."

"Well then," Lady Sybil said. "That means someone thinks this wizard knows something. Assembling things in a logical order, I would conclude that someone is Augustus Rhenn."

"But why?"

"A good question. Unfortunately, not one for which I have an answer. I suppose we should start by inquiring as to the nature of the Wizard's Prophecy. Because, as I was getting around to saying, I think this whole mess stems from the fact you're a witch."

Marissa blinked. "Excuse me?"

"You have something Augustus Rhenn wants. The only thing he's ever been interested in is power. You have power, of a magical nature, which is right up his alley. It's why he showed up in Westfyld to try to coerce you into dropping everything and haring off to St. Giles. Once you're there, he has you under his control."

She considered. "Wyvrndell rather hinted at the same conclusion. So did Francesca."

Lady Sybil looked blank. "Who is Francesca? I thought your maid was named Briana."

"Briana is my maid. Francesca is my…my cat."

A knock at the door heralded the entrance of Rose, the housemaid. "M'lady, a boy just delivered this note for you. He said he was told it was urgent."

Marissa glanced at Lady Sybil, who said, "Perhaps from your errant knight?"

"Thank you, Rose." Marissa took the paper. She cracked the wax, which bore no identifying seal or insignia. "If it's from Morgan, he was in an awful hurry, and didn't bother to use his ring to seal it."

She unfolded the paper and scanned the message. As the blood chilled in her veins, she wordlessly handed the note over to Lady Sybil. The pictures on the wall danced a sprightly reel before her staring eyes.

"If you wish to see Morgan McRobbie again," Sybil read aloud, "come alone to Perseverance Tower. A friend." She sneered. "A friend? Bah! Now what the devil has that boy gone and gotten himself into this time?"

Marissa could only shake her head. Her throat was so constricted she felt as if words would stick in it and strangle her. Taking a steadying breath, she rang for brandy and glasses. When they arrived, she poured a generous tot for Lady Sybil and herself. "I don't normally do this quite so early in the morning. Under the circumstances, a certain amount of fortification may be justified."

Sybil raised her own glass in salute and took a healthy sip. Marissa, not bothering to sip, gulped the spirits down. She immediately felt the brandy's warmth coursing through her, restoring her equilibrium a bit. She glowered at the note, which Lady Sybil had placed on the table between them.

"Any idea where this Perseverance Tower is?" she asked, rereading the message again. "Good heavens, what a name."

"It's a moldering old pile up the coast a ways. Named for Cape Perseverance, which is no place any sea captain in his right mind would want to go. It's right on the cliff, overlooking the waves crashing on the rocks below. I was there once years ago with Martin, for some party, I imagine. Last I heard, it was abandoned."

"So it fits as a handy spot to hide someone away from prying eyes."

"Admirably. Shall we go and investigate?"

"We?" Marissa narrowed her eyes. "I think this invitation is only for me, Lord knows why. 'Come alone,' it says. It may be dangerous."

"Then all the better if you have someone at your back, eh?" Lady Sybil's eyes glinted with a fierce light. "I'll fetch my sword parasol."

Where a moment before she'd been completely drained, Marissa felt a surge of hope. She closed the distance between them and hugged Lady Sybil tightly. "Thank you," she whispered.

"Yes, that's all very nice, but we've got a bit of a trek ahead of us. It's not exactly a short drive to get to this blasted seaside holiday."

Hmmm. She hadn't considered that. Marissa thought furiously. Time was of the essence. Perhaps...

"Just a moment," she told Lady Sybil. "I want to try something." Without waiting for a reply, she reached out in her mind, calling to Wyvrndell.

She was met with silence. Normally the dragon responded before she even finished uttering his name. Now her call seemed to fall unheeded. Where was he? He was always around when it was time for her lessons, never giving her a moment's peace. Now, when she needed him, the blasted creature was off gallivanting somewhere. Well, he had said he was going away for a few days. Did dragons go on holiday? This thought was so incongruous that she had to stifle a giggle. This was no time for humor.

She called again. Still there was no reply. Looking up at Lady Sybil she said, "I tried to contact the dragon. I thought he might be willing to bear us to this tower. Unfortunately, he seems to have vanished. Much like Morgan. Oh!" Marissa's eyes flew wide. "I wonder if one has something to do with the other?"

Sybil McRobbie grasped her hand. "It doesn't matter right now, does it? We'll go by coach. Have your maid summon one while you get ready. You're dressed for tea, not for battle, and I've a feeling there's not going to be much tea where we're going."

Twenty minutes later, Marissa arrived back downstairs. Lady Sybil was waiting, brandishing her parasol. "You really should get one of these, my dear," she said.

Marissa couldn't help but smile. "Like as not, I'd stick myself instead of a villain," she said.

"Suit yourself," her companion replied. "But then, I reckon you've got other means of wreaking havoc at your disposal."

"Magic, you mean? Nooo, not so's you'd notice. I'm only beginning my lessons, and I don't think Wyvrndell is particularly pleased with my progress thus far. I can barely manage to create a little ball of light. He says my focus needs work."

Further conversation was interrupted by the clattering arrival of a coach. Together they walked down the steps and climbed into the conveyance. The coachman's boy closed the door, secured the steps, and scrambled up next to the driver. With a sharp crack of the whip, the team set in motion.

Marissa said, "Did you notice that he didn't inquire our destination?"

Grimly, Lady Sybil replied, "Yes. Yes I did." She rapped on the sliding panel which allowed access to the driver. The coach picked up speed.

"Hoy!" shouted Lady Sybil, pounding harder on the panel. "Open up, you!" The panel remained unhelpfully closed.

"It's, um, rather dark in here, isn't it?" Marissa ventured. She tugged at the curtain, which revealed a piece of wood nailed over the window opening. Lady Sybil pulled back the curtain on the other side, which was similarly blocked.

"And the bloody doors are locked," reported Lady Sybil. "This doesn't bode well."

Marissa set her back against the seat and aimed a kick at one of the doors. The blow resounded all the way up to her teeth, but the door didn't budge. "No, it doesn't bode well at all." She sat back. "But why all this nonsense about the secluded tower? Just to get us into a carriage? None of this makes sense."

Sybil unsheathed the sword in her parasol. Her teeth flashed white in her dark face. "Whatever the game, we'll be ready, eh?"

At that moment the panel above them slid open a few scant inches. A disembodied hand reached in, tossed something down toward the floor, and slammed the panel shut again.

The tossed object was a small glass phial. Marissa lurched toward it, hands outstretched to catch it in flight. She was too slow, only managing to send the phial spinning in its arc. It shattered as it hit the floor, and a wave of noxious fumes rose up, engulfing them.

Marissa choked out a curse, realized this was a mistake, and tried desperately to hold her breath. Lady Sybil clawed fruitlessly at the sealed windows. Marissa saw her hands begin to waver, and then the older woman slumped in her seat.

Marissa succumbed to the blackness.

Chapter Thirty-Nine

Wyvrndell barely registered the click of talons echoing down the stone corridor. Just one of the guards, or another member of the Council come to berate or jeer at him.

He'd thought perhaps his sire might pay him a visit. But Wyzandar, he knew, was too wily an old dragon to do anything that would bring any further shame upon the family name. He would keep his distance. Wyvrndell certainly couldn't fault him for doing so.

He'd also held out a faint hope of another visit from Aireantha. He had—enjoyed—her visit, and her support during that sub rosa interview with Petrandius. But she, too, should not be associated with a renegade such as himself.

His head flew up and he gave a hiss of surprise when Petrandius said, "Are you receiving callers, young Wyvrndell?"

He bowed his head respectfully, saying, "I am always happy to see you, o king of dragons."

Petrandius snorted. The heat of it washed over Wyvrndell as the king said, "Happy? I wonder. Yet, I'm sure you can tolerate my company easier than some I could name, if less eagerly than one."

There was really no appropriate reply to this. Wyvrndell maintained a studied silence. Petrandius went on, "I have been doing quite a bit of thinking, you know. Mostly about what you have done and said in recent days. And I have arrived at a decision."

Wyvrndell swallowed. Hard. It met a rogue hiccup on its way up, and the collision and subsequent war between them made him send an errant burst of acrid smoke toward the king. "A decision?" he ventured.

"Indeed. A king must always consider what is best for his subjects. This often necessitates putting aside his own personal feelings in a particular case."

Wyvrndell lowered his head. This was it. He was doomed. He was going to die.

"So it is a happy chance," Petrandius continued, "when what is best, and what is wished, happen to coincide. Such is the case now."

A tiny spark of hope flared though him. "Your—your Majesty?"

"If you can indeed accomplish what you claim—bring peace

with the Dwarves and convince this human to help us gain the gift of magic—then it will be of the utmost benefit to dragonkind. I have determined you should begin at once."

The spark of hope burned a bit brighter. He wasn't going to die. At least, not today. Though if he failed…

"If you fail," Petrandius was saying, "we will likely both be done for. Yet I have a feeling you might just succeed. You are young and foolish and take risks any normal dragon would sensibly avoid. This may be exactly what is needed. If so, it would be a feat to celebrate."

Wyvrndell stood erect and proud before his monarch. "Command me, my lord."

"I do. Which task would you deign to tackle first?"

"Lady Marissa, Sire. I believe it will be a fairly simple task to secure her cooperation."

Petrandius nodded. "This is what I thought you might choose. Very well. I will escort you from this cell so you may contact your human."

Wyvrndell almost protested Lady Marissa was not his human. She was her own, subject to no master. But in this case, he supposed, she was his human. Not a prisoner, not a pet. No, she was an ally.

"As you will, Your Majesty," he said.

The guards, wary but knowing better than to question Petrandius, sent fierce glares his way as Wyvrndell emerged from the cell. With unsheathed talons and fire at the ready, they watched in case the prisoner attempted anything untoward. They followed Petrandius and Wyvrndell, maintaining a discreet but cautious distance. Finally they all emerged onto a rock ledge, into the afternoon sunshine.

Petrandius dismissed the guards. They returned down the tunnel, muttering balefully to one another. Wyvrndell stretched his neck, luxuriating for a moment in the fresh air after being cooped up in the cell. He could hear again. He'd never really understood how the cell caverns were shielded so dragons were unable to communicate with any one— dragon or otherwise—on the outside. Now, in the open again, he searched for the familiar, if alien, mind of Lady Marissa duBerry.

And found only silence. He called to her by name, but there came no reply. He cocked his head in a gesture of frustration and tried again. Once more his call went unanswered.

"A problem?" Petrandius's tone was mild, but Wyvrndell knew better than to prevaricate.

"Yes, Your Majesty. Since I began tutoring Lady Marissa, I have always been able to sense her mind, even when she sleeps. Now it is almost as if she does not even exist. There is nothing, where before she was always a definite presence."

"Mmm. Humans are short-lived creatures," Petrandius observed. "Perhaps this one lives no more?"

"She is no hatchling, certainly. Still, she is nowhere near the age where she might expire of natural causes. Yet these humans are by nature a violent lot. Some enemy might have…" The weight of this statement bore down on him. Lady Marissa? Dead? That was unthinkable. Not only because he had such hopes for her to help dragons achieve magic. But also because—because he liked her. She was weak and frail, as humans were, but her mind was keen, her spirit as fierce as any dragon's. Yes, he liked her, and would mourn if she had been taken from him.

Petrandius cocked his huge, hoary head, waiting patiently. Finally Wyvrndell said, "It may be the wizard. The one I spoke of, who wanted to control her. He might have decided to slay her if she continued to resist him."

"Mmm. Who knows, with humans, what they might do? However, our time is short. If I am to be justified in my actions, we need results quickly. We shall put your first scheme in abeyance for now. Let us instead consider the second of your claims: a possible peace with the Dwarves."

Wyvrndell, who had still been calling for Lady Marissa, ceased. "Command me, Sire," he said again.

Petrandius hummed deep in his throat as he thought. Wyvrndell maintained a respectful silence, not wishing to offend by rushing the old dragon. At last Petrandius said, "Hear now my decree. You shall fly to K'var'k's stronghold. You will present my compliments and a proposal for peace between our peoples. Here are my terms…"

Wyvrndell listened carefully as the king laid out his vision for a treaty. He diligently committed each point to memory. It would go ill for him to come back and admit to the Council of Dragons, and to the king, that he had forgotten some key issue.

When Petrandius was finished speaking, Wyvrndell considered for a few moments. Then he asked, "My king, are any of these points negotiable? For while, to me, all you have laid out seems equitable for both sides, the Dwarves may feel otherwise and counter with terms of their own."

"I would be astonished did they not," Petrandius remarked. "Such is always the way with matters of state such as these. Which is why another dragon of my choosing will accompany you. A dragon of wit and sagacity, whose intelligence and steadfastness will offset any, um, impetuousness on your part."

Fire and scale, thought Wyvrndell. *He's going to send old*

Traznfell, who will certainly manage to offend every Dwarf he encounters. Even if by some miracle we do succeed, he's bound to claim it was all his idea and doing. His spirits sank.

Petrandius, seeming not to notice his sudden gloom, went on, "And so I'm sending Aireantha along with you as a negotiator. And as a steadying influence."

Wyvrndell's heart skipped a beat and he almost capered like a hatchling. Forcing himself to remain calm, he observed, "Truly, Your Majesty, a most sagacious choice."

"Yes," Petrandius replied with a smug grin. "I thought you might see it that way."

Chapter Forty

Marissa awoke to the screaming of gulls.

Gulls? Why gulls? It seemed a vital question, but no answers readily presented themselves.

Where was she? Somewhere near the docks? She could smell the sea. Wherever this was, there wasn't much light. A bit filtered in from a small, round, extremely filthy window high on the wall. Not much, but enough to see the room was tiny.

Gingerly she raised her head, an action which elicited a low moan. The throbbing behind her eyes felt as if she'd drunk entirely too much wine, something she hadn't done in years. She certainly hadn't done so now. Had she? The room felt as if it was bouncing and swaying, never a good sign. Marissa grasped the side of the bed, willing the blasted thing to stop its shimmying dance. It didn't help.

The cries of the gulls faded momentarily. She shook her head, which now felt stuffed with cotton wool, her brain as fuzzy as an old sweater. With an unladylike grunt she swung her feet over the sides of the bed, found the floor, and tried to stand.

And went crashing back onto the bed. It wasn't just dizziness, though heaven knew her head was spinning like a child's top. The floor actually was jouncing up and down.

Which meant, what, exactly? She knew she ought to have the answer at her fingertips. But everything seemed so muddled. It was maddening.

She lurched upright again as comprehension seeped through like sunlight cutting a swath through a dense fog. The gulls. The smell of the sea. The bouncing floor. The small room…

She was on a boat.

Now that she'd got that bit, she lay back down. A nice sea voyage ought to be just the thing to cure her malaise. Ocean air would be the perfect remedy to the pounding in her temples. With a contented sigh she closed her eyes and allowed the waves to rock her back toward blissful sleep.

Her eyes flew open again. Why in the world was she on a boat? How had she gotten here? She was supposed to be getting ready for her wedding, along with training in the arcane arts. She uttered an agitated sigh and heaved herself out of bed once more. Lurching toward the door, she prepared to fling it open and begin demanding answers of the nearest person.

The door was firmly locked. Looking around the spartan room— it would be a cabin on a boat, wouldn't it?—she saw only the bed, a chair, a tiny wash stand, and a chamber pot nestled beneath the bed. Well, at least her captors, whoever they might be, had granted her that courtesy.

Still, if she couldn't open the door herself, she could get someone to open it. Opening her mouth, she drew air into her lungs to scream. And let it out again in a gasping wheeze as the lock snicked and the door was pulled open. A man stood in the doorway.

He was tall and lean, his weathered face thin and angular. He had squint lines around his eyes, as if he spent a lot of time looking into the sun. He stood with an almost military bearing, curiously at odds with his being a kidnapper.

Which, Marissa told herself, he most certainly was. She drew herself up, gazed down her nose—a good trick, given his height advantage—and demanded, "Well, sir? What have you to say?"

He raised a brow, giving him an insouciant, almost boyish look. "I was going to ask if you'd care for a cup of tea and perhaps a biscuit or two."

At the mention of tea, Marissa's resolve crumbled. Just a bit. "Fine. Yes. Tea would be welcome." She glared. "As would explanations as to why you have kidnapped me."

"Of course," he said, sweeping a courtly bow. "One moment, please. Davrin," he called over his shoulder.

Another man hove into view, bearing a laden tray. He edged around to the wash stand and set down the tray. Marissa granted him a nod, then turned her attention back to her captor. "May I assume it isn't poisoned?"

He looked shocked at the suggestion. "Of course not. I intend you no harm, Lady Marissa."

She poured tea, inhaled the refreshing aroma, and sipped. Then, calmly, deliberately, she said, "Then please tell me just what the devil you do intend. Because from where I stand, it doesn't look promising."

He nodded. "Very well, I can do that. I…"

She held up a hand. "Before you begin your oh-so-interesting tale, just who the blazes are you?"

The look that crossed his face seemed a combination of wariness and sheepishness. "Obviously my fame hasn't preceded me. I am Captain Tobias Fanshawe, master of this vessel. And"— here his eyes lit with childlike glee— "a vicious pirate."

"Humph. Pirate, undoubtedly. Vicious remains to be seen. Oh, wait, I remember now. What was it? Ah, yes. You're the one who only plunders Rhuddlani ships, aren't you?"

"Mostly," he murmured.

"Someone was talking about it recently. They said you've never attacked a Kilbourne vessel. Is that true? Why not?"

Her captor's eyes held a spark of amusement. "Can one not be a vicious pirate and still be a loyal citizen?" he asked dryly.

This ethical conundrum being a bit beyond her mental capacities now, Marissa decided to ignore it. "Didn't you capture a merchant ship as she was rounding Cape Windrock a couple of weeks ago? Took her cargo, along with the ship's safe, but no one on board was harmed? It was quite a sensation in the papers."

"Um, yes. That was my work all right."

"As I recall, there was a young woman aboard who would have brought a healthy ransom from her father. Yet you didn't take her captive."

"No."

The tea seemed to be working its magic. She felt some of the fog lift as she eyed Captain Fanshawe speculatively. "A pirate with scruples?"

"Call it that if you wish. I don't hold with that sort of thing."

She folded her arms across her chest. "And yet, Captain Fanshawe, I find myself your captive. Which rather puts the lie to your previous declaration. It would seem you do hold with that sort of thing."

"There is a slight difference in this case."

"Sophistry?" She barked out a bitter laugh. "I wouldn't have thought it of the 'Scourge of the Thundermist Sea.'"

His face took on a pained expression. "I really do dislike that name."

She sniffed. "Why? Call a scourge a scourge, I always say."

The pirate shrugged. "As you will. Anyhow, I'm not holding you for ransom. You, m'lady, are bait."

Her mouth dropped open. She stared at the pirate, unable to form a coherent retort. He looked so confident and at ease.

Bait? Visions of being dangled over the side while sea monsters nipped at her toes presented themselves in unwelcome array. "If I'm the bait, just what are you fishing for? Nothing with more legs than is good for it, I trust."

His teeth flashed white against his tanned face. "No, nothing like that. I'm fishing for gold."

This was becoming all too confusing. Especially since her head ached abominably. "But you said you weren't holding me for ransom. Make up your mind, will you?"

"No, no." He waved an expansive hand. "It's dragon's gold I'm after."

"W-what? I…" She sank onto the chair. "You'd better explain. In small words, please."

He paced around the cabin. "Lady Marissa, I'm aware of the dragon Wyvrndell's affinity for you. He went out of his way to save you from the Rhuddlani spy who was causing so much trouble in Caerfaen recently."

Her mouth quirked into a tight frown. There weren't all that many people who knew the truth about that story. "Go on," she said.

"Rumor has it he's also tutoring you in magic."

She just stared. *How the devil does he know all this?*

Fanshawe went on, "So I figure he'll come to your rescue again. Here, I mean. To this ship."

She flapped a hand. "And…"

"And while he's rescuing you, part of my crew will be back at his lair, ready to make off with his hoard. Lots and lots of gold, if the legends are true."

Marissa gawked. The man was mad. There was simply no other explanation. Oh, he looked normal enough. Well, normal for a pirate. Or what she supposed piratical normalcy looked like. Except for the decided lack of the obligatory eye-patch, peg leg, and the metal hook where one hand should be. Weren't such items de rigueur for the modern-day buccaneer? Perhaps no one had explained these things to Captain Fanshawe.

But this wasn't the time or the place, she acknowledged. The point was his plan was mad. It would never…

On second thought… yes, actually, it might work. Except for one thing. A vital oversight this pirate evidently hadn't considered. Because she didn't think the dragon had a hoard. Before she could voice this opinion, another thought crowded it out. "Why on earth did you send a note about Morgan? Just to lure me out so you could take me prisoner?"

Fanshawe's cocked his head, his eyes puzzled. "Note? What note? I never sent you any note."

"But—" Fear welled up, filling her gut like the aftermath of a particularly bad bit of fish. "But the note came, and we got into the coach, and now here I am and…" Realization suddenly struck her with the force of a blow. "What have you done with Lady Sybil?" she demanded.

Fanshawe took a step back, holding his hands up in a calming gesture. "She is ensconced, comfortably if not quietly, in another cabin.

She is a bit—" he paused as if searching for the right word "—a bit feisty, is she not?"

Marissa choked out a laugh. "You don't even know." Then, returning her attention to matters closer to her heart, she said, "You really didn't send me a note saying if I wanted to see Morgan again to come to some moldering old tower?"

Her captor straightened and looked her in the eye. "On my honor as a gentleman and a pirate, I sent no such message. I have no knowledge of Commander McRobbie's whereabouts."

"That makes two of us."

Chapter Forty-One

"Wyvrndell," Aireantha said as they flew. "We can't just show up in the Dwarf kingdom unannounced and expect them to welcome us with open arms. You do know this, don't you?"

"Of course I do," he assured her. "I spoke with R'gm'l just the other day. He has sent letters to K'var'k, his father, telling him of our friendship and of our pledge to end the conflict between dragons and Dwarves."

"Has he received a reply from his sire? Just because you and this princeling have forged a bond between yourselves doesn't mean much. Not unless the king has indicated he'll abide by the course his son has embarked on." Aireantha sounded dubious. "You saw what the dragons of the Council were like. If not for Petrandius they'd have torn you wing from limb for your heresy. Do you expect these Dwarves will be any different?"

"R'gm'l has received word from his father. The king is willing to discuss a peace between our races. So we should be received, if not with a rousing welcome, then at least the welcome accorded emissaries of a foreign ruler."

"I suppose we'll see." She flew closer, until the tips of her wings were only inches from his own. "Wyvrndell?"

"Yes, Airie?"

He could hear the smile in her voice at the use of his hatchling name for her as she said, "I'm proud of you. The way you handled yourself before the Council and Petrandius. The way you look to the future of dragonkind…"

"Even to the point of consorting with humans and befriending a Dwarf?"

"Yes, even that. I've watched you flying about with—what's his name, R'gm'l, and—"

"You've seen us?"

"Yes, I've seen you. You looked like you were having fun. Wyvrndell, when have you ever heard of a dragon having fun?"

He shot a startled look at her. This was something he'd never actually considered, and he said as much.

"Right. Never. Do you know why?"

"No, I suppose I don't."

"Because dragons do not make friends," she said. "Not with one another, and certainly not with those of other races. We make alliances with one another as is expedient. We take a mate." Here she glanced over at him. Almost shyly, he thought. "But we do not make friends. You've changed that. Like you're changing everything. In doing so, you've changed who we are as dragons. Or rather, you're changing who we can be."

"I never thought of it that way," he admitted.

She gave him a knowing look. "Of course not. That's why you need me. To explain things to you."

"Of course," he replied, making a valiant effort to fly level, instead of doing a joyous loop. "I believe I do."

The dragons flew on southward, over forests and fields, rivers and rills, over pastures filled with tasty looking sheep, and over lush vineyards. Ahead the mountains jutted up toward the sky. There lay the stronghold of the Dwarf kings from time immemorial.

"Do you have any idea where we're actually going?" Aireantha asked as the jagged peaks drew closer.

"Now's a fine time to ask," Wyvrndell replied, his wings beating the air in time with hers. He dodged the plume of fire she sent toward him in response. "Yes, R'gm'l has described the place where the Dwarf king's fortress lies. At least as well as he could, since he could only provide a Dwarf's perspective rather than a dragon's."

"And are you going to share this information?" she asked. "Or am I intended to remain content in my ignorance?"

Wyvrndell shot a glance at his companion. Her tone sounded more aggravated than playful. He said hastily, "Of course. My apologies. We are looking for the third highest peak in this range. It is completely flat, as though the top has been sliced right off by a giant's sword."

"A good place for us to land, then." She sounded a bit less acerbic now.

He allowed himself to relax. A little. "Not exactly. The peak is actually a place sacred to the Dwarves. They probably wouldn't appreciate a pair of dragons setting down there uninvited."

"Oh." Her voice radiated tension again. "What else have you neglected to mention?"

Choosing his words carefully, he said, "Um, there's a good chance they will fire arrows and spears at us. Just until I can get across the fact we are emissaries, of course."

"Of course," she said, but her words seemed a bit strangled. He edged a little farther away, in case she decided to try and baste him with flames again. He risked a glance over and saw Aireantha wobble in flight. He realized her entire body was shaking with suppressed laughter.

"You've no idea what you're doing, do you?" she finally managed to ask.

"Certainly I do," he protested. At a sharp look from Aireantha he gave a resigned shrug. "Oh, all right, not exactly. Actually, I'm just making it up as I go along." He'd seen Lady Marissa blush once and wondered if the feeling he was currently experiencing was similar. He'd have to ask her some time.

"Well, you'd better make it up fast," Aireantha said. "There's the flattened peak, and it's simply teeming with Dwarves. A welcoming committee, do you suppose?"

Wyvrndell looked down. She was right. The smooth, circular top of the mountain was spread out below them, and a large group of Dwarf warriors appeared to be readying their bows. "No so welcoming, are they? I did predict this."

"And how are you going to respond? Swoop down and roast them?"

"Aireantha! We are here on a diplomatic mission. That would not be proper."

"I wasn't serious. But they seem to be."

A volley of arrows soared toward them. Most bounced harmlessly off their armored scales, while others sailed by. Wyvrndell casually reached out with his fore talon and grabbed an arrow out of the air. Examining it briefly, he tossed it back toward the Dwarves, following it down.

More arrows rained upwards as he focused on a Dwarf who seemed to be in charge of the company. "*Hold, good Dwarves,*" he said. "*We mean you no harm. We come as emissaries from Petrandius, king of dragons, on a mission of peace. Ow.*" A particularly well-placed arrow found a sensitive spot on his tail.

"Trickery," replied the Dwarf, signaling for another volley. One arrow, heading straight for Aireantha's snout, she dispatched with a small gout of flame.

"*It is no trick,*" insisted Wyvrndell. "*Not only are we emissaries of Petrandius but look.*" He gestured with a talon to the ring on its chain around his neck. "*I am friend and ally to your own Prince R'gm'l, who has gifted me the ring known as the Dragon's Fire.*"

"No doubt stolen," replied the Dwarf as spears and arrows filled the air like so many angry hornets. "Such is the way of dragons."

Aireantha spoke at last. "*Dwarf, this dragon speaks truly.*" She glared down at the phalanx of archers readying their bows again. "*If you*

*will not listen, go and fetch a reasonable Dwarf. Or better yet, send word
to your king. He knows the tale and the truth behind this ring.*"

The Dwarf captain slowly lowered his bow. Seeing this, his
company did likewise, except for one young Dwarf who, in his eagerness
to battle the ancient foe, loosed off another shot. The arrow sailed past
Wyvrndell as he watched the Dwarf captain.

"Very well," said the Dwarf. "None can say that M'zr'k, Captain
of the Grey Company, is not reasonable. If you come to parlay, perhaps
K'var'k will listen. I will send word. He can decide your fate."

"*Thank you, Captain M'zr'k of the Grey Company,*" Aireantha
said, bowing her head in acknowledgement as they hovered over the
Dwarves. "*You are indeed a reasonable Dwarf. But tell me: is there some
place nearby where we may land? We have flown far today, and a rest
would not be unwelcome. As long as we will not cause any panic amongst
the Grey Company.*"

"There is never panic among the Grey Company," M'zr'k
replied. "Not so long as I am captain. But see here. You may land on the
next ridge over, where that lone tree grows, until the king comes or sends
word. But wait." He tugged his luxuriant beard. "I have given my name,
but none have you given in return. Who am I to say has come calling?"

"*I am Aireantha,*" she replied. "*And this dragon, named Dwarf-
friend by your prince, is Wyvrndell. We are pleased to make your
acquaintance, good Captain M'zr'k.*"

"Who should have thought it?" the Dwarf mused. "Well enough.
Though fortune may fail me, I will count this day as lucky, to have met
and conversed with such a courteous and" —he smiled in his beard—
"reasonable dragon."

Chapter Forty-Two

Morgan resurfaced into a state of semi-consciousness. His head ached fiercely. Come to think of it, so did the rest of him. He tried to raise an arm to shield his eyes from the sunlight streaming into the room. There was a problem, though. His arm wouldn't move.

Nor would his legs, or any part of his body. He couldn't even turn his head. *What the—?* He tried to call out but found he couldn't move his mouth to form the words.

"Don't struggle so, Morgan," came a voice. A woman's face swam into his field of vision. "It won't do you a bit of good. The spell has you immobilized."

Spell? What spell? He wanted to shout, to shake her. To find out what the devil was going on. Instead, a victim of his uncooperative body, he lay still, staring up at this strange woman.

Was he drunk? Or dreaming? He certainly felt like he was awake. The light was hurting his eyes. His body refused to cooperate. If this was a dream, it was awfully realistic.

The woman turned away, and he heard her speaking softly to another person out of his limited field of vision. He caught the words "allow" and "speak," and a grunt of reply. A tingling sensation coursed through him, similar to the feeling of a leg having fallen asleep. Then the mystery woman returned to stand over him. "Can you talk now?"

He worked his jaw and found he could actually move it. He tried moving his arms, but they wouldn't respond. "Who are you?" he demanded. "What the devil is this all about?"

"I'm devastated." The woman's voice dripped with mock sorrow. "You don't recognize me, Morgan?"

She leaned over him.

His eyes widened even as memories swirled around him. A dark-haired girl, eyes shining as he'd kissed her so many years ago. This was the same girl, albeit a woman now. But those eyes had changed so much. They were hard now, cold and distant, like the snow-capped peaks of some far-off mountain range.

"Kiara?"

"Ah, so you do remember. Too bad you didn't remember sooner. All this" —she gestured to his helpless form— "might have been avoided.”

He stared up at her, mind racing. “What are you—? Are you talking about those letters you’re supposed to have sent me?”

She gave him a pitying smile. “In part.”

He wanted to sit up and explain. It was maddening, being unable to move any part of his body. He strained every sinew, but to no avail. He was completely immobilized. “I never received them,” he said. “None. Not one. If I had, I’d have answered.”

“Lies!” she shouted. “Don’t tell me lies, Morgan.”

“I’m not,” he protested. “I—”

“No more!” she snarled. Gesturing to the other person in the room, she said, “Silence him. I won’t listen to any more lies.” Morgan found himself struck dumb once more.

“You can listen to me now,” she said. “You toyed with me, casting me aside, when I was a girl. And then, when I’d grown to be a woman and found happiness again, you once more appeared and cut me to nothing. You killed Jermaine, and any hope I had for the future.”

Jermaine? Who—? Oh, right. Randolph said she married Jermaine Northram.

“Now it’s your turn. You will watch as your Lady Marissa is taken from you. You will suffer, Morgan, as I have. Then I will have my justice at last.”

Marissa? This woman was mad.

Which, he realized, didn’t make her any less dangerous, or his plight any less real.

“The spell he’ll cast on you in a few minutes will do it. The binding spell. Once it is wrought, the next person who touches you will die. And you will watch and be helpless to stop it.”

A chill spread through him, colder than a January freeze. Then Kiara’s companion stepped into his field of vision, and his blood turned completely to ice. Augustus Rhenn!

Things clicked into place with a horrifying clarity.

~ * ~

As Marisa glared at Fanshawe, a rough voice called in from the passageway, “Captain? Mist ahead.”

“Blast.” Fanshawe turned back to her. “Please excuse me, Lady Marissa. I’m needed on deck.”

He was quite polite for a pirate and a kidnapper. Well, Xavier had been polite too, even as he’d held knife to her throat. She seemed to attract genteel villains. But then the impact of what she’d just heard clarified. “Mist?” Her eyes grew wide. “Thundermist? It’s real?”

He arched a brow. “Of course. They do call this the Thundermist

Sea for a reason."

"I'm coming with you," she said, rising quickly from her seat. Fanshawe shook his head, but she said, "Captain, you have me prisoner on this vessel. Where do you think I might escape to? Jump overboard? In the middle of the Thundermist Sea? I don't think so. But since I'm here, and there is Thundermist, I want to see it."

He hesitated for a moment, then shrugged. "Suit yourself. But you'd be far safer here. More comfortable as well, for what it's worth. Don't say I didn't warn you." Turning on his heel he opened the door and trotted rapidly up the passageway. He hadn't closed the door behind him. Marissa took this as license, if not invitation, to follow.

She stumbled down the passageway as the boat rocked beneath her feet. How did sailors—or pirates, as the case might be—keep their balance? The ship lurched and Marissa staggered again, clutching at the wall to keep from going down.

A ladder led up toward a hatch through which she could glimpse dim, misty daylight. Climbing slowly, clutching at the ladder's rungs, she emerged out onto the deck. Fanshawe was near the rail, gazing out at the sea. As she approached him, she heard distant thunder.

Fanshawe looked not worried, exactly, but wary. A fine mist had definitely formed out before the bow of the ship. It was still a good distance away, but she could see it spreading all across the horizon. Another rumble of thunder sounded, closer this time. Then another, this time much closer. It rocked the boat at bit, and she grabbed at the rail.

"I did warn you," he said as the ship lurched against the increasingly turbulent waves. One crashed heavily against the bow, sending spray over them even as the thunder grew louder.

"Captain," another voice called sharply. "Lookout reports another ship to stern, tacking to close with us."

A spark of hope flared in her breast. Could it be Morgan? Coming to rescue her?

"Flag?" Fanshawe asked, his tone calm.

"Flyin' a Rhuddlani flag, Cap'n."

Her hopes sank like a ship on the Thundermist Sea. Fanshawe uttered a curse, glanced at her, and shrugged apologetically. He scrubbed a hand across his face, looking suddenly very tired.

"They've been waiting for us," he said. "And I've sailed right into their trap."

"Cap'n!" another voice cried. "Second ship, starboard. Closing fast."

"Right into their bloody trap," he repeated dully. Then he straightened, squared his shoulders, and began calling orders. "Hard to port! Mains'l full on! We'll lose 'em in the mist."

"Aye, hard to port."

"Aye, mains'l full on!"

"Steady on, now," he directed as his ship raced toward the thickening bank of mist obscuring the horizon ahead.

"Starboard side ship's changing course," someone called.

"He's running with the wind," Fanshawe said, mainly to himself. "He'll try to get ahead and intercept us. Ram us, if I'm any judge."

Marissa could see the Rhuddlani ship now, sails full on, charging to cut off Fanshawe's escape. Men were visible at the rails, and sunlight glinted off metal. Swords and grappling hooks, no doubt. A boarding party. The Rhuddlanis were here to extract retribution for Fanshawe's raids on their merchant vessels. She had few illusions about what form that retribution would take. Burning Fanshawe's ship to the waterline would probably be high on the list. Taking prisoners would not.

Nor would rescuing a couple of captive females aboard Fanshawe's ship. Or, if they were taken aboard by the Rhuddlanis, she didn't imagine their prospects would improve markedly. Marissa doubted the crew possessed any of Fanshawe's scruples with regards to female prisoners.

She shivered and called out, "Can't this blasted boat go any faster? They're going to catch us!"

"Us?" He shot her an astonished look. "I'd have thought…"

"If those were Kilbourne Navy ships, I'd be delighted to be caught. The Rhuddlanis, not so much."

He grinned. "It's nice to know my company is preferable to someone's."

"Don't give yourself airs, Captain. They're getting close, by the way."

His eyes glinted with glee in the grey light. "Yes, but so is the Thundermist."

She jerked her head around and stared. She'd been so busy watching the pursuing ships she hadn't spared a thought for the mist. Now she gaped, mouth working soundlessly.

The Thundermist roiled and writhed like a living creature. Jagged streaks of lightning arced through its tendrils, lighting it with a fey luminance. Thunder rumbled, menacing and far too close.

And Fanshawe was taking his ship right into it. Her gaze switched between the bank of mist and the Rhuddlani cutter. He wasn't going to reach the Thundermist before the Rhuddlanis caught them up. They weren't going to make it…

He held up a hand, forestalling her observation of their peril.

"Watch," he said. Then he turned, cupped his hands, and bellowed, "Now!"

The crew sprang into action in what had to have been a well-rehearsed move. Every sail dropped in unison. The ship immediately lost its forward momentum, coming practically to a standstill against the oncoming waves.

Caught totally by surprise, the Rhuddlani cutter shot by their bow with only yards to spare. Fanshawe gave them a jaunty wave, then turned to bawl orders to his crew. As the Rhuddlanis attempted to come around, they were caught in the inexorable tentacles of the Thundermist.

A veritable explosion of thunder rocked Marissa as she stood staring in horror. Lightning sizzled ominously around the Rhuddlani vessel, now fully engulfed in the writhing mist. She heard a sound almost like a growl as lightning flashed in an evil green luminescence. Suddenly the mist-shrouded ship's sails exploded into flame. The thunder rolled again, like the snarl of some giant beast.

"My God." Marissa was torn between looking away and watching in fascinated horror as the Rhuddlani ship was destroyed.

"Rig the mist sails," Fanshawe called. His crew leapt to obey, shouting and cursing. They were drifting toward the Thundermist now.

"We're going in there?" she demanded. "But it—it's destroying that ship. Those men…"

"Too bad for them," he said coldly. "Lucky they have friends nearby."

Even as he spoke, the second Rhuddlani ship swept by on its way to rescue the crew of the burning ship. Men were leaping off it into the sea.

"Mist sails rigged," came a call.

"Mist sails?" Marissa asked.

"A little something I came up with. A wizard was kind enough to accommodate me. For a price." He turned back to the bow of the ship to shout, "Let's get this tub under way. We don't want to be hanging about after this lot retrieve their mates. I don't think we'd find them the least bit friendly."

"'Nother ship, Cap'n, closing from the stern."

Fanshawe grinned. "Late to the party. Three ships, eh? They really must hold a grudge." He looked ahead to where the mist lay waiting. It was thickening by the second, swirling over the rail toward her. Marissa stepped back, shuddering at a strange sensation in the air, almost like a tingling on her skin.

"What are you going to do?" she called over the cacophony of wind and waves.

"Hope we make it though," he yelled back. "Go back to your cabin, you'll be safer there."

She set her mouth and crossed her arms. Then she spoiled the effect by clutching desperately at the railing as another blast of thunder rent the sky. "I'm staying here," she said. "If I'm going to die on this beastly boat, I at least want to watch it happen."

"Suit yourself," he called over the next roll of thunder. "At least get away from the rail before you get washed overboard." Turning away, he yelled "Mr. Carsten!"

Another wave roared up over the side. She decided Fanshawe's advice might not be so bad. She made her way to the wheelhouse. As she entered, he was saying, "I have the helm, Mr. Carsten."

"Aye, Cap'n," replied the burly man at the wheel, stepping back to allow Fanshawe to take control of the ship's course.

"Lady Marissa," he said through gritted teeth as he strained to keep the ship from foundering in the swells. "I do wish you'd go below." As if punctuating his remark, another blast of thunder shook the air around them. Lightning sizzled across the mist-laden sky, although at this point Marissa was having a difficult time telling where sea ended and sky began. It was all just the mist, torrential rain, and seawater combining to turn the world into a grey, sodden deluge.

She grasped a ring set in the cabin wall, evidently put there for just such an exigency. "I'm fine, thank you," she replied. "I'm finding this…interesting."

"Really?" Fanshawe's voice was dry, but it was the only dry thing about him. Mist and seawater were both pouring in through the open window of the wheelhouse. With a tight smile he said, "Perhaps you'd like to take the wheel, and I'll go below."

She barked out a laugh at this, the first since she'd been taken prisoner by these mad pirates. The mist was thickening, to the point where she could barely make out the bow of the ship. She wondered if it mattered. Fanshawe certainly couldn't see where they were going. Probably not, she reckoned. If there was another vessel out here in their path, his ship was doomed, but it seemed doomed anyway, so what was the difference?

But what about the other ship, the third one he was trying to evade now? Would its captain risk entering the Thundermist to pursue them? The swells grew heavier and the pirate captain heaved at the wheel, fighting it as if it were a living thing trying desperately to escape his grasp. The ship rocked up and down wildly. Fanshawe fought on, the cords in his shoulders bulging with the effort. He was, she had to admit, quite muscular.

The other man in the wheelhouse, whom she assumed was Mr. Carsten, now said, "Wind's coming around a bit, Cap'n."

Fanshawe acknowledged this intelligence with a curt nod as he gave the wheel another heave. The sea rose to try to engulf the ship, even as the Thundermist from which the sea got its name tried to shake the vessel apart.

"Was this part of your plan?" she yelled.

Fanshawe looked back over his shoulder at her, his eyes gleaming. "Not exactly," he said. "But it actually works in my favor. Definitely will keep anyone from coming after you. Or me."

A deafening roar of thunder and blistering flare of lightning practically filled the wheelhouse, cutting off any coherent reply. Instead she cried out, throwing an arm up to shield her face.

She could feel her hair all but standing on end from the lightning's sizzling energy. A strange bluish glow surrounded Fanshawe as he labored at the wheel. Wildly, she wondered if she could somehow use her power to keep the ship from being torn apart by the storm.

But when she reached inside herself, to that secret place where the magic lay hidden and waiting, she felt… nothing. There was no hint of veiled power, no fizz of potential magic waiting to blaze into life. Just emptiness. As if she'd never had the magic at all.

Chapter Forty-Three

"You handled that exceedingly well, Airie," Wyvrndell said as they landed on the ridge M'zr'k had indicated.

She eyed him with a smug air. "That's why Petrandius sent me with you. You are our entrée, but I think things may go better if you allow me to do most of the talking."

"I'm beginning to see that," he murmured. "You have hidden depths."

"Not hidden," she countered. "You just haven't been around to notice."

"I've been…busy." If he sounded a bit defensive, well, so be it. "I've been away from Ervantium because—"

"Because you've been off consorting with humans and Dwarves? Busy trying to save dragons from themselves?"

"Exactly!"

"Or," she went on as if he hadn't spoken, "have you been absent because of your hiccups?"

"No!" he began. "And then stopped. Because this was Aireantha. He couldn't lie to her. "All right, yes." He blew out a fiery breath of annoyance. "Everyone was making fun of me."

"So you ran away?"

"I left because I-I didn't want you to laugh at me." He turned his head away, not wanting her to see his expression.

He felt her moving closer. Her long sleek neck twined around his. "Did you really think I would?"

Whatever he might have responded to this was lost. Her attention was suddenly focused on the next ridge. Reluctantly, Wyvrndell swung his head around to see M'zr'k waving to them. "The king grants you an audience. Come."

"We are summoned," Aireantha said. "This is good news. Let's go."

He followed her on the short flight to where M'zr'k waited on a large ledge a dragon's length below the flattened top of the mountain. M'zr'k bowed to the dragons, saying, "K'var'k says you are to be treated as honored guests. And because you are a bit, um, large to meet with him in his great hall, he has deigned to come out to speak with you."

"The king is most gracious," Aireantha replied.

"Of a certainty, he is. And you are doubly honored, for the king is determined to meet with you upon the A'gr'zn peak, which is for Dwarves a place most revered."

"We are honored indeed," Aireantha acknowledged.

"K'var'k has requested you to wait here with me until he comes."

"We will, of course, await the king's pleasure." Aireantha settled back on her haunches and glanced over at Wyvrndell. He did likewise.

"I am afraid I can offer you no refreshment," M'zr'k said. "We are unprepared to entertain guests of your, um, nature."

"Do not be troubled, Captain M'zr'k," Wyvrndell replied, modeling his speech on Aireantha's. *"We arrived with neither notice nor invitation. An audience with King K'var'k is all we could wish for."*

"Mmm, well said," boomed the Dwarf. "Two courteous dragons. Who would have ever thought to see the day?"

Before either dragon could answer, a fanfare of horns sounded from above. "Behold," cried M'zr'k. "The king comes forth. Go up to the A'gr'zn to attend him. And," he added, "may fortune smile upon your meeting. For I warrant this day may be one long remembered in the histories of the Dwarves."

"And of the dragons as well," replied Aireantha, taking wing.

"I hope," Wyvrndell said to himself as he followed her.

K'var'k, when they saw him, appeared arrayed more for battle than for diplomacy. The Dwarf king's armor gleamed radiant in the afternoon sun. Light glinted off the tip of his long spear, and off the well-honed blades of the two battle axes strapped across his back. Only his head was uncovered, his helm borne by an attendant.

"This is the way of Dwarves," Aireantha told him. "To do less would be to appear weak, and such he could not countenance. Do not worry yourself unduly, Wyvrndell, for his head is bared. A good sign."

Wyvrndell, recalling his conversation with Lady Marissa, wanted to ask her if he could worry himself duly. However, this seemed neither the time nor place for levity. They landed in tandem before the king of the Dwarves. Aireantha bowed her head low in a show of respect. Wyvrndell followed her example as they waited for K'var'k to speak.

For long moments he remained silent, gazing upon the dragons bowed before him. At last he raised his spear toward the sky, crying aloud, "Arise, dragons of Ervantium. I welcome you to R'mk'vl, a day and a meeting unlooked for. Yet to me one long wished for. This day I meet Wyvrndell, whom my son names Dwarf-friend."

"Your Majesty." Wyvrndell bowed low once more. *"I am honored to meet the esteemed sire of Prince R'gm'l, who in token of friendship has gifted me this jewel, the Dragon's Fire."* He raised his head and the emerald winked in the sunlight.

"Prince R'gm'l has written to me of your meeting. And of his gift, freely given and accepted. Now tell me, Wyvrndell, how fares my scion in the lands of men?"

"He fares well, Your Majesty, growing apace, and speaking naught but good of the court of King Rhys. Only a few days ago did we fly together, chasing the clouds from the sky for our pleasure. He misses his home here in R'mk'vl, but is content to learn the ways of men, as his father has decreed."

"As does my esquire here, Prince Robert of Kilbourne. He abides here in R'mk'vl by his father's wishes." The attendant bearing K'var'k's helm stepped forward, and Wyvrndell saw to his surprise he was indeed a human boy.

"Please, Master Dragon," said the boy. "Convey my greetings to my brother R'gm'l. And to my parents, the king and queen," he added as an afterthought.

"I will carry your messages when I return to the north, young prince," the dragon replied.

"Now, Wyvrndell, introduce me to your companion," K'var'k said.

"Your Majesty, allow me to present Aireantha. Petrandius chose her to accompany me as emissary. I am only here by my good fortune to have befriended your son. But Aireantha is both wise and courteous, and will conduct our negotiations, if such meets with Your Majesty's favor."

Aireantha bowed her head once more, and K'var'k inclined his to her. "Well met, Aireantha of Ervantium. I look forward to matching wits with you as we discuss the fate of our nations. If you are half as sagacious as Wyvrndell suggests, I shall have to be on my guard."

"Nay, Your Majesty," said Aireantha. *"We seek only an accord which will lead to peace between our races. And for a brighter future for both dragons and Dwarves."*

"An outcome truly to be wished for," murmured K'var'k. "Yet can it ever be so?"

"We can only hope," the dragon replied, fixing her eye upon the Dwarf king.

"You speak truly, Aireantha. So, let us begin." K'var'k thumped the butt of his spear on the ground three times. "But before we enter into our discussions, I must tell you one thing. We stand on sacred ground, of which I will speak more in a moment. This place has had an enchantment laid upon it by Dwarf magicians. Within this ring," he waved to indicate the standing stones arrayed around them, "none outside it, dwarf, man, or dragon, can hear what is said. Thus no dragon in Ervantium, for example, could hear you should you call, nor speak to you here. If this is acceptable, we may continue our discussions. If not, then our audience is, sadly, terminated."

Chapter Forty-Four

It was odd, Marissa thought. Horrible and wonderful, all at the same time. She'd never asked for magic. Really didn't want it. It just made everything so blasted complicated. From the way people now regarded her, as some sort of potential monster, to her relationship with Morgan.

And yet, its absence set off all kinds of alarm bells in her head. This couldn't be right. According to Wyvrndell and Sebastien, she had a tremendous amount of power. How could it just be gone?

She rounded on Fanshawe. "What have you done to me?" she demanded.

"Not now, Lady Marissa," he grunted, struggling with the wheel. "I'm a bit busy trying to keep us alive at the moment."

"What have you done?" she repeated. "Tell me!" Then she recalled Wyvrndell's lesson, seeming forever ago, back when they were at Bryntop. He'd told her about witchbane. About how it could be used to prevent the use of magic. And how it also… The realization of what Fanshawe must have done hit her like one of the crashing waves trying to swamp this blasted boat. "You gave me witchbane, didn't you?"

Fanshawe glanced over his shoulder at her, then turned back to his task. But he said, "Yes, I did. Couldn't have you casting some pesky spell now, could I?"

"How much?"

"How much what?"

"How much witchbane, damn you! It's a poison."

Fanshawe darted a glance at her, his eyes wide with shock. "No, it just—"

"It's a deadly poison if you give someone too much!"

He blanched but didn't answer. Another massive wave struck the bow of the ship. They plunged down into the trough left behind. He clung to the wheel, his muscles straining to keep them on top of the water instead of beneath it. She clutched at the ring just in time. They smacked into the bottom of the trough with an impact hard enough to make the main mast sway precariously.

Marissa's stomach started sending urgent signals up to her brain, indicating it was not enjoying the experience one little bit. With a series of mighty creaks and groans the ship began to right itself again, until the bow pointed nearly vertical. This on the whole didn't seem much of an improvement.

Lightning sizzled around them, providing an eerily spectral glow that gave Fanshawe's face an evil cast. His hair stood on end, and he cursed under his breath.

"Don't mind me," she gasped. "Swear away. I'll join you, in fact."

He grinned. "Right you are, then." He hauled on the ship's wheel as he loosed a torrent of blistering invective.

She was impressed. Some of those words she didn't even know. Piratical, perhaps? She'd have to make inquiries at some point. Assuming she was still alive to do so.

She tried again to reach for her magic, and still it remained stubbornly elusive. "How much witchbane did you give me?" she repeated. "This is rather important. Dying witch over here, possibly."

"Sorry, I've been just a bit, um, busy," he pointed out. "Trying to keep this tub afloat, you know. Mmm, I think I may have even succeeded. Things seem to be calming just a bit."

In answer to this overly optimistic declaration, another blast of thunder boomed all around them, shaking the ship to its very timbers. "Or not," he amended.

But he was right. The waves, though still nothing to sneeze at, were no longer reaching higher than the bowsprit. Marissa's stomach ceased its frantic scramble up toward her gizzard and grudgingly clambered back down where it belonged. The lightning faded into little snapping hisses reminiscent of an incensed turtle. The sky, which had turned so dark as to almost be black, began to recede back to a greenish grey which, while no painters dream, at least allowed one to see more than ten feet ahead.

"Witchbane?"

The pirate loosened his grasp on the wheel just a bit, rolling his shoulders to ease the tensed muscles. He wiped his face with an extremely crumpled and rather soggy kerchief, settled his hat back on his head at a more rakish angle, and gave her an apologetic look. "No one mentioned anything about poison," he said, spreading his hands in a gesture of injured innocence. He spoiled it by grabbing for the wheel again as it began to rotate counterclockwise. "I was merely told a small dose of witchbane would circumvent your ability to use magic."

"Hmmph. Well, as I still seem to be alive, it must have been a less than fatal dose. No thanks to you."

Fanshawe shrugged. "I suppose a heartfelt apology won't

suffice, eh?"

She shot him a quelling look.

"No, I thought not," he said, turning back to the wheel.

Then a thought struck her. Was this what had happened to Sebastien? A coating of witchbane on the knife? If so, it must not have been enough to be fatal, but had put the wizard into a prolonged slumber. She tried in vain to recall if the effects would wear off with time, or if an antidote had to be given. At the moment it didn't matter anyway. There was nothing she could do for Sebastien, and her own case seemed less likely to be the cause of her imminent demise than did the sea.

Then, as if the Thundermist Sea were a thing alive and cognizant of her absence of magic, the mist suddenly engulfed her, swirling through her. It seemed to seep into all the places where the magic should have been, somehow lighting her from within. It was as if the lightning was now contained in her body. Marissa suddenly felt as though if she reached out her hand, she'd shoot bolts of fire right out her fingertips.

The thought was quite appealing, and she considered it for a moment. On reflection, she decided if she managed to blast Captain Fanshawe into eternity, she might well end up joining him there when the ship was sucked under the sea by this wretched storm.

Instead, she cupped her hand and whispered, *"Lluminas acciadio."* The now-familiar ball of light sparkled in her hand for just a moment before she closed her fingers around it, snuffing it out. The pirates hadn't noticed, being too busy with attempting to keep the ship on top of the sea instead of beneath it.

Chapter Forty-Five

As Wyvrndell considered the implications of K'var'k's warning, a rogue hiccup threatened to make its way up his gullet. He barely managed to suppress it and sent stern admonishments to his digestive system. He didn't need the distraction, or embarrassment, of an outbreak of acrid belches during their delicate negotiations with the Dwarf King. Aireantha would roast him.

He'd never contemplated the notion of reaching out to Petrandius for guidance, although he had a sneaking suspicion Aireantha had. It didn't matter now, for if they agreed to K'var'k's terms they'd be cut off and completely on their own. He glanced over to gauge her reaction.

If Aireantha was fazed by this turn of events, she certainly didn't show it. *"This presents no problem, Your Majesty,"* she said. *"We are happy to agree."*

"Excellent," K'var'k replied. "Then let us begin."

Aireantha cocked her head. *"You said you would tell us about this site, so revered by Dwarves. Will you not speak of this first, before we begin our discussions?"*

K'var'k flashed her an appreciative smile. "Well done," he murmured so that only the dragons could hear. Aloud, he said, "This mountain is the place where D'rz'mn, Dwarf of my father's father's father and beyond, did battle with the dragon Greythorn. In lay and in legend are their deeds described."

The Dwarf king's voice was deep and resonant as he went on, "With spear and fire did they strive, with torch and talon, upon this mountain. In that mighty contest was this peak destroyed, laid waste and flattened to where we now stand. I find it most fitting that upon this place, sacred to Dwarves as a monument to death and destruction, we will strive together, Dwarf and dragon, to forge a new beginning and an era of peace between our races."

"You have a profound sense of the ironic, King K'var'k," Aireantha said.

K'var'k just smiled. Turning to his retinue, he said, "Now, hear my decree. Since our esteemed guests are by our enchantments cut off from their own kind in the wide world, so too shall I be cut off from my kin. I will negotiate with these emissaries without benefit of counsel. Save that since Aireantha of Ervantium has her companion, the Dwarf-friend Wyvrndell, I shall name one Dwarf as my aide in these discussions."

He looked around the assembled Dwarves, who chattered excitedly to one another. Finally, nodding to himself, K'var'k declared, "In this matter I choose M'zr'k, Captain of the Grey Company. He shall serve me as aide and counsel."

Several of the Dwarves, whom Wyvrndell suspected to be senior ministers of the king, looked scandalized by this decision. K'var'k, however, gave them no time to protest. He went on, "Yet Aireantha, I would also propose we include a neutral party to oversee our discussions."

"A third party, neither Dwarf nor dragon? Where will you find such a one?"

Wyvrndell understood at the same time she did. The king nodded. "I would propose Robert, Prince of Kilbourne, to be party to our negotiations. He has learned much of the art of diplomacy in his father's court. I warrant he will be a fair arbiter of any points of conflict which might arise between us."

Aireantha nodded. Wyvrndell said nothing. K'var'k went on. "Now all but those appointed shall leave us to our discussion." He waved the hand not holding his spear in a shooing motion. "I will summon you back when we are concluded."

The group of Dwarves, thus dismissed, began to file out of the circle, chattering to one another. Wyvrndell could hear some eagerly discussing the prospect of peace. Others muttered dire predictions of disaster as K'var'k led them into ruin.

Once all had left, K'var'k cast down his spear, stretched his arms, and perched upon a large stone. "Come, sit and be at ease," he told the dragons.

Both Wyvrndell and Aireantha reclined in the open space before the king. M'zr'k stood at attention next to his liege. K'var'k said, "Captain, you are not standing guard duty. You are here to lend counsel as needed. Don't hover like that. Sit down."

"B-by your leave, Majesty," M'zr'k stammered. He perched gingerly on another stone, as K'var'k turned to Prince Robert.

"Robert of Kilbourne, I know you have been thrown into a stew not of your liking. Yet I deemed this my wisest course, to prevent an uproar from those who later will be certain to oppose me."

The young prince bowed low, saying, "Your Majesty, sire of my brother, I serve at your command. I have little to offer, yet what I have is at your disposal."

"See?" K'var'k beamed. "Did I not tell you Rhys has taught him well? Hear my command then, young esquire. Listen well and remember, so that those who question you later will hear the true tale of our discussions. And now, good dragons, let us begin in earnest."

~ * ~

Some hours later, Wyvrndell listened intently as K'var'k and Aireantha discussed terms of the treaty. M'zr'k was desperately trying to smother his yawns. Prince Robert, who had borne up well for the bulk of the negotiations, was currently leaning against a large rock, his eyes closed. K'var'k had agreed to each of the points Petrandius had detailed in Ervantium, with little complaint. He had listed off several proposals of his own, but they were ones for which Aireantha had been prepared. There would be peace between Dwarves and dragons.

Even though the talks were progressing with remarkable smoothness, something niggled at the periphery of Wyvrndell's consciousness. He couldn't hook a talon into it; it was just a feeling, as if the whole of their meeting with K'var'k, the peace talks themselves, were somehow…contrived?

The dragon cocked his head as realization struck, clear as a cloudless sky. He paused to examine his conclusion and found it sound. He was merely a pawn, in some game played by Petrandius. And, by extension, by K'var'k as well.

The others must have noticed his annoyance. They stared at him, Aireantha with dismay, the Dwarf king with bland amusement.

"Is there a problem?" K'var'k inquired politely. Behind him, M'zr'k snored.

Aireantha shot a warning look at Wyvrndell, but he chose to ignore it. *"Not a problem,"* he replied. *"Not as such. I merely wonder how it is you knew beforehand each of the terms King Petrandius would offer and were prepared to agree so readily. And how each of your own terms were ones for which Aireantha had been briefed."*

K'var'k smiled in his beard. Wyvrndell pressed on. *"This wasn't a negotiation, was it? This was simply confirmation of things you and Petrandius had already agreed on."*

"Well spotted," K'var'k said, as Aireantha looked between Wyvrndell and the dwarf in obvious confusion.

"Why?" Wyvrndell kept his tone neutral, despite the anger he suddenly felt. No, not anger. He just felt a fool.

"It was for the best," K'var'k said, is if this explained everything. To Wyvrndell, it explained nothing.

"Best? How was this for the best?"

K'var'k's expression turned a bit rueful. "Wyvrndell, and Aireantha as well, I beg your indulgence. We needed to do things this way, Petrandius and I. Much of being a king, of ruling, is knowing how to put on a good show. Yes, Petrandius and I have been in communication. We discussed the terms of a peace accord and came to a mutually satisfactory agreement. But we knew we couldn't just suddenly announce this accord. Neither of our peoples would have accepted that."

"*So instead, Aireantha and I were dispatched here under the pretense of conducting actual negotiations. We were totally unnecessary, except for appearances sake. You and Petrandius had—*" He broke off as a series of hiccoughs escaped him. "*Bringer of peace,*" he said at last. "*Bah. I've been a fool.*"

K'var'k shook his head. "Wyvrndell, you were by no means unnecessary. Nor was Aireantha. And you were no fool. Indeed, you were essential to all this."

Wyvrndell just glared.

"You don't see it, do you?" K'var'k glanced at the slumbering forms of M'zr'k and Prince Robert. "Since they are asleep, I can speak freely. Consider, Wyvrndell. Had you not taken the chance, of your own free will, to befriend R'gm'l, none of what has been agreed to here today would have been possible. You and my son, between you, forged the first bonds of peace. All else came after. Petrandius and I simply seized on the opportunity you so unexpectedly handed to us."

Still Wyvrndell was silent. K'var'k smiled up at him. "We were at a loss, Petrandius and I, over how we could arrange a peace conference in the face of such strong opposition. You, Wyvrndell Dwarf-friend, took matters into your own talons, as it were. You and R'gm'l determined to change the course of history for both our races, whether we liked it or not. And you succeeded. If not for your timely intervention, all our hopes and schemes would have gone for naught."

As Wyvrndell considered this, K'var'k pressed on, "It may be hard for you to understand now. But one day, should it be your lot to rule, remember what I have said here today. Petrandius did not send you because you were a fool or a pawn. No, he sent you because you were the only one who could possibly force a peace between us. By putting on a show, for both dragons and dwarves. And you have, in spite of everything, succeeded."

And for the first time in his life, Wyvrndell the dragon laughed.

Chapter Forty-Six

With exquisitely precise wrist action, Barlbent tossed his final dart. It landed dead center. The little knot of competitors and spectators moaned or cheered according to their preference. He smiled, scooped up his winnings, and graciously accepted the offer of a pint from the loser.

Retrieving his darts, he stowed them carefully into their case and placed the case into an inside pocket. He took off his spectacles, polished them on his sleeve, and drained the pint. Despite the lucrative win, it looked as if his main reason for coming to the Broken Lance was not going to materialize. He huffed out a resigned sigh and prepared to leave.

It was bloody frustrating. He'd been chasing rumors and will-o-the-wisp fancies for days in an attempt to learn the truth about the wizard's prophecy. No one he'd talked to had been willing to admit they knew anything. This was his last hope.

The door opened and a dark-skinned man stepped into the tavern. Barlbent replaced his spectacles, glancing casually over at the newcomer. His persistence had paid off. The night hadn't been a waste after all. He smiled and engaged in another round of spectacle polishing.

As the man approached the bar, Barlbent moved to intercept him. "Nardis," he said, exuding good cheer. "I was hoping I'd run into you here. I believe I still owe you a pint from our last match."

Nardis Cardion took a step back. "You, owe me a pint? I don't think so, Francis. If anything, it would be the other way 'round."

"Even better. You can buy me one. I'm sitting just over here. Come join me." Barlbent gestured to a table he'd staked out earlier, near the rear corner of the tavern's common room.

Nardis looked a bit puzzled, but game. "All right, give me a moment."

Barlbent returned to his table.

Nardis soon appeared bearing two foaming tankards. Passing one to Barlbent, he took a sip of his ale and regarded his companion silently for a moment. At last he said, "Francis, what's going on? I don't recall any wager, though I'm more than happy to buy you a pint if you're short of funds."

Barlbent leaned forward, in order to be heard without having to shout over the noise of the dart players who started another match. "How is Sebastien?” he asked.

Nardis looked suddenly wary. “Uh, fine, as far as I know.”

“I mean, is he recovering from the attack?” Barlbent said.

Nardis’s eyes widened, and he sucked in a breath. “Attack? What are you talking about? He was fine when I last saw him.”

“A few days ago, a man with a knife tried to kill him outside a café where he was supposed to meet with Commander McRobbie and his lady.” Barlbent smiled grimly.

“So,” Nardis whispered, almost to himself. “So he wasn’t as bloody clever as he thought.”

Barlbent took another sip of ale and eyed the young wizard with renewed interest. “I think you and I need to go somewhere a bit quieter, and you need to tell me things.”

Nardis shot his gaze around the room. “I shouldn’t even be seen with you,” he muttered. “Standing you a pint is one thing. If we’re seen leaving together… Well, everyone knows who you work for. I’ll tell you what. I’ll come to your office. Tomorrow. All right?”

Barlbent shook his head. “No, Nardis, that won’t do. I know what happens when we do that. You never show up, because someone’s decided you know too much, and murders you in the interim.”

“What? Murders me? Francis, what on earth are you babbling on about?”

“In books,” Barlbent explained with the infinite patience of a man who reads to one who doesn’t, “it always happens like that. So no, we’ll not wait ’til tomorrow. I’ll leave now, and you can finish your pint and then leave. I’ll meet you outside.”

Nardis’s breath was rather ragged as Barlbent laid out his plan, but he nodded, if a bit reluctantly. “All right, I’ll do as you say.”

“Good man,” Barlbent said. Rising, he called, “Thanks for the pint, Nardis. We’ll have to have another match soon.” With a cheery wave he strolled out of the Broken Lance, giving an approving nod to one of the players who’d just scored a nice toss.

It was nearly ten minutes before Nardis emerged from the tavern. Barlbent breathed a sigh of relief. He’d been afraid the wizard might try to bolt out the back door. He gave a little “psst,” and Nardis joined him in the shadow of a doorway.

“This way,” Barlbent directed, leading him down the street and around a corner. “I don’t live far from here.” He glanced over at his companion, whose eyes were wide and white in his dark face. “We’ll keep to the shadows, so no one recognizes either of us.”

Nardis said nothing, but he did follow along, which was really all Barlbent could have hoped for. It was only a ten-minute walk to his lodgings, and they encountered only a few wanderers searching for drinks, and a pair of constables making their duly appointed rounds.

As he let them into his rooms he could see the other man was trembling, his face dewed with sweat. "Here, let me pour you a bit of brandy," he said. "Park yourself on the settee and take a couple of deep breaths. You're all right now."

Nardis sat. Barlbent poured him a generous tot. The wizard gulped down the first swallow, choked, and gasped for air. Finally, settling down a bit, he sipped more appreciatively at the liquor. As well he should, Barlbent thought, having brought out the bottle he kept for special occasions.

Sinking into an armchair with a brandy of his own, Barlbent said, "At the Broken Lance, you said 'So he wasn't as clever as he thought.' What did you mean? Was Sebastien worried someone might be after him?"

Nardis rested the snifter on the little table at his elbow, took a deep breath, and closed his eyes briefly. "No, he didn't seem worried. Not about that. He... Look, I'd better explain."

"An excellent idea."

Nardis opened his mouth, closed it again, then took another drink. "Francis," he said, "Why all the interest in Master Sebastien? This is wizards' business. Nothing to do with you."

"It involves an, um, investigation I'm pursuing," Barlbent prevaricated. "You said yourself you know who I work for. Call it professional curiosity. Call it nosiness, if you will. Call it whatever you want. Just tell me about Sebastien."

Nardis pursed his lips. However, he seemed to find this rather unhelpful explanation acceptable. Barlbent listened as he recounted overhearing Rhenn and Skarlatos, of going to warn Sebastien, and of the old wizard's enigmatic words.

Barlbent whistled softly when he finished. "Headmaster Rhenn, eh? So McRobbie was right. He is up to something. Unfortunately, it's likely Sebastien is the only one who knows what. And he can't tell us."

"Where is he?" asked Nardis.

"Ensconced at the home of Lady Marissa duBerry. She's the one who saved his life. Kept things together, literally, until someone could fetch a surgeon to keep the old fellow from bleeding out on the pavement. From what I've been told, he's still alive, but doesn't really seem to be recovering. The knife wound he sustained was serious, but he should have responded to treatment by now. I gather the surgeon is puzzled and is keeping a close eye on him."

Nardis took another sip of brandy, his eyes troubled. Barlbent asked, "All right, so what haven't you told me? Things you know? Things you suspect? Come on, man, talk to me. Damn it, this is important."

"Francis, I told you, this is wizards' business. You shouldn't concern yourself with it. You'll only get mixed up in a real mess if you do."

Barlbent shook his head. "No, my friend, it's not just wizards' business. Not when it spills over onto Lady Marissa and Commander McRobbie. If all you wizards wanted to go off and do one another in, I wouldn't bat an eye. Present company excluded, of course. I enjoy throwing darts against you. But when your internal squabbles and wrangling threaten people vital to the security of this kingdom, then it becomes our business. Lord Holman, and the Office of Spies. And me. So don't put me off with this 'wizards' business' bosh. I need to know what's going on, and how to stop it. And you seem to be the fellow who can tell me."

A look of panic spread over the wizard's face. "Me? No, I've said way too much already. My God, if they ever knew I talked to you, that I even knew you..." His voice trailed off as he seemed to contemplate a very brief future.

"No one will hear it from me," Barlbent assured him. He picked up the brandy bottle and splashed more into Nardis's glass. "So what's going on? What's Rhenn up to?"

"I really don't know anything," the wizard said, after taking another healthy sip of the brandy. "But I think he might be planning to make some kind of play to get rid of Foxwent and take over the Council."

"And this would involve Lady Marissa how? He went all the way to Westdale to see her. He tried to compel her to drop everything and go to St. Giles. From what McRobbie's told me, he would have succeeded if not for the dragon's intervention."

Nardis drank more brandy. Which, Barlbent thought, was all to the good if it helped to loosen the man's tongue a bit more. "She's an unknown factor," the wizard finally said. "She supposedly has these tremendous powers, or at least potential. Whichever faction controls her would have her power at their disposal."

"In power," murmured Barlbent, "lies victory."

"Just so."

He grimaced. "And if you can't control power, you deny it to your opponent. Classic tactics. Plays merry hell with the innocent bystanders, of course. But then the innocent rarely factor into consideration in cases like this."

He took a sip of brandy, his mind racing. "So you feel Rhenn would go so far as to murder Lady Marissa if he couldn't control her? In order to keep the other side from using her?"

"Eliminate her," Nardis acknowledged. "That's what Rhenn, the callous old sod, said to Skarlatos. And Sebastien, well, he knew something. He'd been in the archives all night, he told me. He wouldn't say what he'd found out. He just muttered all this tosh about how I'd be safer if I didn't know."

"But it wasn't tosh, was it?" Barlbent pointed out with a grim smile.

"No, I reckon not." Nardis looked up, his eyes suddenly dark with alarm. "You said he was attacked by a man with a knife. And he's not recovering?"

"That's what Commander McRobbie told me."

Nardis squeezed his eyes closed. "Witchbane," he breathed.

Chapter Forty-Seven

"Have you tried to escape?" Lady Sybil sat on a bunk, her leg extended. Her ankle was swollen and turning a ghastly shade of purple. She'd twisted it during the encounter with the Rhuddlani Navy, and now could barely walk.

Marissa considered retorting that they were in the midst of the Thundermist Sea, and just where would she escape to? Rejecting this as rude, she simply said, "No."

"Mmm. I'd thought perhaps you might try using your feminine wiles on that damned pirate."

She looked down at her disheveled dress and ran a hand through hair so tangled it would take a week's worth of brushing to even begin to feel unknotted again. Lady Sybil took in the wreckage, smiled ruefully, and offered, "Perhaps after a bath then?"

"I'm afraid when they were handing out feminine wiles, I was off somewhere reading a book. I don't think I have any."

Lady Sybil gave a little chuckle. It quickly turned into a larger one, and then she was laughing, great galloping guffaws that reverberated off the walls. She laughed until the tears streamed down her face.

"My girl," she said, wiping her eyes, "I see now why Morgan adores you."

She perked up a bit at this. "Does he? I mean, he says so, and I certainly love him, but…"

"Besotted," reported Lady Sybil.

"I'm sure I don't know why. I mean, it just kind of happened."

"Did you ever consider that perhaps he finds you irresistible?"

"Never," Marissa scoffed. "Anyway, we're getting quite off the topic here. Which is, what do we do?"

"Can you use your magic?"

"That blasted pirate dosed me with something to prevent that. He put it in my tea, of all things! I've been thinking it might well be the same stuff used on Sebastien. It's why he's still unconscious and not recovering."

"Pirates!" Lady Sybil's voice held a lifetime's worth of scorn.

"I felt it—the lack of access to my magic—when I was up on

deck during the storm. It was like it never existed."

"Oh." Lady Sybil's voice was flat. "I see. Well—"

Marissa went on, "But here's the funny thing. In the middle of that storm, with the Thundermist and the lightning all around, it felt as if I was being filled with something new. Different. I managed to test it out, discreetly. I could do magic again."

Lady Sybil beamed at her. "There you are, then. So what are you going to do?"

"Right now, I'm going to let you get some rest. Beyond that, I'm not sure. I'll have to think about it. In my, um, stateroom." She grimaced. "Then, we'll see."

Regarding her swollen ankle with a sour expression, Lady Sybil gave a curt nod. "Very well, go and cogitate. I hope you come up with something suitably horrid to do to these blasted pirates. This ankle hurts like the very devil."

Marissa managed the return to her own cabin without incident, despite the occasional lurching of Fanshawe's ship. She'd barely begun to turn over possible courses of action when a staccato rap sounded on the cabin door. Fanshawe's voice came. "May I come in?"

"It's your bloody ship," she muttered in irritation, "I don't see how I can stop you." Aloud, she called, "Yes, Captain, you may enter. At your own risk."

The door swung open, and he entered, bearing a tray. It contained a mug from which little plumes of steam curled appealingly. A small plate of biscuits rested next to it. "Good afternoon," he said.

She had her doubts as to the goodness of the afternoon. However, the pleasant scent of tea suffused the cabin, dissipating her dudgeon. She heaved a sigh which seemed to come from the soles of her feet. And yet… "More witchbane?" she inquired in frozen tones.

"Good God, no," he replied, looking abashed. "Look here, I really didn't know about it being—"

"Something that might kill me?" Marissa favored him with a ferocious glare. Fanshawe actually took a step back. "Oh, give it to me," she said.

He handed her the mug. She inhaled the refreshing fragrance emanating from it. Taking a sip, she said, "Pardon me for asking, but what next?" She helped herself to a biscuit.

The pirate, seeming to have regained some of his former aplomb, cocked a brow. "What do you mean?"

She downed another healthy gulp of tea. If it was laced with more witchbane she couldn't tell and might as well enjoy it for now. She regarded her captor. "I mean, what next? Either your mad plan worked, and your men have scarpered with the dragon's hoard. Assuming there was one. About which, by the way, I have serious doubts. Or else they haven't, and this was all for nothing. Either way, you can't mean to keep me prisoner. So, what do you intend to do with me? And Lady Sybil, of course."

"Um. Can we back up just a moment?" His face had gone pale. "What did you mean about the dragon's hoard?"

She gave the pirate a brilliant smile. "Captain, to the best of my knowledge, Wyvrndell has shown no interest in accumulating any treasure. And since he hasn't been in Caerfaen all that long and has devoted much of his time to tutoring me, I don't know when he would have done so. My logical conclusion is that you have made a serious error in judgment."

"No hoard?" He asked, slumping against the door.

"If you're asking my opinion, no. Not even a tiny one."

"Damn." He ran shaking fingers through his hair. "Well, I reckon I've made a right muck-up of things. Again."

She smiled grimly. "You might say so. You've wagered on a losing hand, Captain. No treasure means your crew isn't going to be very happy with you. Kidnapping me and Lady Sybil will earn you Morgan's enmity. You've gotten on the wrong side of a quite powerful witch. Not to mention Lady Sybil, who I understand has killed her fair share of pirates in the past. And I don't imagine Wyvrndell is going to be particularly pleased with you either."

"Oh, lord…"

"So, Captain, I ask again: what now?"

Fanshawe shuddered. "We're about to set course for Caerfaen," he replied. "When we arrive, my crew will board with the spoils—if there are any—and you and Lady Sybil will be set ashore."

"No."

He stared at her, confusion spreading across his face. "No?" he repeated dully.

She shook her head emphatically, nearly dumping the remnants of the tea. "No. I don't wish to return to Caerfaen. Tell me, Captain, do you know a place called the Perseverance Tower?"

"Um. Yes?"

"Good. Because that's where I need to go. Immediately."

"But why?"

"I was on my way there when you abducted me." Fanshawe opened his mouth to protest, evidently realized the truth of this statement, and closed it so hard his teeth clicked. She went on, "To rescue Morgan."

His eyes widened. "That note you were running on about?"

She nodded. "Someone sent me a message saying if I wanted to see Morgan again, I must come to that tower. I don't know what's going on, but I plan to go find out. So. Will you put me ashore there?"

"I can't," he began. She narrowed her eyes dangerously and he hurried on, "There's no place to land. Those are treacherous waters. But there's a decent cove a couple of miles down the coast. We can anchor there."

She leapt to her feet. "You'll do it? Put me ashore there?"

"Yes, of course, if that's what you really want."

"It is."

He bobbed his head. "There is one condition."

She squeezed her eyes shut then opened them. "How much? And you'll have to trust me for it. I'm afraid I'm a bit short of funds at the moment. Having been kidnapped and all." She glowered.

"What? No, no, I don't want money. Not yours, anyway. What I meant was, I'm not just going to set you ashore alone to face who knows what. I'm coming with you. That's my condition."

Marissa narrowed her eyes, her mind racing. "Why? I'd have thought you'd want to get back to Caerfaen as soon as possible to learn if your scheme bore fruit."

He looked at the floor. "I'm beginning to believe you might be right. About my error in judgment, I mean. No hoard means I've earned all that animus you detailed, with nothing to show for it. This was going to be one last job and done. Instead…"

She bared her teeth in a fierce grin. "Instead you're banking on helping me rescue Morgan to offset things a bit?"

His face reddened slightly, but he nodded. "Got it in one." He looked like a small boy hoping his offering of a somewhat wilted daisy might persuade his mum not to administer a threatened spanking. She threw back her head and laughed.

"Very well, Captain Fanshawe. I accept your offer. I would be grateful for your company."

Chapter Forty-Eight

"Witchbane? What's that?" Barlbent asked. Whatever it was, it didn't sound good.

"Poison." Nardis started to take another sip of brandy, then eyed the glass suspiciously, as if it might contain witchbane. Giving his head a shake, he drained his glass. "Nasty stuff. In lesser amounts, it neutralizes a magic wielder's power. Given in a higher dose, it can be fatal."

Barlbent nodded slowly. "It must have been on the knife. It obviously wasn't a high enough dose to kill him when the knife wound didn't, but still strong enough to keep him from recovering."

Nardis buried his head in his hands. "Poor Sebastien. He stuck his fingers right in the hornet's nest, all right."

"Yes, that may be so. But we still need to do something about the hornets."

Nardis looked up sharply. "What? Francis, what are you suggesting? You can't—"

Barlbent smiled grimly. "Can't I? Wizard or not, Master Rhenn is still subject to the laws of this kingdom. Conspiracy to commit murder is a crime."

"You're going to the Watch? Francis, they won't do anything. These are wizards. They're—" He trailed off under the force of Barlbent's glare.

"They're what? Above the laws of us mere mortals? Perhaps, Nardis. But we can't just sit by and let Rhenn get away with this. We've got to do something!"

Nardis swallowed with an audible gulp. "Um. When you say 'we', are you including me? Because I'd really, really rather not get involved. My life may not be much, but it's the only one I've got, you know."

"You're already involved. You involved yourself when you went to Sebastien to report what you overheard in that cafe."

"See if I ever do something that stupid again," muttered the wizard darkly.

"Yes, yes, it's bloody easy to just ignore things, pretend they never happened. Most people do. But damn it, Nardis, Rhenn plans to use magic to control Lady Marissa and co-opt her power. Even worse, he might murder her to keep anyone else from doing the same. In addition, he more than likely hired someone to kill Sebastien. Are you going to sit idly by and let him do these things?”

“Yes?” Nardis ventured.

Barlbent sighed. “Come on, Nardis, I know better. I’ve played darts with you. I know you. You play to win, but you always play fair. You can’t tell me you’d throw the game. I don’t believe it.”

“Francis, you don’t understand just what—who—you’re up against here. Rhenn is… he’s not like you or me. I mean, yes, I’m a wizard and all, though only a very junior one. But it’s not just that. Rhenn is… he’s obsessed, I suppose.”

Barlbent raised a brow. “How so?”

“With power. Oh, not just magical power, although there are rumors about that as well. But I mean he’s obsessed with the ability to control events, to be the one in charge. It’s what drives him. That, and besting anyone who gets in the way of what he wants. It’s like a game to him, and he plays to win. No matter what.”

“Doesn’t your lot have rules against this sort of thing? I mean, doesn’t the Wizard’s Council have any control of him?”

Nardis scowled. “The Chief Wizard would love to bring him down. But there’s so much infighting amongst the Council that he doesn’t have the support to do it openly. Too many wizards loyal to, or beholden to, Rhenn.”

“Mmm.” Barlbent pondered this intelligence. “So what if we went to the Chief Wizard? Told him what you overheard, what we suspect?”

Nardis shook his head vigorously. “Won’t work. We’ve no proof, Francis. Even assuming Foxwent believed me, it’s my word against Rhenn. And Skarlatos. No, that’s no good.”

“Then tell me what would work. Come on, this is important.”

Nardis’s mouth turned up just a bit at one corner. “More important even than darts?”

“Yes, even more important than darts. What. Can. We. Do?”

“Well, we could try to heal Sebastien.”

Barlbent opened his mouth, closed it again, blinked, and finally spoke. “Well, yes, we could do that.” He rose from his chair, pacing back and forth. “Why didn’t you suggest this a long time ago? I gather there’s an antidote to this poison? Witchbane, was it?”

“Yes, there is. It may be too late, but it’s worth a try.”

“Oh, you think it’s worth a try?” He worked hard to keep the sarcasm out of his tone. “All right, I’m probably going to regret asking, but what's the antidote? Something readily available, I trust?"

Nardis shrugged. "Mandrake root."

Barlbent narrowed his eyes. "And where, might I ask, does one acquire mandrake root? And if you say from a mandrake plant, I shall throw something at you. I'm just warning you now."

Nardis grinned. "Francis, you cheer me. All right, let's go find some mandrake root."

He glanced up at the clock. "Good lord, it's long past midnight."

Nardis shrugged. "Right. I wasn't really thinking. None of the market vendors will be open, and I'm not going to go banging on doors at this time of night. We'll go as soon as the market stalls open in the morning."

Barlbent nodded. "Yes, that seems sensible. All right tell me this. What is 'the wizard's prophecy?'"

"The wizard's prophecy." Nardis drummed his fingers on the table. "Where in the world did you hear of that?"

"Sebastien. He said something about it to Marissa duBerry right after he was attacked. 'Beware the wizard's prophecy.' That was all she was able to get out of him before he lapsed into unconsciousness."

Nardis looked thoughtful. "I wonder if that's what he found in the archives," he said, almost to himself.

"What?"

"Francis, the wizard's prophecy has always been, as far as I've ever heard, just a legend. No one I know has ever seen it. There's no record of it that anyone has been able to find. I know several of my fellow students were searching for it, but they came up empty."

"Like a fairy tale," Barlbent suggested. "It just kind of exists, but no one really knows why?"

"Something like that. Except in this case, it's less 'no one knows why' and more 'because we said so.' It's a bugbear used by senior wizards to keep their juniors in line."

"What do you mean?" He was intrigued by this peek into the inner workings of the Royal College of Wizards.

"Oh, it's just some vague ramblings. No one really believes it. It sounds terribly alarming until you stop and think about it."

"But damn it, what does it say?"

Nardis screwed up his face in an effort of concentration. "Remember, I'm only giving you an approximation. But it's something along the lines of 'When once the raven and serpent unite, then shall the day of the swordsman to be nigh.' Um, what else? Oh, right. 'The ancient tome shall rule again, and all treasure will be as dust.'"

"Good Lord. You're not serious?"

"That's it, or as close as I can remember. But as I said, no one can find any written record of it. It may have gotten a bit garbled along the way."

"A bit garbled? The whole thing sounds garbled to me." Barlbent snorted. "Sounds like the ravings of a wizard who had way too much to drink one night."

Nardis grinned. "Just so. Which is why no one really pays any attention to it. It's just gibberish. 'The raven and the serpent?' The ancient tome?' A lot of us younger chaps feel it's all just moonshine."

"But Sebastien didn't."

The young wizard sobered. "No, if what you say is true, I guess he didn't. I wonder what he learned."

"Hopefully in the morning we'll be able to find out," Barlbent said. "You can bed down here on the settee. I'll bring you a blanket."

"I don't suppose there's any more of this?" Nardis held out his empty glass.

"Good Lord, no. You've practically killed the bottle as it is."

"All right, all right," Nardis said, laughing. "I was only asking."

Chapter Forty-Nine

Aartis stared around the cave. It was, as he had hoped, empty of dragon. It was also empty of anything else. It was especially empty of anything resembling treasure.

"Well, 'e keeps a right tidy cave, ye got t'admit," Aartis said cheerily.

Sharkey uttered a guttural curse and whirled on Aartis. Grabbing the front of his tunic, the pirate growled, "What says you? Where's the bloody gold?"

Aartis broke the other man's grip on his tunic and straightened out the garment. "'ow should I know? I ne'er claimed the dragon had no treasure. I only agreed to lead you lot out here. Yer Mr. Fanshawe was the one as decided there must be treasure 'ere."

The men who'd been following crowded into the cavern, muttering darkly at the marked lack of gold, jewels, and other valuables.

Sharkey appeared to cogitate amid the hubbub. Finally, glaring at Aartis, he said, "Maybe this ain't the right cave. This blighter might have led us astray. Maybe we should tickle him with a bit of steel to see how he answers." He placed a hand on his dagger.

Aartis raised a brow. "Wrong cave? Good Lord, man, can't ye smell ol' dragon's stench?"

"He's right, Mr. Sharkey," offered one of the pirates. "I've heard tell of how the dragon smells. This place purely reeks with it."

"Hmph. I suppose," Sharkey conceded grudgingly. "All right, lads, let's go. Nothin' for us here, is there? Not that I expected anything else." He herded his men out of the cavern. The slanting afternoon sunlight made their shadows caper among the trees as the big man led the way back toward Caerfaen.

Aartis managed to keep near Sharkey, and he seized the opportunity to say, "You ain't surprised by this, are ye, Mr. Sharkey?"

The pirate grunted. "Nah. I reckoned Fanshawe's luck would run out eventually. Don't much matter. This plan didn't work out, but I've got a little backup plan of me own. And I figure all in all it might serve better anyway."

"Ah, now I never figured ye for a man with big idears, Mr. Sharkey. Wha's this wonderful plan?"

"I'm going back to The Mean Ewe."

"Ah, gonna have a pint or two? That don't sound like a bad plan attall. Though not ver' profitable."

Sharkey waved one large hand in dismissal of pints of ale. "Nope. Gonna snatch that barmaid and hold her for ransom."

"What?" Aartis nearly stumbled and had to run to catch up again. He was startled into forgetting he was playing the part of Arn Porter and dropped his accent. "Who's going to pay ransom for a barmaid? That's crazy!"

"Nah, not so crazy. I knows who her father is. And I reckon he'll pay a handsome price to get her back in one piece."

"I thought Fanshawe didn't hold with this kind of thing. No holding girls for ransom and all that."

"Fanshawe may not, but Fanshawe ain't here. Like I said, his luck's run out, and I don't think I'll be going back to the *Mad Maudie*. Gonna strike out on me own, like."

"I see. You do have plans, Mr. Sharkey. And you're a man who's done his research. You have hidden depths, no doubt about it. All right, be forthcoming. Who is this winsome barmaid's father, who'll pay so handsomely for her return?"

Sharkey barked out a harsh laugh. "Ian Taggart."

Aartis managed to keep striding along by Sharkey, but it took every bit of self-control he possessed not to just stop and stare after the man. A cold pit formed in his stomach, sending ice through his veins.

"Ian Taggart?" he cried, grabbing Sharkey's arm and swinging him around so they stood face to face. "Are you mad, man? Fanshawe just wanted to anger a dragon by stealing from him. No big deal. But you? You want to cross Ian Taggart by kidnapping his daughter. Had enough of life, have you?"

Sharkey shook off Aartis's hand contemptuously. "Taggart? He's naught. He'll pay. Oh, he'll pay, all right."

Aartis took a breath to steady himself, then said, "Mr. Sharkey, you're a stranger to Caerfaen, aren't you?"

"Aye. But..."

"Then as someone who knows the lay of the land, as it were, allow me to present you with a bit a free advice. Abandon this idea. This barmaid, if she is indeed Taggart's daughter, is off limits. You touch her at your peril."

"Fooey. I've made my plan, and I'm sticking to it. I don't need your advice. In fact, I don't need you."

"Sorry, I can't let you do this." Aartis delivered a mighty roundhouse punch to Sharkey's jaw.

The blow should have felled the man. It should, Aartis thought wildly, have jolly well felled an ox. Sharkey shook it off as he might an annoying fly. Then the pirate's ham-like fist came up to meet Aartis's chin, and he fell back as if poleaxed. Stars whirled, the sky closed in, and darkness came to claim him.

He fought it. He couldn't afford to succumb to the welcome bliss of oblivion. Shaking his head, he struggled to raise himself from the hard ground. The puddle he'd landed in was seeping into his clothes. It took several attempts before he managed to gain an upright position.

Wiggling his jaw, he decided it wasn't broken. "Although why not," he said aloud, spitting out part of a tooth, "I'll never know." He massaged his aching head and tried to focus. Looking around, he noted a welcome lack of pirates.

Sharkey. Kate. Taggart. "Oh, hell," he muttered, and started to run.

As he pounded through the forest, Aartis had a moment to reflect on what Sharkey had said. Was Kate really Taggart's daughter? It didn't seem possible, and yet… it did make sense, in a bizarre sort of way. Why else would Taggart place so much trust in her? But why hadn't Ian told him?

Because he was trying to protect her, Aartis realized. He probably hadn't told a single soul. That way no one could get to him through the girl.

He wondered how Sharkey had learned of it. Well, it didn't matter. What mattered was stopping him before he did anything to hurt Kate. Because that would kill Taggart, and he couldn't allow that. Ian was his friend.

He shuddered slightly at the realization that he'd been flirting shamelessly with Taggart's daughter. Such a thing might well have earned him a quick trip to the bottom of a cistern, tied to a large rock, if she'd complained to Ian.

Then another thought flitted across his still-scrambled brain. He also had to stop Sharkey before he did anything to hurt Kate because he cared about her.

Good God, had he really thought that?

Yes. Yes, he had. Despite the fact that she was Taggart's daughter, Aartis cared for Kate.

No, not just cared for her. Loved her, damn it!

Love?

Yes, he decided, loved her. Oh, he'd had plenty of feminine companionship. His reputation was built on it. But he'd never offered any sort of commitment, any promises of anything more than an enjoyable evening together.

If he managed to get Kate out of this mess, he was going to become a one-woman man. And Kate was the woman.

He ran faster.

Chapter Fifty

From her spot in the rear of the jolly boat, Marissa glanced back at Fanshawe's ship riding at anchor on the gentle waves several hundred yards offshore.

Sunlight streamed through a light mist which he had assured her was not the precursor to another bout of Thundermist. It suffused the scene with an almost homey glow.

Although she couldn't see Lady Sybil, she could feel the force of her wrath. Not at Marissa, certainly, but at the situation. Her ankle, now swollen to twice its normal size, prevented her from accompanying Marissa and Fanshawe on their rescue mission.

Lady Sybil had been vociferous in her protestations of fitness. Marissa had invited her to climb the ladder up to the main deck.

Using her sword parasol as a cane she managed to hobble down the passageway. The ladder proved too much for her, and she turned back with a snarl.

"All right, damn it, you win," she snapped, thumping back to her cabin. She turned the air blue with curses normally only heard from stevedores and the better class of lumberjacks.

"At least take my sword parasol," she offered when Marissa came to bid her farewell.

"Thank you, but I think not. I'd be more likely to do myself an injury than to make any effective use of it," she had demurred.

And now here she sat, in a tiny boat surrounded by pirates, on her way to some mysterious rendezvous with an unknown adversary in unfamiliar country. With no weapons, no plan, and no idea what was about to happen.

It didn't matter, she reminded herself. The only thing that mattered was Morgan.

She bared her teeth at this thought. The nearest pirate shrank back, wide-eyed, and the jolly boat lurched to one side as he dropped his oar. "Hoy," muttered his mate irritably.

She mellowed her expression to one of benign uninterest, and the startled pirate settled back to his rowing. In another few moments the boat scraped up onto the tiny pebbled beach.

Two men sprang out into the shallows to haul the prow up onto the shore before the waves could carry it back out again. Fanshawe rose, offering her his arm.

Marissa wobbled a bit as she hoisted herself off the seat, gratefully accepting his assistance to exit the boat onto dry—well, relatively dry—land. Water lapped at the soles of her low boots, and she stepped hurriedly further up the beach as one final wave darted in with malicious intent to slop over the tops.

Fanshawe, after conferring briefly with his crew, joined her. "Which way?" she asked as the rowers turned the jolly boat back around for their return to the ship.

"Up," he said, gesturing toward the twenty-foot-high crag that lined the little cove. "We've got to get up to the top of that first. Then we'll head north a bit. Probably a couple of miles or so, if memory serves."

She regarded the cliff. Shaking her head at her own folly, she muttered, "I suppose I asked for this." Aloud to Fanshawe she said brightly, "Very well, Captain, let's be off. Time's wasting. Lead the way."

"Are you sure you want to do this?"

She barked out a harsh laugh. "Want to? Not in the least. This is something I have to do. Not because I have no choice, but because I chose to do it, despite the inherent dangers. Rather like sailing right into the heart of the Thundermist."

He nodded gravely. "I understand."

Their scramble up the cliff was something she would never really remember. She simply closed her eyes at the bottom, and didn't open them again until he announced, "We're up."

She realized she stood only inches from the edge of the precipice and took a hasty step away. And then another. Fanshawe's lips twitched slightly as he asked, "Did all the cursing on the way up really help?"

Marissa raised her chin haughtily. "Yes."

"Brandy?" He held out a small stoppered flask. "You look like you could use it."

"As tempting as it sounds, I'd best not. I've a suspicion I'm going to need every bit of wits I can muster today."

"Suit yourself." He took a quick sip, wiped off the mouth of the flask and proffered it once more. When she shook her head, he stowed it away in a pocket.

"If I might inquire," he said, "just what do you expect to find in this beastly tower? Besides Commander McRobbie, that is."

"I wish I knew. I don't know who, and I've no idea why. All I know is someone wants me here…" A flash of comprehension glinted like fairy gold, elusive and incalculable. "I wonder," she muttered.

"Me too," he agreed. "What?"

But Marissa held up a hand to stem his banter. "I wonder if Wyvrndell's absence is a coincidence. I wonder if whoever lured me out here to the middle of nowhere knew he'd be far away and unable to communicate with me. Because the only reason Headmaster Rhenn wasn't able to overwhelm me with his magic was the dragon. With him gone…"

"…and no one around to help," put in Fanshawe.

"I'd be a much easier target."

"All right, assuming you're right, where does that get you?"

"I don't know." Frustration and fear clouded her voice. Then she stopped and considered. "Perhaps I do. Know your enemy, isn't that what they say? All right, I know Rhenn. I know what he can do, or at least what he has done. And I know how to counter it, thanks to Wyvrndell."

She paced back and forth along the edge of the precipice, looking out at the sea. "Of course, I don't know everything he's capable of. But it's a start."

Fanshawe looked troubled. "I hate to point this out, but if this Rhenn chap went to the risk of kidnapping Commander McRobbie just to lure you here…" He straightened and looked her in the eye. "I'd say he's planning something more than just trying to convince you to attend his academy. Something—"

"Drastic?" she suggested.

"Well, yes, dash it."

"You're probably right." Her eyes hardened as she spoke. "But it doesn't matter. I have to go. I'm Morgan's only hope."

"So you're just going to walk blindly right into a trap?"

She smiled. A bitter smile, tinged with equal parts fury, determination, and hopelessness. "Oh, not blindly." She recalled the fizz of the Thundermist as it had coursed through her during the storm. "Not blindly at all. With my eyes wide open."

He regarded her with a mixture of approval and trepidation. "I hope you know what you're doing. Shall we go?"

She laid a hand on his arm. "Captain Fanshawe, you don't need go any further. Point me in the direction of the tower, and I'll consider any obligation discharged."

"Not a chance," he said. "Miss the opportunity to see you in action?" He quirked a grin. "Against someone other than yours truly? M'lady, for what it's worth, my sword is at your command." Drawing it, he knelt before her, holding the weapon in his outstretched hands. The blade glinted in the sunlight.

For once, she found herself speechless. Finally she recovered enough to murmur, "Nicely done, Captain. Arise, and let's go storm the tower."

Chapter Fifty-One

"I don't know, Francis," Nardis said. His voice was tinged with disgust. "I wouldn't have thought it would be this blasted difficult to find a bit of mandrake root."

They'd explored the narrow, twisted back alleyways of the bazaar, where the purveyors of stolen goods, magical items, and other ephemera lurked. They'd gone from booth to stall, always met with head shakes, glares, or simply stony silence.

"There certainly doesn't seem to be any abundance of it," Barlbent agreed. "Shall we try down here?" He gestured to another alleyway lined with stalls and shops. Nardis shrugged, but followed.

In the fourth stall, as their hopes dwindled to naught, a wizened old crone with a face like a year-old apple had allowed that, "Yes, dearie, I've a bit of mandrake."

Barlbent felt a thrill, even stronger than when he scored a bullseye at darts, course through him at her words.

"Show me," Nardis demanded.

"Fresh this week," she cackled as the young wizard examined the root. Barlbent noticed his companion shake his head slightly at this declaration, but he seemed satisfied. Since he had no notion if age affected the efficacy of the mandrake root, and since a root in the hand was better than nothing, Barlbent wasn't in a position to question.

He also had no notion of the going rate for mandrake root, so her price of six shillings tuppence seemed reasonable. He did manage to bargain her down to six shillings flat, but that was just for form's sake. One didn't strike a bargain here without a bit of rudimentary haggling. But when the old woman adamantly refused to part with the mandrake unless he took a guaranteed love potion, Barlbent found his patience wearing thin. Thrusting a crown into her outstretched palm he grabbed both mandrake and potion and fled, Nardis in tow. As he led them back through the maze, he could hear her calling, "Just you drink up that potion, dearie, and come back to see me." He blanched and hurried on, Nardis chuckling in his wake.

Barlbent set his course for Queen Street, where Lady Marissa maintained her townhouse. He walked swiftly now, eager to put the marketplace well behind them, and to set in motion the preparation of the antidote for Sebastien.

His shudders continued all the way to Lady Marissa's townhouse.

~ * ~

Aartis stumbled out of the forest, puffing hard, heading toward the East Gate of Caerfaen.

He'd thought himself pretty fit, but the evidence seemed to weigh against it. His legs wobbled, his lungs burned, and his head pounded abominably. He pressed doggedly on.

Reaching the gate, he halted before the guards, gasping for breath. One of the sentries, evidently of a slightly more curious nature than his companion, inquired, "What's been chasin' you?"

Aartis shook his head, still puffing hard. Finally he recovered enough to ask, "Did a large group of men come by here recently? Led by a big brute of a fellow?"

The curious one considered. "Yep. Not so long ago. If ya hurry, ya might catch 'em."

Aartis just nodded and set off again at a trot. He still had a good way to go to reach The Mean Ewe, but at least Sharkey didn't have too much of a head start. And Aartis knew the city intimately. If he could keep up a brisk pace, he had a chance of getting there ahead of the pirate. Be waiting for him…

Setting his mouth in a grim smile that soon turned into a grimace, he ran.

If there was a record for crossing the city from East Gate to the docks, he figured he'd broken it. He only hoped he was in time. Sharkey didn't seem like one to waste time. The Mean Ewe was dead ahead as he rounded the last corner. Instead of the normal raucous hubbub which normally emanated from the tavern, the Ewe seemed strangely silent.

"Oh, hell," Aartis muttered. "I'm too late." With a final burst of speed, he crashed through the door, entering into a surreal tableau.

The patrons of the Ewe seemed practically frozen in place. No one spoke, no one moved. They all just stared.

Sharkey, his back to the room, loomed menacingly over Kate. She stood defiantly before him. "Yer comin' with me," he was saying.

She gave him a look mixed with incredulity and disdain. "I'm not going anywhere. I've a bar to run. And, no offense, but you're just not my type."

He beckoned with one hand. "Make it easy on yerself. Come along quiet like and ya won't get hurt."

"Sharkey!" Aartis yelled from across the room, just as Kate flung the contents of the two tankards she held at the big man's face.

Sharkey whirled at Aartis's yell, and the ale soaked his back instead of his face. He didn't seem to notice. His beady eyes were focused on Aartis. He didn't look pleased to see him.

"You again," he snarled.

"Me again," Aartis agreed cheerfully. "Just a bad penny, always turning up when least wanted."

"A'right, let's finish this," the pirate said. He pulled a long dagger from his belt. The watching crowd gave a collective gasp.

"Let's." Aartis produced a knife of his own from its place of concealment at the small of his back. Sharkey's mouth creased into an evil grin.

"Aartis, no!" cried Kate.

Sharkey pulled up short. "Aartis? Thought yer name was Arn?"

"My name," Aartis said quietly, and with a good deal more confidence than he actually felt, "is fate."

Sharkey shrugged. "Name's gonna be 'dead'," he advised, moving toward Aartis with his knife hand extended.

Aartis circled but was immediately cut off by a table that had placed itself unhelpfully in his path. Sharkey's laugh echoed off the rafters.

In a perfect world, Aartis thought wildly, the table would be just right for grabbing by a leg and crashing down on Sharkey's head. In the world he unfortunately inhabited, the table was solid oak, weighed about five hundred pounds, and would take three men and a mule to budge. He dodged around it.

The onlookers had migrated back along the walls, out of the arena of combat. Over the sound of the blood rushing in his ears, Aartis could hear wagers being laid on. The smart money, it seemed, was on Sharkey. Aartis was too busy figuring out how to stay alive to resent it.

Out of the corner of his eye he spotted another table lurking, ready to reach out a leg and trip him up. Or at least halt his circuitous progress around the room as he attempted to keep out reach of Sharkey's forays with the dagger. Sharkey saw it as well and, evidently realizing this was his best chance, came on in a crouching rush.

Aartis saw no sensible reason to just stand there and be skewered. Since the table was there anyway, he hopped onto a chair and then up to the table's top, sending tankards cascading to the floor along with a flood of spilled ale right into the pirate's path. As Sharkey hurtled toward him, unable to stop on the ale-sodden floor, Aartis used the pirate's momentum, along with a hearty boot to the back of the head, to send him crashing into the bar. When the pirate turned to focus on Aartis, his expression was murderous.

Which was, Aartis figured, all to his own advantage. His opponent's judgment would be clouded by his rage, giving Aartis an edge he desperately needed. He was outclassed in bulk, reach, and cutlery. His only advantages were in speed and clarity of thought.

Sharkey came charging in again, uttering a bloodcurdling roar like some primeval forest beast. Aartis managed to dodge sideways this time, but not quite far enough. Sharkey's long knife scored a slice across his left shoulder.

The wound wasn't severe, but it stung like blazes, and was bleeding freely. There was no time to staunch it. Gritting his teeth, Aartis readied himself for the next onslaught. He needed to end this little game, and quickly.

Sharkey, knife held high for a downward slash, came rumbling in like a dung wagon. Aartis dived toward the floor to the pirate's left—the side away from the knife—and rolled as Sharkey tried to stop his rush and come about. As the big man went by, Aartis's knife flashed, catching his leg just behind the knee. Sharkey went down like a felled tree, bellowing in agony and rage. The pirate lashed out with his knife hand; Aartis slithered hastily out of range.

Sharkey's bellows were abruptly silenced. Kate appeared, fire in her eye and her stout cudgel in her hand. She brought it down with a satisfying thump on the pirate's head, and he slumped down with a contented sigh.

"Are you all right?" she asked. Aartis could see the anger and concern in her face.

He pushed himself slowly up off the sticky floor, giving her a grin. "'Tis just a scratch," he said.

Her gaze took in the spreading stain of blood on his jacket. Rolling her eyes, she gestured for him to follow. "Come on, conquering hero. Let's get you patched up before you add more blood to the mess in here." She shook her head. "Good lord, what a wreck. Donal!" She summoned the barman, a short, stout, fatherly-looking fellow. "Get some constables in here to take this"— she aimed her cudgel at the fallen pirate— "somewhere uncomfortable. And then start cleaning up."

"Aye, Miss Kate," the barman acknowledged. "All right, you lot, get out," he said, chivying the patrons toward the door. "The Ewe is closed for repairs."

She started off again, then paused as she realized Aartis was still just standing there. "Are you coming?" she demanded.

He shook himself into motion. "I'm coming. We need to talk."

As she led the way back to her room, he heard her mutter, "Oh, God."

Chapter Fifty-Two

Gasping, desperate to suck air into her tortured lungs, Marissa flung herself up the tower's last few steps. Now, at the highest level, she stood before the door to the tower's chamber.

As doors went, this one wasn't particularly impressive. No carved figures or inset panels. Its one virtue was of solidity. As she slumped against it, panting, she felt for the latch.

It turned smoothly enough, but the door stubbornly refused to open. Locked, blast it. And no mat under which the key might hide.

She glared at the door even as fatigue and frustration threatened to overwhelm her. She shook them off. There was no time. She gathered her will, the magical forces deep within. The ones she still had no idea how to control. But she remembered what she'd had to do, what seemed like a lifetime ago, when she and Sebastien had been trapped in the portal at the cathedral.

Narrowing her eyes, she hurled raw, untamed power at the door.

The door didn't just open. It exploded inward, splintering into a million pieces, the hammer-blow force of the spell deafening in the little alcove. Marissa cried out in agony, clapping her hands to her ears in a futile effort to prevent her head from suffering the same fate as the door.

"Oh," she said. Her voice came out raspy. She cleared her throat and tried again. "Oh. My."

She could hear the sound of feet on the stairs below, but there was no time to wait for Fanshawe. She had to find Morgan. She stepped through the shattered doorway and into the tower room.

She was up above the clouds here, the turret bathed in brilliant sunshine. Marissa didn't even care to speculate how high she was. She'd never been good at heights. Even climbing a tall tree when she'd been a girl had resulted in terrible dizziness. She'd had to beg her father to clamber up the tree and carry her back down again.

Large windows, inset with glass in a myriad of colors like those of a cathedral, were set into the rounded walls, shedding rainbows onto the floor. It was…lovely.

Or at least, it was until she saw the room's occupant.

Morgan lay motionless on a stone table that resembled nothing so much as an altar. Black cords bound his arms and legs to the stone.

More wrapped around his torso. Another twined around his throat.

"Oh, God. Morgan!" she cried. But some tiny inner voice cautioned her against rushing to him.

"Go to him," crooned a voice.

She whirled, looking wildly around.

A dark-haired woman stepped out of an alcove where she had obviously been waiting. "Go to him, take him in your arms."

Her voice was almost like that of a child reciting a nursery rhyme. Marissa took a hesitant step toward where Morgan lay motionless, her gaze flitting between him and the strange woman.

"Who are you?" she asked. "Why are you doing this?"

The woman glared with such a fury Marissa took an involuntary step back, as if from a physical blow.

"I've been waiting for you. You've taken much too long to get here."

"I got here as soon as I could," Marissa protested. Then, recalling the situation, said, "Never mind that. What is going on here?"

"Go to him," the woman repeated, and Marissa saw that her eyes were clouded by something that might have been fury or madness. Or both. "Embrace him and be done with it."

Marissa swallowed hard. This strange woman wanted her to touch Morgan? Why? Why lure her here just for this? There had to be some diabolical reason, some trap...

"Why don't you touch him?" she asked.

This evidently was the wrong question. The madwoman dashed at her, catching both Marissa's arms in her grasp. She struggled, but the woman's grip was like iron shackles. Slowly, inexorably, the woman began to drag her toward the stone altar where Morgan lay.

Cold fear warred with hot rage. She kicked wildly, hoping to land a blow on her captor's shin and force her to release her grip. The woman stepped out of the way of the kick, even as her hands tightened harder around Marissa's arms.

"Rhenn," yelled the woman. "Subdue her."

Rhenn? Marissa looked behind her as Augustus Rhenn stepped into the chamber. He lifted a languid hand, splaying his fingers. She could practically see the power emanating from him. The woman was pulling on her arm again, trying to drag her toward where Morgan lay. *On a bier? Was he dead?*

Rhenn's teeth bared in a wolfish smile as he prepared to launch a spell at Marissa. He never saw the flicker of movement behind him.

Fanshawe said, "Don't move, wizard. Don't breathe. Don't even think."

All motion in the tower stopped. No one breathed. A sudden gleam of steel, reflecting the rainbows of the window, had appeared across Rhenn's throat. The wizard froze as Fanshawe went on almost conversationally, "You may be thinking you're faster than I. That you can loose a spell before I can slit your throat. And you know, you might be right." He shrugged, and the edge of the blade drew a tiny red line across the wizard's exposed throat. "But then again, you might not be quite fast enough. Are you willing to take that chance?"

Rhenn sighed and lowered his hand.

A cry of fury erupted from the strange woman. With renewed strength she began shoving Marissa toward Morgan. "Touch him, damn you!" she screamed.

Eyes wide with fear, Marissa fought against her. It was like trying to hold off a mountain rockslide with a gardener's trowel. Inexorably, she was forced closer, ever closer to where Morgan lay.

"Why are you doing this?" Marissa wailed.

"Did Morgan never tell you?" The woman's voice was raspy with strain. "Tell you of Kiara, his first love? The one who adored him beyond all reason. The one he cast aside like an unwanted dog?"

"No," Marissa managed to choke out as she struggled to keep this crazy woman from dragging her closer to him. "He never mentioned you."

"Then he never told you how, once I found love again and married, he killed my Jermaine? Killed him mercilessly in battle?"

Marissa found herself suddenly overwhelmed by emotion. If this woman was mad, she had earned it. "You poor thing," she said.

Kiara dragged her closer to the bier. "I need no pity, no kind words from you. I need vengeance. And I will have it. Just as he destroyed my world, now I will destroy his. He will watch you die."

"Watch—? Wait, he's alive?" Marissa's heart leapt within her suddenly too-tight chest. He wasn't dead. There was still hope. If she could manage to get him away from whatever this woman had planned.

The words of Elthebesa rang through her mind, almost as if written in the air in fiery letters. "To save what you love, you will have to choose what you are to be."

Choose what you are to be. Choose what you are to be. The words echoed in her brain, and then suddenly her path was clear. "I choose," Marissa said through gritted teeth. "I choose to be what I am. To wield my magic. *Lluminas accadio!*"

It was the only spell she could recall in the heat of the moment. It was a silly, pointless spell. But she put all her will and focus into it.

The ball of light bloomed in her hand like a fire-flower. Kiara gasped, her grip loosening for an instant. It was enough. Marissa yanked her arms free, spinning away from where Morgan lay. Fanshawe and Rhenn stood stock still as statues, frozen into place. If Fanshawe relaxed his guard even for the briefest moment, the wizard would be free to cast some killing spell. There would be no help from that quarter.

Marissa, panting and gasping, straightened to face the other woman, her eyes blazing like the ball of magical light in her hand. She prepared to hurl the little ball of light at Kiara. But in her fury, as she pulled her arm back to throw it, the light of her spell began to change.

Marissa stared in shocked amazement as the ball of light began to elongate, stretching out into a long line of near-flame. The line morphed again, so swiftly her eyes could barely follow it. In another instant she held not a ball of light, but a sword of fire.

Kiara's eyes widened as the sword flared crimson in Marissa's hand, and she flinched away.

Marissa's mouth tightened into a grim smile. "Yes," she said softly, raising her other hand, palm up in a gesture of acceptance. "I will become the witch I was meant to be. And you…" she returned her gaze to Kiara, who shrank back toward where Morgan lay prone on the bier. Morgan, who still lived, and could be freed of whatever foul spell these fiends had laid on him. "You have dared to cross me?"

Marissa brandished the sword. Its edges flickered like flame, although the hilt didn't feel hot to her hand. But she knew instinctively this was no illusion. It was a true weapon, capable of injuring, even killing. If she so chose.

"I-I wanted him to suffer, as I have suffered. To know the pain of infinite loss. I—" Kiara choked back a sob. Then she raised her eyes to meet Marissa's. "I have lost, yet again," she said, and to Marissa she seemed to bear the weight of eternity. "It is over. Kill me." Kiara stepped toward her, chin raised in defiance, her eyes steady, hard, and cold with resolve.

Marissa sighed and lowered the sword. "No." She forced the word out. "Even after all you have done, all you have caused to happen, it is not for me to take your life. You will be taken back to Caerfaen. There you will answer to the king's justice. I pray for your sake he will be merciful."

"Mercy?" spat Kiara. "I care not for your mercy, or your king's either. It is death I seek. Death which calls me to its endless embrace."

Before Marissa could move, Kiara whirled, placing her hands on Morgan's prostrate body. As the spell laid on the enchanted knight took her, she froze. A rictus of horror spread across her face. Then she sank bonelessly down to the stone floor and was still.

There was a sharp, strangled sound from Fanshawe. Marissa spun to see Rhenn, a look of triumph on his face, standing over the fallen pirate.

"You!" hissed Marissa as he turned toward her, his long thin fingers moving in the beginning of some deadly arcane spell. "To her I showed mercy, for she was driven to madness by her grief. But you, who are supposed to be of a higher order, you took advantage of her madness to further your own ends."

Rhenn smiled, but his expression held no humor. It was the smile of a predator about to seize its prey. "Just as you say," he said agreeably, and released his spell.

A sense of calm washed over her. Everything was suddenly moving unbelievably slowly, as if the entire world, or at least her little bit of it, was coated in treacle. He loosed his spell, and she raised her fiery sword. It flared into a blinding brightness, deflecting the energy the wizard had sent toward her. He narrowed his eyes.

"And your plans included eliminating Morgan and me," she went on conversationally, though she glanced sidewise at the sword of fire. Could she keep this up? Rhenn was an exceptionally powerful and competent wizard. She was simply a novice witch with no experience, especially in a contest like this. All she had were fear and rage to bolster her defenses.

Still she went on, goading him, hoping to throw him off balance. "Your designs have failed. Release Morgan from this vile enchantment. Leave this place before I smite you."

Rhenn laughed. "Smite me? With that?" He gave a contemptuous wave at her flaming sword. "I think not." He uttered another spell and sent it hurtling her way.

Marissa managed to deflect the energy of his magic again, but the strength of the spell sent her stumbling back.

He scowled. She tried to quiet the trembling in her limbs as she prepared for his next onslaught. *How long can I hold out?* The wizard had years of experience and undoubtedly a deadly arsenal of spells to wear her down with. It would only be a matter of time until the inevitable.

He launched another spell, and she swung the magical sword wildly. It deflected his magic again, but she could feel herself weakening. The sword was not nearly as bright as it had been, its flames fading more to embers.

"Bah. It's time to end this, witch. You may be the one the prophecy warns of. It doesn't matter. It won't save you. You and your knight will be together soon enough, in the eternal sleep of death."

Driven back by the force of his spell, Marissa found her back literally to the wall. She barely managed to deflect the next one, sending it caroming into the tower's wall. The energy of the blast melted a good-sized hole in the stone, letting in a shaft of light that fell on Morgan.

"To save what you love, you will have to choose what you are to be." Elbethesba's words rang in her head once more. Well, she had chosen. If she had to join him in death, so be it. But she wouldn't go without a fight.

"Hmmph!" grumped the wizard. "Enough. The time for play is over." With that he sent a jagged bolt of magical energy flying at her.

She squared her shoulders, swinging her fiery blade to deflect the spell once more. But this, she realized, would be the final time. Her strength was ebbing fast. She wouldn't be able to hold off Rhenn's attack again.

Instead of sending the deadly energy of his killing spell harmlessly to one side, her blade met it head on. The energy of the spell rebounded, hurtling directly back at the wizard. Overconfident in his own strength and ability to breach her defenses, he had relaxed his guard. He had no chance to dodge.

His own spell struck him dead center. Dead being the operative word, she thought wildly. Rhenn's eyes widened in horrified knowledge of his failure, his mouth forming a silent "O" as the spell worked its deadly magic.

He stiffened. "Well played," he managed to murmur. Then, with a gurgling gasp, he began to…evaporate.

That was really the only word for what happened, she thought. His robes fluttered to the floor, empty. His staff toppled across them.

"Well," she said, regarding the fiery sword. "I certainly didn't expect that." She released the energy of her own spell. The flaming sword dissolved, leaving her standing with an outstretched hand.

She hadn't expected to be surrounded by bodies, either. Kiara. Fanshawe. Rhenn's empty robes. Morgan…

Morgan! With a cry she dashed to where he lay. She didn't touch him—she wasn't sure if it was safe to do so—but by leaning close, she could just make out the gentle rise and fall of his chest as he breathed. Not dead, then. In fact, his eyes were open, staring at her. Could he see her? He didn't move, nor did he speak.

"Bother!" she exclaimed. "What in heaven's name do I do now?" Looking desperately around for some clue, some guidance as to how to release Morgan from whatever remained of the spell which bound him, she saw… nothing. There would be no help for her, or Morgan, in this blasted tower.

"Wyvrndell?" she called, hoping against hope the dragon had

returned from wherever he'd been gallivanting instead of coming to the aid of the needy. If she could reach the dragon, perhaps he could fly to her aid and bear Morgan back to Caerfaen, where Sebastien or someone might remove the enchantment.

"Wyvrndell!" Marissa's inner voice was sharp and shrill, on the edge of hysteria. But no answer came. She was alone.

All alone, surrounded by Rhenn's victims, with no one to help her. She didn't know what to do. Damn it, what was the point of being a powerful witch, the witch all these prophecies spoke of, if she couldn't do what was needed in a time of crisis? For all she knew, Morgan might even now be slipping away into some horrid trance from which he might never be recalled.

"Wyvrndell!" she screamed.

Nothing. Only the wind, whistling through the hole she managed to blast in the tower wall. It moaned like a soul in torment. It… Marissa whirled around.

"Ohhhhh, God," came the raspy voice of Tobias Fanshawe.

Chapter Fifty-Three

"So," said Kate as she deftly cut off the arm of Aartis's jacket and snipped at the sleeve of his tunic. "Would you care to tell me what in the world that was all about?"

Aartis winced as the fabric, which was stuck firmly to his wound, pulled away. The cut began to bleed once more, and Kate used the remnants of the tunic to stop the flow. "Mmm," she said, pulling away the cloth again to examine the cut. "I think you'll live to brawl another day. It's a nasty slice, but nothing that won't heal up, given time." She began to bandage his wound. "All right, tell me."

"The jolly gentleman you just encountered," he said, "is Mr. Sharkey. Doubtless you've seen him in here before with the rest of the pirates. He's Fanshawe's first mate, and evidently a man of both ideas and initiative. We'll get to him in a moment. First, allow me to bring you up to date on recent events as experienced by your correspondent. Until now I've been under the watchful eye of Mr. Sharkey, and unable to let you know what was happening."

"Oh, I wasn't worried," Kate replied with an airy wave. But she could see Aartis, watching her eyes, stifle a smile. It was really rather endearing of him.

With the air of a new recruit reciting a report to his sergeant, Aartis gave her a précis of Fanshawe's scheme and its disappointing (if you were a pirate) outcome.

"Robbing the bloody dragon?" She gaped in wonder. "He must be mad."

He shrugged. "It would have worked, except there was no treasure to be had. The pirates, who I must point out are not nearly as clean and tidy as advertised, were not on the whole a happy lot. But here's the nub of the thing. Your friend Mr. Sharkey had a plan held in reserve. His plan was to kidnap you and hold you for a nice fat ransom."

"Me?" She was thunderstruck. "But no one—"

"Mr. Sharkey," he went on doggedly, "was quite convinced your father would come across with a goodly sum to get you back safe and sound."

"My father? But…" She didn't like the sound of this. Not one bit.

"He was quite certain of his facts," Aartis said, his expression bland.

"No," she whispered. "He couldn't."

"Couldn't he, Miss Taggart?"

Kate buried her head in her hands. She suddenly felt as if her entire world was crumbling into a little heap. "He—he told you?"

"He did. And I have to admit, at first I thought him as crazy as Fanshawe. But the more I considered it, the more I realized it made all manner of sense."

"Oh, God," she moaned. "Nooo."

"I also realized Sharkey was right. Ian Taggart would pay any price to keep his daughter safe."

Kate sat up, gave an extremely unladylike sniff, and wiped her eyes. She wasn't crying. Not really. It was just…strain. That was it, strain. "I don't like where this is going," she said. "Not one bit."

"Neither did I when Sharkey told me," he replied. "I tried to dissuade him, but he was rather adamant. Forcefully so, in point of fact." He smiled, displaying a broken tooth.

She stared into his eyes, not wanting to ask the next question, but knowing she had to. "Did you try to dissuade him," she asked, "so you could use that knowledge yourself?"

His head jerked around so fast she was surprised it didn't just keep going and fly right across the room. He narrowed his eyes. "That hurts, Kate. No, not from any ulterior motives of my own. No, I dragged myself out of the forest and across the city to stop Sharkey for only one reason. You."

She stared at him, her eyes wide.

He went on. "Whatever Mr. Sharkey may lack in subtlety and a certain spirit of comradery, he more than makes up for in oomph and ugly. But did this daunt our noble hero? No, not at all. Recovering from Sharkey's tender ministration out amongst the trees, he sped through the city, determined to save the girl he loved from—"

"What?" Kate's mouth dropped open. "Did you just say what I thought you said?"

"Um, which bit? Ugly brute? Noble hero? Valiant rescue?"

"Umm. The bit about love."

"Damn it, that part slipped out, did it? I'd rather hoped I'd just imagined saying it."

"It did. And you can't. Love me, that is."

"That's just what I kept telling myself, ever since the first moment I laid eyes on you. Unfortunately, I don't seem to be very convincing. Because despite my best arguments, I still seem to be quite firmly in love with you."

He spread his hands, then winced again, the wound no doubt making its presence known once more.

"Nooo," Kate groaned, letting her head fall back into her hands. "No, Aartis, you can't. Forget it. Forget me. Now that this pirate business is over, you can just go back to being dashing Captain Poldane and capturing the fancy of all the ladies at court."

"I know I'm not worthy," Aartis went on, as if she hadn't spoken. "But there's only one lady whose fancy I wish to capture, and you are her. She. Whatever."

She had to stop this. Make him see it wasn't possible. "You, not worthy of me? That knock on the head must have scrambled what little brains you possessed in the first place. You're not thinking right. It's me who's not worthy. I'm the daughter of the man who controls most of the crime in Caerfaen. You're a knight, a man of honor. You don't want to be dragged down into the muck of my world. Go back to the Legion, and forget you ever met me."

He reached out his hands, grasping hers. "Kate," he said softly.

Her name sounded almost like a caress on his lips. His hands felt wonderful, strong and comforting. She pulled away.

"No! You're just letting a passing fancy run away with you. I won't allow you to throw away your career and your good name."

He barked out a laugh. "My good name? Tell me another one. You know my reputation. And I'll be the first to admit I've earned it. So actually, when you think about it, marrying you might go a long way toward making an honest man out of me."

With a rising sense of dread, she held up a hand to stop the flow of his words. This wasn't going the way she hoped. At all. "Marrying me?" she demanded incredulously. "Who said anything about marrying? I thought you just wanted…" she trailed off, unable to speak.

"I know, I know," he said, capturing her hands again. "I'm progressing a bit fast here. Let's just leave it for now at 'I love you, Kate'. The rest can come later. You know," he said thoughtfully, "you said yourself no one really knows who you are. You've made yourself into a successful woman. Why should your father even enter into the thing?"

"Because, for all his sins, he's still my father. I can't change that. And I won't run from it, either. I can't change who I am, Aartis. So thank you, but…"

"But Kate," he protested. "You've already changed who you are."

She bristled. "I've done nothing of the sort."

"You told me you own this place. And others as well. Do you

own them? Or does Ian?”

“What does that have to do with anything?” Her bristles sprouted bristles. “Dad loaned me enough to buy the Ewe. I’ve since paid it back, in full and with interest. Neither of us would have had it any other way. As for the rest, everything else was done completely on my own.”

“That’s what I mean,” Aartis said with a maddening smile. “You did it all, made yourself into what you are today. Not because you’re Ian’s daughter, but in spite of it.”

“Hmmph. All right, I suppose I have, at that. But it doesn’t change the fact. You can’t be in love with me. Can’t marry me, even if I wanted to.”

“Do you?” His voice was suddenly breathless at her words.

“Do I what? Want to marry you? I— Aartis, I don’t know. Yes, you’re handsome, and charming, and entertaining, but so is Donal’s parakeet. I don’t think I’d marry him either. Besides, this is all a bit sudden, you have to admit. I mean, you just dash in, save me from that ghastly pirate, and expect to just carry me off on your white horse…”

“He’s black.”

Kate took a breath, glared at him, and ignored this commentary on the coloring of equines. “And think I’ll agree to marry you. Aartis, a girl, even one like me, likes to be wooed, at least a little bit. And then there’s still my father. Whether you want to accept it or not, he’s part of the package.”

“Well, all right, but does he have to come along on the honeymoon?”

She sent her eyes rolling heavenward. “How many times do I have to say this? There is not going to be any honeymoon. Marrying you is not an option at the moment. At the moment, all I want to do is throw the flower pot at you.”

His face fell. “I’m sorry, Kate. I’ll go.”

“Good.”

“But I won’t let this be the end of it. Wooing, eh?” He brightened. “That sounds like it might be fun.”

“Good.”

“What?” He whirled to face her, hope dancing up in his eyes.

“Go! I said go. That’s all, just… go.”

“Right.” There was that maddening, dazzling smile again, the one that made her heart do strange fandangos. Treacherous heart. “I know what I heard.” One hand on the door latch, he sketched an elegant bow. “Miss Taggart, prepare to be wooed.”

She threw the cushion at him as he fled. But even if her eyes were suspiciously moist, she found her mouth turning up unaccountably at the corners.

"Idiot," she muttered. And wasn't at all sure if she was referring to Aartis, or herself.

Chapter Fifty-Four

Marissa stared. Fanshawe stared back, blinking wildly as if to clear his vision.

Hauling himself up on one arm, he surveyed the carnage. "Pardon my language," he croaked, "but what the hell just happened here?"

"Oh, Captain Fanshawe, I am glad you're still alive."

"That," Toby said, staggering to his feet, "bloody well makes two of us."

"I promise I'll tell you all about it later, in exquisitely gory detail. Right now, however, I need your help. Morgan is alive. We've got to get him out of this dreadful place and back to Caerfaen."

Bracing himself on the wall, Toby shook his head like a fighter who's taken a stunning blow. "Just give me half a moment to find my feet," he said. He shot a glance at McRobbie. "Do you think it's safe to, um, touch him now?"

Apparently she'd been considering this very point. When she spoke, it was with considerably more confidence than he suspected she really felt. "I believe so. I think the trap was sprung when that madwoman touched him herself. I can't believe it would work more than once."

"Hmm. That's a heap of supposition, isn't it? Begging your pardon, of course, but..." He shrugged. "Still, you've been pretty spot-on thus far, so I reckon we might as well try." He moved to McRobbie's prostrate form.

She neatly blocked him. "No, Captain Fanshawe. I claim first touch. Just in case I'm wrong. If that foul enchantment is still on him, better it be me than you."

"As you wish, m'lady," he replied. "I hope you know what you're doing."

"Of course I do. I'm a witch, aren't I?"

His only response was a smile. He was glad she judiciously ignored its implication. Turning to McRobbie, she bent and kissed his lips. Hard. With every ounce passion she possessed, as if willing him whole again. Toby discreetly studied the ceiling.

Nothing happened.

Good lord, that kiss should have roused a dead man, he thought with keen appreciation. Someday perhaps he'd find a girl who would kiss him like that. Although, he admitted, if somewhat uncharitably, pirates didn't often get kissed at all. Perhaps that's why they were so blasted pirate-y.

But that was all beside the point. Something best left for consideration at another time and place. Right now they needed to get away from this tower of death and despair. "No, um, ill effects?" he queried.

"No ill effects," she reported, staring down at McRobbie.

Toby retrieved his knife from where he dropped it when that blasted wizard had zapped him. He cut the cords binding McRobbie to the stone alter, sheathed the blade, and hoisted the unconscious man into a sailor's carry with a muffled, "Whoof."

It took over an hour to reach the base of the winding stone stairs and stagger out into the blissful afternoon sun. He'd had to stop several times to reposition his cargo, which kept slipping in a most unobliging way. And to catch his breath.

Toby laid McRobbie on the ground, plopped down next to him, and wiped sweat from his brow. "He's not an overly large man," he observed, "but he certainly is solid."

"So are you, Captain Fanshawe," Lady Marissa said. "Solid indeed. My thanks."

Toby shrugged. "A man does what needs doing,"

"*Sicut necessitas postulate*," she replied. "As needs must. That's the McRobbie family motto. I gather it gets them into all manner of difficulties." She flashed him a weary smile. "Like this."

Toby looked around rather than at Lady Marissa, to mask his blush. And with a sinking feeling, he said, "I hate to be the one to bring up tiresome questions when you've just snatched victory from death's jaws. But do you have any idea how we're going to get out of here?"

Her mouth pursed in an expression of extreme annoyance. "Well, I certainly can't well ask you to bear Morgan any further. I can see you're about played out as it is."

"Oh, I can probably—" Toby began manfully. But she wasn't listening. Her attention was drawn to something else, a discordant noise, just on the edge of hearing.

"Bells," she breathed.

Toby gestured in helpless confusion.

Lady Marissa's face broke into a broad grin. "The Tzigani," she said, and laughed exuberantly. "The Tzigani are coming."

So they were. The sound of the bells grew louder. In a few

moments, he could hear singing, and men's voices calling orders. A wagon rolled out of the trees and into the clearing.

Lady Marissa straightened her skirts and strode eagerly toward the wagon. "Greetings," she called, "and well met. My good fortune has not deserted me, for in my time of need, you appear."

A swarthy Tzigani in striped trousers, a flowing crimson tunic, and sporting a magnificent moustache, reined in his mount before her. He bowed from the saddle.

"My compliments, Lady Witch," he said, grinning broadly. "It would be an honor to render what aid we may."

Toby watched agog as more and more wagons, horses, and Tzigani poured into the clearing. One of the wagons contained a cage housing a huge brute of a bear. The Tzigani all greeted Lady Marissa with respect and, in some cases, seeming fondness.

Finally, the last wagon halted. A tall, striking woman with a crown of red-gold hair leapt down and embraced Lady Marissa, kissing her on each cheek. "You have made your choice, eh?" she said, gazing into Lady Marissa's eyes.

"I have indeed. I have chosen to embrace what I am. I have used what I have to save what I love, as you foretold."

The woman nodded slowly. "I see. Tell me." She took Lady Marissa's hand in hers, heading her across to where Toby stood watch over Morgan McRobbie.

At the Tzigani's urging, Lady Marissa launched into an abbreviated account of their adventures. She left out, Toby noted with no little surprise, his role as pirate and kidnapper. Instead she extolled his stalwart efforts on her behalf in her quest to rescue her beloved.

Toby was half tempted to glance around to see if she meant two other fellows entirely. But the Tzigani chieftain wrung his hand cheerfully, saying, "You seem to have acquitted yourself well, Captain Fanshawe."

Toby was almost abashed by the effusive praise. Then he remembered why he was here at all. Because he had kidnapped the betrothed of Kilbourne's Knight-Commander in a desperate grab for gold. Toby studied his boots.

The red-haired woman approached him. When Toby raised his head, she looked deep into his eyes. Then, taking his hand, she turned it over and traced one slim finger across his palm. Nodding once as if she'd glimpsed something she had anticipated, she said, "Captain Fanshawe, I see into your future. As did Lady Marissa, you will have a choice to make. The lines branch, and which way you will take I cannot say. I also cannot tell you which way you should go. But one path will ultimately lead you to fortune and renown. The other, I fear, will lead you into ignominy and despair."

He grimaced. "The story of my life," he muttered. "But how will I know what path to take? That's always the problem, isn't it?"

She nodded vigorously, sending her red hair swirling about her face. "Ah, you are wiser than many. For you recognize the difficulty. But by aiding Lady Marissa as you have done, you have perhaps begun down one of those paths. Reflect on that. And think why she did what she did, risking all to rescue her beloved."

"All for love," he said with an airy wave of his fingers.

"Just as you say," the Tzigani agreed. "Though you speak in jest, your words hold truth."

"For some, perhaps. It doesn't seem to work that way for—" Toby halted mid-sentence, his tongue cleaving to the roof of his mouth.

A girl was approaching them. A marvelous girl. An extraordinary girl. From under long lashes her eyes flashed a startling blue, like the azure of a summer twilight's sky. Shyly she said, "Thank you, Captain, for your brave service to Lady Marissa."

The red-haired woman smiled fondly. "Captain, allow me to introduce my daughter, Antonettia."

"Toni," corrected the loveliest girl Toby had ever laid eyes on.

Elbethesba said, "We are preparing to take you, Lady Marissa, and Commander McRobbie back to your ship. You can then return them to Caerfaen. While we do, why don't you regale Toni with your adventures, Captain Fanshawe. Who knows? Your path may become clearer…" And with a smile and a swirl of skirts she was gone.

He stared after her for a moment, his mouth opening and closing once. But he couldn't force any words past his lips.

And then Toni, she of the enormous blue eyes, said, "Yes, please tell me about life at sea, Captain. And about your many bold adventures."

"Call me Toby," he told her, as both chills and a sudden, unimaginable warmth coursed through him simultaneously. "Please, call me Toby."

Chapter Fifty-Five

"Wyvrndell," Marissa called once more. The Tzigani caravan was making its way back to where Fanshawe's ship waited. Morgan still lay cold and unmoving, his eyes open but unfocused. She needed to know what to do, how to break the—

"I hear you," came the dragon's sudden reply.

She nearly dropped the mug of tea she'd been sipping. "Oh, thank heaven! Why haven't you answered my calls before?"

"My apologies, Lady Marissa. For a time I was in a place where I was unable to hear you. Then when I tried to speak with you, I could not reach your mind at all. For the last two days I have been in R'mk'vl, engaged in extremely delicate negotiations on behalf of my king. A Dwarf enchantment has prevented me from hearing you. Now. What is wrong?"

She poured out her tale. When she'd finished, there was only silence from the dragon. After several long minutes, she called his name once more.

"I have been consulting about your problem with a—a friend," he said at last. *"She concurs with my opinion. Your best course is to return Morgan McRobbie to Caerfaen. To the wizard Sebastien, in fact. He should know what to do."*

"But—you mean you can't do anything?"

"No. I have no magic, and he is under some enchantment. Seek out Sebastien, Lady Marissa. He will know what needs to be done and will have the ability to do it."

Marissa heaved a sigh. Once Wyvrndell had made up his mind on something, there was little point in arguing with him. "Very well, Sebastien it is. Tell me, though, who is your friend?"

"Her name is Aireantha. She is fierce and loyal and quite intelligent. And beautiful. In fact," he went on with what sounded to Marissa suspiciously like a draconian chuckle, *"she rather reminds me of you. Now, I must bid you farewell. My negotiations are not yet done, and I have much to do. But I will come to you as soon as I may, for we have much to discuss."*

"Thank you," she called, but there was no reply. Perhaps he was right. Sebastien would know what to do. She would just have to trust.

She placed a hand over one of Morgan's as he lay still and silent. Closing her eyes, she breathed a prayer.

When Elbethesba woke her, Marissa was still holding tight to his hand.

"We are near the place where your Captain Fanshawe says his ship is anchored," she reported.

"I cannot thank you enough. Both for your timely arrival, so unlooked for, and for your generous aid. Going all this distance out of your way, just to help us."

"It is our nature." Elbethesba smiled. "We Tzigani always help our friends. And when we are in need, those friends repay with their help."

"Yes, and how can I help you in return?"

Instead of answering, Elbethesba asked a question of her own, "Tell me, what do you think of Captain Fanshawe?"

"He's a pirate," she replied instinctively.

"Is he? He tells me he only raids the ships of your enemy, the Rhuddlanis. That he shares out the spoils with his crew, takes a small percentage for himself, and turns the rest over to the crown. I believe this is what is known as a privateer, is it not?"

"Oh." Marissa considered this. "Yes, I suppose so. If he has a letter of marque from the king. That would explain why he only goes after the Rhuddlanis."

"Indeed so. I have examined him. I see no evil in him. Far from it."

"But—but he kidnapped me. And Lady Sybil, Morgan's mother!"

"Yes, he did indeed. But reflect a moment, if you will. If he had not, would you have been in a position to rescue your beloved? And without him as your ally, would you have succeeded in your mission?"

Marissa opened her mouth to protest. Then she closed it again as the truth of Elbethesba's words struck home. "No," she said simply.

Elbethesba flashed her a gentle smile. "Then what I will ask of you should not be too onerous. Help Captain Fanshawe restore his name and his honor among your people. He is, at heart, a good man. Impulsive, certainly, and a definite rogue."

Marissa started to speak, but Elbethesba held up a finger. "Yet rogues, especially charming ones such as he, have their uses. And their needs. So this I ask of you. Do what is in your power for Captain Fanshawe."

"But—"

She gazed at her, and Marissa grinned. "Oh, very well, of course

I will, if you so wish it. But why? You don't even know him."
	Elbethesba's face creased into a grin. No, not really. But I have a feeling I soon may."

Chapter Fifty-Six

Their return to Caerfaen was little more than a blur for Marissa. The voyage was short, and thankfully uneventful. No Thundermist, no Rhuddlani ships in pursuit, and little in the way of rough seas. The skies were a brilliant blue and the sea was calm as a child's bath. Marissa hardly noticed.

She and Lady Sybil watched over Morgan. At first, they'd taken turns, but eventually they just sat together, mainly in silence. After a while, at Lady Sybil's urging, Marissa related all that occurred in the chamber at the top of Perseverance Tower. Sybil's mood swung from shock to horror to outrage and back again. All the while, he lay unmoving, his open eyes fixed on the ceiling. Marissa wondered if he could hear what she and Lady Sybil were discussing.

"In the old tales my mother used to tell me," Sybil said, "the princess was always woken with true love's kiss."

"Don't you think I tried that first thing? As you can see, it didn't work. And yes, he is my true love, forever and always," she added, just in case there was any doubt on that score.

"That poor, mad girl," Sybil mused. "Kiara, I mean. She was obviously out of her head to do something like this. I suppose she was driven to it by grief. But even when she was young, I always felt there was something a bit odd about her. Unusually intense, if you know what I mean."

Before Marissa could reply, a rap on the door of their cabin was followed in short order by Fanshawe. "We'll be in Caerfaen port within the hour," he said.

Lady Sybil just glared at him. In her book, Marissa realized, a pirate was a pirate and no two ways about it. Although, given her history with them, Marissa couldn't fault her for that. She recalled Morgan relating how pirates had kidnapped Lady Sybil's sister, holding her hostage to keep control over her father, an Admiral in the Orskan Navy. Lady Sybil and Morgan's father had together staged a daring raid to rescue her sister and deal with the pirates. Lady Sybil, he told Marissa, had leapt through a window like an avenging fury and killed the leader of the pirates herself.

As for her, she felt Fanshawe had redeemed himself. She would, as she had promised Elbethesba, do what she could to aid him when things settled back to some semblance of normal.

"Thank you, Captain," she said.

"Ladies."

He turned to leave, but stopped in his tracks when Lady Sybil barked, "Wait a minute, young man."

He slowly turned to face her, his expression studiously neutral.

"Marissa," Lady Sybil said, "has told me how you came to her aid in the tower. How you bore my son back here."

"Well, just down to the ground level," he demurred. "The Tzigani…"

"Bah. You did what needed doing. That's been the McRobbie family's motto going back generations. So I'll say this once, and only once." She looked Fanshawe dead in the eye. "Thank you."

He executed a bow, tipped his hat, and left them to their vigil.

"That was exceedingly generous of you," Marissa remarked.

"He may be a pirate, but when things got dicey, he did show his true colors, I'll give him that."

"I don't think he'll be a pirate much longer. Or rather, a privateer."

"Oh?" Lady Sybil looked up with interest.

"If the Tzigani, Elbethesba, is correct, his activities are sanctioned by the Crown. He raids Rhuddlani ships and turns a good portion of the spoils over to Kilbourne. But this whole scheme of his was intended to finance his retirement. And I could see he was quite smitten with one of the Tzigani girls. She would, I think, be the making of him."

"Yes," Lady Sybil pointed out. "But you don't think his plan worked, do you?"

Marissa shook her head. "Not really. I'm fairly certain Wyvrndell doesn't have any treasure stored up. So the men he sent probably came away empty handed."

"How's he going to get out of being a pirate? Privateer. Whatever. He's going to need to do something."

"I don't really know. But I'm sure I'll think of something."

Lady Sybil looked horrified. "You'll think of something? But he kidnapped you. Us."

"Well, yes. But if he hadn't, he wouldn't have been there to keep Rhenn at bay while I dealt with Kiara."

"I suppose," Lady Sybil said, her tone grudging. "Although I think I could have done just as well, had I been there."

Marissa rose and threw her arms around Morgan's mother. "I'm sure you would have performed splendidly," she agreed. "You and your sword parasol. If you'd like, you may give me one as a wedding gift."

"Now you're talking." Lady Sybil grinned.

Chapter Fifty-Seven

Once Fanshawe had his vessel anchored in the harbor, he accompanied Marissa and Lady Sybil ashore. He commandeered a chair for them, since Lady Sybil's ankle was still too swollen and sore to bear her weight. "And anyway," he said, "these docks are no place for two ladies to be wandering around alone."

A couple of his crew carefully placed Morgan into a second chair. Marissa gave the chair men directions to her townhouse, then turned to him. "What are you going to do now, Captain?"

He shrugged. "I really don't know. Find my first mate, Mr. Sharkey, and see what happened at the dragon's lair, I suppose." He didn't look particularly excited about the prospect.

"And if my theory was right?"

"Get out of Caerfaen before my crew turns on me. I don't think they're going to be too happy if this scheme didn't pan out."

"Tell me something, Captain," Marissa said.

He cocked his head, waiting.

"If you had gotten a big haul from Wyvrndell's cave, what would you have done?"

"That's a pretty personal question, Lady Marissa," he said, although he didn't sound upset.

She flashed him a brilliant smile. "You kidnapped Lady Sybil and me. Despite this fact, neither of us plan to press any charges against you. After all, you did help me no end at the tower. I probably wouldn't be here if you hadn't. But all in all, I think you owe me this one answer."

"Oh, all right, if you're going to be that way. If the scheme had panned out as hoped, I would have paid off my debts and given up this career for something a little more…respectable."

"You used to be a naval officer, didn't you?"

His face clouded, rather like the Thundermist. "I was," he said stiffly. "I was cashiered."

"It took me a while," she said, "but I remember hearing discussions about it. Morgan and his friends in the Legion were talking about the case. I gather they felt you'd been unfairly treated."

"It doesn't matter at this point," he said.

"No? If you say so. But tell me, Captain. Are you indeed an

actual pirate? Or do you have a letter of marque from the king?"

He gaped. "How—"

"I have my methods," Marissa replied, a bit smugly. He didn't need to know Elbethesba had divined his secret. "Are you a privateer, in service to the crown?"

He gazed out across the water before he spoke. "You have it right. Someone approached me with an offer I couldn't really turn down, and—here I am. The Scourge of the Thundermist Sea." He quirked a grin. "I've actually done fairly well at it. You saw how eager the Rhuddlanis were to get hold of me. I've put a real crimp in their shipping."

"Your crew doesn't know this, do they?"

"No. I let them think we were true pirates. It's easier that way. They just had to play by my rules. Which were a bit out of the norm, I suppose, but they seemed to get used to my ways. We've had a surprisingly good run, up to now."

Marissa pressed on, "So you would have paid off your crew, paid off all your debts, and made a triumphant return to society?"

"Hmm. I don't know if I'm really interested in society at this point." His eyes took on a faraway look.

She wondered if he was thinking of Toni. "I've a suggestion. You're planning to find out if a bunch of angry pirates are out for your blood. Before you do, why don't you come with us? I'm taking Morgan back to my house. You can rest up, get cleaned up a bit, and get something to eat."

Fanshawe gave her a startled look. "You…want me to come with you? Why? I'd have thought you'd be happy to see the last of me."

"Captain, I've had it pointed out to me that if not for you, I probably wouldn't have been able to save Morgan. So yes, I want you to come with us. Then, if you wish, you can go deal with your crew. If you're still in one piece after that, perhaps you can go pay court to Toni."

He stared. "You really are a witch," he murmured.

"No, just observant. She's a lovely girl, and I think Elbethesba—her mother, and their clan leader—rather likes you. She was trying to convince me to take up your cause."

"Really?" Suddenly he looked extremely interested.

"Why don't you ride in the chair with Morgan? You can keep him from getting knocked about." Not giving him a chance to refuse, Marissa clambered into the chair and closed the door.

Fanshawe assisted Lady Sybil into the other side. Then he got into the second chair with Morgan.

"I didn't think he'd actually do as you asked," Lady Sybil said.

"I wasn't sure either. But Captain Fanshawe, for all his bravado, is a practical man. And what could be more practical than doing what I want him to do?"

Chapter Fifty-Eight

Once the chair men stopped outside her house, Marissa hurried up the stairs to open the door. Two of them, along with Fanshawe, carried Morgan up and into the house. The other two assisted Lady Sybil up the steps.

She expected to find only her servants in residence. Instead, when she opened the door, she revealed a seething mass of humanity in the foyer. They were all talking at once and trying to shout over each other. Briana, of course, and Kevin Jacoby. There was Bishop Randolph, and Captain Jenks of the Watch, along with that funny little sergeant, MacGwyn. And that nice Mr. Barlbent. Finally, a strange man she didn't recognize, who looked as if he must be an Orskan.

As Marissa and her entourage entered, disheveled, bedraggled, and carrying the unconscious Morgan, all conversation died away. The entire group crowded into the hallway turned to stare. "We're back," she said brightly.

The hubbub that erupted was almost as loud as the storm when they'd entered the Thundermist. She couldn't make out any individual questions or statements. It was all just noise. Which came to a sudden halt as someone—ah, Captain Jenks, she saw—blew a loud blast on his whistle.

"Quiet," he bellowed.

"Thank you, Captain," Marissa said. Dismissing the chair men with thanks, she turned back to the group at large. "I'll give you all the gruesome details later. Right now, there are more important things to deal with. Is Sebastien awake yet? I need him."

"Not yet," said Mr. Barlbent. "He does seem to be rousing from his trance, or whatever it was. But he's not fully conscious yet."

"I think he was given witchbane," Marissa said. "It's—"

"Yes, he was," said Bishop Randolph. "Thanks to Wizard Cardion here, Sebastien's been dosed with root of mandrake, which evidently is the only sure remedy. But it's taking its sweet time."

"Blast," she said. "I was hoping he'd be awake. Morgan is under an enchantment, and I was hoping Sebastien would be able to break it."

The Orskan sketched a bow. "Nardis Cardion, at your service, Your Ladyship," he ventured. "I'm a journeyman wizard and a friend of

Master Sebastien's. I would be honored to help Commander McRobbie if I'm able."

"Oh, thank you. Can we carry him into the morning room? Lay him on the settee?"

This was accomplished. The young wizard shooed everyone out except Marissa. "You can stay," he said, "but please be quiet. I need to concentrate so I know what I'm up against here."

She collapsed onto a chair. "Please, just help him."

Cardion closed his eyes as he bent over Morgan. Running his hands lightly over the prostrate figure, he muttered under his breath. Marissa held her questions in check so as not to distract him.

Finally, the wizard straightened. "He's definitely under an enchantment. It seems a fairly simple one. I should be able to break it."

"It won't hurt him, will it?"

He shook his head. "No, it shouldn't. He may be stiff and groggy for a while, but that should be it."

"Then do it," she urged. "Please."

"It might be best if you wait out there with the others. I need to focus, and any distraction might…"

She cast an entreating look at him, saw the wizard was resolved, and nodded. "Very well."

He bent back over Morgan as she stepped toward the door, laying his hands upon him, and muttering words in a tongue she did not understand. She slipped out.

"Mwrow."

Marissa looked down to see Francesca staring up at her, green eyes gleaming. Before the cat could speak, Marissa said, "Don't even start with me right now. I've got too many other things to worry about."

"I was merely going to say, well done."

"Oh. Well. Thank you. I'm not sure I want to know how you know, but we'll deal with that later." She glanced into the front parlor, where all her visitors seemed to have congregated. "Why are all these people here?"

Francesca yawned and flicked her tail. "You'd better ask them. They just gabble and argue, and the priest has drunk up most of the good brandy."

"I shall." She stepped around the cat and moved to the doorway of the parlor. Fanshawe was in there, scrunched up against the wall and twisting his hat into complex knots. If he was trying to look inconspicuous, he was failing miserably.

The rest of the party, if one could call it such, were indeed gabbling and arguing. She could only catch snatches of their conversation. Lady Sybil seemed to be relating their adventures to anyone who would listen, but her audience kept getting distracted. Captain Jenks appeared to be questioning Mr. Barlbent, with Sergeant MacGwyn trying to take notes.

"Excuse me!" Marissa called. The only person who even glanced at her was Fanshawe.

"Hello!" she called again. Still no response.

"Quiet!" she yelled into the vortex. Finally, they stopped talking long enough for her to speak.

"Now. While I'm certainly glad to see you all, could someone explain just what you're all doing here?"

She took a step back as the chaotic chorus broke out again. The pirate gave her a rueful grin. Then he jammed his hat back on his head, cupped his hands around his mouth, and bellowed, "Pipe down!"

The words echoed off the walls. Mouths dropped open, and a blessed silence reigned.

"Thank you, Captain," Marissa said, favoring him with a nod as she stepped into the room. "Would someone like to explain just what's going on here? Why you're all here? Is there anyone who thinks they can handle it?"

The occupants of the room looked at each other and back at Marissa. Slowly, Mr. Barlbent raised his hand. "I'll give it a try," he ventured.

"Thank you." She looked around at the others. "While he's talking, everyone else please be quiet."

Mr. Barlbent brushed his hair back from his eyes, adjusted his spectacles, and said, "I'm here because you and Commander McRobbie asked me to begin an investigation regarding the wizard's prophecy, and the attack on Master Sebastien. And how they might be connected. After a good many false trails, I found Journeyman Wizard Nardis. He was able to provide information about both these things. He also located the mandrake root needed to heal Sebastien and came here with me to prepare and administer it.

"Captain Jenks and Sergeant MacGwyn," Barlbent continued, "are here because the Watch located the man who attacked Sebastien, sleeping in a bush outside Commander McRobbie's door. Further investigation revealed the disappearance of yourself, Lady Sybil McRobbie, and the Commander. They ended up here in the course of their investigations and decided to stay for a bit to see what developed once Sebastien recovered."

"His Excellency, Bishop Randolph, came because of—" Here Barlbent hesitated for a moment, and then managed, "well, because of your cat."

"Ah, Francesca. Why am I not surprised?" Marissa murmured.

"Mwrow," came a soft response from near her feet. Marissa ignored it.

"The cat, um, evidently convinced your maid and Kevin Jacoby to go to the bishop, this morning, to determine if he could contact the dragon, in order to locate you or the commander. When this effort failed, His Excellency returned here with them." He smiled ruefully. "You do seem to have accumulated a rather full house."

Captain Jenks stepped forward. "M'lady, I really need to speak with you. I believe there are number of inquiries which you might be able to shed some light on." He glanced meaningfully at Fanshawe, who returned his gaze with a bland disinterest.

She began, "I'm afraid this isn't a good time, Captain. I—"

At that moment the wizard, Cardion, staggered into the room. "It was a bit stronger than I realized," he said, scrubbing a hand across his face.

"Did it work?" she demanded, Jenks forgotten. Cardion nodded, and she raced down the hall.

Morgan lay on the settee, twitching. Marissa knelt next to him, taking his hand in hers. His arm jerked, nearly pulling his hand from her grasp. "You did it!" she said to Cardion, who had followed her.

"It would appear so," he agreed. "It may take a bit of this jerking about before his ability to move fully returns."

Morgan's entire body spasmed this time. He groaned, then turned his head so he was looking up at Marissa. He worked his jaw for a moment, then croaked, "This has been…interesting."

"Oh, thank God," she breathed. "You're back. Do you want some water?"

"Help me sit up," he said. She did so, and he slumped over against her.

"Don't try to stand, Commander," Cardion said. "Give yourself some time to get your feet back under you."

"Don't worry," Morgan said. "Right now my legs feel like jelly. Actually, everything does."

"Water?" she asked again.

He shook his head. "What I would like," he said, his voice a bit stronger now, "is some of that brandy your father sent up. The stuff bottled by monks with kid gloves, under a full moon on the last day of summer. A large glass of it. Better make it two."

She put her arms around him and kissed him soundly. "Now I know you're all right," she said. "When you can make jokes about it…"

He managed a weak grin. "It got you to kiss me, didn't it? Best medicine of all. By the way, young man," he said to Cardion. "I've no idea who you are but thank you for ridding me of that blasted spell. Orskan, are you?"

"Yes, Your Grace. Nardis Cardion, journeyman wizard. I'm happy to have been of service."

"Come see me in a couple of days, once I'm back on my feet again. We need to discuss a reward for your assistance."

"That's not necessary, Commander," the wizard protested.

"Don't argue," Morgan told him.

"All right, I'll come," said Cardion, heading for the door. "I'll leave you now."

"How do you feel?" Marissa asked wrapping her arms tightly around him.

"Like Wyvrndell sat on me. But I'll be fine in a bit. About that brandy?"

"All right, all right, I'll have Briana fetch it. If Randolph hasn't finished it all." She went to the door, gave orders, and came back to sit next to Morgan again. "Do you know what's happened?" she asked.

"Well, I know what Kiara told me, as she and Rhenn were trussing me up on that stone table. And I was able to see at least some of what you did at the tower." He shook his head. "And I heard you talking to Mother about it on the way back." He shook his head. "I can't believe we're still alive. You were remarkable. You…"

"Umm. We'll talk about that later." She shivered as mad memories of the tower crowded in on her. It wasn't something she wanted to relive, at least not yet. "Right now, just concentrate on getting back to normal."

"Normal? What's that?" he asked as Briana entered with the brandy and two snifters.

"Normal," Marissa replied, pouring each of them a healthy portion of spirits, "is you and me, together against all adversaries." She raised her glass, and he touched his to it. They drank. Then, with the taste of brandy on his lips, he kissed her. Thoroughly.

"Amen to that," he said. "Did… Are… No, you're right. We'll hash it all out later. Right now, I suppose we'd best go out there and face the mob, eh?"

"Stay here," she told him. "If you're up to it, they can come in here. If not, they can just cool their heels until you are."

"Mmm. I suppose we'd best bring 'em in and get this over with."

Marissa herded the crowd from the hall into the morning room, shushing them all the while. Once everyone was assembled, Morgan and

Marissa between them told their tale, each picking up as the other left off.

"So Kiara and Rhenn are both dead," she said at last. "There's no one to arrest. Unless it's me, for killing them." She glanced over at Captain Jenks, who shook his head.

"Sounds to me like this Kiara woman took her own life, bizarre as that may be," he said. "As for Rhenn, well, I reckon he got what he deserved, all things considered. I've got no problems."

"What about the fellow who attacked Sebastien?" Morgan said.

"Funny thing," said Jenks. "We found him. Outside your house, in fact, dead asleep in the hedge. Your description rang bells with a few of my constables. Dog-ear Donovan, a two-bit thug for hire. He's locked up now and won't see the light of day for quite some time. We wanted to talk to him about a number of other things. So that's all wrapped up."

"Captain Fanshawe?" Morgan looked at the pirate.

Marissa saw him gulp. Then he squared his shoulders and stood straight. "Yes, Commander?"

"I want to publicly express my gratitude for the assistance you provided Marissa. She seems to think neither of us would be here if you hadn't been around to help. So we'll forget about any incidents of a more, um, mercenary nature, and focus on your actions in the tower and after."

Fanshawe stood looking straight ahead, not saying a word.

"An officer in the Kilbourne Navy," Morgan went on, "would likely receive a commendation for such actions. As an officer myself, I know what a commendation is worth. That and a shilling will get you a rotten cup of tea."

She saw Fanshawe's lips twitch. Other than that, he maintained his ramrod posture, staring at the wall.

"So instead of a commendation, I'm offering you a bounty. We'll have to work out the details once I'm up and about again. And before you say no" — Morgan gave him a tight smile— "keep in mind that I have access to both a witch and a dragon, and I know how to use them."

"Thank you, Commander," Fanshawe said. "I'll be there."

"Well done," murmured Marissa.

Randolph harrumphed. "I should like to say something."

All gazes turned toward him. The bishop beamed. "I don't know if this is really the time to make such an announcement, but I figure it's better you hear it from me than from gossip." He stepped over to Marissa and offered her a hand to rise. Puzzled, she took it, standing next to the big priest.

"I've spoken to King Rhys and Queen Gwyndolyn," he said. "By their decree, I now present to you the first Royal Enchantress of Kilbourne: Lady Marissa duBerry, soon Duchess of Westdale."

"Royal Enchantress?" Marissa sputtered. "What are you talking about?"

"Their Majesties simply agreed with my impeccable logic. You are to be recognized not only for your power, but your loyalty and dedication to Kilbourne. There will be a ceremony soon, where you will be commissioned, and granted the protection of the Crown."

"I…see." She didn't really, but perhaps she just hadn't the wits at the moment to understand it.

"So, no more Witch of Caerfaen?" Morgan asked.

"Exactly." Randolph beamed. "Royal Enchantress has a much nicer ring to it, don't you think?"

She nodded, now comprehending. "Thank you, Randolph. That was extremely thoughtful of you. And of the king and queen. Now, what about Sebastien?"

"He's…"

"Still tottering about," said Sebastien, coming into the room. "Rumors of my demise were evidently premature. Although if there is any of that brandy left," he pointed toward the bottle, "it might find a good home here."

Marissa brought him the bottle and dispatched Briana for another glass. "Actually, since this seems to have turned into somewhat of a celebration, you might as well bring a lot of glasses, including enough for yourself and Kevin. And more brandy."

Soon Kevin and Briana returned with a cart loaded with glasses and several bottles of brandy. Toasts were raised, praises were sung, and spirits flowed. Marissa plopped down onto the settee next to Morgan. As she did, her reticule tumbled to the floor, its contents spilling out.

He bent to pick them up for her. "What's this?" he asked, holding up a small object.

She glanced at it. "Oh, that? Just a book. I found it in the tower when we were getting ready to leave. It seemed a shame to leave it there to molder away. I just tucked it into my reticule, and never thought about it again."

A ferocious hissing came from the vicinity of his feet. Morgan looked down to see Francesca. Her back was arched, her tail spiked, and her ears lay flat. In an urgent voice, the cat said, "Put that book down. Now."

His mouth fell open. Was he still feeling the effects of that damnable spell? He shook his head to clear it, recalling Marissa telling him about her familiar.

"Francesca?" Marissa asked. "What's—"

"Put. It. Down," the cat said adamantly.

Morgan dropped the book back to the floor. Francesca backed away hastily, as if loathe to touch it.

"Oh, we are in such trouble here," said the feline.

**Other Books By
Keith W. Willis**

**Desperate Knight
Traitor Knight**

Acknowledgements

Like all books, this one is the result of a lot of hard work. A writer doesn't just sit down and toss off an easy hundred-thousand words, call it a book, and send it off to the publisher. It takes countless hours of drafting, revising, frustration, juggling, and piecing it all together. Then you go on to the next sentence…

So why go through all that? A couple of reasons. The first is that when it's done (and trust me, no book is ever truly done—ask any author) and you hold that copy in your hand, it's an amazing feeling of accomplishment and validation. The second is that I'm doing this for you, the readers. The fans who have reached out, either electronically or in person, to say "Hey, I read your book and really enjoyed it." The knowledge that I can help to give people a few hours of enjoyment in this hectic, cantankerous world of ours—well, to me it's all the reason I need to keep going. So here's to you—the readers, the fans, the dragon-lovers. Without you, we writers wouldn't exist.

Producing a novel isn't as solitary an activity as people think. Sure, the writing is. But after that? For me, at least, it's team effort.

Thanks to my fabulous editor, Nikki Andrews. Nikki has worked on all three of my books, and it is such a joy to have her as part of my team. Her insight, expertise, and guidance have helped to shepherd *Enchanted Knight* into being a much better story, and I'm grateful not only for all her help, for her friendship as well.

Thanks to Cassie Knight and her team at Champagne Book Group. I'm proud to be part of the Champagne family, whose attention to detail and focus on quality are superlative. A special shout out to Melody Pond, who has produced such amazing cover art for not only this book, but also for new editions of *Traitor Knight* and *Desperate Knight*.

Here's to Myles Mazurak. I was thrilled to bring back M'zr'k, the mighty Dwarf warrior, for a return engagement. Myles, I hope you enjoy meeting the dragons.

To all the folks who put on the amazing Renaissance Faires we attend over the summers in order to bring you Kilbourne books in person—your hard work and dedication to these events are a true inspiration, and I'm grateful for the opportunity to be a part of them.

And to all the faire-goers who took a chance on my books; and especially to all of you who came back for more. Support like that is simply overwhelming. I can only say, quite humbly, thank you.

Finally, to the one person without whom none of these books would have been possible—my amazing, patient, supportive wife, Patty. She has throughout my journey been friend, cheerleader, partner, story consultant, taskmaster, and proofreader. I'm so lucky to have you on my side and by my side. Thank you for sharing your life with me.

About the Author

Keith W. Willis graduated (long ago) with a degree in English Lit from Berry College, which has the distinction of being the world's largest college campus. He now lives in the scenic Hudson Valley/Adirondack region of NY with his wife Patty. Keith is certain those rumbling noises attributed to Henry Hudson's crew are really just the dragons grumbling. Keith and Patty have one grown son, Matt, who actually thinks it's pretty cool that Dad writes books.

Keith's interests include reading classic fantasy, sci-fi, and mysteries; camping and canoeing; and cutthroat games of Scrabble. He began writing seriously in 2008, when the voices in his head got too annoying to ignore. When he's not making up stories he manages a group of database content editors at a global information technology firm. *Enchanted Knight* (Champagne Book Group, 2020) is his third venture into the magical world of Kilbourne, following *Traitor Knight* (Champagne Book Group, 2015) and *Desperate Knight* (Champagne Book Group, 2017).

Keith loves to hear from his readers. You can find and connect with him at the links below.

Website/Blog: http://www.keithwillisauthor.com/
Twitter: https://twitter.com/kilbourneknight
Facebook: https://www.facebook.com/TRAITOR-KNIGHT-191368320972613/

~~~

If you enjoyed *Enchanted Knight* and want to see how Morgan and Marissa met, their adventures began in *Traitor Knight*, book 1 of the *Knights of Kilbourne* series. Just turn the page.
~~~

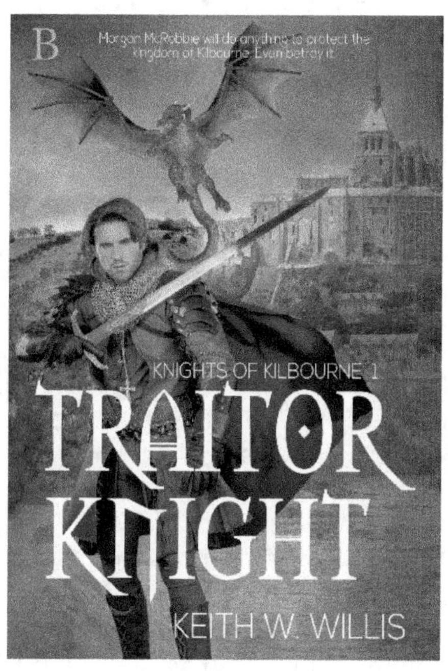
Morgan McRobbie will do anything to protect the kingdom of Kilbourne. Even betray it.
KNIGHTS OF KILBOURNE 1
TRAITOR KNIGHT
KEITH W. WILLIS

Chapter One

A clamor of rooks exploded through the trees, nearly drowning out the woman's scream.

Morgan straightened in the saddle. Trouble, at last. The patrol had been boring up 'til now. He set his heels to Arnicus's flanks and the big gray gelding quickened his pace along the narrow trail. The birds flapped off, their raucous calls fading in the distance. A watchful silence overtook the woods, broken only by the thud of Arnicus's hooves on the summer-dry earth.

Morgan peered through the trees, searching for the source of the cry. He knew no good reason why a woman, screaming or otherwise, should be in the middle of the king's forest. But no matter the reason, he had to find her. Help her, if possible. He'd never been one to shy away from trouble. No soldier was, or he didn't remain a soldier for long. He loosened his sword in its well-worn sheath.

Another shriek split the air. Arnicus leapt forward, nostrils flared and ears laid back. Morgan bent low over the horse's neck, scanning ahead for danger. It might be a trap. The trees thinned slightly, the mottled light of the forest replaced by brighter sunshine that heralded a clearing. Suddenly Morgan jerked hard on the reins, causing Arnicus to toss his head in equine complaint. He paid little heed.

Just ahead, the trail opened out onto a serene sun-dappled clearing. The little meadow, dotted with bright patches of wildflowers, would have been charming if not for the hulking blue dragon crouched in its center.

"My God!" Morgan whispered, half curse and half prayer. Arnicus pawed the ground nervously, suggesting a strategic retreat might not be such a bad idea. Morgan didn't blame him in the least. "Steady on, fellow," he whispered, as much to himself as to the horse.

Despite the generally accepted notion that dragons had been extinct for centuries, this one looked pretty damned corporeal. Iridescent azure scales covered the creature's enormous body. Huge green eyes gleamed with an alien intelligence from beneath bony brow-like ridges. Vast leathery wings rested on the creature's back, twitching slightly as if eager to lift off into flight. Curls of steam vented from its snout, forming delicate patterns in the air.

Blast! The standard-issue dragons had been bad enough. This was one of the fire-breathing ones. And he didn't have time to call up reinforcements from the Legion garrison at Caerfaen. This was his problem.

The dragon held a dark-haired girl in its talons, and its attention was focused exclusively on her. Which was both good and bad. Good, in that it hadn't noticed him yet, giving Morgan a brief moment to reclaim his scattered wits. Bad, in that its attention was focused on the girl in its talons. He was going to have to act at once to have any hope of saving her.

Morgan swung down from the saddle and drew his sword. The steaming nightmare inspected the girl much as a cook might a particularly savory delicacy. She strained to free herself, wriggling and even managing to land a fierce kick on its snout. The dragon didn't deign to notice. A surge of adrenaline fizzed through Morgan, familiar as the hilt of the sword in his hand. Well, he'd been looking for excitement, and he was about to get it. Likely a lot more than he could handle.

"Unhand that maiden!" he shouted, storming toward the monster and probable death. "Release her and prepare to meet your doom!"

The dragon, hissing like a brace of tea kettles, turned to face this interruption of its mid-morning snack of maiden flambé. Ominous rumblings sounded in the beast's superstructure. The girl struggled harder now, a wild hope lighting her eyes.

If nothing else, perhaps he could force the dragon to drop her. Then she might have a chance to escape while Morgan kept it occupied with killing him. He heard the deep rumbling again, herald of his own doom. With a wild yell he darted forward to strike the first blow.

The sword ricocheted back off the protective scales, nearly cleaving Morgan's head in two. His hand throbbed as if he'd just launched an attack at an anvil. *Curse it, that just wasn't fair!* Fire and armor, against his insignificant sword and a worse than useless shield. Definitely not fair. He stubbornly hacked again with roughly the same effect as the girl's kick.

The dragon tracked his progress, taking careful aim like an archer sighting on a target. Well, if he had to die, Morgan thought, it might as well be in combat with a dragon. Perhaps after he went up in flames he might go down in song. Assuming anyone found enough in the charred remains to tell who he had been. But without a doubt his death was going to be quicker and messier than it was glorious. From what he'd seen on battlefields over the years, death usually was.

The dragon opened its mouth to flame. Like a fighter desperate to get inside his opponent's reach, Morgan flung himself directly toward the beast, clutching at its haunch. He scrabbled one-handed for purchase on the smooth scales, using the dragon's body as a shelter against the fiery death intended for him. A roar like a thousand forges being lit at once nearly deafened him. Then the flames came, passing just overhead. The heat slammed into him like a blow from a giant, sending him reeling.

Quitting his refuge before the dragon decided to squash him, Morgan dodged around the massive hindquarters. He spared a glance up at the girl. At least the fire hadn't harmed her. Yet. She was still trying to break free. He made another quick foray with the sword, but it was like trying to drive a butter knife into a boulder. Then a huge clawed foot lashed out, catching him in the chest. Morgan went flying.

He hit the ground with a wrenching thud, skidding on his back until he crashed against a large rock. He fumbled around for the sword. It lay halfway between him and a very smug-looking dragon. When he reached for the weapon, blinding pain shot up his arm, exploding in his scrambled brain. It didn't seem to really matter. He was going to die, with or without the sword. Morgan swore like the Legion soldier he was.

He spared a quick glance at the girl. She watched his imminent demise with an air of resignation. Her expression almost seemed aggrieved, as if she resented having her hopes raised only to see them dashed again so quickly. The dragon took careful aim once more, opening its jaws to deliver the *coup de grace*. Morgan struggled to his feet and raised his shield. It was pointless, he knew, but instinct was driving him now. He stared into the gaping maw and waited for death to overtake him.

But instead of deadly fire, what emerged was a little plume of steam and a loud "Urp!"

Morgan stared. The dragon stared back, as if daring him to snicker. It took another sulphur-laden breath and gave forth what was probably intended to be a mighty roar. The effort was punctuated with another series of hiccoughs and a large wisp of acrid blue smoke.

The dragon tossed its head in a gesture of what Morgan could only interpret as frustration. It made a final effort to produce a flame, but more spasms shook the massive body. Shaking off his trancelike state, Morgan made a dash for the sword. Not that it was going to do him any good, but at least he'd have made the effort.

Looking rather sheepish, the dragon hiccoughed twice more, dropped the girl, and unfolded its wings. With two flaps it began to rise, the ascent marred by its ongoing hiccoughs. Morgan grabbed his sword in his left hand—his right still felt useless—and slashed savagely at the dragon as it gained altitude. The blade bounced off its scales again, and

Morgan growled in frustration.

The spiked tail lashed almost idly in his direction. Another shudder spoiled the dragon's aim, and what should have been a killing blow flashed harmlessly by. Morgan stood captivated as the dragon winged drunkenly away over the treetops. One final "Urp!" echoed back to him.

Good God, I'm still alive! And still had all the important bits attached.

A feminine voice broke in on his reverie. "Don't just stand there gawking," it commanded. "Help me up!"

Chapter Two

The girl lay sprawled in a tangled heap. Morgan sheathed his sword and extended his hands, wincing at the pain throbbing through his right arm. He ignored it and when she took his offered hands he pulled her upright.

She swayed for a moment, as if she might topple into his arms. A little part of Morgan's brain, one he had thought well suppressed, suggested this might not be such a bad prospect. He slammed the door on this notion. He didn't have time for such distractions, no matter how pleasant they might be.

Anyhow the girl either regained her balance or thought better of the falling-into-his-arms motif. She made a rather futile attempt to smooth out her tattered, mud-stained dress. Morgan noted a telltale trembling in her hands, but when she finally spoke her voice seemed calm, betraying no hint of her recent horror.

"Thanks," she said. "I really didn't think anyone would hear me scream. I figured I was going to end up as the dragon's breakfast."

"My lady," said Morgan formally, "I'm happy to have been of service. Did you take any injury from your... from the..." His voice trailed off, his brain refusing to allow the word past his lips.

"Dragon," the girl finished for him briskly. "Most definitely a dragon. I've seen drawings in the old storybooks, and in history texts as well. Rather a magnificent creature, wasn't it? And no, thank you, I don't seem to be at all hurt. Are you? He caught you a pretty good kick there. But we're both still alive, so I guess things could have been worse, eh?"

Morgan gaped.

"You did cut it a bit fine though, didn't you?" she went on, as calm as if she was commenting on the weather. "Another few seconds, and I would have been part of the history texts myself. First girl eaten by a dragon in three centuries. My claim to fame."

She laughed at Morgan's startled expression. "Don't worry, I'll be fine. Although in about five minutes, I'm probably going to have screaming hysterics. You won't mind too much, will you?"

"I...what?" Morgan opened and closed his mouth like a gaffed fish. She should have been quivering in horror, not bantering like this. She had as much self-control as any battle-hardened veteran. Most women—men as well, he conceded—would have already succumbed to those screaming hysterics. He was having a hard time suppressing them himself. But if she could manage it, so could he. "No, of course not," he said. "Who could blame you?"

But as the tension of the moment drained away, it was being replaced with a strong curiosity, itching to be satisfied. "At the risk of being thought rude, who are you?" he asked. "And what are you doing out here? The forest is no place for a girl!" He looked around, but no one else emerged from the safety of the trees. "And you're all alone, aren't you? No escort?"

"No, no escort," she replied with a shake of her head, the gesture a mixture of defiance and wariness. Subtle golden flecks in her brown eyes gave her a slightly exotic look at odds with the plain sensibility of her green walking dress and sturdy boots. Morgan wrested his attention back to her words as she added, "I've never needed one before."

Interesting. This girl was no delicate flower if she traipsed about the forest on her own. As far as Morgan could tell, most of the ladies at court felt quite daring if they chanced to stroll through the palace gardens. A tramp through the woods? Not likely.

Which made her an object of suspicion. Because this would be an excellent place for a clandestine rendezvous. Well, except for the dragon, of course. But all in all, this secluded clearing, far from prying eyes, would be an ideal meeting place for someone with treason in mind. Someone passing sensitive information to agents of King Varsil, monarch of Kilbourne's aggressive neighbor to the north, Rhuddlan.

Someone was doing just that, as Morgan knew all too well. There was a traitor in their midst, someone highly placed. In all likelihood one of the men on the Royal Council, of which Morgan was a member. That person was funneling political and military intelligence to the Rhuddlanis. Information that would make it much easier for them to mount another invasion attempt into Kilbourne territory. One Morgan and the Legion he commanded would find hard to halt this time.

Morgan's current assignment, known to only two other men, was to determine the source of the leak and stop it. Was it possible this girl was a courier, acting for the traitor? Had he unwittingly stumbled on a lead to his quarry? He scanned her face for some trace of duplicity, but found none. Actually, all he could see were those fascinating gold-flecked eyes.

She regarded him in turn with less enthusiasm than might have been expected from someone who'd just been rescued from certain death. Of course, Morgan temporized, her reaction might be due to the realization that her rescuer wasn't the typical knight in shining armor.

His unusual heritage was writ plain to see in his features. They didn't call him the Dark Knight for nothing. Although not to his face, at least not anymore. He thrust this thought away and resumed his scrutiny. Their eyes met for a brief moment and Morgan felt a sudden chill course through him, as if the sun had passed behind a cloud. Odd. Perhaps she was up to something.

Yet his instincts told him she was more likely just an innocent victim of circumstance, in the wrong place at the wrong time. He'd long since learned to trust those instincts. Still…

"You're a frequent visitor to the forest?" Morgan kept his tone mild, but added just a touch of steel. He needed answers. Needed to be sure she wasn't linked to the traitor he was supposed to uncover. The traitor most people assumed was Morgan McRobbie, Knight-Commander of the King's Legion. The Dark Knight.

"Actually, yes," she replied.

He couldn't decide if she looked guilty, or merely annoyed at being challenged. But he pressed on. "All right, I'll ask again—who are you, and what are you doing out here?"

Morgan found himself on the receiving end of a fierce glare. "If you were going to be beastly," she said, biting off each word, "perhaps you should have just left me to my dragon."

As Morgan choked on this, her belligerent expression softened. She gave what might under other circumstances have almost been a faint smile. "Oh, very well. I suppose, since you rescued me, you have the right," she conceded. "My name is Marissa duBerry. I'm lady-in-waiting to Queen Gwyndolyn. I'm here because I came to collect flowers for the queen's boudoir." She indicated with a gesture what once might have been a basket, now trampled flat under the dragon's weight. "Oh, look, the foul creature sat on them!"

Either she was an excellent actress, or her story was true. To his surprise Morgan found his credulity still intact. *Trust your instincts.*

She continued, "I often walk in the forest, gathering flowers for the queen's pleasure. The day was so pleasant that I went a bit farther afield than normal. But bandits and ogres wouldn't dare come around here. And I certainly never thought to encounter a dragon." She shivered at the memory. "I didn't think dragons even existed anymore."

"Neither did I," Morgan admitted, relaxing his own guard a little. "If I hadn't seen it with my own eyes, I wouldn't have believed it." He rubbed his aching arm. It wasn't broken, by some miracle, although he was going to have a marvelous batch of bruises to show for this little escapade. If he hadn't been wearing a mail shirt, the dragon's kick would have likely torn him in two. As it was, it just felt like it had.

"You should be safe now," he said. "I don't think it will be back, now it knows there's a knight here to challenge it."

"Let's hope so." Her voice was dubious, and she glanced up toward the sky. "Although," she murmured, "it didn't seem so much concerned as indisposed. Ah well..." She cocked her head, reminding Morgan of a pert and inquisitive sparrow. "And so, bold knight," she went on, "having saved me from the dragon, what reward would you claim?"

Morgan bowed. "None at all," he said. "Your thanks are payment enough. It's my oath-bound duty to see justice done and evil banished from the kingdom."

Her eyes narrowed. "My word! Did they teach you that in knight school?" The sarcasm dripped from her voice like honey from a hive. "A pretty speech and a most noble sentiment. It does you credit, I'm sure. But you shall have some reward. I won't have it said any man had a claim on me."

Morgan shook his head. "Nay, m'lady. You have thanked me, and that will suffice."

Her eyes flashed dangerously and her voice was filled with agitation as she demanded, "Would you deny me?" Her hands began to tremble again. She quickly clasped them together and smiled up at him. It was a bright and brittle smile which looked as if it could dissolve into either sobs or hysterical laughter without warning. "I wish to grant you a boon. Are you churlish enough to refuse a lady so?"

Hmm. Was her offer intended to distract him from asking more questions? He mentally tossed a coin, which came up on the side of *no*. "As you wish," he replied. "I will accept your gracious offer, since you insist. You may satisfy your obligation by having dinner with me this evening."

Morgan blinked in surprise. *Good lord, why had he made such a request?* His dratted instincts taking over again, no doubt. With all the concerns he had to juggle at the moment, he couldn't afford the distraction a girl would present. No matter how interesting her eyes might be.

"Have dinner with you?" she repeated slowly, as if the concept were completely alien to her.

Morgan nodded, not trusting himself to speak. Having made his request, he was not about to go back on it now. *Instincts, trust your instincts.* The refrain rang through him almost like the toll of a bell.

"Why?" she demanded, hands on her hips. She brought to mind a stern schoolmistress from his distant past, challenging why a certain young boy didn't have his sums completed. It was rather daunting. Under the force of her glare Morgan grasped desperately for explanations. Unfortunately the only thing he could come up with was the truth, and it was something less than diplomatic.

"You're… different…" He trailed off, heat rising to his hairline. Damn it, he wasn't good with words. Give him a sword any day. Although right now he just wanted to fall on one.

She grimaced. "Not exactly a courtier, are you? If that was intended as a compliment, I think I should return it for repairs. It seems to lack a certain something."

Morgan groaned to himself; she must think him a babbling idiot. That impertinent part of his brain piped up again, wondering just why he cared. He ignored it.

"I'm sorry, I'm not putting it well," he said, scrambling to think how to explain without offending her any further. "All right, look. Ninety-nine girls out of a hundred, having been snatched up by a dragon and rescued in the nick of time, would have murmured 'My hero!' and swooned at her rescuer's feet."

"A bit hard, all that murmuring and swooning," Marissa observed.

"That's exactly what I mean! You have a different outlook on things. No swooning, no murmuring. Instead, you calmly dust yourself off and start in by berating me for my tardiness. I've never met a woman—anyone—like you, and…" He looked at her helplessly. "Dinner?"

Chapter Three

Marissa regarded her rescuer with a mixture of curiosity and suspicion. He'd been so bold as he had faced the dragon. Now he just looked nervous. As if he was unsure of himself? Or of her?

Well, it didn't matter, did it? If a dinner together was the worst she had to endure, so be it. After all, he *had* rescued her. She had a good idea what reward most of the so-called "gentlemen" of her acquaintance would have exacted. On the whole, the attentions of the dragon would be preferable. One evening in this knight's company should be tolerable in exchange for her life.

Decision made, she replied, "Very well, Sir Knight, I will accept your invitation." She narrowed her eyes again. "Peculiar though it and your explanation both seem. But first, tell me your name. You seem to have neglected to do so."

Her champion hesitated. Finally he said, "I do beg your pardon, m'lady. Sir Morgan McRobbie, of the King's Legion. At your service." He made an elegant bow.

"Morgan Mc…" She recoiled as if another dragon had suddenly hoven into view. "Oh! That…" She couldn't stop the look of burgeoning horror she knew must be spreading across her face.

She should have recognized him before. If only because of his dark complexion, so different from almost every other man in Caerfaen. In the excitement of the moment she'd just chalked it up to a man who lived his life outdoors, exposed to the sun and weather. But no, this was Morgan McRobbie all right. Morgan the half-breed, some called him. And worse. Although not within his hearing.

And he wasn't just "of the King's Legion"—he *was* the King's Legion. Knight-Commander, in fact, and dashing hero of the wars against the Rhuddlani invaders. Of all the people who could have come to her rescue. Morgan McRobbie. The man everyone whispered had turned traitor against Kilbourne.

Was he out here to meet an enemy agent? To hand over information the Rhuddlanis could use to try and invade Kilbourne again? Had she—and the dragon—interrupted something sinister?

Her expression must have given her away. Sir Morgan heaved a sigh. "Aye, m'lady, that one," he acknowledged. "And now, should you wish to decline my invitation I will certainly understand. There are few enough who wish to be seen with the likes of me."

She'd been about to do just that. Then Marissa caught an unexpected flash of despair in Morgan's eyes, so overwhelming as to crumble her resolve under the weight of it. *Does he suffer so because he's a traitor? Or because he isn't?* Well, it didn't matter. It wasn't in her to refuse him.

"I have already accepted your invitation," she told him. "I would not be counted false. Even if you are as black as is rumored…" she trailed off as he grimaced. Marisa flushed, realizing the statement cut two ways. She gathered herself and soldiered on. "Still and all you did save my life, and I'm in your debt. I suppose my reputation can stand a wee bit of tarnish."

"Lady Marissa, you don't have to…"

She cut him off with a raised hand. "Sir Morgan, I have given you my answer. Shall we stand here and debate it until the dragon returns?" She glowered. "At what hour shall I expect you?"

It looked like he was about to choke, although whether from annoyance or amusement, it was difficult to tell. He finally seemed to regain control enough to reply, "Half past seven, if it suits your convenience."

"I shall await…" A shadow fell across them, nearly blotting out the sun. Looking skyward Marissa spied the dragon, high overhead.

Its great wings were outstretched and it rode a current of air in an aspect of silent menace. Then it wobbled slightly. Another hiccough? If the dratted thing regained its ability to flame, it likely would be on them again, looking to continue the fight. Looking to gobble them both down. As they watched, the dragon roared, and then produced a spectacular gout of flame. *Drat!*

It began a lazy descent.

Marissa tore her gaze from the dragon and back to Sir Morgan. "I think," she observed, "it knows there is a knight here who would challenge it. Do dragons, I wonder, *enjoy* a challenge?"

He ignored this well-aimed barb, changing from nervous to confident again in an instant. It was an amazing transformation. A fierce gleam lit his eye as he scanned the terrain, no doubt picking a spot from which to make a stand. He exuded a palpable air of confidence and competence. Indeed, even of nobility.

It was a little disconcerting. Rather like watching a rabbit suddenly turn about and begin to hunt a fox. This was definitely a man to be reckoned with, she realized with a little frisson. If he was a traitor to Kilbourne, he would be a most dangerous one.

"M'lady," he said, "I should get you back to Caerfaen at once. If the dragon returns you'll be in grave danger while I fight him. Having managed by sheer luck to rescue you once, I wouldn't wish to tempt fate a second time."

She wasn't about to let him get the last word in. "You mean he'd swoop down here and char both of us on the spot, don't you?" she observed. "Very well, let us away. I wouldn't want to be roasted and eaten quite yet. You've promised to stand me a dinner."

Morgan stared at her, his mouth opening and closing, but no words emerged. Finally, shaking his head he said, "So I have." He turned and gave a sharp whistle.

An answering whinny and the pounding of hooves heralded the appearance of a huge gray horse at the edge of the clearing. It galloped toward them, stopping in a cloud of dust and rearing to paw the air with steel-shod hooves.

Marissa eyed the stallion in awe. "He's magnificent!" she exclaimed.

"This is Arnicus," Morgan informed her proudly. In an undertone, he muttered, "He's rather a show-off when he's got an audience." The horse nickered and regarded Morgan with an air of reproach. Marissa stifled a chuckle as Morgan continued, "He's served me well over the years and has gotten me out of several tight spots in our time together."

"Good, he can get us out of this one. Less talk and more leaving, Sir Morgan. The dragon's on his way. I don't know about you, but I don't relish the thought of a second engagement."

Marissa found herself practically tossed up onto the horse's back. Morgan mounted in front of her. "You heard the lady," he told the horse. Marissa grabbed at Morgan's waist for support as he shook the reins. "Now, Arnicus!" he cried, and the great horse leapt forward at a speed which was almost dizzying.

Marissa had not been on a horse in years, and never one as fast, or as enormous, as Arnicus. Corded muscles like steel bands rippled beneath her legs as the great gray ran through the trees. She looked down. It was a long way to the ground from up here!

She clutched at Morgan in a determined effort to maintain her seat as they crashed through the forest, stifling a wild laugh. Had she been saved from the clutches of a fearsome dragon only to be killed by falling off a speeding warhorse ridden by a traitorous knight?

Behind them, the dragon roared. In frustration at their escape? Or in triumph at having driven them off? She decided she didn't really care to find out which.

"Can't this nag go any faster?" she yelled into Morgan's ear.

He spared a quick glance back at her, shrugged, and kicked the horse's flanks. Arnicus shot through the forest paths like he had been hurled from a catapult. The dragon roared again.